The Advocate

THE HISTORICAL COLLECTION
BOOK THREE

KATIE CROSS

KCW

Author's Note

This story has been brewing in the back of my mind ever since I wrote THE DRAGONMASTER TRILOGY, years before I had any proper plans to release THE ADVOCATE. The right time never presented itself.

Then I began the SISTERWITCHES SERIES, which picks up from the moment that the DRAGONMASTER TRILOGY leaves off. I realized *what better reintroduction to the world of the Dragonmasters than Charlie and Maximillion?*

Charlie and Max wrote their own story. The characters inside this tome, Faye in particular, knew exactly what they wanted from the beginning. I had little to do with it. This book came together unlike any novel in my experience.

My dream for you is that you relish THE ADVOCATE and your time with some of our favorite characters again. Then hold on tight.

More is on the way.

—Katie Cross

Chapter One

MAXIMILLION

Twelve-year-old Maximillion saw the livid shades of red in Pere's eyes from across the room.

He should have jumped out the window, but he realized the mistake too late. Years of living under Pere's heavy fist had taught him the finer points of survival: keep objects between you. Don't make noise. Pere thrived on the sound of pain. Run, never look back. Return only when hunger prevented him from sleeping in the marsh, or the cold became so deep that breath billowed through the rain.

Tonight? All the rules went out the door.

A low-ceilinged wall stood at Max's back, the table to his right, another wall to the left. He was cornered. His second idiotic mistake. Max crouched, eyes wide, as Pere stomped across the room.

"Maaaaax!"

Pere closed in, faster than a man of his colossal size should be able to move. He clenched the broken wooden leg of a chair in his hand like a club. Pere would smash that piece of wood into Max's brain, hide his body, and live his ipsum-soaked life. Only Abbi next door would miss Max.

No escape.

Instinct, combined with sheer terror, moved Max as the chair leg vaulted toward his face. He ducked. The wooden leg shattered against the wall. Pere regarded it through crossed-eyes, bleary with drink.

A visceral flow of magic bubbled inside of Max. With it came power.

No, he thought. *Not now.*

Pain surged alongside the magic. A gripping agony, like a leather strap around his brain. These erratic, recurring headaches had dropped him into strange dreams before. Unconsciousness, of a sort. A world of darkness, sometimes with slivers of light like paths. Twice, he'd almost died because of them.

Pere grunted, spun.

"Rotten, stinking son of a whore!"

Max dropped. The remains of the splintered chair leg slammed into the wall again. Pere lurched forward, caught himself on the edge of the table.

Desperation drove Max to throw a kick. He caught Pere in the knee. A crack followed, then a howl. Pere staggered to the side. Finally, the ipsum worked against Pere. In his semi-delirious state, he struggled to stand. A belligerent grunt followed. The same sound that came before Pere's fist.

"I'll kill you!" he bellowed.

Out of the corner of his eye, Max saw the incoming strike. He ducked to the side. Pere's knuckles grazed the top of his cheek, scraping delicate skin. Tears in his eyes, Max shoved his foot into Pere's chest. Pere toppled like a dying house of cards. Too quick to make sense for a witch so drunk, Pere's arm swung out and grabbed Max's ankle with a roar.

Max resisted, but his puny legs were no match against Pere's brute strength. While Pere yanked him closer, Max scrambled for the splintered chair leg. It clattered just out of his grasp.

Garbled shouts filled the air. A hand closed around his shirt, yanking back.

The magic surged again.

Blackness.

Pain.

He didn't know where the pain that Pere inflicted began, or the magic. What threatened his life more? This pounding headache or Pere? Blood and fury and desperation raced through his body, washing past his ears in a *shush, shush, shush* sound.

The tip of his finger grazed the splintered chair leg. Against all odds, and with the last of his strength, Max lunged. His grasping fingers found the chair leg. He snatched it, lifted it high, and swung. The jagged wood connected. Pain reverberated from his clenched fingers all the way through his shoulder.

Pere gave a muted shout. His skull *thunked* on the floor, eyes glassy. Crimson boiled out of his nose in a dark stain. He released Max, arm lolling uselessly to the side. Beads of blood slipped to the floor, slashing red across his mottled skin.

Max hurled the chair leg across the room with a terrified cry. He scrambled away. His trembling back pressed into the wall. Through the magical blackness that threatened, he could barely see.

Only blood.

More blood.

He pressed a hand to his throbbing head. His shaky voice broke the sudden, strange stillness.

"Pere?"

Pere's chest didn't move. The vein in his forehead no longer pulsed. His neck lay still. Not a breath in his body.

The dizzy maw swelled within Max's chest. Darkness. The

expanding magic threatened him from deep within, rising higher like a steamy fog. His stomach lurched. He turned to the side, vomited. Shadows moved over his vision, like night-dancers. He groped with his hands for something to hold.

He had to leave.

Race out of here before Pere awoke.

No, Pere's eyes wouldn't open. Max killed him. Darkness covered Max's vision again with another surge from the headache. He panted, throat raspy, and stumbled farther away. A silver line cut the darkness in half.

A . . . path.

"No!" he shouted. "I won't go there again."

Moments before the inky cloud overcame him, it retreated. The sensation of a jerk at his navel and the feeling of dropping back into his body escorted him into reality.

To Pere.

The dizzy whirl faded as he pressed his back to the door. Emotion dissipated. Pere wouldn't hurt him again, but someone else might. They'd throw him in Carcere for murder. They'd consider him a criminal.

Another tide of magic bloomed through his chest. Max repeated the oft-used transportation incantation that Abbi taught him for the worst nights, when Pere obliterated himself with drink.

The strange magic tangled with his spell.

They swept him away.

Darkness, pressure, pain followed. He screamed, but no one could hear him. The agony pressed on his chest—he longed to breathe—until he felt the grip of consciousness fade. He wouldn't make it. Couldn't survive. How long had he been in the transportation magic?

Where did he take himself, anyway?

Why did he fool with magic?

A moment before he succumbed to the darkness that

could only mean death, the magic thrust him free. Hard ground met his shoulder, jarred his teeth. His aching head rattled on the impact.

Something cold lay beneath him. The chill seeped through his threadbare shirt onto his skin. Max groaned, rolled onto his back. Wet cobblestones pressed into his knobby spine. The sounds of hard-falling rain and distant shouts—a pub, perhaps?—came from not far away. The pounding water revived him.

Rain slammed onto his forehead. It washed away the boggy air, the smell of ipsum. A baptism from the sky.

He'd made it out alive.

"Hey, you all right?"

The sound of a voice brought Max out of his mental meanderings. His eyes flew open. He stared into the freckled, green-eyed gaze of a boy his age. A bright white smile bloomed across his pale face.

"Merry meet. I'm Charlie."

Chapter Two

CHARLIE

Charlie Dauphin had faced many obstacles in twelve years of life.

Losing his Mama when he was born—which he couldn't remember, so he didn't take credit for his own survival. He'd broken five bones, successfully avoided Mr. Tate's willow branch switch when he filched an apple off the cart in the market, and staved off death by fever no less than four times.

But avoiding Papa's questioning glare beat all else.

He smiled grandly, which disarmed most adults. Papa, however, had a firmer countenance.

He didn't sway.

"I saved him, Papa! He was laying on the street in the rain and looking like he was about to starve to death. What was I supposed to do? *Leave* him there?"

"I didn't ask that, Charlie."

"What would he have done without me? Died in moments, I imagine."

Papa rolled his eyes.

Charlie pressed a hand to his chest, sweating now. "Pearl loves to take care of lost souls, Papa! You know she always has witches coming to her that need help. It only seemed appropriate to bring this lad home to Pearl. You would want a stranger to do the same for me, Papa. It's the Dauphin legacy!"

He lifted his chin.

Papa folded his hands behind his back. "I didn't ask about Pearl. Nor did I ask about your motivations for saving this unfortunate soul."

Charlie ignored that. If he could distract Papa *away* from the fact that he'd been outside in the middle of the night, he had a prayer of making it through this interrogation without losing his freedom.

"He clearly needs a place to stay. I'm confident we'll be best friends."

Warning lined his tone when Papa drawled, "Charlie."

Frustrated, Charlie switched tactics. He had to do it on the fly so much it had become second nature. Clearly, diversion wouldn't work. He should have known Pearl would write to Papa and tell him that Charlie brought a boy to her in the middle of the night. Papa held to his rules like a dog to a bone.

Charlie pressed a hand to his forehead.

"What are we going to do with him, Papa? I'm worried. He can't be my best friend if he's dead and I have an open slot for the position."

Ranulf Dauphin lifted an eyebrow. The pale blonde strands held deep judgment.

"Charlie, you won't distract me. Yes, you saved the boy's life. When he wakes up, we'll get his story. That isn't what we're discussing. *Why* were you outside, in the middle of the market, at 3:00 in the morning?"

Charlie swallowed.

A heavy lump filled his throat. How to explain? He chewed on his bottom lip. Arguing would be useless, he could see that, but the time for capitulation hadn't come yet.

No, he had too big a goal to quit now.

He had to find a place in which to house his secret society. Somewhere hiding in plain sight, where no one would know they gathered, but it might still be secured . . .

Not to mention check on Faye.

"Well, Papa . . . you see . . ."

Ranulf wagged a finger. "None of that, Charlie. I'll have none of it. A straight answer or you're locked in your room for the weekend."

Charlie's brow fell. With an eye roll, he gave a martyr's sigh. "Fine. Papa, I couldn't sleep. I know you understand how that is." He swept an arm out. "Just look at you! Awake at 4:15 in the morning!"

"So you ventured into the market stalls?"

"No!" He recoiled, as if offended. "No, I went for a walk."

A deadpan expression overtook Ranulf's face.

"In the rain."

Easier to hide with, Charlie thought. Few witches bothered to get wet, though it was easy enough to step in front of a fire and dry off. Of greatest benefit, however, was the noisy effect of the rain.

Very difficult to hear over.

"It's quite refreshing," Charlie chirped. "I'd tell you to try it sometime, but I don't want you to take a cold. You're pale these days, Papa."

Papa's eyes tightened. He stood next to his desk, near a snapping, bright fire. "You're twelve, Charlie. I have a hard time believing you can't sleep."

"Sometimes, a man can't make it happen."

Papa huffed. "A man?"

"And when a man can't sleep, he requires vigorous exercise."

"Tell me you weren't trying to see Faye again?"

Charlie's jaw dropped. The astonishment was genuine enough. That Papa had guessed was almost embarrassing.

"Papa! I'm a gentleman."

"You're twelve."

"And a gentleman!"

"I never said otherwise. Charlie, leave Faye alone. I commend you for bringing the boy to safety. Pearl said he'd been roughed up by someone and she promised to bring him to Wildrose in the morning when she starts work. In the meantime, you're restricted to the manor for the full day tomorrow."

"Papa! How will I check on Faye? I'm her protector. She's not safe where she lives! She needs somewhere else."

Papa lifted his hands. "Argue with me and I'll make it two days, if I must. Leaving during the night is not safe, Charlie."

"But—"

"I will look into Faye's living arrangements if that will stop you from going out there."

Charlie readjusted his coat with a grumble. "It will. It's horrid, Papa. You won't believe the way those witches treat her. She sleeps on the ground outside, did you know that? She could work at Wildrose with Pearl. I'll teach her how to read! She's so smart."

Papa breathed a long exhalation through wide nostrils. "Then it's agreed. I will look into Faye's living situation, you will leave Faye alone. Stay off the streets when it's dark. Do you hear me?"

Charlie pressed his lips. Tough go. A full day in the manor? Terrible. He'd already learned all Wildrose Manor's secrets, which made for a very tedious day. Restriction made it difficult to help Faye, but it wouldn't be impossible.

Everything came down to subtlety and timing.

Still . . .

His pride stung. If he hadn't brought the boy to Pearl's, he would have avoided capture. He didn't regret it. Clearly, the boy needed help. He should have left the boy in his room until the morning, then made up a story about finding him with the chickens.

Next time.

The lad also stood as a prime candidate for best friend. Faye already held the title of soulmate, though she had yet to realize it.

Ranulf drew himself higher. His broad shoulders cast a wide shadow that danced over a painting of Sarah, Charlie's mother.

"I'll take your silence as agreement," Ranulf said. "No leaving the manor today. If more problems with your behavior arise, it will be two days."

"Yes, Papa."

"How are your dizzy spells?"

Charlie's face heated. "Fine. They're not dizzy spells. They're . . . something else."

"They occur with the headaches?"

"Yes."

"Any pain now?"

"No."

"Hmmm. Well, Pearl is relatively confident that you're about to transition into the power of a Watcher. Which, to be honest, I'm not very happy about. A difficult power to wield."

Papa's hand rested on top of something on his desk. A glazed, distant expression overtook his face.

"Society . . ."

He cleared his throat.

"Never mind that. Keep me updated on what you're feeling. According to Pearl, the headaches will stop when you officially receive the power. If that *doesn't* happen, then we'll find another Apothecary. Either way, we'll know soon enough."

Charlie had left the house after midnight because the intermittent, thudding pain in his skull had finally stopped. No potion prevented the steady ache. He had to wait it out.

"May I go to bed, Papa?"

Amusement riddled Papa's tone when he drily asked, "Have you finally tuckered yourself out like a man?"

Charlie puffed up. "I have, thank you."

Papa shuffled behind his desk. Charlie glanced quickly at what Papa had been reading before their discussion. An open newsscroll, the *Chatham Chatterer,* brightened in the firelight. A bold headline crossed the top.

Big Leo Apprehends Watcher at the Border.

Papa waved to Charlie. "Go to sleep, my boy. I'll see you at a late breakfast. Yes, you have to be up by 9:00. I don't care if you're tired. You stayed up all night. You can be miserable about it for the rest of the day."

Charlie turned to go.

It will be worth it, he thought. Faye occupied his mind as he strolled down the hallway, toward his bedroom.

Chapter Three

MAXIMILLION

Heat warmed the front of Max's eyelids.

A fire? A torch? No, they had neither most of the time. Pere couldn't afford coal, and the wood from the marsh was far too wet.

Groggily, Max forced his eyes open. The left eye struggled more than the right. He expected to see the cracking walls of his home, a mouse as it scuttled over the floor, and broken ipsum bottles along the seam of the floor.

Instead, a hearth.

Brick climbed the wall in a fireplace as big as the closet Max slept in. Flames bounced around, emitting languorous waves of heat.

He blinked once. Twice.

Where *was* he?

His gaze darted to a low ceiling. Dusty crossbeams ran lengthwise toward square windows, beneath which paintings, books, and a cluttered desk filled the space. A hard divan cradled him close to the fire. Near enough to keep him sleepy and warm. Candles sputtered on a holder near shadowed shelves.

Recollections whispered through him. Pere's rage-twisted face. The chair leg. Streaks of terror when the magical darkness threatened. Pere collapsing, then blood sliding out of his nose to drip on the floor.

A rainy street.

Bright eyes.

Waves of fatigue rolled through him. He closed his eyes, almost submitting. Where had he landed after transporting? Obviously, Pere hadn't followed.

Wouldn't.

Pere was dead.

Which meant he was safe. For now. He'd . . . figure out all the rest later.

Night rolled away outside the windows, giving way to a lightening sky. Day hailed. He should leave now, before he had to confront anyone. This wasn't the first time a stranger had helped. Max tried to swing his legs out of bed, but they wouldn't listen. His arm lifted, yet dropped as quickly.

Too weak.

Too tired.

When had he last eaten?

He couldn't recall through the muddy layers of his brain. Didn't need to worry about that now, anyway. Pere couldn't hurt him, and whoever helped was clearly kind. He could afford another wink or two of sleep. Then he'd leave. Find a new life or . . . something.

He tucked deeper into the cushions, the weight of his blankets pressing on him. Sleep stole back over his mind.

In a second, he succumbed.

* * *

"Well, you're awake!"

A chipper voice startled Max out of sleep. He vaulted up

with a gasp, attempting to dive off the couch. A firm hand stopped him.

"Calm down. No one's going to blow a trumpet in your ear."

A pair of kind eyes set inside a round face blinked at him. A woman with fluffy hair in curls around her head and a dress that buttoned to a lacy neckline. Max leaned away when dizziness swept through him.

Not the magical, fuzzy, going-somewhere-else sensation that had kicked up recently, either.

The laying-down-too-long-haven't-eaten-enough kind.

"I'm Pearl," the woman said. She used the common language, which is all Pere ever spoke, despite living in the Eastern Network. "Charlie brought you here last night. Do you remember?"

Vague clippings of memory. The smell of rain on dark cobblestones. A pair of friendly eyes, a firm hand on his shoulder. Did they hobble down a road together? Recollection of a supporting arm around his back, a reassuring voice. At some point, all turned to darkness.

The back of his eyeballs pulsed with a mild headache. Not unusual for the last several weeks.

A tray lowered to a table in front of him. Pearl sat heavily in a chair that hurried over a second before she would have dropped to her bottom. A basket of yarn balls appeared.

Without looking, she grabbed one with knitting needles stuck into it and set it in her lap. Her short, chubby legs lifted into the air, resting on an ottoman as it arrived.

She peered at him with deep curiosity.

"What's your name?"

The smell of breakfast distracted him, or he might have been more careful. Buttered toast. Porridge. Was that a crock of cream?

Sugar!

His mouth watered. He reached for the petite bowl. A spoon stuck out the side.

"M-maximillion."

"You're ten, I'd guess?"

He nodded.

Twelve, but she didn't need specifics. He'd always been little, like the orphans that ran around the streets. Pearl made a noise in her throat. Most of her attention focused on the tangled yarn around her fingers.

A silver dome lifted off a nearby tray. The succulent smell of ham wafted toward him, drifting through the air. Bacon, was it? He'd only had it once, when Mere was still alive. He nearly fell off the divan he reached for it so quickly. In seconds, he'd stuffed a slice of meat in his mouth and snatched the toast.

Pearl glanced up, then back down.

She said nothing.

His stomach growled as he chewed through the salty meat. Each bite flew down his throat to ease the constant pain. He might choke and die—but it would be worth it. Halfway through his frenzy, Max froze. Pearl swayed side to side as she counted stitches, hummed under her breath.

He chewed the piece of bacon, then swallowed. "S-s-sorry," he stammered. "I can't pay you. I—"

She scoffed.

"Payment? Bah. Don't worry about it. It's only bacon and porridge and breakfast and tea. About the cheapest breakfast you can find in the Central Network."

Central Network.

Max registered the fact with some shock. How did he transport all the way to the Central Network? He blinked at the tray, processing the fact. He'd never left his small fishing village in the Eastern Network marsh.

To magic away so far . . .

In a daze, he remembered the tangling of the painful magic and the transportation magic. The painful magic brought welling darkness, coinciding with Pere's attack.

Attack.

His veins turned to slush. He lifted a hand to his left cheek, touched the skin there. How had he forgotten?

The good gods, he'd killed Pere. Slammed the wooden leg right into his nose. The sickening crack as bone shoved into brain replayed through his mind. He attempted to summon up remorse, but couldn't find it.

Only fear.

Would they come after him? What would the East Guards say? Eventually, someone would find Pere. Abbi would search for Max when she hadn't seen him. Well, they couldn't find him here. He transported away in the middle of the night. Not a soul would search for him.

Not even aunt Serafina.

The dump of panic ebbed. Nauseated, he leaned back. He shouldn't have eaten so fast. He'd be lucky if he didn't vomit it all back up right now . . .

"No rush, my boy. You've got all the time in the world to be here, if you need it. No need to go back to whoever gave you those bruises. You're safe with me."

The low croon of her voice quelled the white-hot panic teeming under the surface. His urge to run, and the desire to stay, battled.

I killed my pere, he longed to say.

To speak the words would make them real and concrete. It would put them into the world where he could make sense of their meaning. Their . . . stolidness.

He slumped back to the couch.

There he stayed, legs tucked against his chest, as he stared at the flames. The clack of Pearl's knitting needles and the snap of the fire lulled him into another desperately needed sleep.

Chapter Four

CHARLIE

Maximillion looked more like a Max.

Charlie studied him with a tilted head. Pearl claimed Max was ten, but he *highly* doubted it. He might be thin, but was definitely older. Like him. Destined to be best friends. He could feel the truth of that. Like Faye, his soul knew this witch. Such a revelation wrapped him with affirmative certainty.

He knew this boy.

He didn't really, but he did at the same time. It made sense, yet . . . not at all. Like most things in this world.

From across her little cottage, Pearl asked, "How are your headaches, Charlie?"

He scowled. "Why is everyone asking me about the headaches?"

"Because you'll transition soon enough, if you're a Watcher. We should find out soon. Otherwise, you're just a kid with headaches."

"They're fine," he mumbled.

Relentless, he should have said. More nuisance than painful. Sometimes, they caused a welling dizziness, but otherwise simmered in the background. Once or twice, he thought he saw lights. Not flashing dots, the way some witches complained.

More like . . . trails.

Charlie leaped back to his feet and paced. The sound of his shoes hitting the floor would, with any luck, wake Max up. Why did he sleep so late? Didn't he understand they had things to *do*?

Charlie had finally done it. Shortly after breakfast with Papa, he'd found the perfect hideout for his secret society. He needed someone to join it with him. No, not just somebody.

His best friend.

Pearl paused halfway across the room, a coffee mug in hand. She peered at Charlie with a practiced eye.

"Are you allowed to be here today?"

Charlie waved that off. Pearl lived a suitable distance away from Wildrose Manor—twenty minutes by carriage, almost an hour on foot. To Papa's chagrin, Charlie had learned transportation years ago, before he should have known how.

With Papa occupied by a work meeting, Charlie had only a few more minutes before he had to return to Wildrose and appear repentant for leaving last night. *Restriction to the manor* was more of an idea than a rule, anyway.

"Don't worry about that, Pearl. Can I wake him up? I want to take him back to Wildrose with me."

"He's resting!"

Vexed, Charlie waved a hand toward him. "It's almost noon!"

"He's woken up twice to eat, then fallen back to sleep. He clearly needs it! You won't wake him up for one of your wild ideas."

"It's not wild. It's brilliant!"

"I'm sure it is. Now, take your brilliance back to Wildrose. When he wakes up, I'll bring him with me. Tell your father I'll be there when he's strong enough. Ranulf wrote this morning, said there's a new girl staying at Wildrose?"

Charlie grinned. "Her name is Faye. Papa rescued her."

"Like all the witches that come to Wildrose," she muttered. "Fine, I'll set her up in a room as soon as I arrive. Show her where the sheets are?"

"Already done, Pearl. Honestly, you insult me."

She gave him a long suffering glare. "Then I'll see you shortly. Now scuttle back home before you get into more trouble!"

Her dismissive tone left no room for protest. Charlie left, Wildrose bound, with an impatient huff.

* * *

Thick eyelashes framed by a pair of almost-black eyes peered at Charlie. Faye, a fresh new dress covering her from shoulder to ankle, peered at him between slats in the staircase. Her thin fingers gripped the wooden planks.

He grinned from where he stood below.

"Hullo, Faye."

She fled, folded white sheets clasped to her chest. A giggle floated behind her as she ran, umber hair streaming down her back. The clothes were a little too big, but with proper food, she'd grow into them fast.

Papa's admonition to leave her alone rang in his mind. He let her escape. His cheeks warmed at the sight of her though. Her hair looked so soft. He wanted to touch it, but didn't dare.

Faye, sweet Faye. The love of his life. He'd give her the spot of best friend, but she was destined for greater.

Soulmate, and all that.

Plans filled his mind as Charlie jogged down the grand staircase toward the bottom floor, where high ceilings with painted murals and dusty shelves populated. The shining wooden floor echoed his hurried footsteps. The indistinct murmur of Papa's voice meant Charlie had returned just in time.

Charlie headed toward heavy double doors at the back of the manor. Within minutes, he jogged a steady clip across the grassy grounds. Water collected on the grass stems, wetting his shoes.

By the time he arrived at the hidden cellar door, his head pulsed with a fresh headache. He dropped to his knees to feel for the latch through the grasses. How hadn't he thought of the cellar before? The perfect headquarters.

Underground, tucked next to the manor.

No one would know!

He winced. Goodness, but this headache was worse than before. The pain tightened like a band of tension around the back of his head, his temples, and his forehead. He attempted to shake it off, but the agony pounded harder.

Charlie diverted his attention.

Headquarters.

Secret society.

Best friend.

Big things happening today.

The cellar door groaned as he yanked it open. Later, he'd oil the hinges, or find a grimoire centered on hiding things in plain sight. For a secret society, such an obvious entrance would *not* do.

Moldy smells filtered through the air. He grimaced. Their pungent aromas worsened the headache. Through the blackness encroaching from the sides of his vision, he peered into the dank hole. A wooden ladder crossed the space from floor to top. Charlie regarded it, and thought twice about his plan to venture inside.

Nausea welled back up.

No, not today.

He dropped to the grass, rolled onto his back. Shadows wafted over him, pulled him closer, like a gentle tug on his lapel. Easy. A persuasion, not an insistence. He went willingly, for where it took him, the headache didn't stay.

A velvety forest backdrop met him. Not unlike the space where he slipped right before sleep claimed him. A soothing spot.

Charlie felt his body, but couldn't see it. He saw nothing except a friendly penumbra. He existed outside of himself, but only in mind.

Somewhere magical.

A single ray of light appeared at his feet and raced backward. He whirled, gazing behind. The light hurried into the darkness, creating a floor. He stepped closer. Nothing stopped him. No innate awareness to remain.

He continued.

Light brightened as he closed in on a fuzzy luminescence. Charlie reached for it, but it had no substance. His fingers touched through a gauzy mist.

Wispy, like a dream.

Another appeared. Then a third. More grew behind those. They stood as tall as him. Apparitions of smoke, perhaps? The avenue diverged. It grew and budded and spread. Trails, paths. Incandescent spiderwebs cut through the inkiness.

"Merry meet?"

The sounds didn't echo, but he heard himself speak it. A peculiar sensation replaced the peaceful nature of this world.

A tug.

A . . . return.

From a distance, a voice called his name.

Faye?

"Charlie? Charlie! Wake up! What's wrong with you?"

Charlie closed his mind to the magic. He didn't know

how he did it, just that it worked. The murkiness dissipated. Brightness cut into his vision. With a hand held high to block the light, he opened his eyes.

Daylight flooded the world, profiling Faye's concerned face.

"Charlie?"

Chapter Five

MAXIMILLION

The silence woke him.

Max's eyes flew open. He stared at the underside of a vaguely familiar ceiling. Thick beams. Dust motes. Cobwebs. A remote humming and prattle and the smell of fresh bread.

Pearl, was it?

Slowly, he sat up. His entire body rebelled. Pere had only hit him twice, but he felt as if a tree had fallen on him. There was the sprawling headache and his body was clenched, stiff, and exhausted. The otherworldly shadows constantly nagged him. He slept, but not really.

Strange dreams populated. White trails streaking ahead of him. Ethereal spots of smoke. A weird representation of Abbi. Serafina, too. Pearl, though that made no sense at all. Why would so many witches haunt his dreams?

Too much food before bed, perhaps. Abbi always said *food is the seasoning of dreams.*

Carefully, Max swung his legs over the side of the divan. He attempted to sit up, but an explosion of pain filled his skull. He moaned, leaned back again. As if summoned, Pearl appeared at his side.

"Max?"

"Maximillion," he mumbled.

Only Mere had called him Max.

"What's wrong?"

His palm lightly patted his temple. He attempted to speak, but another wave of discomfort renewed. It crept in from the edges, like a slow wash. He battled it. He wanted to stay here with Pearl. Pearl who lived quietly, so that he might rest.

Instead, he vaulted back into the waiting gloom. The peaceful tenebrosity came in a welcoming starburst.

Confusing twists of light grew in front of him, filled with witches he didn't know. Fat lines, thin ones, populating endlessly from his feet. The boy that saved him. Pearl. A man with a mustachioed face and accommodating eyes. Aunt Serafina.

Their vague expressions solidified. Witches he didn't know, witches he thought he knew. Not Pere.

Never Pere.

Did dreams not reveal the dead?

An explosion rippled through him, one that meant . . . *something*. The strange surreality fractured, and everything became a little easier to see. Magic had broken, given way. Pressure released in his brain. The pain evanesced.

For dreams, these weren't all that bad. Could definitely be worse.

Pearl spoke from a distance. He heard her only vaguely until she disappeared. Sounds faded. He stood firmly in his dream world, surrounded by witches.

Yet never so alone.

* * *

Pearl's voice brought Max out of the strange wanderings. The paths he trod, the things he saw. Vague. Confusing. Blurry and unclarified.

"Well, we transported him to Wildrose without issue, which is a miracle. I've never transported someone unconscious."

A deeper male voice replied.

"It's a bit easier."

"He woke up, claimed a headache. Or, so it seemed. There is some magical ability and intelligence in him."

"I agree."

A pause.

"The odds are impossible, Ranulf!" she cried with irritation. "Two boys, around the same age, develop the same rare magic at the same time? It cannot be."

"We have no definitive answers, Pearl. It's a mere suggestion. According to your reports—and Faye's as well—both boys dropped into a sort of . . . unconscious state . . . at the same time. They appear to be sleeping, and we know Charlie has had a headache the past month or two. We know nothing of Maximillion, except his name, but he did motion to his head. *As if in pain.*"

A huff, a rustling skirt, and a chorus of mumbles replied. They sounded an awful lot like *impossible* and *never in my life* and *how could it even!*

Max groaned. The ache in his body had subsided, like the descent of a fever. The bizarre dreams, oddly grounded, shifted through his head. What did they mean? Were they dreams at all?

They lacked the nonsensical nature of illusions, the wafting, uncapturable essence. Everything remained clear in his mind.

"Charlie is waking, Ranulf, sir," said a young, melodic voice off to the side.

"I'll be right there."

The smell of chamomile filled the air right before a body sank next to him. He laid on a . . . divan? A bed? Carefully, his eyes fluttered open. Low daylight flooded them, like a sky inching toward night. He swallowed past a dry throat, ravenous and thirsty and filled with energy.

Pearl's face moved into his view.

"Max?"

"Maximillion," he muttered again. The recourse came out coarse and dry. A delighted smile zipped across her face.

"Well, you certainly haven't changed in the last two hours. Are you feeling all right?"

He nodded.

No headache pulsed through his skull. In fact, he felt . . . lighter. Each passing moment escorted him more firmly into real life. He cataloged a new place. Pearl's homey cottage had disappeared.

An old-world, ornate room sprawled around him. Dark wood, gleaming windows, furniture with clawed feet and rough tapestry. Leather-bound books shone in the muted light. In a hearth decorated by ornately carved wooden panels, a low fire snapped. A slight chill filled the room.

"Where am I?" he croaked.

"Wildrose Manor."

Vague remembrances came to mind. In the dreams he'd seen this room . . . hadn't he? Confusion deepened.

Gently, he sat up. His body gave no protest, but moved readily. Pearl directed a wary eye on him, but seemed pleased with his movement.

"Tell me, Maximillion. Have you struggled with a headache?"

He regarded her, the metallic taste of distrust ripe on his tongue. Remembering the click of her needles, the warmth of her food and tea infusing his barren stomach, he relaxed. Pearl asked nothing of him, yet gave much.

"Yes."

"Hmm. How long have the headaches bothered you?"

He shrugged.

"Did any potions ease them?"

He frowned. "Potions?"

"No one gave you potions to ease the misery?"

He shook his head, scoffed. Who would have given him potions? The motion caused no pain. Her gaze tapered until her eyes resembled slashes. After some thought, they fluttered wide again. A bright bounce lifted her voice.

"Don't worry about that. Did you have any strange dreams?"

Again, he nodded.

Unbothered by his wordless replies, unlike Abbi, who always crabbed at him to *use your words*, Pearl scooted closer.

"Were there lines of light in your dreams? Set against a backdrop of darkness?"

Max could only blink at first. How did she know? In astonishment, he whispered, "Yes."

"I see. Were they in front of you or behind you?"

"What?"

"The paths. Apparitions. Images of witches, or . . . things. Did they occur in front of you or behind you?"

His breathing sped up. He pushed off the divan, straightening. Panic gripped him.

"How did you know?"

She waved an errant hand.

"I'll explain in a moment. Forward or behind?"

"Forward."

The strain left her body with a breath. "Good. Good. I can work with that. How many lines or apparitions did you see?"

"So many."

"Hmm . . . who was in them?"

He opened his mouth to reply, but stopped. Everyone. Witches he didn't know. Not Abbi. Nor Pere. Nothing of the East, except once when he saw Serafina.

The young boy that saved him, mostly. Charlie, did they call him?

"I don't know."

Pearl tapped a finger against her lips. "Huh."

"Why do you ask?"

She smoothed the ruffled fabric of her skirt. Dust billowed in gentle swells beneath her ministrations. "I have the same question. What *is* happening here? Unprecedented, whatever it is."

"Is it . . . magic?"

"Does it feel like magic?"

"Yes."

Pearl's lips pressed into thin lines. Whatever the ridges between her brows meant, he couldn't fathom.

"You're a Watcher, Maximillion. Part of a big magic. A secret magic. It's something we didn't ask for, but it found us anyway."

Her hands folded demurely in her lap. Her voice developed an oddly wooden note.

"From now and for the rest of your life, you'll carry an ability that allows you to see future chances. They appear in paths, with what we call wisps. The wisps change based on what witches decide. Agency swings the course of fate all the time.

"Sometimes, what you see will happen, sometimes it won't. Most of the time, a strange variation of the event comes to pass. It's a gift that feels more like a curse. Until you learn the intricacies, who you see for, what it means . . ."

Her voice trailed away. He fell quiet, lost in his own thoughts.

Watcher.

Carry an ability.

Future chance.

Strange variation.

"How?" He choked over the word. "How did . . . what . .
."

Pearl didn't touch him in those awful moments, which might have been the only saving grace. He didn't leap out of his skin, sprint across the room, and never return.

"In some ways, the Watcher power will be your greatest blessing. In others, it will almost drive you mad. The faster you accept it, the more beneficial it can be. Don't fight it, Max. That's the only advice that I can give you right now. You're on the cusp of something so fathomless . . ."

Before he could form the words to ask, the door slammed against the wall. He jerked back. Over his shoulder, he glimpsed a wild-haired Charlie standing near the door. Max pressed his fists into the divan, canting his body to face the door.

Why did he feel calm?

Safe?

Suddenly . . . relieved?

Charlie's expression illuminated.

"Max?"

He opened his mouth to correct him, but stopped. He knew this boy. Charlie, the one Pearl had been speaking about with . . . Ranulf, was it? Charlie, the boy that saved him. Who hobbled with him through the streets and over to Pearl. Charlie carried most of Max's weight as they struggled to a dry, warm place.

The boy that stood in dozens of wisps, more than any other witch.

An older-looking gentleman stood behind Charlie, oddly similar in facial structure. He had blond hair, where Charlie's spiraled in wild strands, like a fire. Max licked his dry lips. He felt as if he'd known Charlie his whole life, but that made no sense.

"Charlie."

Charlie's shoulders sagged. A harried expression pulled his eyes down, dropped them toward his jaw.

"Good. You know me."

Pearl straightened, hands clasped. She looked at the older gentlemen. Presumably Charlie's father, Ranulf.

"A Watcher, for certain. I've just discussed it with him."

Ranulf frowned. With a warm hand on Charlie's shoulder, he said, "Tell Pearl what you saw."

"It happened the way you described Pearl, except for one thing."

"What's that?"

"The paths appeared behind me."

Pallor crept over Pearl's expression. Her cheeks slackened and breath stopped entirely. Eventually, she closed her lips and swallowed.

"Behind?"

Charlie nodded, perplexed. Max watched her cautiously. Surprise meant nothing good.

"Behind," Pearl repeated. "It means . . . it means you're a Defender, not a Watcher. You see possibilities for the past, not the future. What was presented?" Pearl hastened closer to him. "Tell me what you saw, Charlie. Did any of it seem confusing? Or was it familiar?"

"Familiar." He shrugged. "It's the past. I saw the past, for certain."

"How do you feel?"

"Ready to show Max what I found outside."

Panic flashed across her eyes. She whirled around to stare at Max, then Charlie. Her frantic motions added to the building tension. Ever-so-slightly, she edged herself to the right until she stood in between Max and Charlie.

"And how do you feel about Max?" she asked, carefully. "Do you feel . . . anything?"

His brow crashed together.

"Max? He's my best friend! I already told you that. About time you're awake," Charlie called over her shoulder, then waved a hand. "C'mon. Now that we wrapped all this headache business up, I have something to show you. Hurry! I've been waiting all day!"

"Wait!" Pearl cried. "You don't feel any sort of . . . emotion toward Max? A sense of violence?"

"Violence?"

"Yes, violence!"

"No!" Charlie blew a flabbergasted raspberry. "I just want to show him something. Can we go?"

Max scooted back, an eye on Ranulf. He hadn't moved. His curious expression remained, but that meant nothing. Pere hid behind curiosity all the time.

Pearl wrung her hands together. "Fine," she mumbled. "Fine. A-a-nd you're certain? You don't want to hurt him or anything?"

"Hurt him? Honestly, Pearl." Charlie spun toward the door. "C'mon Max! Gotta show you something."

In a blink, he was gone. Reluctantly, Max edged his way out of the room. Ranulf and Pearl's eyes followed until he popped into the hallway and followed Charlie's retreating steps.

Chapter Six

CHARLIE

Floorboards creaked beneath Charlie's feet as he crept down the edge of the hallway the next evening. Wildrose Manor, over a hundred and fifty years old, reminded him of an old lady: cantankerous, complicated, filled with shade and shimmer and too many groans.

When a low moan accompanied a footstep, he paused, winced, and waited. Papa's unwavering voice meant he hadn't heard Charlie approach.

Yet.

Papa had ears like an elephant.

Charlie avoided the squeaky board on the left. By the time he made it to Papa's office door, his heart thudded. As far as Charlie's usual overt operations went, this was by far the calmest. Clammy palms aside.

Papa's words drifted through a crack in the doorway. He spoke sedately, the way he conducted business. Darkness filled the windows. Flickering light cast shadows on Papa's desk, where candles dropped hot beads of wax. Several hovered around him. A giant quill bobbed up and down, clutched in Mr. Harry's hand.

Papa's solicitor.

Charlie frowned. So he hadn't imagined carriage wheels cracking up the cobblestone drive. A witch who came stealthily in the night had secrets to keep.

Oh, how he *loved* secrets.

He almost recruited Max to snoop with him, but held off at the last moment. Only a day had passed since Charlie shifted into a Defender, and Max to a Watcher. Max hadn't lost the glossy-eyed terror yet. All day, he hid in his room on the other side of the hall.

Slept like the dead, too.

Try as he might, Charlie couldn't get him to wake up.

A stirring of life, maybe magic, came from Max's room every so often. Charlie felt it like shifting oil in his chest. The intriguing sensation made him want to draw closer, follow the soundless, yet melodic, tune.

Well, there would be plenty of time for them to sleuth together. For now, he had other questions to answer.

Why did Papa invite Mr. Harry over so late at night?

"What is your desire for Wildrose in the event of . . ."

Mr. Harry, his profile visible, lifted invisible eyebrows higher. His bald forehead gleamed.

"The manor will go to my son, of course. The Dauphins have always bequeathed Wildrose from father to son. Just as Wildrose has always been a sanctuary for those in need, it will also continue in the line of our progeny.

"Above all, Harry, I want Charlie taken care of first. Wildrose second. I would hope Charlie would do all in his power to keep Wildrose within the Dauphins, but . . . anyway. With the way we have structured my affairs, the two should work together. Charlie cares for Wildrose. Wildrose cares for Charlie."

"Charlie is only twelve. And a bit . . . impetuous, if I might add. Is it wise?"

A rolling chuckle answered.

"He won't be twelve forever, Harry. Charlie is brilliant, don't let his affability fool you."

"I have noted him as the inheritor of Wildrose Manor, including all outlying properties and your investments in Berry."

"Yes," Papa mumbled, as if he'd forgotten. "The orchard, of course. An asset he might sell, if he needs it. Wildrose requires a good deal of currency to keep functional."

"You will bequeath all."

"We'll need to hurry this through the verification process, if the Apothecary is to be believed. I'd rather be prepared."

A sheet of ice formed under Charlie's skin, crackling.

Apothecary?

Prepared?

Mr. Harry asked, "Does the Apothecary feel that it's so urgent?"

"It could be. I may survive years, I might die in a week. He said there's no way of knowing."

"Are you going to tell Charlie?"

"No. No reason to taint whatever time we have left with worry over it."

"I'm sorry, Ranulf."

Gently, Papa said, "Me too, Harry. Me too."

"Charlie is a good boy. He'll be just fine. Pearl and I will look out for him whenever that time comes. You know that?"

"I do. Thank you. I appreciate the help more than I can say."

A long silence passed before Mr. Harry read from a parchment partially unrolled. Charlie's stomach knotted. Shock froze him into place. He didn't move, could barely breathe. His fingers curled around his knees and squeezed until all the blood blanched out.

Every few moments, Papa made a noise indicating agreement. Mr. Harry scratched something and pressed on. Parchments shuffled, dry but explosive in his ears.

An hour later, Charlie remained.

He soaked in every word, memorized it. The *uncanny intelligence* that Papa tutted over cataloged the facts. Papa and Mr. Harry said nothing concrete, only prepared for a vague future event precipitated by an unknown illness Papa didn't disclose. All business would happen later.

When grief choked Charlie.

When the emptiness of Wildrose Manor and his inherited legacy pitted him against the texture of the world.

Without his parents.

The looming event hovered like a dark specter in the night. A promise. A swooping goblin from the bowels of Wildrose that had been waiting all along. The same foul creature that stole his Mama in childbirth.

Mr. Harry gathered his things, murmured a few genuine platitudes, and shuffled out of the office. Charlie crouched behind a bookshelf, not bothering to hide with magic. Mr. Harry never paid attention unless it was to words on paper, so he didn't see Charlie lurk in the background.

Once Mr. Harry turned out of the hallway, Charlie crawled to the door and peered through the gap.

Papa stared at the wall, skinny fingers folded on his lap. Shadows snapped like long creatures, tossed by the flames. All manner of creepy ghosts that inhabited Wildrose and her ancient halls appeared there. Dragons. Birds flying. Ghouls chasing. Papa dissipated the wraiths with a clearing of his throat, startling Charlie out of half-awake dreams. His eyes burned with exhaustion.

Papa reached for a potion bottle. A cerulean liquid lay inside. He uncorked it, tossed it to the back of his throat, then winced as he swallowed.

The glass from the vial shattered in the fireplace when Papa tossed it inside. An explosion of sparks drifted up the chimney. The brilliant colors faded to gray ash that hovered.

All at once, the fire extinguished.

Chapter Seven

MAXIMILLION

The cellar door groaned as it opened.

"Demmed heavy thing it is," Charlie muttered, cheeks blooming red. He grunted, then dropped the thick wooden door. Mud coated the inside edges. Dust motes and an acrid scent drifted out of the black hole.

Dazed, Max could only blink at the cellar dug out of the ground, alongside the magnificence of a place like Wildrose Manor. A lovely, gothic countryside home with tall windows, sharp gables, and endless oddities inside.

Wildrose boasted four floors, with a smaller apartment on top for the master and mistress of the house. Gables, patios, and staircases existed everywhere. Magnolia Castle was the largest building he'd ever seen.

This manor might war for that title.

Max studied the sparkling window panes and stone facade, aged by weather and time. At the top, gargoyles perched on each corner. Flames emitted from their mouths. *Enchanted,* Charlie said the other night. *They pop on and off whenever they want. Not sure why.*

New growths of ivy twined lazily up a trellis behind them.

Sprouts of green grass populated from rich earth, leading all the way to the forest.

The fathomless, mysterious, and reputable Letum Wood. Letum Wood towered on three sides of Wildrose, like a too-close hug. Those unnerving trees. Max shuddered. The south edge of the property faced the road, far enough away that carriages could be seen, but not in great detail. A cobblestone drive led straight to the manor.

Max tore his hungry eyes away.

"What are you doing?" He squinted against the bright spring sunshine. Charlie hovered above the cellar, copper locks burnished and glowing.

"We're checking out our new headquarters."

"*Our* headquarters?"

"Of course! Think it's any fun running a secret organization by yourself? I've been studying and reading books about this for years. The Cudans really had it locked down, you know? Secrets, I mean. Anyway, it's not as easy as you might think."

"A secret society for what?"

Charlie shrugged. "Dunno."

"Do you know anything about the details?"

"Not yet!" Charlie laughed. "We have to figure out the big stuff first."

He leaped into the hole.

The last four days blitzed through Max's mind. Clues added up to a ragged picture, accompanied by thoughts of Pere. The blood dripping from his nose, the twining of two magicks that brought him . . .

. . . right here.

"Where am I?" he muttered.

"C'mon!" Charlie called. "I'll explain everything in here."

"Your father wanted us inside."

The thought of upsetting Charlie's father set him on edge.

Who were these witches? Where was the edge of Ranulf's impatience? This man might be an additional problem.

"We'll get there in a second," Charlie said. "Pearl and Papa just want to talk to us about magic and paths and stuff. There are witches that hate Watchers, so they want to teach you how to protect yourself. Big Leo in the East is one of them. We have that for the rest of our lives. C'mere."

Despite his better judgment, the one that told him to flee before another household sucked him in, Max followed Charlie into the black hole.

A dank, moldering smell surrounded him. Crumbly dirt walls, a distant screech. The cellar was bigger than he expected. Old shelves, filled with empty glass jars, cluttered the sides along with discarded furniture repurposed as storage and boxes of crumbling parchments marked ESTATE TAXES and MISCELLANY. Cold air drifted like a cloak.

"This is what you were so excited about?" he asked. Even to his own ears, he sounded imperious. Taciturn. He didn't mean to be, but couldn't force his voice to bend, his fear to break.

Charlie didn't notice.

"Yes! It's perfect."

"But . . . why?"

"Well, it's below ground, for one. That makes it harder to detect. The size is a bit small. At least thirty paces by thirty paces. We'll need to expand, for sure. I think it runs alongside the basement, though. We could fit ten desks and chairs in here. See that far wall? Pushes against the house. Wouldn't take long to dig through it, create a tunnel."

"To what?"

"A tunnel to the basement, of course! What good is a secret headquarters without an escape?"

"What do you need a secret headquarters for?"

Charlie put his hands on his hips. "Dunno yet. We're

going to figure that out." He pressed a fist to his face, brows scrunched in concentration. "It'll come. We'll find something necessary. Wildrose Manor has always been a haven for those seeking refuge, which means I can fulfill my family obligation of providing it. We're best friends now, Max." He thumped himself in the chest. "We're meant to be, don't you think?"

"Needs candles," Max muttered. He wiped something off his forearm.

Charlie laughed. A breathy sound that made Max want to curl into himself. He didn't belong here. Charlie would see that soon enough. Or maybe he wouldn't have to. Now that he felt his strength restored, Max could leave in the morning.

"You'd never know it's here," Charlie said, "if you didn't know to look. With a few spells, we can make the grass grow right over the top, then we can just transport inside. I love that about it. Wildrose Manor is always surprising me."

Max stepped back up the ladder to help relieve his claustrophobia. Charlie was mad, wasn't he? Frantically energetic, with thoughts for days. Knocking a hole in the cellar wall could have ramifications for the earth above it. What if it collapsed? How would he stabilize it?

These thoughts accompanied Max back to the surging spring air. Charlie followed, prattling about ideas of what to do with their new headquarters.

Wildrose's giant windows drew Max's curiosity. What secrets thrived within the sprawling rooms?

Charlie continued speaking, oblivious.

"You just never know, do you? You think you do, but you don't." Charlie laughed. "Strange."

Max stared at him. What was he talking about?

"Where am I?" he asked.

"At Wildrose."

"No, no. Where is Wildrose?"

Charlie sobered.

"Oh, right. The Central Network. The northern part of it, near Newberry. Come to think of it, you have a little accent. Eastern Network?"

Max nodded once, and *that* was as far into his life as they'd go.

Charlie spread his arms.

"Welcome to Wildrose, Max! If you like creepy places, follow me. I'll show you the cemetery, then we'll go into the basement. I think I know where it shares the wall with the cellar. We can start digging. Just don't tell Papa, all right?"

"Your Papa wants us inside."

"Oh, right, Watcher classes, or whatever. Sure. We'll do that first, then Papa won't suspect anything."

Watcher classes rang through his mind.

Well, maybe he'd stay a few more days.

Charlie took off across the lawn, discussing *weight distribution ratios* and *a book I read on household improvements,* while Max considered the fact that Charlie asked no questions about his life in the Eastern Network, or why he showed up on a rainy night. Charlie could be so loud . . .

. . . but maybe not so bad.

* * *

An envelope floated in the air above Max.

Was it a dream?

Not at all.

He pushed off the bed in the overly large room Ranulf had given him. A soft mattress and a dazzling lamp lent a surreality to his situation.

Was *any* of this real?

The letter lay horizontally as it floated. Scripted handwriting crossed the front in his name, first and last.

Maximillion Sinclair.

With a trembling hand, Max touched the outside. He recognized Serafina's hand in the swooping lines. A similar letter had arrived shortly after Mere's funeral, after Pere had slugged him in the face then collapsed into an unconscious heap and pissed all over himself.

Why now?

Why did Serafina write *this moment* of all times?

Dozens of fears bubbled to the surface. Did she know he'd killed Pere? Maybe she warned him away. Guardians might search for him, the twelve-year-old murderer that wandered loose.

If he touched the message, would it burn him?

Max snatched the letter, hopped out of bed, and chucked it into the fire. If he didn't see what it said, it couldn't hurt him. The paper sat on top of the coals for a second before smoke wound out from beneath it. The gauzy curtains surrounded the letter until a hole burned through the middle.

The whole thing caught on fire.

He turned away, hid back under the covers, and closed his eyes.

Chapter Eight

CHARLIE

Sleep eluded Charlie that night.

The next night.

The two that followed.

While Max hid in his bedroom down the hall, Charlie assessed headquarters, planned out the furniture, and removed all the old stuff. The physical exertion, combined with the additional urge to stop everything and drop into the paths, exhausted him.

Yet once he lay down to rest, he couldn't sleep.

Charlie tapped a rhythm on the sheet with his fingers, mind whirling. Shadows swirled in the recesses of his room. Thoughts of Papa, Apothecaries, Faye, Max, and magic cluttered the landscape. He closed his eyes, slipping easily into the Defender paths.

The magic Pearl feared.

She didn't say it in so many words, but her reservations showed in her actions. She eyed him warily. Every time he entered the room, she monitored his mood. Watched him. From her mannerisms alone, she clearly expected something awful to happen. What that might be, he couldn't imagine.

In the magic, the paths populated behind him. The welcome darkness soothed his rattled nerves. His emotions felt like teeth loose in his skull. Loud. Obnoxious.

His whole day laid out, branching into details that revealed what *could* have happened, but hadn't. Though Max snuck from room to room in Wildrose all day, blithely avoiding everyone, opportunities had existed for them to spend time together. Fishing in the forest stream. Berries. Digging the tunnel from headquarters to the manor.

All manner of trouble, if the angry twist of Pearl's face through several events meant anything.

Amongst all the possibilities lingered familiar and not-so familiar faces. Witches in distress, he assumed. In the wisps, they hugged Pearl, clung to Papa. Filled the kitchens, cluttered the grand staircase. Vagabonds from the forest, more than likely. Wildrose always brought in the needy, the searching. As if its wide windows and sweeping porches invited them. A silent magical call to the disenchanted and hungry.

Charlie closed the magic with a thought, returning to his room to stare at the ceiling.

A shuffle of sound caught his attention, followed by a muttered curse. A sensation like a string tugging at his navel pulled him out of bed and to the window. Down the way, a shadowed silhouette stood on the balcony.

Max.

He disappeared. A flash of color drew Charlie's attention to the grass. Max had transported there and strode toward the forest. A knapsack on his back likely meant he didn't plan to return.

Panic coursed through Charlie.

With barely a thought, he transported into Max's path. When he arrived, they stood face to face.

Max startled, eyes wide.

"Where are you going?" Charlie asked. "Can I come?"

A glower formed on Max's serious brow. Before he could answer, Charlie spoke again.

"I hate staying in the house at night. Kind of creepy, the way it creaks. After a hundred and fifty years, you'd think it would have settled as much as it could. No. It still has some complaining to do."

He turned to walk at Max's side.

"Is that why you're leaving?"

Taken aback, Max slowly followed. He walked, one arm stiff, the other clutching his knapsack with a too-tight hold. The faint odor of fresh bread drifted out.

No answer came.

"Where are we going?"

Max swallowed hard. "Ah . . . I don't know."

"I'd avoid the roads if I were you." Charlie hooked a thumb to the west. "There's a small village that way. Pershington. That's where I found you. Wildrose helps keep Pershington alive. At least, it used to. With just me and Papa, the manor doesn't require much now. Pearl lives there. Loves the Pershington library."

As he prattled, Max unwound. They shuffled through ankle-high grasses and into Letum Wood. Darkness enveloped them. Max canted a wary gaze overhead. A few paces in, he stopped.

"I'm leaving."

His trembling pronouncement created no surprise. Charlie spun, hands in his pockets, to face Max.

"I know."

"And you're going to let me?"

"Sure."

"Why?"

"Why would I force you to stay?"

Max opened his mouth to reply, then shut it again. Several searching moments passed before he croaked, "I don't know."

"Where are you going to go? If you need a few suggestions, I can give them."

"I'm . . . not sure."

"Back to the East?"

Max's glower deepened, but Charlie felt no fear. Such a cutting gaze would have torn through Faye, who shuddered when he entered a room and avoided contact with him. They hadn't met officially yet. Both seemed to avoid each other.

"Never."

"Then Pershington might have some work in stables. I hear that Chatham Castle is always hiring fireboys, though you're already too broad in the shoulders for that."

"I'm smart."

"If you were older, you could be a tutor."

"Not at twelve?"

Charlie laughed. "Well, maybe if you're teaching four-year-olds. You'd be more nanny than tutor, and I can't see that being a good thing for a kid like you. Better to live off the forest. C'mon. There's a stream up here. Let me show you where the best fishing hole is."

Reluctantly, Max followed. Movement allowed Charlie's thoughts to roll out. They tripped over each other, all of them good thoughts, brilliant ideas, ways to save Max from. . . . well . . . whatever he needed saving from.

"What's it like, seeing future possibilities?"

The question rolled out of him unexpectedly. Of all there was to say, that wasn't what he had anticipated.

Max startled, but eventually said, "Confusing."

"Same here. The past is all bungled up. I see what happened, but also what *could* have happened, and sometimes I can't remember which is which. As time passes, the images, whatever they are, become more clear."

"Pearl calls them wisps."

"Right. Wisps." Charlie rolled the word around his lips

several times. "That's right. It makes sense. They're . . . not real."

Minutes later, they arrived at the stream. Charlie stared at the vague dimness of his reflection, dimly visible through the dark. Pale face, abundance of freckles, and disarming eyes. Witches said he had a delightful smile.

Whatever that meant.

But what if he didn't?

The question haunted him. What if he *wasn't* what everyone expected him to be? Heir to the Dauphin legacy. Manager of Wildrose Manor. Layers of generations weighed on his shoulders. Unspoken requirements.

You are the heir.

You are Wildrose.

But what, he said to the voices that whispered from the grave, *if I wasn't exactly what you wanted me to be?*

The water shifted, clearing his image. He gazed away. Max stared at Wildrose over his shoulder, taut as a rock. The manor lurked amidst the trees in spectral lines. A lone candle in Max's window gave it away.

"If you didn't want to go," Charlie said, "you could stay forever with me. You might not want to be the best friend to anyone. With whatever you've survived in the past, maybe you have no reason to trust me and Papa. But I'd like you to stay. Papa wants you to stay. Pearl, too. She helps witches like us, you know. Watchers with questions come to her. We could go to school together when it starts next spring. A Network school. My exams were high enough to get me in early, and we could bring my tutor here to catch you up this winter. Faye will be at a girls school then, too. They're both sort of local Network schools. They wouldn't refuse a friend to the Wildrose heir."

Max said nothing.

Charlie stepped away. A twig crackled under his foot. The

blip and sigh of water as it slid over rocks, hurrying elsewhere, faded.

"See you later, Max."

With that, he left the shadows, Max, and all his fears behind him. Max would return.

Charlie could feel it in his bones.

/ Chapter Nine

MAXIMILLION

Dawn crept out of the sky like a plodding spider. Max watched while he slumped against a tree, waiting for the misery of outdoor life to end. Dirt. Bugs. Chilly air that made his lungs want to seize.

Not his thing.

Abbi told stories of witches in the Central Network that lived in haunted Letum Wood. The same forest he hunched in now, attempting to restore some sense of order and pride to his life.

So far?

Failing.

They live there, Abbi said with a hoot, laughing in a toothless way that sent air whistling through her puckered lips. *Can you believe that? Probably wake up with ghosts in their hair, trying to eat their brain.*

To be sure, he brushed a hand through his.

Nothing.

The small marsh town where Pere had imprisoned Mere and Max lay close to the Central Network border, swathed in swampy lands. Witches inhabited the only slightly elevated portion in all of it. Slugs, leeching wetness, and giant reptiles too small to be dragons, but not far off.

He shuddered, remembering the weight of the sticky air. The bugs that sucked blood from the bottom of his feet. The way the water lapped around everything, destroying whatever it caressed.

Trees littered the swamp just like here, but they were so different. Was the Central Network another world entirely?

Felt like it.

With a shiver, he thought of Pere. Had Abbi gone looking for Max yet? Did they know he murdered a family member?

Over a week had passed since he left his sodden town. Surely, someone had peeked into the shack. A debt collector, perhaps. Or a neighbor that needed help with their nets. When not tipsy, Pere's giant fingers held real skill with the complicated woven patterns.

How Pere was gentle with gossamer strands Max would never understand.

Dawn crested the horizon. He leaned forward, his back cramping from the cold. His conversation with Charlie had been more revealing than expected. Finding a house where he could be hired as a tutor had been his primary plan. Charlie had, without meaning to, torn it to shreds.

Foolish plan.

Max had no formal training. He might be intelligent, but lessons by starlight with a half-dead old woman from stolen books had nothing to do with true learning. Ingenuity—a rare idea he chased. He loved to be smart. Craved the power of wisdom and cleverness. Everything that Pere wasn't.

What now?

Where to go?

Charlie's offer held more temptation than he wanted to

admit. Live in Wildrose, an elegant, stately home that felt . . . safe. Walls everywhere. Doors that locked. Windows that closed all the way. Pearl or Ranulf or Charlie made noise all the time. There was no succumbing to the elements, like several of Pere's shack-like homes.

Only stability.

Max craved the manor the same way he hungered. Ravenously. Constantly. Three meals a day, plenty of clean water, nightly baths in a bubbly tub, if he wished, had soothed the puckered, dry parts inside.

He yearned for more, though he didn't deserve it.

You're housing a murderer, he thought. *Do you know that? What if they come for me?*

He scoffed with a gentle misting of breath. Who would come for him? Who would want to, or even think of, avenging a witch like Pere? No one. Abbi might be happy for Max, assuming he'd taken off and had no plans to return. His fingers tightened into a fist.

What other option did he have *but* Wildrose?

A dark feeling settled like a low fog. One other option. One glaring, frustrating choice that he almost didn't acknowledge.

Circumstances forced him to think of her. Serafina, his mother's sister. His aunt. The aunt who had left him with Pere. The aunt on whom he blamed every gash, every bruise, every night when his body trembled while he hid under the bed and Pere frothed himself into a wild, drunken rage.

No, Serafina wasn't an option.

She was a loose thread to his past. One he tucked away yet again and forgot existed. He'd promised himself never to reach out. Never make himself known or visible.

When she didn't attend Mere's funeral, Serafina made her feelings known. She sent a note stating her regret, but that was all. His only ally had abandoned him to remain in her place of honor in Magnolia Castle.

A place he could never go.

The same burning rage that kept him alive all those nights fueled him now. He'd survive just to spite Serafina. To show his aunt that fighters existed without a High Priestess swooping in to save them.

Mere may have given up, but he would not.

He turned to Wildrose again, thoughts centered on Charlie. Charlie had a wildness about him. A streak of energy that Max could hardly bear to look at. Once he put on weight, grew to his natural size, would he be boundless like Charlie?

Was this his chance to find out?

Before he stood up and trudged back to Wildrose, he already knew his answer. He knew what he wanted.

Wildrose.

Food.

Safety.

To the greatest extent, a family. This desire he tucked away. No one would see the tender, burning glow that fed fire to the rest of his will to survive. It kept everything else from smoking to ash.

If Charlie meant what he said, Max would take the offer. He'd do it without pretense. Ranulf and Charlie would know *exactly* who they invited into their homes and lives.

A flickering candle on a bottom floor window in the front, overlooking the long drive that extended from the road, drew him closer.

Ranulf's office.

The forbearing witch was already awake, starting on the day. Charlie, as Max had observed through listening at the seam of the door for the last week, would sleep until well past the sun rose.

Max steeled himself as he headed toward Ranulf.

Time for total honesty.

* * *

The knock echoed on Ranulf's wooden door.

Lifetimes stretched out before a pair of slippers crossed the floor, opening it up a sliver. Ranulf peered out, then reared back when he saw Max.

The smell of mud and dying leaves and other dead things wafted off him. Max fought not to wrinkle his nose or apologize. Into the dredges of his gut he reached, attempting to find a modicum of courage.

"Mr. Dauphin, may I speak with you?"

Ranulf stepped back, the door opening. "Only if you agree to call me Ranulf. Mr. Dauphin is my father."

Max nodded, though he suspected too late that Ranulf meant to make a joke. A somber air followed them as Ranulf sat behind his cherry wood desk, filled with parchments, and motioned Max into a chair right across from him.

Bookshelves ringed the cozy office. Some of them filled with squared-off cubbies of various sizes, meant to house scrolls. Enchanted handwriting scrawled along the wood to dictate an organizational pattern. A counter spell could erase the writing. If touched, the ink wouldn't flake off. A chill lingered in the room, despite a healthy fire and a fresh stack of wood. Potion bottles scattered the top of the desk, two of them half-empty.

Max lowered into the offered leather chair.

"What can I help you with at this . . . early hour?" Ranulf asked, fingers braided in front of him. His brow rose in curious inquiry.

All the words Max had shored up failed. They fled like startled guppies. His mouth bobbed open, then closed. Heat built in his throat. Finally, he squeaked out something between a sound and a sob.

"I want to stay, sir."

With a clearing of his throat, Max pressed a hand to his mouth and yanked himself together. Ranulf's shoulders melted back. He lifted an eyebrow.

"Oh?"

Max closed his eyes, released a breath through his nose. The pause gave him a chance to hide his flailing fears. When he opened them again, Ranulf waited patiently.

"At Wildrose." Max cleared his throat. "Charlie said . . . he said that I could. I would like that. I wanted to see if . . . if that was a promise he could make."

Ranulf nodded. "Yes, Max. Of course you can stay. I told Charlie as much myself. He didn't speak idly."

Something breezed through him. Relief, only infinitely stronger. Hope! That was it.

It had been so long . . .

He felt vaulted into the air. Tossed out of darkness and finally within reach of something better. The chair grounded him.

"I'll work as a stableboy," he blurted out. "Or someone to clean. I'll figure out how to cook or—"

"Is that necessary?" Ranulf asked.

"I . . . I don't know."

"What if you stay as a young man?"

Max reared back. "Sir?"

"Just like Faye. She stays here without working."

"You would do that?"

Ranulf gave him a weary smile. "I don't know your past, Maximillion. I would like to, if you feel safe sharing it with me, but I feel it's wise to assume you came from a difficult place. You must have done a lot to stay alive. I can appreciate that. Perhaps you had to clean and work to prove yourself. I'd wager you've never been able to just . . . be a young man. To get into trouble for the right reasons, not the wrong ones. To attend school?"

The searching tone wrinkled his composure. Max leaned away, breath fast. Oh, no. This had been a huge mistake. Ranulf would find out and send him away. This would just disappear and be a dream. He'd wake up with Pere screaming, eyes bloodshot.

He remembered the chilly nights in the swamp. The way Abbi gummed her food down because her husband knocked too many of her teeth out before killing himself on a boat. How Pere chugged ipsum until the sides of his mouth streamed with froth and soaked his shirt in broadening stains.

Max dropped his gaze.

"No, sir. Never attended school."

"You strike me as a smart lad."

Defensiveness drove his tone. "I am. I'm very smart."

"Good. I have an excellent tutor that can do some testing, figure out where you're at and then get you ready to start into a school with Charlie next year. It would be a couple of years early, but they're short on young boys these days. Charlie already tested into it. I believe you might as well. If not, we'll find you another position, equally helpful."

"The currency, sir. I—"

Ranulf waved a hand. "No, Max. Don't insult me. I'll take care of it."

"But . . . why?"

Here, Ranulf paused. Lines formed around his eyes, pushing them into deeper, thoughtful structures.

"Because good witches still live in the world. I hope that's a lesson I can teach you before it's too late. What happened between you and your past is not your fault."

His heart turned to a thick spring mud. Dank. Difficult. He'd felt this heaviness before, when Abbi dragged him out of the swamp and saved his life. When the thought of Serafina at Mere's funeral cast the light of hope into his bleak days, then she never appeared.

Surely, such recollections drove his next words.

"I murdered my Pere."

Ranulf considered that, then calmly stated, "Tell me more."

The truth streamed free. Each morsel of the story as he remembered it. The jagged, fractured memories. Incomplete, loaded with emotions that blurred the edges.

He said the words this once. One time. After this, he'd never say them again. Pere would disappear like smoke, his fists a legacy of ashes. No one would remember him. Forgetting Pere would be Max's final revenge.

At the end, he whispered, "I didn't mean to, sir. But . . . I'm not sad."

Ranulf's sympathetic face blurred when hot tears popped into Max's eyes. Oh, how he loathed the rising tide of emotion. He swallowed them back. Any smart boy tucked dangerous sentiments like *hope* and *courage* and *resistance* down. Down deep. Deep enough, they didn't exist. Deep enough, Pere would never know they arose, as if he could sniff them out like the swamp bloodhounds that chased anacondas.

"Do you know what self-defense means, Max?"

"Yes, sir."

"You're aware that doing whatever you can to prevent your own death, even if it accidentally results in the aggressor's death, means you are innocent? If you were to stand before the Highest Witch of your Network, they would not find you guilty."

Max bit his tongue.

In fact, he didn't know. All he saw was dripping crimson. A growing stain. Felt the panic of an unknown magic clawing at him. Even now, with all the heightened emotions, the magic wrapped around him like a vague promise to cart him to safety again. A prickling sensation, step-brother to fear.

Ranulf leaned back in his chair, contemplative as he peered up at the ceiling. "For my part, I consider you a survivor, not a murderer. Your Pere received the inevitable result of such a life. You extracted yourself from a hellacious place and brought yourself here. Let's make something of you."

"Repayment—"

"Is an insult," Ranulf said gently. "Never speak of it again."

A ball of heat lodged in Max's throat. He nodded once.

Ranulf's gaze dropped to the vials sitting on his desk, then back. "In fact, my boy, we may help each other out. Charlie will need someone at his side when . . . well, he already has great affection for you."

A world of tenderness, even distress, lingered in the words. Suddenly, Max understood. The potions treated illness.

Ranulf wasn't well.

"When?" Max asked. Supposition loaded the single-word question, but Ranulf understood.

"I don't know."

"I'm sorry."

"Me too."

"Sir, thank you. I—"

"It's enough, Max." Ranulf smiled kindly. "It's enough. Now, who is going to tell Charlie that you will remain? He'll not stop talking for days. He'll be so excited."

Max cracked a weak smile. Charlie, his only . . . friend. If one could call him that. What else would he be? Charlie, who spoke so he didn't have to. Charlie, so unaffected by Max's contrary opinions. Charlie, who let nothing deflate his drive and excitement for life.

A stranger witch didn't exist.

"Don't imagine that any of your appearance at Wildrose Manor is an accident. You and Charlie stepped into the exact same magic system at the exact same time. And it all occurred after he broke the rules on a particular night, only to find you on a rain-soaked street. Like it or not, Maximillion, you're meant to be here. It's an honor to have you."

CHARLIE

One year later

Charlie peered into the dust-scattered cellar with a frown. In nine months, could not one soul look after it? Dust ballooned through the air. Already, he could see it lining the shelves, the old table he'd dragged down there and almost smashed.

What a depressing headquarters.

No matter.

He'd returned. Time to whip it back into shape.

Charlie placed one foot onto the ladder to descend. A shuffling near the corner of his right eye stopped him. He spun to see Faye standing in the depths of the cellar, hands propped on her hips, a scowl on her face. Her dark skin camouflaged her against the wall. She wore her long hair tied away from her face with a cloth, the bright red fabric a brilliant zing of color in the dark.

His lips twitched to hold back a smile. Faye. His soulmate. The zest in his soul. How he had missed her!

He dropped off the ladder. With a cry, he spread his arms.

"Faye!"

She held out a hand to stop his advance. He stalled a few paces away, heart thready like a hummingbird.

"Oh, no!" she cried. "You don't get to greet me like we're best friends after you stopped writing."

The power of her frown cut through him like a hot knife.

Faye, angry with him?

"What?"

She propped both fisted hands on her hips. "Why didn't you write, Charlie? I waited for a letter from you every day at school. You can't imagine how insufferable it is living with so many girls, and not a one of them with an ounce of adventure in their heads."

Her imploring tone weakened him.

"I wrote. Every week."

Her nose scrunched. "I didn't get any letters."

"They wouldn't let us send them. Just to parents this year. First-year rule, or something."

He held out a hand. In his bare palm, a pile of envelopes appeared, tied by twine. He handed them over.

"Organized by date. Every one of them is for you."

Her eyes widened. She clasped them to her chest with a delighted cry, then astonishment. "By the good gods, Charlie! What sort of magic are they already teaching you over there? You're thirteen and can conjure?"

Conjuring was nothing compared to what he *really* wanted to learn. She ran her thumb along the edge of the envelopes. Her full lips hinted at a brilliant smile.

He plopped onto a chair, set his hands on his knees.

"Tell me everything, Faye."

"Everything?"

"Everything." He swept a hand in front of them. "Tell me everything you have to say. What's happened? What has the school taught you? Have you gone back to the West to find your family?"

She eyed him, finger held up to scold. "Don't think you can avoid my questions by asking me first!"

A charming grin stole across his face. He pressed a hand to his chest, faking shock. "Me? Faye! Never. Tell me, please! I'm curious what the girls' schools are like in comparison to smelly, dodgy young boys. We stink."

Hesitantly, Faye nodded. She relaxed, melting into the chair across from him. Her hands rested in her lap, eyes alight.

"I struggled at first, but your father hired a tutor for me."

"Good."

Her nose scrunched. She held the letters more tightly. "It's an awful lot of currency, Charlie."

He snorted. "Papa loves to provide education, you know that. It's the Wildrose in him. Look at what he did for Max! Now Max is attending a more elite Network school than me."

An annoyed eyebrow tilt replied. Of all the things they had to discuss, Max would be the absolute lowest on her list. Right above *moldy socks*, but below *edible types of larvae*.

"We aren't talking about *him*," she muttered. "Having him with us at Wildrose during the spring is bad enough."

Charlie laughed. She'd never love Max the way he did. Her spine stiffened at the topic.

"Max is upstairs," she said, frosty now. "He arrived this morning."

Charlie grinned wider. "Is he cranky?"

"Isn't he always?"

"Come now, Faye! Don't be jealous of Max."

An equally irritated expression crossed her face. Her arms tightened around the letters.

"I never said I was jealous."

He laughed. "Good. Max as my best friend means nothing

in comparison to you. You're my soulmate. That's far more powerful."

Her vexation melted into the same sense of disbelief she always wore when he said it.

To his bones, he felt the truth. They would be together for the rest of their lives. He'd known it since she showed up in Pershington, abandoned on the roadside and seeking water.

A winding coil of hair fell out of her bun and over her left ear. She absently tucked it away before he could reach for it himself. They couldn't be more different. His pale, freckled skin contrasted with her tawny, rich tones. Bright red hair, carroty against her dark-as-night locks that fluffed around her head when she didn't put it in braids.

With an elbow, Charlie nudged her toward the ladder.

"C'mon, Faye. I've seen enough here. We'll clean it up later. Tell me everything I've missed while I've been gone. Pearl has been keeping track of Apothecary visits, hasn't she? Will she tell you about them?"

She sent him a sly smile. "You know I can get it out of her."

"I taught you well!"

With a laugh, he gripped the ladder first. She followed, trailing at his heels like a veritable puppy. Once in the warm spring sunshine, she tilted her head back. A radiant smile brightened her features.

"I've missed the sun."

A figure strode toward them. Thirteen years old, but surly as an old forest lion. Max stalked closer, a crisp white shirt under a black vest. Faye snorted. Max's signature sense of impeccable style humored her.

Max had a penchant for perfection, particularly with fashion.

"He never relaxes," she muttered.

"He likes to be prepared." Charlie lifted an arm to wave. "Max!"

Max didn't pause, but continued to barrel toward them. The last year had been good to Max. He put on weight, lost the gauntness in his eyes. Faye slipped away, murmuring, "See you later, Charlie," under her breath, letters in hand.

Disappointment zipped through him, but he set it aside for later. He'd sneak into Faye's room after bedtime. It was more fun to see her in secret, anyway.

The moment Max slowed, Charlie threw his arms around him. Max stiffened like an ice pillar as Charlie thumped him on the back.

"How are you, Max?"

"Fine." The flinty glare softened by degrees. "I'm . . . glad to see you again, Charlie."

"Are you really?"

"Yes."

"Me too. How are things going? Papa says you've been working like a dog to get up to speed in your classes."

"School has been fine." Max hungrily scoured the grounds, eyeing the ring of forest behind the carpet of fresh green grass. The gazebo on the far side, the open cellar door. The perusal stopped at Wildrose. Affection softened his intensity.

"Just fine?"

"Yes, but I'm glad to be home," Max said tentatively, with undeniable tenderness. Charlie glanced at Wildrose, saw nothing but an ancient old structure that never moved, and couldn't fathom the draw.

Bored with those thoughts already, Charlie jabbed him in the rib with an elbow again. He steered them toward the manor.

"Then let's get started!"

Max cast him a sidelong glance. "On what?" he drawled. His lack of immediate rebuttal heartened Charlie.

"On practicing. What kind of secret society doesn't have all the invisibility magic memorized? C'mon. I filched a few books from the library on invisibility incantations, and some others with summoning. We can practice them in the cellar!"

* * *

The scent of roses drifted past Charlie a week later.

Max stood tall at his side, eyes narrowed to shrewd lines. Both of them leaned against the exterior of Wildrose, climbing roses scraping their necks. The miniature buds emerged from their vines, tiny as a hummingbird heart. Rapid growth over the next week would lead to the giant, variegated petals that decorated the walls.

Charlie tutted. "Whatever is making all that racket in the forest, it's definitely something dangerous."

"A mortega," Max muttered. "Not a dragon."

"I never said dragon."

"You implied it."

"That's a lot of moving branches for a mortega that lives on the ground," Charlie drawled. "Unless they grew wings?"

Max glowered.

Sunset washed a bath of colors over the top of the forest. Simmering hues of the brightest pink and radiant orange swirled near the skyline. Clouds on fire drifted by, bellies glimmering. The sound of clattering wheels hurried up the drive, bumping over cobblestones. Charlie tensed. Max's perpetual frown deepened.

"Another Apothecary," Charlie said.

Max gave no reply.

"Will you—"

"No. I will not look into the paths for you to see what happens. Besides, I see only for myself, not others."

Charlie sighed. Max always refused the request. *There is no good answer, Charlie,* is all he ever said.

"Pearl told Faye that the Apothecary comes every two weeks now. Used to be monthly. She's not sure what they're doing. I don't think Papa realizes that we're tracking him."

A stubborn silence seemed to insist otherwise until Max broke the quiet.

"You have always loved being sneaky."

Charlie would have laughed, but a somber feeling overtook him. The door to the carriage closed. The wheels creaked as they slipped away. A sudden thickness burdened the air. Out of the woods came a staggering figure—the source of their original curiosity.

Max straightened.

"Not a mortega," he drawled.

"Not at all."

A witch fell to their knees, then their face. Charlie shoved away from the wall, drawn by power. Tingling curiosity.

An otherworldly . . . something.

The same sensation that called to him when Max used the Watcher magic. Like a light flooding him from the inside out. The radiance curled, pulling him closer. A visceral tug of energy that faded shortly after it began.

In silent accord, they sprinted toward the fallen witch. As they closed in, Charlie called, "It's a Watcher!"

Max's sharp green eyes cut over. "How do you know?"

"I told you. I can *feel* them. Not as powerfully as I feel when you use your magic, but enough."

The coy flare of desire ended. The witch, a middle-aged woman with streaks of gray in her blonde hair, lay face down. Blood turned the edge of her scalp pink. Dirt coated her fingers, which lay slack on the grass.

Max dropped to his knees.

"Madam?"

Charlie put a hand on her shoulder. "She's breathing. Not heavily or fast."

"Find Pearl."

Charlie hesitated, then obeyed. Max would be the better one to stay. A second later, transportation dropped him in the middle of the kitchen. Steam luffed off a boiling cauldron, set in the heart of a crackling fire. Pearl stood at a wooden counter, a large knife in hand as she attacked turnip greens and beets.

Faye smiled from where she stood near the window, kneading a surging bowl of dough. Heat filled the back of his neck when he winked, then twirled to Pearl in utmost soberness.

"Pearl, a Watcher has come."

Pearl's head jerked up.

"What?"

"A woman. She's older, I guess. She's hurt. Just stumbled out of the trees. I felt her magic when she arrived."

Pearl set the knife aside, wiped her hands on an apron tied around her waist. "Take me to her."

Charlie dodged to the door, unable to transport all three of them at the same time. He could only transport himself short distances, but his ability increased daily. Once outside, he pointed to the far edge of the field. All three of them separately transported to Max's hunched figure.

Max had taken his coat off, draped it around the unconscious woman. Twilight settled, making it difficult to see her profile.

Pearl crouched down.

"Oh, Amee."

Charlie's head jerked up. "You know her?"

"She's a member of the BLAUS and a friend of mine."

"What is the BLAUS?"

Pearl impatiently batted that aside. "The Berry Literary Society for Ancient Texts and Upholstering. It's just a front for a group of Watchers that get together every month." Sorrow filled her voice as she pressed a lock of hair out of Amee's eyes. "Her sister is married to Leo Giuseppi, in the Eastern Network. If she's here, nothing good has happened."

The name rang a faint bell in the back of Charlie's mind. Where had he heard that before?

Max's face hardened. "The Eastern Network Head of Guardians," he said. "A lech, and a known Watcher hater. Rumor states he's been gathering up Defenders to find Watchers with their draw and kill them."

Oh.

Right.

That Leo. Big Leo of the Eastern Network. A petite man with medals almost as big as him. Also a known confidante of the High Priest, Dante Aldana, and a man determined to wipe Watchers out of Alkarra. Despite the fact that killing Watchers had no effect on the magic, Big Leo staged raids, planned executions, and forced prison time on innocent witches. Anything to rid the populace of Watchers.

A simmering rage nudged out Charlie's curiosity. Someone should have protected her. She should have had somewhere to go that was safe.

She should . . .

An ideal bubbled to life in Charlie's mind. His eyes widened. He sucked in a sharp breath, the sound lost as Pearl gently turned Amee onto her back.

The good gods.

He had it.

He knew *exactly* what he wanted.

Amee groaned, which jerked him out of his thoughts. Faye gasped. Bruising bubbled under Amee's left eye. A scratch crossed her upper cheek, as if someone with a ring hit her with a fist.

"The good gods," Pearl muttered, with a shake of her head. "Come on, then. I'll transport her into the kitchen. Faye, fetch the oils and herb chest out. It's in Ranulf's office for—well, it's in there. Charlie, Max, find Ranulf and bring him, too. He'll want to see her."

Chapter Eleven

MAXIMILLION

Charlie's thoughts bubbled like a stew. Max could almost hear them from the other side of the room. Only a few paces away, Amee lay in the bed, on her side, tucked safely into the basement where no one would stumble on her.

Max watched Charlie carefully, aware of just *what* that level of concentration meant.

Trouble.

Faye bustled to the linen closet for heavier blankets, while Pearl and Ranulf spoke quietly in the hallway. Heat swelled into the cool room from a snapping fire. A thin, horizontal window at the top of the wall hinted at a night sky speckled with stars.

Too late, Max realized Charlie wasn't just plotting. He stood entirely too still. When Charlie connected ideas, his body moved.

Constantly.

No, Charlie didn't plot anymore.

He eavesdropped.

Annoyed he hadn't thought of it first, Max cast a spell. Ranulf's voice filled his ears, along with a brighter pop of fire that made him wince. Why listening incantations couldn't be more specific, he'd never understand.

"Of course she can stay, Pearl. For as long as she needs."

"The BLAUS would do more to help her, but I think they're afraid. If it *was* Leo, the way I highly suspect, they don't want to draw Defenders to them."

"Understandable. Your Watchers are being wise. Please, allow us to help. This is what Wildrose is for."

Distress coated Pearl's voice as she pressed on, oblivious to his calm replies. "I don't think she would bring any danger to Wildrose by being here, as no one knows she's here. At least, I assume not. But without knowing what happened . . ."

A rustle of cloth, as if Ranulf reached for Pearl, followed. "I'm not afraid of a few bullies, Pearl. Wildrose has its own penchant for magical protection. We'll know."

"What if Leo comes looking?"

"He won't. How would he know to find her here?"

"He might have had her followed!" she squeaked. "He'd sense that I'm a Watcher and maybe burn down the manor!"

A low chuckle followed. "Dear woman. We have many places we can hide you and Amee here. The secret passages, the hidden closets, all of that. The sheer number of rooms! She'll be safe until you can discover the story, heal her up, and we'll find her a better situation. If Leo Giuseppi comes, I will deal with him personally. I doubt he will. We aren't even sure that her injuries stem from him. There could be an entirely different story."

Pearl, far calmer, sniffled. "Yes, you're right. Thank you, Ranulf. You're good to me. I just . . . I don't want harm to come to you or Charlie or Max or Faye."

"Your concern is most appreciated. I believe we're quite safe."

Pearl snuffled one more time, composed herself with a

couple breaths, and the *tap tap tap* of her retreating footsteps sounded next.

Max closed the magic. Charlie shot him a knowing look. Max nodded once to show he'd heard. Charlie returned to his mental brew, fingers tapping against his thigh. Ah. Contemplation had returned.

Meanwhile, Max studied Amee. She had fine-bone features and a handsome face. Wispy blonde hair curled off her temples like a sigh. Faye had tenderly cleaned the blood away.

When would Leo come for him?

Memories of Pere interposed over Leo until he didn't know the two apart. A feeling like hardened iron sank in his gut when Ranulf stepped inside. The hinges on the door squeaked, then quieted.

Ranulf stood in the doorway for several moments. "If it was Leo Giuseppi that attacked Amee, we may have a bigger problem on our hands."

Charlie spun to face his father, a gleam of interest in his eyes. Max fought off a sigh.

The good gods, but they were in it now.

"Problem?" Charlie drawled.

Ranulf frowned. "This attack would mean that Leo has crossed into the Central Network with his Defenders to attack Watchers here. Once we can confirm the story, which I feel is likely, we need to contact the High Priest."

"Rabid dog," Max muttered, offended at the thought. Attacking Watchers was horrific enough, but the political climate of the Eastern Network on a hunt?

Ridiculous.

"Yes." Ranulf fell into deeper thought. "If Leo continues to attack, I'll tell Pearl to let her Watcher friends know Wildrose is a safe place, should they need it."

Charlie grinned.

Clouds of concern overwhelmed Max. Would this plan be wise if it put Wildrose in danger, as Pearl had said?

What about the manor?

He silenced his fears. He trusted Ranulf.

Fire cut across Ranulf's face, illuminating hollow cheeks. In this light, he appeared gaunt. Daylight didn't cast such starkness on his features. Max hated that he could see such obvious illness at all. He tried to ignore the affection he felt for Ranulf, something he couldn't feel for his own parents, but couldn't help himself.

He owed his life to Ranulf.

"Will you tell the High Priestess?" Max asked.

Ranulf snorted. "Not until we know for certain. We must be careful. Greta would use it as an excuse for another war, which we don't need. The High Priest would be open to discussion over it."

Max filed that information away for later. High Priestess Greta had become an increasingly controversial subject at his school, Mr. Shad's School for Boys. Mr. Shad milled political issues into every subject, a fact that thrilled Max daily.

Stacking government structures, the complications of minuscule problems that became sprawling ones over broad populations, sent a frisson of excitement through him with each class he gobbled up. Catching up to his compatriots had been harrowing, almost as difficult as erasing his Eastern accent, but worth it.

Ranulf turned to Charlie. "Do you feel her power?"

Charlie nodded.

"Why do you think Charlie doesn't feel the same hunger to hurt me or other Watchers?" Max asked.

Ranulf shrugged. "Pearl believes *you* have inoculated him against it."

"Do you think that's true?"

"As I'm not part of the magic, anything I can contribute is

a guess. Might be a simple, misunderstood nuance. Or the Eastern Network might create this issue in Defenders, knowingly or unknowingly. Time will tell."

Amee shuffled. Her head twitched to the side, fingers jerking. All three of them paused. Silence spread through the room. With a sigh, Amee returned to sleep. Faye appeared in the doorway, blankets in her arms. A teapot followed, steaming. Charlie brightened with a smile he reserved only for Faye. She shyly returned it.

Max turned away.

Lovesick doves.

"Mr. Ranulf," Faye said. "If it's all right with you, I'd like to stay the night with Amee. She might need someone to take care of her when she wakes up, and I wouldn't mind. That allows Pearl to visit the other witches in the BLAUS. Their secret society will need some warning."

Charlie shot him a wry look that Max pointedly ignored.

Ranulf continued. "When rumors that Leo might cross borders to attack first circulated, Pearl had the BLAUS tighten ranks, so to speak. It seems that time may have come again. Faye, I would be most appreciative if you cared for Amee. Thank you. Please notify me if you need anything."

Faye nodded. She settled a blanket on top of Amee and kept a worried gaze on her. Pearl hadn't returned. Likely wouldn't, for a bit, if what Faye said was true. Max itched to speak to Charlie about this. Set free whatever terribly stupid idea brewed in that red head.

One Max might, if pressed, admit he looked forward to hearing.

Minutes later, Ranulf left, hands folded behind his back, expression contemplative. Charlie winked at Faye, then cast Max a gaze over his shoulder. With a tilt of his head, he motioned to the hall.

Max followed.

* * *

Charlie led them to the cellar.

Er—headquarters.

Of course.

Max dodged a hanging root, obliterated it with a spell, and used another incantation to remove the dust from an old divan. He lowered onto it uneasily. Fortunately, he'd learned several spells to clean soiled clothes, so *headquarters* wouldn't stain the pieces he had.

He loathed this place, but didn't dare tell Charlie.

Charlie placed an unusual amount of attention on this cellar, particularly for him. His mind hopped from one place to the next. He brimmed full of thoughts, most of them ostentatious or translated from a different language or completely out of context. With school momentarily out and a break stretching ahead of them, Charlie would have more energy than ever.

Part of the dirt floor had been covered by uneven wooden planks Charlie found in a back garden. Two of them popped up if stepped on in the right spot. More than once, Max had nearly tripped over a board that stood higher than the rest. An incantation to root the boards into the ground, a thorough sanding, and a coat or five of polish would make them serviceable. Cast offs, all of them, but not ineffective.

Charlie planned to stack stones along the wall to hold in greater heat, hiding the muddy walls that oozed with rain. Weak magic, more hope than skill, kept the cellar from collapsing.

Charlie paced, his feet thudding along two particularly long boards. He gesticulated in front of himself.

"I've got it, Max! Amee has inspired me. Finally, the secret society has come together. This will be the headquarters for an organization to help Watchers and Defenders. Mostly Watchers."

Max frowned.

"What?"

Charlie laughed. "I can't believe I didn't see it before! You heard Papa. Big Leo has ventured into the Central Network to steal Watchers here."

"Allegedly."

Charlie waved that off.

"An obvious attack on our witches. You and I can't do anything about it politically—that's on other witches for now —but we could do what Wildrose has always done: provide a safe place. It's our legacy, Max!"

Your legacy, he almost said, but stopped the words. Desperately, he wanted it to be *his* legacy as well. The walls, the gables, the stones of Wildrose cradled his heart. He loved this property with fierce adoration.

"We're thirteen, Charlie. Still in Network schools! Will you run this organization during lunch and dinner?"

The scathing note of reality completely rolled past Charlie.

"If I must," he said brightly, head tilted back. He gazed on the ceiling, but deeper thoughts claimed him. The good gods help them all, but Charlie might actually try it.

Max let out a long breath. "Charlie . . ."

"I know, I know." Charlie flapped an impatient hand. "We're young, we're in school, and all that. But I don't see why that should stop us. We have holidays and an occasional weekend. I've been saving my allowance and could pay a witch to finish our headquarters."

"What are you going to *do* here?"

Charlie set his hands on his hips, then shook his head. "Haven't the foggiest idea, honestly. Practice magic. Gather other witches that want to help. Make it safe. A place to escape. Maybe protect it with a spell that only allows certain witches to transport in? We'll figure it out. We're obligated Max."

Max didn't disagree, but couldn't grasp the logic that drove Charlie.

"Why?"

"Because we've found each other! We're a match in the magic. We both see for only ourselves. I think there's something there. We can't be the only ones, right? Pearl agrees. Each Watcher has a paired Defender, like you and me."

"You're guessing."

Charlie threw up his hands. "Aren't we all?"

"Why does that—"

"Because I don't attack you like Pearl says some Defenders attack Watchers. Maybe we've figured something out that we can share with other Defenders. More than just helping Watchers, we might stop this problem entirely. And also protect Watchers," he tacked on.

The words sent a shock through Max. A cold thrill. The idea of helping witches in need appealed on a powerful level. Hadn't he been the recipient of such selflessness? The headquarters? Not so much. Not when they had all of Wildrose at their disposal.

What Charlie spoke of was something bigger. He wanted to dig to the source of this problem.

Well, that fired all the nerves that Mr. Shad taught him. *Government,* said Mr. Shad's voice in his memory, *is only as good as the roots. When an issue arises, you don't react. You seek. You find the source, take it out, and fix the circumstances that cause negative repercussions in society.*

Despite his better judgment, Max nodded.

"You have my attention."

Charlie hooted. "I knew it. We're magical twins, and there's no way around it."

Max rolled his eyes.

Charlie laughed harder. He dropped into a chair next to Max. The brightness of a new plan illuminated Charlie from the inside out. Like a candle in a hall of mirrors, he glowed.

Max couldn't help himself: he craved such incandescence. Wished that Charlie's light could pierce the darkness of his soul that crept in while Max was away from Wildrose. When dreams of Pere clawing out of the grave to snap his neck kept him awake at night in his shadowy room, alone.

The temptation to slip into the paths, see how much this cellar might feature in his possibilities, swept through him. He ignored it. Searching wouldn't help. Might actually frighten him. Still, the desire surged within.

Future possibilities had a tendency to reveal a heightened chance of anything new. Naturally, he moved his life in those emerging paths and patterns, which often diluted reality. The future was complicated and nuanced. Too cluttered. The magic insisted that he step into the paths daily and the demand annoyed him, yet once the darkness bathed him with its cool, kind escape, the release bolstered him.

"I'll always be at your side, Charlie. Just don't be stupid?"

Charlie nudged Max with a friendly jab in the ribs. "Wisdom, Max. Wisdom."

CHARLIE

A moldering scroll fell apart in Charlie's hands later that night.

He tried to piece it back together with a spell, but it disintegrated under the weight of magic. Carefully, he set it aside. Information on the world's greatest underground organization had once filled the page. He'd long ago copied it to a new one, but something powerful drew him back to the original.

He returned to his work.

Four other scrolls filled the wobbly desk where he sat in headquarters, hastily scratching in near-illegible notes. Structures filled pages, scrolls the width of the table. He didn't stop.

Couldn't stop.

Magic or excitement or distraction filled him. When he sank into adventure, helping others, and disguises, he didn't think about Amee on the bed. Didn't remember that Apothecaries visited Papa with increasing urgency. Didn't consider the fact that he couldn't stop the suffering.

His desire to save witches who couldn't save themselves came from somewhere, and it didn't matter where.

He wrote.

The system flowed.

Sometime around four in the morning, he popped out of the chair with an exultant cry. The damp walls chilled him through—the top of his skin felt like a layer of ice. Candles sputtered, nearly out of the wick, on the table next to him. None of that mattered. He'd set fire to the roots crawling out of the soil, if he had to.

With a flourish, he crushed all four scrolls together in a pile, then scrawled the final words on a piece of parchment that lay on top.

The Advocacy.

* * *

When the door latch clicked open, loud as an explosion of heated sap, Faye jerked awake.

Her small silhouette lay on a divan close to where Amee slept. Faye pressed up, hair askew as she whispered, "Charlie?"

He slipped inside.

Buttery light coated the room in steady flickers as he made his way to her side, then sank to the floor. Amee twitched, mumbling something.

"She's woken a few times, mostly after dreams."

Faye scooted closer to him. He put his arm around her shoulder. She shivered.

"Has she said anything?"

"Not much. I bet she'll wake up fully in the morning, then Pearl and your father can find out more."

"I'm going to stay. Listen in."

"They might not let you."

He scoffed.

"Remember, Charlie," she whispered. "We're only thirteen."

What does that matter? He wanted to ask. Why did witches always remind him of his age? If there was any time of his life to form and follow through on big plans, shouldn't this be it? Natural energy compelled him. Sickness didn't plague his body. All of Wildrose and his inherited legacy pressed on his shoulders. Generations of family that held power in the grave. Their silent portraits lined the hall.

Laconic expectation.

His fingers curled around the stacked parchments he brought with him. He had opened them all, then placed them one on top of another. They were rolled together in one giant scroll. A paper, tied by the twine, fluttered from the knot.

The Advocacy.

He handed it to Faye.

"Do this with me, Faye?"

She hesitated, then tugged at the twine. A slip of parchment with *The Advocacy* fell into her hand. She regarded it, breath held, then opened the scrolls.

Plans, pictures, and images followed. An idea to dig through the wall of the cellar and connect it to the house. The doorway between the two would hide behind a bookshelf. He'd cover the current cellar door overhead with dirt and grass.

The ultimate hidden headquarters. Utterly inaccessible except for transportation or a secret spell in the hidden basement.

A safe place.

Charlie kept his gaze steady as she riffled through the pages, reading slowly. Faye did nothing fast. Like a sloth compared to a hare. He didn't mind waiting. He needed someone else to believe in it and he wanted that witch to be her.

Doubts plagued him. Concerns he didn't want to give space. Maybe he *was* too young to do something big. Maybe there was no dent in the evil of the world he could make.

Or maybe he could.

Long after she finished reading, curled the parchment back together, and clasped it in her hands in her lap, Faye stared at the fire. She tilted her hand to return the parchment.

"It will take time to set up, Charlie."

"I know."

"It could be dangerous. You're talking about disguises, pretending to be what you aren't, and things that thirteen-year-olds don't usually do."

"I know that too."

Her brow lifted. "You still want to do it?"

"Yes."

"Your father won't like it."

"He doesn't like a lot of my ideas."

Faye met his gaze. Something like admiration brimmed in the reflecting firelight. He wanted to touch the sensitive skin around her eyes, but didn't dare. She loomed in front of him like a precious, breakable porcelain doll that wasn't his, but he wanted so badly.

"If anyone could make it happen, Charlie. It's you."

"Will you—"

She leaned into him. "I'm always at your side."

Chapter Thirteen

MAXIMILLION

One year later.

The letter landed in front of Max like a precocious bird.

He stared at it, upper lip curled over his teeth.

He shouldn't be surprised that a specter of the past visited. Serafina wrote every year around this time. He suspected, though hadn't confirmed, that his birthday was in the spring. Or some other vague reason she'd write, which could be anything. Mere had died around then, now that he thought about it.

Max plucked the message from the air. He leaned forward to chuck it in the dining room fire, but stopped. He hadn't opened the last one, and it haunted him. While the ink had burned, fire chewing away at the parchment until it became ash, he'd wondered if he made a mistake.

What if Mere was actually still alive?

What if Pere hadn't died?

What if Serafina warned him of unknown danger that lurked from Eastern shores?

As unrealistic as the questions were, he couldn't help but

listen. The sounds of milling boys filled the room with low chatter. Guffaws. Filthy jokes. The sharp tone of a lad attempting to be a man, but not quite sure how.

Max tucked himself in the far corner of the study hall and returned to his book. Only a single desk and chair filled this spot, so the rest of the students left him alone. The other second-years, anyway. The third-years chortled over the lilt in his accent, which he worked diligently to erase. Year by year, it lessened, nearly dissipated.

He fingered the edge of Serafina's letter, sorely tempted to open it. He'd long ago erased his blood family from mind. The Dauphins were all the familial ties he needed, and he'd only known them for two-and-something years.

Unable to stand it, he flipped the envelope over, tucked a finger under the flap, and slid it sideways. A letter slipped out, likely enchanted. Trust a High Priestess to use magic on such luxuries.

He felt sick to his stomach as he read the *Ilesan* script.

Maximillion,

My thoughts are drawn to you now, as always. You and my sister. I hope you're well.

I sent Guardians into Morrisanna and the outlying marsh villages to inquire after you. Neither you, nor your Pere, are anywhere to be found. They reported that a neighbor woman, Abbi, says you disappeared years ago.

Your Pere is dead. Did you know? Abbi said you left, and then he died. I'm worried.

I've sent other inquiries, but can find no sign of you. I've put a special incantation on this letter—a rare one, not well known.

It will search for you for a week. If it doesn't find you, then it will return to me.

I don't know how magic can find a witch with a spell, certainly not if so much land separates us, but I have to believe in something.

Forgive me, my sweet nephew. If you didn't know about your Pere's death, and this is your first update, know you have my love and condolences.

Please come home.

Yours,
Serafina

Max read it once, twice. The background of guffaws, then scraping wood on wood, and the beginnings of a brawl followed. Ink flew across the room, spattered the wall. A boy shouted, another groaned. Teachers filtered in to break up the ruckus.

Max ignored them.

He devoured the words a third time, drunk on what they meant. *You have my love and condolences.*

Abbi had covered for him, after all. She told the Guardians that Max left, *then* Pere died. He had nothing to fear.

Elation swept his heart higher. A momentary rush of joy followed, so intense it made him dizzy. He wouldn't be sought after. Exoneration, that's what she'd given him.

Sweet old Abbi.

He owed her something.

He stood, pitched the letter into the fire, and watched it burn until the heat turned it to ash. All remnants of his former life disappeared. The wax melted onto bright coals, beading away.

Max gathered his paperwork, stuffed it together, and wound around the still-jeering boys, split into groups on different sides of the room. Idiots, all of them. Their parents had paid for their placement in a school they didn't deserve.

The Central Network would intentionally make *these* fools its leaders. *Fix it at the source,* Max thought as he headed up the stairs, a candle bobbing with him.

The Central Network had a lot of work to do.

* * *

Morrisanna smelled like old leaves.

The quiet hush of the swamp created a soothing symphony. Springtime in the marsh led to knitted quilts of emerald. The canopies and teeming life alternated between dark and light. Scents wafted in the breeze, some were floral, and others more difficult to parse out.

Water. Everywhere, water.

Max ignored the bone-numbing cold. The tips of his fingers turned to ice. He tried to forget the memories that assaulted him as he stood, invisibly, across the road from his old shack.

Why had he come?

A gloomy sky grumbled above a mat of fog. Drops of water spritzed from the roiling foam. Across the way, several shacks stood in a row. No candlelight issued from inside any of them. No friendly fire, not even smoke from a hearth. Abbi would be huddled under all her blankets, singing to herself, probably.

He hesitated.

Despite being almost fifteen years old now, part of him wanted to throw himself through Abbi's old door, rush into her room, and seek shelter. She hadn't been much of an ally on a day-to-day basis, constantly half-drunk herself, but she'd provided a safe space.

On purpose, he avoided his old shack. Ghosts of a little boy would haunt him if he glanced there. Hardly a child at all, he'd been solemn, half beaten, and mostly starving. Well-fed Max, with shoulders he used to dream about, and more intelligence than Pere held in a fingernail, was something that little boy could never have dreamed of.

Serafina's letter floated through his mind.

Twice, Max attempted to cross the quiet dirt track. Tried to force his feet to move to Abbi's house, thank her. No justifications gave him the courage. He couldn't go back there.

Besides, he shouldn't have come. Shouldn't have transported this far. Mr. Shad would punish him when he found out, because Mr. Shad always found out.

Still, the past cried louder than the present.

"Thank you," he whispered.

He sent a box stuffed with food into the shack. Baguettes, *pittas,* olives, and fried eel slices. All the saved currency he'd made from tutoring the other idiots had bought it for her at the local village. Food she'd love and understand. Not the dense Central Network meals that gummed his body.

A cry issued, familiar enough that everything nervous inside him settled. She lived. Abbi was fine.

A head peered out the window, gazing around. Toothless in the front, with ragged strands of thinning hair. He hoped she still had her molars.

Max transported away, satisfied.

* * *

Ranult had moved into a different office.

A smaller one.

The crowded walls required less firewood, though he did little work these days. What tasks he couldn't handle, his company distributed to other witches. For the time being, Mr. Harry oversaw Wildrose's currency and functioning.

Only half of Max's third year had passed, and a silent understanding already existed that Max would take over the responsibilities of Wildrose when he graduated in the spring. After that, he'd work for Mr. Shad for a year as a paid Assistant.

Charlie would stay away for an extra year, also. He accepted an apprenticeship with a witch in the Southern Covens that specialized in transformation on a stage. He would work with costumers, set design, thespians, and play-wrights.

Tongues wagged all over Pershington at such a wild, unprofessional idea. *So unlike Ranulf,* hen-pecking women whispered. *Not at all responsible.*

Mr. Harry's mustache bristled in annoyance every time Charlie entered the room.

"Doesn't matter what they think," Charlie always said, laughing. "They can hate me all they want. Can you imagine how all this transformative magic will change the Advocacy?"

Always the Advocacy.

Ranulf sat in a plush, high-winged chair by the fire. Another seat waited a few paces to the side, typically the one Mr. Harry occupied on his visits. Max sank into it, relieved to escape the brighter lights and conviviality of the kitchen.

"How are you?" Max asked quietly.

Ranulf gazed over, chuckled, and back to the flames. A single hand rested on the side of his face, as if his neck were too weary to hold up his head.

"Do you forget you're fifteen, Max?"

"No, sir."

"Sometimes, I do. I forget that you're not a grown adult. You came to us far too old for your age, my boy. It's not fair."

Max said nothing.

After several moments, Ranulf shifted in the chair. He turned to face Max more fully. Interest and questions and curiosity gleamed in his fatherly eyes. Max could hardly believe he'd only known the Dauphin's for years. Felt like lifetimes.

Though Ranulf's body wore away, his brain did not. Which was worse? To lose the mind, but not the body? Or to lose the body and not the mind?

The questions scattered to the wind when Ranulf asked, "Are you prepared for me to die, Maximillion?"

His throat closed off.

How to answer such a question? After attending Mr. Shad's School for boys for almost three years, it required something impressive to startle him.

Ranulf did.

"I am, you know. Dying, I mean. Actively, if you want to put a word to it. My body crumbles more every day. My Apothecary tells me it's a slow process. That every day will be a little more difficult, and witches tend to cling at the end for a little too long."

A macabre humor filled his throaty laugh.

"I have an honest Apothecary, if you can't tell."

"I'm sorry, sir."

Ranulf waved a hand. "This is life, Max. There's more in the lands and lives beyond, whether or not you believe in it."

Max certainly didn't, but that had no place in this situation.

"Ranulf, how can I—"

"Charlie."

"Charlie?"

"I know you have an affection and friendship for Charlie that, frankly, might not make much sense. You're serious and level-headed where he is playful and full of dreams. It's that very thing that lends the strength you'll need to get through this mess."

"Which one, sir?"

Ranulf grimaced as he leaned back. A wince wrenched his features, then settled on a breath.

"Greta. She's a disaster of a High Priestess, and it's only going to get worse."

Max's nose wrinkled. If there was one name he *didn't* want to hear on the day they decided would be his birthday, which was today, it was Greta.

At Mr. Shad's, he'd written six different papers on how diplomacy could have been used in place of her brute-force tactics. While other boys lauded her no-nonsense attitude in place of negotiation, he countered the other side. The rift between him and the boys at Mr. Shad's had only grown.

He suspected that Mr. Shad had made him an Assistant not only out of necessity, but safety. A wing of shelter. A desire to keep Max from the constant physical aggression instilled from the other boys. His second-year had been a fight for his life.

Mr. Shad needn't have feared. Max would never let another witch have the upper hand on him again. His daily training regime ensured that. Running. Weights. Push-ups. Constant pushing of ability and mental weakness.

"Greta," Max muttered.

Distaste coated his tongue.

"There's a rumor of a war with the Western Network. Her lack of controlling witches at the border irritates Dostar, and tensions escalate."

"We're already quibbling with the Southern Network," Max countered. "Our Ambassador, Dahlia, is the only thing holding this Network together."

Ranulf nodded a wry agreement. "Alas, we're here to talk about you and Charlie, not another of our epic debates about how the Network should run. Charlie will need you when I die, Max. He'll need help with Wildrose."

"He's too fixated on the Advocacy. It consumes him."

"He does it to forget my pain."

Max stared at Ranulf, at a loss. In all the months that he and Charlie had discussed the Advocacy, how it might work, how to recruit help, how to get news out about it to hidden Watchers, he'd never once considered the root of Charlie's wild beliefs.

"Sir?"

"Charlie buries himself in the dream of saving other witches that can't save themselves because he can't save me. Maybe he doesn't see that yet, but I hope that he will. Probably with your help."

Ranulf leaned a little closer to the fire. Max stood, grabbed several pieces of wood, and stacked them on top. The motion gave him an opportunity to think, away from the thickening intensity of this discussion.

He wanted to squirm away from the uncomfortable topic. Not what he wanted to discuss, but he recognized it for what it was.

An affirmation.

Max was an almost-man. At sixteen, a graduate from Mr. Shads School for Boys, he'd enter the workforce. Many boys didn't get out of the Network school system until eighteen. Nineteen for others. Ranulf's influence, grit, and determination helped to push him through at a young age.

Max crouched at the fire, poked it with a stick. Flames climbed the chimney.

"You want me to take care of Wildrose."

"Charlie will, too. There's no reason to nudge him out, but . . . he might think of it last. Once I die, the currency will only run a few years. You'll both need to work to maintain expenses at first. Until you become more established in your careers, and your currency is higher, it will create lean times."

"I see."

"He'll need your level-headed way of thinking."

To this, Max had no argument. Charlie was brilliant, in many ways, but he wasn't focused. Unless it was on the Advocacy.

"Yes, sir."

"He'll also need you. I'd like to know, Maximillion, that you'll stick around. That you'll be here for Charlie when . . . all feels darkest. Perhaps this is unfair to ask, yet I'm asking it."

"Not unfair." Max set the poker aside, returned to his seat. He leaned his forearms on his knees. "You could ask anything of me, Ranulf, and I would do it for you."

Ranulf set a shaky hand on his shoulder.

"Thank you."

In silence, they let the logs burn. Max's mind ran through the avenues it must in order to pull things back to order. Already, so much lay on his plate. His new position as Assistant, his classes, the looming tests that would commandeer all his time.

Now, Wildrose.

Ranulf.

Charlie.

Yet, he wouldn't trade the burdens. They were duties of family, of belonging. They were what he'd craved all his life.

"Stay close to Charlie and the two of you will be fine. Wildrose will be safe, and that's all I ask. Keep the manor in the family. It's always been a challenge to maintain, but I know you're up for it."

Max met his ardent gaze with his own. Though loath to admit it, he loved Charlie with a fierce and brotherly love. He already knew he'd do anything for him, his magical twin, his brother.

His friend.

"I promise, Ranulf."

"But, I beg of you, please don't underestimate Charlie.

He's keen, deep-feeling beyond what you might think, and sharp as a point. He might surprise you. You ground him, he lifts you up. Oh, he has Faye and he loves her, but she can't do for him what *you* do. Charlie will need witches like you to surround him, help him control his own genius.

"Without each other, you'd both be a right mess. Not even Pearl could fix you, nor would she want to. And above all of that, remember, that you will always be a Dauphin."

Chapter Fourteen

CHARLIE

A year and a half later.

Summer rain poured into the grave.

It pooled into a shimmering puddle broken by falling drops. They rippled across the surface, sending out languorous waves.

A stream of water ran from the crown of Charlie's head and down his neck. Slowly, his shirt saturated. The creeping sensation crawled over his chest like a cool kiss, frosty as the breath of death.

Death.

Papa.

Two workers from the manor carefully lowered Papa's casket into the hole in the ground. The rain made the tightly wound ropes creak. They could have done this with a spell, but no, they didn't need a spell.

Ropes were fine.

Papa would have preferred them. Similar to the way he preferred tea over coffee in the morning. Coffee was too bitter.

He drank it, though, and used the grounds in the greenhouse, where he planted his favorite turnips.

Turnips.

A squeeze of his arm brought him back to life. Faye held onto him. He leaned on her so much she staggered to the side. He readjusted. To his right, behind his back, in a greatcoat that drew his shoulders out even broader than before, stood Max. A glowering specter that would frighten death away.

Yet, he came too late.

Charlie's fragmented thoughts kept him from drowning. Pearl sniffled quietly at Faye's other side, while a woman at the top of the grave sang out a blessing of peace and rest. The invocation drained into a chant, requesting a blessing of remembrance.

From whom did they ask?

And how could he ever forget Papa?

The deluge continued long after the two workers grabbed their shovels and, with a nod from Max, tossed the ropes into the chasm. The *thud* of their falling weight on top of the coffin sent a jolt through Charlie.

Max flinched.

Faye's hold tightened.

Another nod, and the two workers began to shovel. One of them cried. The other pressed his lips, brow low over light eyes. Charlie stared at the disappearing coffin, struck by the desire to throw himself in the great maw.

There to stay.

"Charlie, I'm going to take Pearl inside," Faye whispered. "She's going to catch her death in this weather."

She tilted her head back, a denizen of silent questions hidden there. At seventeen, she took his breath away. Shorter than him, but she always had been. Her face sharpened into lovely angles and lines. Ebony hair framed her broad cheeks, her dark eyes, wide lashes.

She peered at him with unabashed concern. Water trailed down her hair. She'd been standing outside Pearl's umbrella to hold him tight. All of them would get sick from this rainy chill. Fog crawled out of the forest with long fingers, grasping for the lives that stayed.

Charlie reached up, hand on her face. She leaned into his cold palm, closed her eyes. The gesture soothed like balm across a scraped heart.

Reluctantly, she untangled herself, wrapped a soggy arm around Pearl, and guided the sobbing woman to the manor. The rhythmic *thunk, thunk, thunk* of falling dirt clods and rocks pinged the coffin. Max stood stalwart at his side, silent. Overhead, the damp gargoyles were inert and fireless in the rain.

Max and Charlie stayed until the final shovel finished.

Candlelight guided Charlie later that night.

He moved at a fast clip through Wildrose, a pickaxe, a shovel, and several burlap bags thrown over his shoulder. The somber air of the manor seethed under his skin, hurrying him along.

He had to get out of here.

The soggy grass created boot prints as he strode to the eastern edge, where the cellar awaited. The grass had long over-grown the door—he let it happen. He hadn't slipped into the headquarters without a transportation spell in . . . months.

Ages.

The deadening effect of time, combined with graduation from Mr. Chu's School for Boys, then apprenticeship with Master Dillantay, had kept Charlie too busy to think of what the headquarters would look like. Papa dying two days after he completed his internship left him with giant holes.

So he'd do what he'd always planned to do: forge his *own* purpose.

With the pickaxe, he chewed at the grass, yanking it off the wooden door and all around the edges. By the time he finished, sweat trickled down his spine, wet his shoulders. The humid night clung to him, a welcome reminder that he was home at Wildrose. Without Papa, it didn't feel the same. Maybe that would change.

He tossed his hair out of his face, yanked the cellar door free, dropped his tools down, and followed.

Time to get to work.

* * *

A blaze of torchlight drew Charlie out of a haze.

How long had he been staring at the wall, lost in wild thoughts? Too long. The blazing floated down from above, then paused mid air. He scrunched his nose, held up a hand, and winced. Behind the glow, Faye appeared. Her haunting eyes crinkled with concern as she waved the torch to the far corner.

"Charlie?"

Sweat dripped off his arms, rolled down his bare back. Mud coated him. His hair had thickened from moisture and sweat. He panted.

Mounds of dirt occluded the ground at his feet, filling the cellar in undulating mounds. A warmer draft of air whistled through a hole in the far wall closest to the manor, where an opening the size of Charlie's fist led to the basement.

He destroyed the wall, finally creating the path between his dreams and his obligations.

No elation followed.

Faye regarded the hole, then him. No surprise appeared. A cream-colored shawl hung off her arms, giving her gauzy wings as she opened them for him. Her black hair rustled in the interchange of air, drifting around her face.

"How can I help?"

All the welling pain he'd attempted to keep at bay broke free. With a cry, he crossed the room, crushed her in his arms. A sob escaped.

Tenderly, her hand found his head. She murmured something in *Breeta*, her tribal language from the West. Like a singsong, she hummed it gently in his ear. Her fingers kneaded into his scalp, imparting comfort. Grace. Love. His knees gave out. He sank to the ground, clutching her to him.

She tightened her arms, and Charlie cried.

Chapter Fifteen

MAXIMILLION

Two weeks later.

The letter arrived unexpectedly.

Elegant *Ilesan* script meant the message hadn't come from the High Witch of Pershington, for whom he worked. But it definitely came for Max.

Serafina.

Midsummer heated the world with broiling ruthlessness. Her imploring letters normally arrived near the end of winter, early spring.

A break from her yearly routine, then. A clutch of fear assaulted him, made him think that something terrible must have happened. That made no logical sense, either. He had no ties to the East but her.

Five years had passed since he integrated himself into the Central Network, banished his accent, worked for Mr. Shad for a school year, and ingrained himself in the political system as the lowly Assistant to the High Witch of Pershington. Such proximity allowed him to live at Wildrose.

He didn't need Serafina anymore.

The clock on the wall chimed. Max peered over Ranulf's desk, which was depressingly barren of paperwork in the wake of his death weeks ago, and to the clock on the wall.

Nearly noon.

Harry would be here in minutes. Grateful to get this visit over with, Max tucked the letter into his pocket, smoothed his suede jacket. He had business to execute, emotions to stuff aside, and a manor to secure.

He had no time for forgotten family.

* * *

A knock sounded on the office door at precisely noon. Harry bustled inside, mustache twitching. He nodded to Max. Max responded in kind. Faye, who saw Harry in, closed the door behind him.

"Maximillion." Harry set a briefcase on the desk, let it drop to the side. "Merry meet. Good to see you again."

Max struggled to say the same. He satisfied conventional formality with another nod. A clamor sounded at the door before it blew back open. Charlie slipped inside with a broad smile. Behind his usual conviviality lurked another fiend.

Grief.

How well Max knew that monster.

Still, something *else* was different. Grief haunted all of them now. A common enemy that no one sought, everyone accepted, and none attempted to evict. Such would be pointless.

Despite himself, Max tensed. The past several years tensions ran high between Charlie and Harry, particularly since Charlie's advent into the playacting world of transformation. Harry saw Charlie as a buffoon. A waste of the privilege that wealth and positioning bought.

Amused by such judgment, Charlie constantly rose to the

occasion. He ever acted the fool around Harry, who was the only social outlet they had at this point.

Charlie crossed the room, arm extended to Harry. Dirt rimmed his fingernails. A clod drifted to the floor as they clasped forearms. Harry's nose wrinkled, then quickly smoothed out.

Charlie laughed. "Oh, sorry about that, old boy! Just got out of the greenhouse, you know. Love gardening. Plants in the summer. Very important."

Harry nodded blankly, clearly confused.

Max couldn't help but feel the same. What was wrong with Charlie? He spoke in short, clipped sentences that belied the tenebrous air. Nervous chuckling? Too-bright smiles? He may have just lost his father, but he didn't need to attend the reading of the will with a shirt untucked, dirt all over the place.

Ranulf's death left a gaping chasm in his own chest, one he found difficult to breathe around. It should have positively wrecked Charlie. And it had. Yet, he pasted that insipid smile on, anyway.

Why?

A crawling suspicion told Max that something wasn't right.

"Well," Harry said with a quick clearing of his throat. "Let's attend to the business, shall we? As always, Ranulf was extremely detailed in his work. It shouldn't take long to conclude the reading of the will. Thankfully, no surprises."

Charlie nodded. His features appeared paler than usual. The freckles stood in sharp relief to his light skin. Whether that was a result of Ranulf's loss or his time in the depths of headquarters, burying himself in the same earth that now held his father, Max couldn't be sure.

The three of them sat. Harry cleared his throat, brought a monocle to his left eye, and began to read. Details followed. Wildrose, all surrounding properties, and all holdings would be bequeathed to Charles Ranulf Dauphin immediately. Max snuck a glance at Charlie. A glazed expression filled his friend's eyes. Charlie blinked, snapped out of it, and refocused on Harry. Minutes later, the distant expression returned.

Meanwhile, Harry droned on.

At the end, a single line caught Max's attention. "Finally," Harry drawled, "Mr. Maximillion Sinclair is to hold the title of Manager of Wildrose and executor of all business."

Dread pooled in his gut.

Harry nodded once, as if to punctuate it. "Charlie holds all ownings, but you are in charge of Wildrose, Maximillion. Ranulf was abundantly clear."

The revelation came as no great surprise, but there had always been a question of whether the documentation would dictate the obvious. Ranulf had said as much a year and a half ago, and confirmed it again closer to his death when the end loomed, hanging over Wildrose like a wicked pall.

Max would bear the weight of Charlie's birthright.

To his surprise, relief shone through Charlie. He jabbed him in the ribs with an elbow, a gentle move that still irritated Max. "Manager *and* executor. Well earned, Max. There's no more suitable witch!"

"You're sure?"

Charlie laughed. "Certain! Better you than me."

Relief colored the words. Harry regarded them both through narrowed eyes, but his assessment lingered on Charlie.

"All manor business will go through Maximillion," he said carefully, as if testing the water.

"Yes, yes. I think it's wise!"

Astonishment laced Harry's voice. "All of it? You don't mind."

"Not at all. Max is family. Wildrose is staying in the family and will be better taken care of this way."

A jauntier-than-usual tone filled Charlie's voice. Just enough to set Max on edge, but not alert Harry. Entirely constructed.

False.

Charlie was definitely up to something.

He wouldn't mind Max managing Wildrose. He never felt as passionately protective of the manor as Max. This . . . personality . . . that he was affecting boggled him, though. To what purpose did he act like an idiot?

Harry let out a wheezy, tired breath. Max couldn't stop the wish that *he* had died instead of Ranulf.

Unjust, but true.

"I know you won't like this suggestion." Harry's gaze lingered on Max, though it fluttered to Charlie for a moment. "But obligation compels me to say it. If you're wise, you'll sell Wildrose."

Shock rendered Max mute.

Rage hardened his reply.

"Excuse me, sir?"

"Wildrose is a liability. A very expensive one. I've worked with this estate ever since I began my legal work and it's never been easy. Wildrose is too big. Ranulf worked too little up to his death, which lowered his income. Taxes are going up with Greta at the helm. You can't possibly keep all of it warm, the staff fed and paid, for more than a year with what's currently saved."

"You're bold," Max hissed.

Harry sighed. "I know. That's all I'm going to say about it."

Charlie's eyes bounced between Max and Harry.

"I will take it under consideration," Max muttered through clenched teeth. "I have heard you."

Wearily satisfied, Harry nodded to the closest quill. "Then

let's complete this. I need both of your signatures on the corresponding lines."

While Max signed, and Charlie chatted with Harry, he did a quick review of the documents. The total sum of available currency was much lower than he'd like, as Harry indicated, considering how much Wildrose required. But the situation was not impossible.

Max's salary alone wouldn't be enough, but it would be a buffer to shore up against later times. Now that Charlie had graduated with highest honors and completed his apprenticeship, he would also work.

Satisfied, he slid the paperwork to Charlie.

Charlie signed it without looking, and on the wrong line. Harry regarded it, opened his mouth to say something, then stopped. With a roll of his eyes, he blew on the wet ink.

"Well, that's that. Maximillion, contact me with questions. Charles . . . good luck."

"Thank you, sir!" Charlie said brightly, waving. "Most appreciative of your kind words and help with my father. Be safe out there."

The door closed behind Harry.

Max glowered.

Charlie met his gaze, hands folded behind his back, with a twinkle in his eye. The too-smooth facade faded into the calculating expression he'd become used to.

"Not to worry, Max. Not to worry."

"Don't be a fool."

"All in my plan," Charlie said smoothly. The jauntiness and almost-wild tinge that set Max's hair on edge ended. "All in my plan. Do you trust me?"

Max hesitated, but only for a moment. Charlie already knew the answer.

"Of course."

"Then I ask you to extend it now. By the way, with the

current state of the manor, we only have nine months of currency, not twelve. That's not factoring your income into it, though I don't think I can ask you to supplement."

"Of course I will," he snapped.

Charlie shrugged. "Up to you. Either way, I have a few things up my sleeve with the Advocacy. We have nine months."

Max's jaw almost dropped. Charlie turned to head toward the door, but Max stepped in his way.

"What did you say?"

"Nine months," Charlie repeated. "His calculations were wrong. We have nine months left if we do nothing else. If you supplement, it would be longer, so we have plenty of time to figure out a plan for supporting Wildrose. Because of our nine month cushion, there are some Advocacy things I plan to do before I sign into a career."

"That is insane, Charlie. You can't—"

He lifted a hand. "Rumor of an attack on a Watcher in the Eastern Covens of the Central Network has circulated."

"From where?"

Charlie grinned. "I spent a fair amount of time amongst vagabonds and more unsavory types while with Master Dillantay, Max. I have my sources. The attack is supposed to be this weekend. I'm going to prevent it. After that, I'll figure out what's next in my life. Probably a job."

"The Advocacy doesn't count as work."

A somber expression crossed Charlie's face. "To you, maybe not. To the Watchers I plan to save this weekend? You better believe it does."

"Charlie—"

"Max, you'll never dissuade me. Please, don't waste either of our time in your attempts. I will run an undercover operation that only a few witches know anything about. The Advocacy *will* save Watchers imprisoned by the Eastern Network and bring them to safety here in the Central Network. This is what I was born for. This is how I carry on the legacy of Wildrose, and all the generations that come before me. Papa spent my entire life pressing that obligation to me."

"Yes, but—"

"It's a yes, or it's a no, Max."

The firmness of his voice left no room for argument. For convincing him against insanity. A dozen rebuttals to Charlie's plan surfaced, but Max forced them all back. Charlie had just lost his father, his anchor. He knew what that felt like . . . sort of. Not so much with Pere.

But Serafina.

Mere.

If the Advocacy gave Charlie something to hold on to while he transitioned out of this place of grief, then who was he to block it? After years of dreaming the Advocacy to life with Charlie, he wouldn't deny obligation, maybe hope, for it to come to pass himself.

"Fine," he muttered. "A week, then you need to do something real. Something productive."

Charlie bowed, then winked.

"What was that fool's facade you put on just now?" Max tilted his head back toward the middle of the room. "You didn't even sign on the line. And since when do you go by Charles?"

Charlie laughed. "Again, Max, I beg your trust. Go with it. Call me Charlie in private around Wildrose, but I'll be Charles to the world. It's all part of my plan, and it's already well underway."

"The Advocacy," Max growled, "doesn't count as work, as a plan, as a life or career choice. You realize that?"

"Yes."

"You understand you'll need something else?"

"You're spot on, Max. The Advocacy could never run by itself. To do what I want to do? I'll *definitely* need more."

The words sent an ominous feeling through him. The good gods help them. What was Charlie doing now?

* * *

Dear Max,

I hope my yearly letter finds you well. Alive. Sometimes, I torture myself over what you must look like as an adult. Dark-haired, like your mere? Light-haired, like your pere?

The only poor comfort I have is that these letters never return as undeliverable. I hope you're reading them. You might as well be burning them. That would be well deserved.

I know this is outside the time for my usual yearly letter, but . . . I was thinking of you. Missed you. Daily I call to mind you and my sweet sister. Life in the castle is . . . nerve-racking.

Sometimes, I just need to remember who I am. You help me do that.

Yours,

Serafina.

Chapter Sixteen

CHARLIE

Two false rumors of Watcher assaults, a fake attack that turned out to be nothing more than a horrific joke gone bad, and two wasted weeks later, Charlie stared at the wall of the growing headquarters in consternation.

Something must be done.

This haphazard guessing, and by himself at that, was no way to run an Advocacy.

With spells and sheer tenacity, he'd greatly expanded the size of headquarters. Quadrupled it, really. Three of the four walls were finished with wooden boards, giving the room a brighter ambiance. He'd hammered sconces into place. Soot marks already burned the wood behind them, which lent less of a brand-new energy. The atmosphere lightened considerably without dirt and mud on all sides. The scent of pine filled his nose with a delightful zing.

Charlie paced across the completed floor, spun, then strode to the other side. He accomplished fifteen full strides before he changed direction. Thick timbers crossed the ceiling, as a support, then paid workers had placed a dry, white ceiling between the beams, enchanted to prevent accumulating water during the rain.

After a month of solid work, he felt more than reasonably certain the headquarters wouldn't cave in.

A note from Pearl fluttered in front of him.

Heading to the BLAUS and will return in the morning.

—Pearl

He squeezed his eyes shut in a moment of self-recrimination.

The BLAUS.

Of course! Why hadn't he thought of it before?

The *Berry Literary Society for Ancient Texts and Upholstery Repurposing*.

What a dolt he'd been. That group of Watchers would be the perfect place to gather more information. He should have thought of it long before, but that didn't matter.

With a chuckle, Charlie stood up and transported away. Time to do some real reconnaissance. He wouldn't show himself at the BLAUS. Several of them wouldn't trust a Defender, even if Pearl vouched for him.

He just wanted to listen in. Max had attended the BLAUS once, gave Charlie only an eye roll in response, and never went back.

Tonight?

Time for sleuthing.

* * *

The *Berry Literary Society for Ancient Texts and Upholstery Repurposing* delighted Charlie.

Four witches sat in a circle in Pearl's living room while he crouched upstairs, hidden in shadows. He came here often as a young boy. Enough that he knew the hiding places in her house. She'd be so busy with guests present, she wouldn't find him. Invisibility certainly helped.

For good measure, Pearl laid out swathes of upholstery. Another witch had brought a chaise laundering project that a spell worked on while he jabbered, and ancient texts populated the table in a tower between snacks.

"No further updates," said a man with a round face, wide glasses, and cornflower blue eyes. "Everything in my life has been smooth and stable. Very little upheaval, except for what Greta causes. I find that if I watch for news on Big Leo only once a day, instead of all day, fear doesn't consume my life."

Pearl raised a teacup. "Hear, hear."

Kole, an elderly gentleman with thinning lips and saggy cheeks, said, "Leo is one in a line of witches afraid of us. He'll eventually go away too. They all do. Keep your secret, live your life. That's what I've always said."

"A witch with a prodigious amount of power," Pearl retorted tartly. "And a history of killing Watchers!"

While the conversation continued downstairs, Charlie clasped his arms around his knees and focused. Little pulls of magic came now and then. Rarely. Not *predictably*. Just enough that he noticed. Like when Max accessed the powers, only less intensely. These purls on his mind, like tugs from a rope, distracted him but little else. More like recognition, than power, he would say.

A knock came on the door. With it, a rush of sensations all at once. Desire ballooned through him, hot as a fire born of magical power. Charlie lurched forward, a strangled cry in his throat.

As quickly as it came, the surge left.

"Yaz has come!"

"Yaz! I haven't seen her in ages."

"She's been visiting family."

"Oh, how lovely!"

Pearl's feet crossed the floor downstairs and her door creaked open. Charlie held his breath, heart slamming. The urge to rush downstairs, throw himself into the midst of such magic, nearly overcame him. More easily than he thought possible, he wrestled it back.

A tinny voice entered the house, indistinguishable amongst a rush of greetings that followed. Charlie tamped aside the rising surge of hunger that came with the swelling emotion.

He focused on his breath.

Thought of Faye.

Within a minute or two, the impulses ebbed away.

So, then. There *was* something to the rumors. To what Leo in the East, and the ever-climbing Ambassador, Cecelia Liam, proclaimed about the thirst Defenders experienced for Watchers.

He'd need to investigate more.

Chatter continued for the rest of the evening. Updates about family, the magic, and other things that had no pertinence. Constantly, he thought of the tugs, the way they bloomed and faded, when Watchers accessed and closed their power.

That night, he lay in bed, staring at the shadows that stretched across his ceiling. Papa floated through his mind, then back out. He didn't want to think of the dead. He wanted to focus on the living.

With a spell, he conjured a wavering blue cloud. Cobalt, twisting to sapphire. A unique spell. By changing the words, it altered the colors as they presented. He flipped words around, extracting them from a *Yazikan* poem taken out of the Southern Network. He'd learned it while apprenticing with Master Dillantay. When he recited the poem with certain changes, it produced an ever-altering vision.

The color morphed to mustard, then emerald, back to blue. Rotating the details, focusing on a bigger picture and tweaking the overall experience settled him. All the roaring questions of Defenders and Watchers and death and permanence faded into shifting minutiae.

When he let the magic rest, the colors deepened. He altered a consonant, and the most vivid form of blue illuminated the room.

Freedom, he thought, thinking of the blue skies Papa would no longer admire.

He closed his fist. The magic ceased.

Tomorrow, he'd go to the Eastern Network. Nothing here would move the Advocacy forward. In the East, he'd form connections, meet witches. Watchers, if he could find them. Tell them about the Advocacy and all he offered. That was the next step.

Tonight, the BLAUS taught him that Watchers retreated to stay safe. They knew so little about their own kind, their own magic.

He'd find them.

He'd save them.

Charlie fell asleep.

Chapter Seventeen

MAXIMILLION

Max passed through the filthy, streaming streets of Chatham City. He glared at the watermarked cobblestones, ignored the piles of refuse outside a window, and attempted not to get rained on. Dwindling summer days led to cooler climes. The first month of fall lingered just around the corner. With it, more rain.

Blasted weather.

Aggravating storm aside, it felt good to be out of the stuffy office.

Zaya, a witch who couldn't find her way out of a room with one door, had complained about tax fraud against the High Witch of Pershington, for whom he worked. Nothing too alarming. Zaya had no proof, and they had excellent accounting, but the rebuttal required far too many trips back and forth from Chatham City to clear the accusation.

Which meant Max conducted those trips.

Arguably, Chatham City must be the filthiest place in the Central Network. The stormy weather made it worse. Worms littered the stone roads. Mud slaked by, past gushing rain barrels long since full. The plinking moisture drowned out the sound of rats as they scurried across eaves.

He tugged his collar a little higher and glanced up. Chatham Castle loomed overhead, the shadowy turrets and spires a gigantic backdrop to the bustling city. Sharp-gabled houses and slick roads gave way to sprawling Letum Wood, or the towering castle. Either loomed larger than life.

Instead of taking the angled road that would require ten extra minutes—though fewer rats—he darted across a busy street during a lull in carriage traffic. No witches populated the narrow alley he rushed into. Only the quick clip of his shoes filled the narrow space with sound as he hurried through.

Halfway there, he paused.

A thin, recessed gutter, put there several High Witches ago, slipped down the left side of the alley. It had been dug into the ground and lined with stones. Thankfully, it rid the alley of standing water and dramatically decreased the spread of water-borne illnesses.

Not that Greta cared about population life span.

At the top of the surging gutter lay a dark bundle on the ground. A mop of saturated, unruly blonde hair drew his eyes. He sucked in a sharp breath.

A woman.

He hurried to her side. Blood stained the cobblestones and her dress. Someone had ripped the front half of her bodice open. Crimson stains around pillaged skirts, the bruising on her cheekbone, told the rest of the story. Raped and left in the alley to die.

Liquid rage slipped through him as he felt for a pulse. She stirred, moaned. Relief swept through him.

Alive.

Or was that better?

He went down on his knee.

"Madam?"

No response. A gentle touch to her good cheek yielded no consciousness, only a low sound in her throat.

"Madam, my name is Maximillion. I can help take care of you. With your permission, I'm going to pick you up, transport you to my home. It's warm and safe there. A woman named Pearl or Faye will take care of you."

She winced, her face contorting. The barest nod came, so quick, so fleeting, it might have been only hopeful on his part. Would she agree to a stranger yanking her out of the rain?

Taking it as permission regardless, he carefully pulled her into his arms. Standing, he gazed around. No other signs of evidence. Only scuffles in the dirt, most washed away by the torrential downpour. She trembled. He regarded her in surprise.

So young.

Sixteen, perhaps? Only just younger than him. Max steeled himself. She may not be a Watcher, but she was in need. Wildrose awaited.

* * *

The woman lay on the side of the bed, her back to him. Pearl had cleaned her up, braided her hair, and left her to sleep. A warm fire kept away the chill. Her breathing had evened into repose, no longer jagged with pain.

He closed her door, wound his way through the halls. Rugs softened his approach down the stairs to the kitchen.

"She's tired," Pearl said from behind a counter in the middle of the expansive room. Copper pots hung overhead, near dried collections of herbs. Her drawn expression showed deeper fatigue. She had a sip of her beloved coffee, then another.

"Did she speak?"

"Didn't say a word, but cooperated. Sort of stared at the

wall when she was awake. I gave her a drink as well as some potions to help with pain and sleep."

"Thank you, Pearl."

She sniffled, tears in her eyes. "Can you find them, Max? The men who did this to her?"

"No." He frowned as he said it, and stared at the fire. "I went back while you helped her clean up. There's no evidence. I took two Guardians there, but there's little they can do. She can give a statement and they'll keep an eye out."

"What about Charlie?"

He shrugged. "I don't know. He sees only for himself in the paths."

Pearl frowned. "A more powerful Defender would certainly help in this moment, wouldn't it? They'd be able to identify the witches responsible, at least."

"And who would believe them? Defenders are subterranean, hardly known about at all. Watchers have commandeered all the attention for the last hundred years. Besides, any Defender might lie, unless there was a way to pull someone else into what they saw. Extremely unlikely."

She opened her mouth, then closed it again. Resignation flooded her tired features.

"Well, I'm glad you found her. She's sleeping, so I'll return home. Expect me in the morning to fix your breakfast, as usual."

"I can manage, Pearl. Faye is gone, and you've left plenty of bread and cheese. I believe there's some beef left. I don't mind throwing a few things around in the kitchen."

She tweaked his ear as she passed, a note of humor in her voice. "I'm not ready to give Wildrose up, even if you want to boot me out of it. But all right. Eat your own breakfast."

"I haven't booted you out."

"Not yet," she said with a witty smile.

"Desire has nothing to do with it. And I would never release you, Pearl."

The last addition came out more gruffly than he intended. She laughed and snagged her coat off a hook in the wall. Her face furrowed with concern as she yanked her sleeves on.

"Watch over her tonight. I don't want her to wake up, frightened, in a house she doesn't remember. And leave out some food for her, just in case she gets hungry. I have a feeling she'll be a night owl after all this napping."

After she left, Max leaned both palms on the counter and fell into thought. The two landscapers he had to release from their positions yesterday darted through his mind. It hadn't been easy, but that's why Ranulf left him in charge of Wildrose. Charlie focused entirely too much on the Advocacy, anyway.

He'd let the lawn run wild, if he had to, to conserve currency. Charlie was comfortable with nine months of squandering currency before they figured out a plan, but he wasn't.

Feasibly, they had six months of savings reserved, now that Charlie finished paying those he had hired to complete headquarters, which gleamed like a shiny pentacle. Six months to figure something out, and now a new mouth to feed. The paths he saw seemed to show she could be around for a while. The witch would decide that, of course. Everything could shift once she awoke and made her own decisions.

He had a feeling, however, everything had just changed.

The witch awoke that night.

Max stood near her fire, staring into the popping flames, when she sat up with a terrified gasp. He stepped away, back to the wall, and met her horrified gaze. His hand came up in a placating gesture.

"My name is Maximillion, and I mean you no harm."

Her braid had dissolved into wild, unruly strands. Several of them kinked off her shoulders. Her muted eyes, so wide with fright, seemed to have lost all color. Slowly, the terror in her gaze faded. Her breath ebbed into a normal pattern. She swallowed, winced.

A hand lifted to her neck, then touched her heart.

She licked her lips.

"W-water?"

Max nodded to a small pitcher and glass of water next to her. She reached over with a shaking hand, grabbed the glass, and brought it to her lips. After a tentative sip, she downed the whole thing.

Her wary gaze returned.

"I found you in an alley in Chatham City. You were in the rain, half in a gutter, covered in blood. Do you remember me bringing you here?"

A vague lift of one shoulder. At the words *Chatham City*, her expression dropped.

"Pearl cleaned you up. She helps at Wildrose, which is the manor you're currently staying in. It's located just outside of Ashleigh."

She regarded him with a blank, uneasy stare. Any witch in the Central Network would know the two principal cities—Chatham City and Ashleigh. Her blank expression could only mean she had an exceptional talent at hiding her fear, or she didn't know where he spoke about.

"You're welcome to stay for as long as you like, or you can go. We have a carriage that can take you where you need. There's also food next to the bed. Stay the night, at least, and give yourself a chance of recovery. We were going to send for an Apothecary, but wanted to wait for your permission."

She blinked, then gave a bare nod.

He paused.

She said nothing.

With a little bow of his head, Max headed for the door. As it closed behind him, he thought he heard her say, "Thank you."

Chapter Eighteen

CHARLIE

A petite clearing of the throat drew Charlie's gaze higher.

He sat behind his father's desk, skimming through a grimoire on complicated spells and their successfully truncated versions. Faye, hands on her hips, glared at his feet propped on the edge of the desk.

With a blush, he lowered them.

"Why were your feet on the desk?"

"Seeking a more comfortable position."

She tilted an eyebrow.

He shrugged sheepishly. She studied the grimoire, then him. Annoyance morphed into questions.

"What is that grimoire for?"

Excitement shuffled back through him, like bolts of lightning. "I'm returning to the Eastern Network. Heard another rumor from a local there about Leo and Cecelia teaming up. The source said something about Cecelia teaching Defenders how to find Watchers, while Big Leo and East Guards conduct the raids."

"Huh."

An unreadable expression followed.

Charlie set aside the grimoire, slowly rose. He reached for her, and she didn't resist. Her soft fingers fit perfectly against his, a sensation he'd never tire of.

Frustration rumbled through his tone. "I have to do *something*, Faye. All my work with Watchers has been frivolous so far. While lovely witches, the BLAUS society has no information. Everything I try to find out just fades into nothing. Fake rumors. Gossip. I need . . . a better vantage point."

"Like what?"

"I don't know. I think I'll find it in the East."

"Well," she said brightly, "at least you have a headquarters. It's complete and lovely."

"Too bad I don't have a plan to *use* it."

She curled closer, tucked under his chin. "You'll figure it out, Charlie. It's been just over a month since Ranulf died. Surely, you're allowed some uncertainty."

He tightened an arm around her shoulders, the smell of her minty soap filling his nose. The familiar scent eased his tight frustrations.

Grass had grown over the top of the old cellar door in a clean carpet thanks to spells and a steady summer that faded into the first month of fall. An unobtrusive bookshelf in the basement of Wildrose hid the entrance he'd hacked out of the dirt with a pickaxe and sheer might. Inside, wood lined the floor, ceiling, walls. Desks and chairs and shelves and candles and torches gave a warm touch.

Perfectly functional.

And utterly barren.

"We need *witches*," he said with feeling. "We need witches to help us do this work. I can't do it on my own. We need informants and workers and . . . things we don't have." He dragged a hand through his hair, and could feel the way the locks stood on end. "We need things I'm not even aware of, Faye, and it frustrates me. Max won't tolerate me focusing solely on the Advocacy for long. Two more weeks, at most. It's weeks longer than he was initially willing to give me."

"So you're going to throw yourself into the Eastern Network and spy? Sounds reasonable."

He recoiled, laughing. She tilted her head back, eyes glittering with mischief. He ran the tip of his finger over the bow of her lips.

"No, my darling. I'm going to go for a walk, and it will happen to be in the Eastern Network, along a particular beach. I might decide to be invisible while I do so, and I'm going to gather information if certain witches are also scheduled to arrive at the exact same moment. That's all."

"Sounds dangerous."

The wobbling of her usual bravado startled him. He pulled her close. She wrapped her arms around his waist, her ear to his chest. His fingertips slipped through her hair, comforted by the rough strands and the way they lined her scalp. Faye snuggled against his neck with a sigh.

His heart galloped at her touch. Faye, the love of his life. The soul in his blood. Though Advocacy business nudged him to the East, he stopped thinking about it. These moments with her filled the gaping ache that Papa left behind. Reminded him why it was still so good to be here.

Faye stopped the encroaching sadness from absolutely swallowing him.

"Max stormed out of his office this morning," she murmured against his chest.

He broke the dream of snuggling with her under a tent of warm blankets on a rainy morning to say, "What now?"

"Currency."

"Oh."

"Prices are going up, and Harry delivered news that the tax on Wildrose is going to increase."

"Greta."

She nodded.

A ripple of thoughts followed. There were other assets. Things they could put into place . . .

"Are you going to find a job?" she asked carefully.

He held back another laugh. When it came to him finding a job, Max and Faye walked on eggshells. Neither of them wanted to ask him to deal with his grief, stopper up the Advocacy, and get a job already, but he felt their nervous tension all the same.

"I've applied for several. Just waiting to hear."

Her shoulders slumped. "Oh."

With Faye in his arms, his mind wandered to other roads. Over to the East, down to the island of Carcere.

So many places for him to keep busy . . .

He broke free of those tangling thoughts to say, "I'll talk to Max tonight. How is the girl he brought? What's her name?"

"Lucey."

"Yes, how is Lucey doing?"

Faye pulled away to see him better. "She's very nice. A little strange. Keeps asking if I know a Drago, or whispering about him. She doesn't seem to know much about the Network."

"She hasn't spoken a word to me."

"She avoids Max, too. Not that I can blame her," she added in a low mutter that made Charlie laugh.

"Is she going to stay?"

"I assume so. She's been here a week already. I caught her sweeping upstairs yesterday. This morning, Pearl taught her how to make bread with fig pieces in it. She'd never had figs before, can you imagine? I'd say she wasn't from the Central Network if her accent was mostly familiar to here. Had no idea what covens are, either. She spends most of her time in the library, poring over books."

A niggling suspicion wriggled in his brain, but he let it go. No use conjecturing about a witch he didn't understand. He tried searching for her in his paths, but she interacted with him so rarely, nothing appeared.

"Well, I'm glad she found shelter here," he said gently, "after all that she's been through. Perhaps we can recruit her to the Advocacy."

Faye rolled her eyes.

She stepped out of the ring of his arms. He felt the loss of her warmth keenly. He wanted to curl his body around her, tuck her deep inside, and stay here with her all day. They could lie in front of the fire, wrapped in blankets, and toast bread on long sticks so they didn't burn their fingers.

A lovely scene for another day.

Advocacy business called. These Watchers couldn't protect themselves from Leo—not alone, anyway—and he had to satisfy the itching question that kept asking, *what will Leo do next?* Which was quickly followed by, *and how will the Advocacy stop him?*

"Tonight," Charlie said, a hand still on her hip. "Have dinner with me?"

Faye reached up, pressed her palm to his cheek. "Of course, Charlie."

Relieved, he smiled.

"Be safe, please? I know how much you love the Advocacy, but I love *you,* and don't want another funeral only a month after your Papa's. To lose you would gut me."

* * *

The Eastern Network had far too many gulls.

The annoying birds hopped around the surf, seeking the dead amongst the tidal wash. Beaks pecked, cawed, attacked.

Charlie watched them as the sea breeze shuffled his hair in flurries around his head.

An empty beach, humidity in the air, and an incoming storm weren't bad for a first impression of the Eastern Network shoreline. Having never been this far east before, transporting had been fraught with peril, but it worked out well enough. Left a mild headache behind.

He shuffled through the sand, enjoying the feel of the granules through his toes. No one stood close enough to see the moving sand, so he kept at it, but had an ear tuned. Eventually, he began to walk again.

Other witches didn't see him as he shifted past. The temptation to transform into a rock and listen nearly drove him to do it, but he decided against it at the last minute. If it went awry, disaster would result. Images of his upper body sticking out of a boulder led him to greater caution. Besides, rocks had no life form and might not hold intelligence. Better to practice that magic at Wildrose before doing it here.

He stepped out of the sand and onto a water-splashed dock. A hustling sailor nearly crashed into him, but he swerved at the last moment. Tenacity helped him hang on to his invisibility spell, but only just.

In the distance, beyond the small pier where witches buzzed and shouted in a market, he thought he saw a change in the unending ocean scenery. A blip that appeared and disappeared against the rolling waves.

La Torra island.

The distant place housed Carcere, an enchanted prison where, rumor had it, the High Priest Dante housed any Watcher found in the Eastern Network. Charlie tucked his hands in his pockets, stared out with tapered eyes. Carcere made sense.

Watcher imprisonment did not.

Several small boats lined the pier, filled with witches clambering in and out. They loaded boxes, some containing clucking chickens, barrels marked fresh water in *Ilese*—one of the languages he felt moderately comfortable speaking, though he'd had no formal training—and a couple of rolls of muted fabric.

"Let's go!" bellowed a thick-jowled man with a beard. "We're rowing against waves to beat the incoming storm. We'll be lucky if we don't capsize!"

Then Charlie saw her.

Huddled at the bottom of the boat, bound and gagged, laid a girl not much older than twelve. Thirteen, perhaps. A puddle of water surrounded her. Her teeth clattered, body trembled.

Charlie clenched his fists, dodged out of the way of a witch carrying an open cage of fluttering hens, and stepped closer.

How hadn't he seen her before?

Oh, they'd taken pains to hide her. A heavy blanket wrinkled over the top of her tiny body. A woman sat in the middle of the boat, perched like an eagle. Seeing the blanket had wrinkled and revealed the child's face, she quickly replaced it. Her gaze darted around.

Charlie's teeth ground together. Well, he'd finally found a Watcher, all right.

Three younger boys hopped onto the skiff-like boat and shoved away. A rope dropped into the greenish waters, then sprayed droplets on the pier when they yanked it back out. Wind swept up, hurrying them into choppy waters. The woman in the middle steeled herself, white knuckle grip on the board where she preened.

The call of a bird caught Charlie's attention.

He glanced overhead and saw several spiraling giants in the air. Massive for a bird, if they were this large from so far away. *Aquilas*, he recalled. A native of the Eastern Network, and dependent on the ocean for food. A shot of delight stole through him. One creature he and Faye had planned to discover when they set out to travel Alkarra.

Aquila birds were capable of a little magic. They could change size to be bigger or smaller as they wished, depending on how they hunted. In their normal state, the length of their wingspan would be twice the height of a witch. Most of them had pearlescent wings, riddled with different colors. Some were black, others mottled brown. Several showed a sharper tan.

They caught fish with talons and their sharp beaks, like a sea-faring dragon crossed with an eagle in the sky.

Fierce.

Also, an opportunity.

* * *

Becoming an *aquila* bird should have been much harder. Whether his excited emotional state led to snappy magic, or all the time he spent studying transformation during his apprenticeship aided him now, Charlie didn't know.

He *did* know that the gliding of air under his wings was an intoxicating caress. The flow of currents gave a deep thrill. White-capped waves littered the world below, crashing against each other as moisture fell from the sky.

The tiny skiff, set against such a large ocean, didn't seem to have a chance of a successful crossing.

Charlie soared ahead, beating his massive wings into the wind and sky. Other *aquila* birds made aggressive strokes his way, at first. They didn't like a new one in their crowd. As he broke off, leaving them behind, they stayed away. Sharp screeches warned him not to return.

He headed toward La Torra, the transformative magic a low constant in the back of his mind. This bird had a great deal more intelligence than he'd expected. Transforming into an animal had many risks—particularly when done without practice. The witch would, during the transformative process, typically take on the intelligence of that creature.

Cats were of utmost ease for transforming, for they held a great deal more mind power than many gave them credit for. The ability to remain a cat, observe one's surroundings, and commit it all to memory, was unparalleled.

It might be so for an *aquila*.

With great effort and straining wings, he closed the distance between him and the island as it appeared on the horizon. Wind tossed him. The more he sailed into it and stopped resisting the currents, the less he tumbled.

When he dropped his eagle-like head, he could see the skiff bobbing in the waves, not quite halfway across. The sailors heaved against the ocean, straining.

He pressed harder.

He dodged closer to La Torra, circling. When he opened his throat, a delightful scream issued. He swooped low, startling a Guardian, who shrieked. The layout of La Torra left little to the imagination. A circular, turret-like building with a stone exterior and flat top. Sparse bushes and white sand.

Guardians.

Little else.

Except . . . *lots* of Guardians.

Rarely did he feel the temptation to slip into the paths of his magic on a daily basis. After Papa died, he found more memories than he wanted to grapple with. Emotions, too. He'd step in sometimes, see if he should have done something else in a different or better way, to help the Advocacy.

Now, he felt an urge to do it that he didn't understand.

Dismissing that, he renewed the transformative magic and dove closer to La Torra. With such a storm brewing, and rain pelting through the air, he expected more Guardians to duck inside.

At least thirty ringed the entire island, several of them on the pier. One of them peered out, hand slanted over his eyes. Presumably waiting for the boat and the Watcher at the bottom.

Clearly, Charlie would have to get the girl *before* they arrived. There'd be no helping her after. While his wings soared, he flexed his talons. Giant, razor-sharp weapons. Could he grab her without hurting her? Visions of streaming blood and a screaming innocent filled his mind.

He dismissed them.

He could do this.

The temptation to land on top of La Torra momentarily distracted him, but he saw no other *aquila* birds in the air, nor near the island. With six Guardians ringing the top, he doubted *aquilas* often landed, which would draw attention he didn't want.

From his perch in the wind, hovering in the same position thanks to the storm, he could make out the East Guards shouting at each other. The broken *Ilese* was difficult to decipher over the wind.

"It's our first Watcher from the West!" one shouted. A middle-aged gentleman with thick jowls and very short hair. A gleeful expression filled his face. "She's young. If we can catch them before they grow into their full abilities, we may stop their magic with Carcere's suppressive ability."

Charlie struggled against another gust of wind. Rain slammed into his feathers, peeled away as quickly. His energy flagged, fighting these gusts.

Calculations, ideas, and plans raced through his mind like the storm. A more stolid figure stood next to the first Guardian, at the end of the pier. Despite the ocean churning beneath the violence of the wind, he didn't move.

An implacable, stalwart figure.

Leo Giuseppi.

It had to be. Here to greet their first victim from the West, no doubt. Troubling on several levels. First, Leo had a coldness to him that sent a shiver down Charlie's spine. He'd heard much about Leo's frosty stare, and none of it overstated.

Second, that they'd branched their kidnappings into the West meant they'd soon start pulling watchers from the South, perhaps the North.

What would stop them?

Only fighting back, which meant that the Advocacy needed massive growth *now*.

Charlie's magic remained strong as he puzzled through a simple plan. The intelligent *aquila* bird had more mind power than expected, but that didn't allow for complicated ideas. Simple would be safest.

The little skiff appeared not far away now, the huddled, freezing occupants barely visible. Oars were pulled rhythmically through the churning water. From Leo's viewpoint, the boat must appear and disappear as it cut through the troughs and peaks of waves.

There would be one chance to save the girl.

One chance to build an opportunity for them to spy on La Torra more consistently. He couldn't be too obvious because he didn't want them to suspect the *aquila* birds. Otherwise, greater chances in the future would be lost.

He'd have to cast transformative magic *and* a spell on the girl.

In fact, he'd have to drown her.

Chapter Nineteen

MAXIMILLION

Lucey stood in front of Max with clenched fists, a tipped back chin, and a frightened gaze. She didn't appear afraid of him, but of something else.

She'd been haunting Wildrose like a mouse for weeks now. Faye had formed a quiet alliance with her, though it would be a stretch to say that Lucey had made friends with anyone.

Today, Lucey came to see him at work.

He stood in the middle of the High Witch's office in Pershington, a heap of scrolls in his hands. A lone carriage rolled through the middle of the village, the horse whinnying as it tugged the wooden box along. Three buildings were scattered through the area: a bakery, a blacksmith, and a dressmaker.

Max set aside the scrolls and met her gaze. Lucey's clenched fists showed white knuckles and a general terror of what she'd just accomplished.

Transported here.

Her pallor appeared greener for it, but she'd sustained no injury. Transporting could be hard to adjust to. Faye said she'd been accomplishing each benchmark with the awkwardness of someone unaccustomed to magic.

Max stared at her in unfettered surprise.

"Lucey." He straightened. "Welcome."

"Thank you. Sorry to surprise you," she said steadily, but with the rote tone of someone who had practiced what she'd say. "I'm here to thank you for all you've done for me. For your shelter and food, I owe you better than what I've given. I've been quiet and haven't said much."

A half-wince crossed her features, then righted. He dissolved the urge to step into the paths to see what populated ahead. Why it would matter, he didn't know.

"No apology necessary. We're happy to help."

"Your manor is lovely."

He opened his mouth to counter that it wasn't his home, but stopped. Charlie had insisted that, if at all possible, they convince witches that Wildrose was Max's.

Trust me, he said when Max asked why. *Should my plans realize, it'll be better for the Advocacy if I'm not associated with Wildrose. The secrecy of headquarters will be paramount. If possible, no one in the Advocacy will even know that Wildrose houses headquarters.*

Despite his better sense, Max *did* trust him.

"Thank you," he said. "Wildrose is a special place. Many witches have found refuge there, yourself included."

"I grew up as a . . . what do you call them, here? Forester?"

He nodded once.

"My family is rid of me. I have nowhere else to go." Her voice wobbled, then righted with a swallow. "If you don't mind—"

"Stay as long as you wish."

She exhaled. "Thank you. I want to be of service and would love to learn magic. More magic, I mean," she hastily added.

Max shrugged. "You may help Faye, if you like. There's always something to clean or cook at Wildrose, it seems. Faye is a natural educator, so I'm sure she'd be happy to continue your lessons. She teaches many witches that roam through there."

"Thank you, but . . . I'm thinking about something a bit more . . . involved."

He lifted an eyebrow.

She wrung her hands together, but didn't break eye contact. He wondered how much courage it required to meet his gaze after what she'd been through. Any attempt to soften his expression went unnoticed.

"I want to be an Apothecary. I want to . . . help witches in physical pain. Emotional pain too, if I can."

"Admirable."

"How do I do that? I'm . . . overwhelmed. Not sure where to start. I have no . . . currency, as you call it?"

Another nod.

She frowned. "Nothing to my name but the clothes you've given me, and even that was charity. I . . ."

Tears threatened. Max spoke quickly. He'd rather hang by his thumbs than endure a woman in tears.

"There are schools that teach one how to be an Apothecary. You seem intelligent enough. You can read and write?"

"Of course!"

"With foresters," he muttered, "one never knows. There are entrance exams, I believe. Basic herbology, anatomy, that sort of thing. I'll hazard a guess that you don't know what the Network school system is?"

She shook her head.

"It's an educational opportunity, essentially. One for which you might be too old. You don't have to attend a Network school to become an Apothecary, but it certainly helps. I'll pull some books from the library tonight and leave them out for you. Study those. I'll make some inquiries about getting you a placement test, and we can go from there. It's bound to be difficult."

"That's fine. I'm assuming it costs something?"

"Yes."

"I have no way to pay for it."

"Wildrose might sponsor you."

Her brow rose. "Really?"

No, he thought, with a stab of annoyance at himself. He had no right making promises like this. Currency dwindled faster than expected due to tax hikes and difficulty obtaining basic flour, thanks to increasing Guardian ranks from their inane High Priestess.

War hummed along the Western border, which drove up the price of everything. He couldn't even buy a slab of pork without wanting to gasp. Yet he couldn't help himself—something nudged him to aid her. After she left, he'd look into the paths and see what lay there.

"I would do anything to help pay for the costs of my education. Clean, cook, work during the day and study at night. I'm smart. I just . . . want to make something of myself out here. Home isn't an option right now." Her voice broke. "I can't. Not until I can take care of myself."

Eagerness infused her now, the first sign of life he'd seen since he carried her to Wildrose. Relief swept through him. She'd be fine. There would be nightmares and memories to haunt her for a while, but she'd pull through. He could sense it in her. A depth.

The grimace she usually wore returned. A hand pressed to her temple. The color had leached from her face.

"You need a break," he declared.

"Yes. Thank you. I'd appreciate your help with the books tonight, and for . . . everything else."

With a snap, she was gone.

* * *

The darkness of the Watcher magic often soothed Max. Today, it made him more jittery than ever.

In fact, it made no sense.

He stood before a wisp of a blondish witch with intelligent eyes and a stubborn frown. She was young, perhaps six. She stood alone. No paths connected to her, no other wisps appeared around her.

He frowned, turned away. When he looked back, she disappeared.

Finally, normalcy returned. He shucked off the strangeness of that lone witch to study the paths sprang to life in the darkness. To his surprise, Lucey littered his trails at almost every turn. Not just Lucey, but Lucey in less-than-safe circumstances. Rarely did he see Charlie and Lucey in a possibility together, yet Lucey and Faye appeared together constantly.

Other witches too, always witches. Wisps populated endlessly around him on paths. Always branching, moving, altering. Every few seconds, they morphed. Some solidified. The nuances of future-seeing never ceased to boggle him.

How could one make sense of it?

Amongst the possibilities lay a sense of deep and abiding power. The magic asserted fathomless reservoirs, which always made him wonder about the source. From whence did the magic come?

Snorting, Max brought himself back out of the magic. Well, he didn't know how, but he certainly needed to put Lucey through an Apothecary school. If he had to hazard an interpretive guess about what the future held—a skill he did not excel at yet—he'd presume she had a future with the Advocacy. Though he rarely saw her with Charlie, a detail he'd puzzle together later.

Charlie would be delighted.

The unknown witches dissipated, fading to darkness. Max was glad to see them go. For a man that yearned for solitude, he certainly had enough witches around him all the time.

His return to the office at Pershington met with little but the same drudgery as before. Witches milled in the street below. The dull tones of Gabbi, the High Witch, as she spoke to someone in her office dissipated to a blur in the background. Gabbi was competent, at least. Most of his work kept him doing actual errands on her behalf, which helped.

All of it, routine.

Boring, really. He'd been in this position a little over a year and already had it figured out. In fact, any recent graduate of a Network school could do this work.

He needed more currency.

Flashing headlines on the newsscroll caught his gaze.

Peace Talks Fail.

Max curled his upper lip over his teeth as he skimmed the article, bypassing ridiculous truths such as *Central Network Ambassador Dahlia Sigard failed to meet on common ground with Dostar, High Priest of the Western Network* and *Rumors of a romantic relationship between Greta and the Western Network Ambassador, Odet Shein, abound.*

Newsbooks from the Eastern Network fared little better in updates. *Leo Giuseppi and Cecilia Liam to join forces in their hunt against the magical antagonists known as Watchers, with High Priest Dante Aldana's approval,* crossed the front page.

Charlie had been mumbling about obtaining more visibility into the Eastern Network for a while now. The Central Network headed right toward a cesspool with sycophants like Dahlia Sigard speaking to bullies like Dostar.

In fact . . .

Max stood up, infused with a new purpose.

He needed more currency and a career far more challenging than Pershington could offer, though being close to Wildrose had provided a breath of fresh air, particularly in the wake of Ranulf's death.

Time for something different.

He reached for a quill, grabbed an empty parchment.

Ms. Dahlia Sigard,

My name is Maximillion Sinclair, Assistant to the High Witch of Pershington, outside of Ashleigh Covens, and manager of the Wildrose Estate, formerly owned and run by the late Ranulf Dauphin.

I graduated early, and with the highest honors, in my class at Mr. Shad's School for Boys. My ambitions are great, and I have long admired your work.

He swallowed back the rise of acid that crawled up his throat while writing the words. Oh, how he loathed flattery.

Still, with a witch like Dahlia . . .

Would you be available for lunch together? I have many questions I'd love to ask, if you have time or favor for such a thing. Also, if you have any openings for an Assistant, I would like to put my name forward for the position.

Yours in regard for the Central Network,

. . .

Maximillion

He perused it once, twice, sent it off with a flutter of parchment. The sordid reality was likely that Dahlia would never respond. She must get dozens of letters requesting the same, and he'd given no offer for something in return.

All politicians were the same. They didn't serve one unless—

A reply hovered in front of him.

He blinked.

The Golden Guinea Hen in ten minutes.

—Dahlia

Max read it twice, forced his heart to beat again, and scrambled to his feet.

* * *

Witches filled the Golden Guinea Hen almost to bursting.

Outside, carriages sped by. Loose dogs jogged through the seething alleys. The cobblestone road ended here, leading to dirty streets filled with dried mud that carriages rattled over.

Meanwhile, he assumed the High Witch of Highways napped with how terrible highways had gotten these days. Ditches and holes that nothing but magic could fix had already formed.

Max stepped inside the Inn, then immediately off to the right. The mouthwatering smell of pot roast filled the air. A witch approached him wearing a white apron around her waist, a bushy braid over her left shoulder.

"Can I help ya?"

"I'm looking for Ambassa—"

"This way."

The girl led him off to the right, behind the Inn, and into a quieter back room. As he left the chaos behind, he slowly relaxed.

Sitting alone at a table was a witch with an elaborate knot of hair on top of her head. The folds of hair were shiny, well kept, and a light blonde. She peered at a menu, nose slightly wrinkled in thought.

"Miss—"

"Have a seat, Maximillion. Trixie, please get us the beef pot pie, with a loaf of bread on the side, and firm white cheese."

"Yes, Ambassador."

So, that was how it would play.

Dahlia studied him as he lowered to the chair across from her. Her brow rose higher in a blatant perusal. She settled her hands on her lap, hiding a gaudy cord of engagement on her left wrist. Despite his less-than-pleasant impression of her, the melody of her voice had a pleasing note.

"Your message took me by surprise and arrived at just the right moment."

"I'm glad to hear the latter."

"You seem well spoken enough." Her gaze dropped, taking him in. "You're well dressed and present handsomely."

"Is this a test?"

"Absolutely." She reached for a cup of tea, motioned for him to do the same. One steamed lightly in front of a small plate filled with flat, oval biscuits. Max refused, but said nothing.

Her lips twitched.

"Are you serious about wanting a position as my Assistant?"

"I never joke."

"Hmm . . . I can sense that in you. Why not?"

"Who has the time?"

"Fair. You're quite young."

"Age is a frame of mind," he retorted. "I turn eighteen this winter and have already accomplished more than most men at twenty-two."

She laughed. "Also fair. Well, you're certainly confident in the way you speak, I'll give you that. Is that a flaw or a strength?"

"It's both. Outspoken people like myself often intimidate witches, which can be a good or a bad thing depending on the situation. I know how to dial it down," he added quietly.

She said nothing.

Trixie returned with two plates of bread and a shared plate of firm cheese with a bright red rind. Pink faded into the cheese from the edge. His stomach growled, but he waited until Dahlia reached for hers before he did the same.

"Tell me your opinions on Greta," she said.

"First," he instantly replied, "please regale me on whether you're a witch intimidated by another witch who knows their own mind and opinion. Even a witch as young as seventeen."

"No."

"Then Greta is a fool. She surrounds herself with syco-phants, dotes on witches that tell her what she wants to hear, and bumbles around the Network government structure instilling fear in everyone. When she comes up against an enemy like Dostar, who is not afraid of her, she fails. She'll take the Network down with her."

Dahlia's expression didn't change, except to sharpen slightly in her gaze.

"And relationships with other Networks?"

"Immeasurably important, if we're talking about maintenance of peace and life as we know it."

"I recently met with Dostar, in the West."

"I know."

The tip of her index finger trailed along the top rim of her glass, sending a ring into the air. The low hum rippled past, setting his hair on edge. Max ignored it, wouldn't pull his gaze away.

"Tell me your opinions."

"I don't think you want them."

A smile crossed her lips—a little tighter than before—as she leaned forward. "Oh, I'd *love* to know what you thought of my negotiations with Dostar as presented in the *Chatterer*, Maximillion. I can tell you're a man brimming full of truth and power and authority. The type of witch who can do no wrong, are you?"

He paused, irritated by the cat-like curl in her words. An overwhelming feeling of being caught in her paws, the mouse to her feline rapacity, froze a scathing reply in his throat.

Dahlia smiled with ice.

"First lesson of diplomacy, Maximillion. Don't assume you know everything just because you read the headlines. You have a youthful arrogance that's irritating and small-minded. What's worse? You don't even *see* it. Judge Greta, if you must, but you're no different."

Astonishment quelled him into absolute silence.

Her words stacked up in his brain like stone walls, forming a rudimentary picture of what she said. Dahlia leaned back. Her flinty gaze looked less feral now, the irritation fading into concern. Ridges formed between her eyebrows.

"There are those of us still fighting for the Central

Network. Maybe Greta is attempting to take over with an unprecedented show of power-hungry moves, but not all of us bow to her every will. Perhaps every negotiation with Dostar doesn't go the way I'd like, but at least there was a negotiation. That *I* went instead of Greta was a win itself. Also, don't believe everything you read in the Chatterer. I don't always release the details of my negotiations with other Networks, so they make garbage up to have filler. Did you know that?"

"No," he whispered.

"Imagine. Something your wise seventeen years hasn't seen. I'm disappointed. With your educational background, I had hope for someone with a better moral compass than self-righteous judgment and indignation. If you really want to be an Assistant and make a difference to this Network, you'll set aside your own prejudices first and admit you have much to learn."

A shrinking feeling overtook Max, reducing him to a pile of rubble in his own body.

By the gods.

He'd never met a woman with such a sharp tongue, and so much truth in it.

Wearily, Dahlia rubbed a hand over her brow. She opened her mouth to speak, but Trixie bustled back in, a long-sleeved glove over her arms as she bore a bubbling, brown-topped pie their way.

After she settled it in the middle, plopped a spoon inside, and bustled out, Max met Dahlia's gaze. They stared at each other in implacable silence.

Finally, he rasped.

"You're right, Ambassador Sigard. Forgive me. I hadn't seen that my own prejudices gave way to judgment and ill feelings. I deserved every bit of that."

Slowly, her lips parted. She swallowed and said, "Thank you for being willing to see it. Listen, Maximillion, you had me intrigued by your letter. I have three hundred applicants that all want to replace my Assistant, who leaves next week. Only yours drew my attention, and I don't know why. I was on my way here when I received it and took a chance.

"I want you to be a great candidate, and I want you to serve the Central Network well. It's no secret that the Assistant to the Ambassador typically takes over as the next Ambassador, though history has seen other circumstances."

The smallness inside him shed, welling into something that almost felt like hope.

"I won't live forever," she continued, and something stark altered her voice for a moment. "And the good gods can damn me to Halla if I leave the Central Network in a more precarious position after I'm gone. I want *you* to be the one that learns how to do it right from me, because I don't plan to have another Assistant. Will you do it? Will you set aside your ego and learn?"

"Yes."

The immediate reply, born of desperation and hope and sincere desire, rushed out of him. It startled both. She reared back. He held his breath. Dahlia set that searching gaze on him again, then said, "All right."

Disbelief froze him.

"All right?"

She lifted both hands, motioning to him. "You're hired. You will start next week. Whatever you're paid now, I'll double it. You can live wherever you want, but I expect you to work at least nine hours a day. Sometimes fifteen. You'll attend all negotiations and meetings with me. Normally I don't pull my Assistant into everything but . . . I have a good feeling about you."

"I won't disappoint you."

Amusement tilted her lips. "I hope not. Now dig in. We have much to discuss, and I'm starving."

Chapter Twenty

CHARLIE

Frightfully choppy wind tried to press Charlie back as he hovered far above the little boat that skipped the top of a foamy sea. Eastern Network tradition lent a far-greater-than-normal belief in the goddess of the ocean, Prana, though the popularity of the goddess paradigm waned.

If true, Prana must be in a violent fit to cause a storm like this.

The blanket the witches in the skiff had thrown over the young Watcher remained in place, despite all odds. Charlie calculated his risk, the energy in reserve, and the magic at his fingertips. Just enough, he'd wager.

He had to dive, capture, and return to Wildrose.

Alerting none of them.

For the first time since Papa died, life infused him again. His heart banged against his ribcage. Excitement flowed through every facet of his body, sending tingles down his hollow bird bones. One minute until he acted.

The Guardian who stood next to Leo shouted something over the rain. As the skiff approached the pier, Charlie issued an invisibility incantation. He didn't want the *aquila* birds thought of as this happened.

His timing must be perfect. He lowered into the air, giant wings flapping, and closed the transformative magic.

He plummeted.

Wind whistled past his ears for only a moment. The world moved so quickly. He had to force his eyes to remain open. Time slowed as he hurtled toward the ground, freezing air whistling past him.

Three seconds.

They tugged the Watcher girl up from the bottom of the boat. As expected, her legs wouldn't hold her weight. She cried out, muffled by a gag.

Two seconds.

Charlie held his breath.

Don't move her, he thought, *don't move.*

The East Guard, holding her arm, turned to bark something at the pier.

One second.

Charlie started the transportation spell. He reached out, snatched her arm as he sped by. The force of his momentum jerked her out of the East Guard's grasp and into the icy water with him. They crashed into the ocean. His invisibility spell slipped over her just as the transportation spell completed.

* * *

Bella sat at the table at Wildrose, slurping her third bowl of warm soup. Lucey sat nearby, hovering like a mother hen. Pearl eyed her from the hearth, where she stirred a cauldron with a long-handled wooden spoon.

Charlie shucked the blanket off his back, stretched it across a drying rack near the fire. He'd transformed before they returned to Wildrose, donning a dark-skinned alter ego with jet black hair that matched Faye's and strong shoulders. He deepened his voice, just in case, affecting a vague accent.

Faye's glittering gaze told him she knew he lurked under the layers of magic, but Lucey and Pearl's curious glances meant they did not. Ideal. If they would keep the Advocacy safe and push his plan to its inevitable end, no one could see Charles Dauphin at Wildrose.

Not even Pearl, nor Lucey.

Bella didn't stop speaking. Lucey stared at her, as if she could understand, but given the blank expression on her face, she didn't comprehend a word.

In broken attempts at a popular tribal language she knew from the West, Faye asked, "Can you speak the common language?"

Bella held up two fingers in a pinching motion " . . . stolen . . . family!" she cried through half a sob. A spoon full of egg noodles and diced carrots dropped into the broth. "Da!"

"Da means father," Faye said with a sigh. "I'm assuming she was captured from her family."

Max stepped out of the shadows. "Can you ask her from where?"

Bella whirled around with a startled squeak. Her eyes widened. He cut a frightful figure, standing in the dark corner with his resonant voice and intense green eyes. In this light, they almost appeared emerald.

Faye attempted.

Trembling, Bella said, "Shecca."

"Shecca is a congregation area for tribes."

Faye used magic to conjure a scribble of glowing lines in the air. Open rifts and valleys on a desert funneled toward a starred point in the middle. The scripted word *Shecca* appeared next to it.

"Her tribe must roam through there."

Max turned away from the girl. "Tell her to finish the soup. We'll help her find her family."

After Faye attempted to help her understand, Bella's tears dried. She scooped more food into her mouth, babbling questions Faye could barely decipher, if her confused expression meant anything.

"Please give Bella another bowl of soup. After she's done, I'll take her back home."

Faye nodded. Meanwhile, Bella dove back in for another slurp. Lucey watched with quiet amusement, then returned to the book sprawled in front of her. Max strode out behind Charlie. He muttered to Charlie as he passed.

"Come with me."

With a whirl, Charlie obeyed.

Max led them to the study, a room that Charlie had carefully avoided since Papa died. The tobacco leaves, the old books, the quiet fire, all reminded him too much of Papa. He avoided ghosts.

He didn't court them.

Charlie kept his reservations silent as he stepped to the window and peered out on the grounds. The transformative magic from earlier bled away, revealing himself in the pale reflection against the glass panes.

The study overlooked the forest. Darkness had returned, sweeping the landscape in tones of shadow and question. The steadiness of it soothed him.

His mind vaulted back to the East. To Leo. To Carcere. The close call with Bella. The retrieval had been far too simple. In hindsight, he'd set them up to fail later. Now, Leo might not row Watchers out.

He should have returned to Carcere immediately, observed

their response to learn more about them. Were they livid? Frustrated? He hoped so. Tonight, he'd go into the paths, replay the events. Figure out how to do it better next time. He wouldn't make the same mistake twice. He must transform his looks from the beginning, as well.

Max cleared his throat, drawing Charlie's gaze. As Charlie turned, a letter popped into the air in front of him. Familiar-enough handwriting scrawled his name on the outside. He snatched it, turned it over, and read the hasty words on the back.

Ah.

Just as planned.

"Well," Max said. He leaned two hands back on the desk, glared at him with all the power of an old man.

"Honestly, Max," he drawled and pitched the letter into the fire. "If I didn't know any better, I'd think you were my father. Why are you glaring at me like I stepped on your cat?"

"You retrieved a Watcher."

"Finally! The Advocacy does something right. We should be celebrating."

Max eyed him. "So why aren't you?"

"You noticed."

An inclination of his head was all he replied.

Something hid there.

Charlie lifted a questioning eyebrow. Irritated, Max snapped, "You're not the only one invested in a safer world for Watchers. If you're going to take matters into your own hands, you could do the rest of us the courtesy of letting us be involved somehow."

Charlie stifled a smile.

Ah, so Max was jealous he missed out on the fun. Such an easy observation. Max didn't even realize how transparent he could be. For his part, Charlie never wanted to be the one to inform him.

Charlie sighed. "Well, Max, I never could hide anything from you. Yes, I'm grateful to have saved Bella. Seeing Leo at Carcere was a confirmation of several rumors. But, if we're honest . . ."

He trailed away, lost in swampy thoughts. With forced practice, he extracted himself.

". . . this isn't going to work. The Advocacy can't run with only me, as you've mentioned. Certainly not with rumors, or hopes, or suicide missions. We can't be random about it unless randomness is our strategy. In that case, it needs to be a planned strategy that appears random. Leo is quite intelligent. He'll figure us out. Our structure has to change."

A loosening of Max's glare told him all he needed to know. "I was going to say the same."

Charlie paused behind a chair, put his hands on the back. "I'm restructuring the Advocacy, Max. We're changing everything."

"There's not much to change."

Charlie snapped two fingers. "Exactly. This is how we're going to do it. We're going to create an image of a man. A . . . name. Someone that others can follow. Watchers haven't cared about an organization so far. They don't trust organized protection."

Reluctantly, Max assented with a nod.

Charlie spoke faster. "Now that we rescued Bella, we're going to spread the word that a secretive, powerful witch under the name of the Advocate has saved her. Watchers will talk about us, try to find us. Then we'll gather information and save another Watcher. And another. As we save them, we'll recruit them, their families, their trusted witches, to our cause."

Max's jaw tightened. The meditative look of his eyes meant he stewed in thought. Charlie plowed onward, sensing what might be his only opportunity.

"The reputation of the Advocate, and the supportive Advocacy, will grow quietly. The key is absolute secrecy. No one, except for you and Faye, will know about me. No one will know the Advocate."

"Are *you* the Advocate?"

"Yes."

Max's brow furrowed. "They'll know. If you're saving them, then—"

"Transformation, Max! Our number one rule is that you can never be who you are. They must adopt a persona to protect their identity. The headquarters of Wildrose that I've spent so much time on will be the center. Newcomers must be transported in. The majority of witches will transport in and out. Only those seeking refuge will travel through the book-case, into the basement."

"And will they leave the basement?"

"No, never. Wildrose cannot be known as the location of headquarters. Do you see? If we have persona's and alter egos, no one will know."

Max's pervasive silence bred hope.

"Faye will help!" Charlie cried. "So will Pearl, Lucey."

"Will they know you are the Advocate?"

"No. They cannot."

"Pearl will figure it out. So will Lucey. They were here tonight."

"And I was not. They saw a different man."

Max's eyes widened. He sucked in a sharp breath and paused, as if replaying the previous scene through his head. All at once, his bunched shoulders deflated.

"Oh."

He turned away.

Charlie could almost see the direction of his thoughts. Pearl spent less and less time at Wildrose since Ranulf died. She knew that Charlie built a project in the basement, but had never been inside. Since Faye left formal schooling, she'd taken over as mistress of the manor.

"Perhaps they wouldn't," Max finally conceded.

"If anything, they'd think it was *you*."

Max scowled.

Extracting the building thoughts from his mind, laying them in front of Max gave an undeniable, deep relief. The pressurized thoughts had built all day, expanding until he thought he'd explode.

"You remember Harry?"

Max cut a sharp glare. "How could I forget?"

"Remember how I acted with him?"

"Yes."

"That's the answer." Charlie's eyes widened. "I won't be Charlie anymore. At least not in public. To you, to Faye, to Pearl, yes, you may always call me Charlie. In private. I'm about to step into someone else."

Charlie motioned to the fireplace with a wave of his hand.

"I've just received news that I'm to become the Assistant to Council Member Stiles. He needs someone new, and he's an absolute newt, as far as morals go. But he sits in the center and hotspot of gossip in the Network. Harry helped me pull owed favors from Papa's former confidantes."

"Harry thinks you're an empty-headed idiot, Charlie."

He grinned. "I know."

Slowly, understanding showed in Max's gaze. "You are . . ."

"Charles Dauphin." He bowed, his voice brightening into something insipid. "A witch that loves to garden, thanks for asking, and thinks politics is all too boring, really. Don't you have better things to do with your life?"

"Charlie—"

"It's the ultimate game, Max!" he cried, advancing a step. "We beat them at their own rules. There's a pattern to the witches that Greta chooses to trust, and it's an easy mold to fill. I'll be the idiot they love to employ, get the information the Advocacy truly needs, and funnel to you. You can make assignments to other Advocacy members. You'll be my screen. Send Lucey or Faye or whomever we recruit that wants to help. Do you see? If I live at the castle and hear all the *real* details, then the Advocacy can prosper."

"It's too much."

Charlie waved a hand. "It's not! It's what we must do, Max. You can see it, can't you?"

"Wildrose—"

"Is a place that will be exceptionally hidden. No one can see outside of headquarters, and if they need sanctuary, we'll have the basement locked down. The windows are too small to see more than Letum Wood, anyway. And when I come back to help, I'll transport and transform to someone else. I'll be a worker. Someone that no one suspects. The Advocate will be at large, and you will be the only one who knows who I am."

"Not Pearl or Faye, as you said."

Charlie sobered. "I must tell Faye. She is my soulmate, Max. We'll both need her. But not Pearl. As much as I love her, I don't know if we can trust her with a secret this . . . expansive. To protect her. And Lucey? No. She needs to focus on getting into her Apothecary training."

A reluctant scowl crossed Max's face. Long moments passed while they stewed over the implications.

"Your currency as a Council Member Assistant will certainly help remove pressure from the manor. I was just promoted to Assistant Ambassador this afternoon."

"No!"

"Later." Max waved it off. "My salary has doubled, but so has my work involvement."

Charlie blew a raspberry. "Congrats, Max! And all the more reason to pull other witches in. Wildrose will run easily between the two of us, and what's left can go to the Advocacy.

We can ask Watchers to donate to the cause. Not currency, because precious few have that. I'm thinking of time, clothes, spaces to hide, you name it. If we have the Advocate's name to gather under, the Watchers will follow. I've been to enough BLAUS meetings the past several weeks to know that they're hungry for a leader."

Max stared hard at him, a glittering gaze cold as stone in his eyes. It didn't bother Charlie.

He knew love when he saw it.

"I thought you were a fool, you know," Max said. "Chasing the Advocacy to grieve over Ranulf. Seeing Bella today. I . . ."

He stopped. The glower intensified.

"Charlie, you . . . you have no dead ancestors to impress. You were enough for Ranulf as you are."

The perpetual knot that lived in Charlie's chest tightened. "I know."

Max challenged him with a piercing stare. "You don't have to do this."

"Yes, I do."

"There are no requirements gripping you from the grave."

"The Advocacy is a fulfillment of the Wildrose ambition . . and so much more."

Max sighed.

"I see that."

"You'd want an Advocacy, wouldn't you? If you were a young kid like Bella, thrust into a magic you didn't ask for. At any moment, your life is in danger simply because you were born a certain way. Witches are abandoning their children to keep themselves and their family safe. Watchers are hiding and almost dying."

Max nodded. "Yes, of course. With your plan, it has a fighting chance."

"Fighting chance!" he cried, laughing. "A bold lie. We're

going to do it, Max. All we have to do is stabilize. We'll use Bella to build up the Advocate reputation. I'll glean information. Together, we'll save Watchers, recruit more workers, and do it over and over until we have our own protective force. You see? With information from the castle and your work at Wildrose, we'll save Watchers everywhere."

Chapter Twenty-One

MAXIMILLION

Five and half years later

The moment Max felt briny sea air on his face, he knew he'd made a mistake.

Surreptitiously attending old Abbi's pathetic funeral had cut him to the center, weaning him from stoic resolve. He hadn't interacted directly with her in years, though he sent food baskets as often as he could manage. No one in his village would be likely to remember him, the desperate imp that scrounged for food in the swamp. He didn't stop to talk to any of them to find out if he knew them, either.

During Abbi's burial, Max stood outside the cemetery, invisible. Wetness thickened the air with the smell of mold. A young boy called out an invocation and blessing on her grave. Two poor, hired lads shoveled dirt into the hole in the ground. A witch from the local coven dedicated to the sea goddess spoke about Abbi. There had been little to say.

She existed, now she left.

Inevitability at work.

Now, Max stood on the beach and stared at Magnolia Castle.

His coat flapped in a gusty wind. The sea frothed not far away as it rushed closer, then retreated. In the distance, two small children played in the ocean. Near them stood a slim, dark-haired woman. Her hand elevated just over her eyes, peered at the waves. She laughed.

Serafina.

The delighted sound of her laugh made his stomach hurt.

As if drawn by a string, Max transported closer. East Guards clomped through the outer grounds of Magnolia Castle, muttering to each other. If they sensed his invisibility magic, they gave no sign.

You're an adult, he thought with sharp reproach. *You're above spying, begging for attention. Serafina made it clear where her loyalties remained years ago, after Mere's death. You seek absolution amongst the dead.*

Scathing inner voice or not, he pressed closer.

Around a sprouting green bush of fronds, he crouched. No one could see him with magic in place, though a gardener could happen by, but he felt better with something between him and his aunt.

She stood down the shore, watching the two young scamps in the waves. Water soaked the bottom of her dress and clung to her ankles charmingly. Her dark hair, pulled high, tumbled around her shoulders. Age swerved around Serafina, leaving her young and lovely as ever.

The wind whistled past his ears, occluding another peal of laughter to mere hints of sound. An exhalation drew his attention to the left.

"Oh, Your Majesty."

Max froze. He pivoted, still crouched behind that blasted bush like an imbecile, then stopped. Cecelia Liam stood only a few paces away. She wore a simple, pearl-colored dress, with glittering diamonds on her ears and wrists. Underskirts fluffed around her legs a few layers deep.

Decorative, woven walls built for climbing flowers in the summer hid her from sight of the beach.

They hid Dante, as well.

The two of them stood in a lover's embrace. Bodies pressed close. His arm held her at the waist. Indrawn breaths preceded a ravenous kiss that continued for minutes. Max's shock ebbed.

Well.

How very bold.

A shriek of laughter rang through the air during a lull of wind. One child danced away from foamy sea kisses, arms waving overhead as they sprinted across the sand. Serafina caught the little girl and tossed her higher.

Cecelia pulled away from Dante, palms on his chest.

"Dante, no."

"They can't see us," he insisted. "Cecelia, it's been too long since I've held you in my arms. You make me crazy."

She almost capitulated to his stormy gaze. A long, intense stare in his eyes nearly swept the courage out of her.

"Yes." Her thin fingers reached up, tucked a lock of hair off his forehead. "Even ten minutes away is too long, *masuna*. But this is no life."

"It has to be enough, for now."

Cecelia scoffed. "You're the High Priest, Dante. You can say it's enough because no one will challenge you. But me? If word spread . . ."

Her trailing voice shocked Max more than their indiscretion. With Dante, she effused warmth. Affection, even, but Cecelia had presented herself as a haughty woman for the last year or two. Unprecedented for a female in this Network to gather such power and acclaim. These intrigues helped her spirited rise in the Network structure make far greater sense.

Dante gathered her closer, if possible. "Then I will simply keep you close. Protect you however I can. With my name, my position. We will be together one day, *masuna*. I swear it. I will always care for you."

The far off tap of approaching shoes brought another step of distance between them. After a look brimming with despair, Cecelia disappeared. Dante straightened his shirt, pulled in a deep breath.

Two seconds later, Leo approached. He leaned outside, saw Dante, and lifted his brow.

Max stiffened.

Big Leo in the flesh. Rarely did he see the Head of Guardians in his Ambassador work with Dahlia. His upper lip curled.

"I have updates, Your Highness," Leo said.

With a troubled sigh, Dante folded his hands behind his back and followed Leo down the hall. Max stayed rooted to the spot, though sorely tempted to trail them. Instead, he remained behind the fronds to watch Serafina on the beach, his heart in his throat.

* * *

"Well, that's a rotten twenty-third birthday, Max."

Charlie's subdued tone, so different from the pandering, jovial voice he used with the rest of the Network, set Max's teeth on edge.

Even five years later, nothing felt as unnatural as Charlie attempting to be Charles Dauphin, Assistant to Council Member Stiles. Because of the obvious disparity between his personas, Max still struggled to transition between the two of them.

Even in the safety of Wildrose.

The study closed around them with dusky walls filled with

books, quills, parchments. Ledgers of Wildrose expenditures from Faye, including costs of caring for transient Watchers and costs relating to new Defenders, populated down the desk. They reconciled, but not easily. Currency wasn't tight with both of their political positions and donations to the Advocacy, but they didn't have any to spare.

Max spun, the scent of the Eastern Network still heavy in his nose. "I don't celebrate birthdays," he muttered. "And that's why. Sets one up for constant disappointment."

Charlie softened. "Well, I'm sorry about Abbi. You didn't mention her much, which tells me you cared a great deal about her."

Not a hint of sarcasm filled his tone.

Max could only nod.

Charlie leaned back in the chair, eyes glimmering. His ankle crossed his knee in a lazy flair only he could execute so well. Fatigue lines tugged at the corners of his lips. He'd never admit that his dual role in society—the elusive Advocate, the idiotic Assistant—tired him, but the signs manifested in the quiet moments.

Just as Max opened his mouth to ask how Charlie really was, a gentle tap came on the door.

"Come in."

Faye peeked inside, saw Charlie, and illuminated like a tree filled with fire. With a hop to his feet and a wide grin, Charlie crossed the distance between them and clasped her tight. While they whirled in the middle of the floor, Max turned away.

They'd need a moment.

They *always* needed a moment.

He could only explain the tightness in his chest when near them as annoyance over their generous amounts of affection. Certainly *not* jealousy over how much Charlie cared for and adored her.

No, not that.

Max had his social life nailed down easily enough. Caterina and Bella helped him deal with his more carnal appetites.

As empty as that sometimes felt.

Max accepted the opportunity to slip into the paths. Nothing exceedingly surprising there. More work with the Western Network tomorrow, but he expected that. Dahlia set up appointments near the border . . .

Out of nowhere sprang a new wisp.

A female witch.

He'd seen her before. Many, many times before. Often enough he recognized her immediately. Blonde hair, streaked with darker brown in places. An attractive expression, with inquisitive eyes and a sharp gaze. The first time he saw her, she was a rambunctious looking child. Now, a gangly teenager. She smiled like Charlie, with her entire face.

"Who are you?"

Neither the wisp nor the magic responded. They never did, but he continued to ask. He strode around her, studying each nuance. An attempt to find the trail that led away from her led to nothing. In fact, there was no trail. The magic had given him a simple moment in time with absolutely no attachments. That had never happened except for with *this* witch.

It meant something.

As quickly as she came, the girl disappeared.

Chapter Twenty-Two

CHARLIE

The rustle of Pearl turning a page in her romance book was the only sound in the room. She sighed, reached for another Leto nut, and popped it into her mouth.

Charlie put a hand on the trembling shoulder of a young man that stood next to him. Rolf. Brawny through the shoulders, with thick hands that felled trees in Letum Wood. He sold them for lumber, so he always smelled like sap.

"Easy," Charlie murmured.

Charlie stood before Rolf in his typical Advocacy disguise. Light brown hair to his shoulders, pulled back in a braid. Not a hint of freckles on his tawny skin. Near-black eyes with sparse lashes. Lean through the shoulders, the legs.

Entirely forgettable.

"I can't stay here," Rolf gasped. His pale green eyes blew open, panicked. "I can't. Her Watcher magic is driving me mad! I have to stop it!"

Pearl yawned.

Charlie gripped Rolf's shoulder. Rolf panted, shoulders heaving.

"Remember what I said? Deep breaths through the chest.

Expand them in your stomach. You can *think* this away. It's power, that's all. You're recognizing their abilities. Like a craving for a sweet, it'll pass."

Breathing heavy now, Rolf squeezed his eyes shut. His giant hands flexed into fists. Charlie eyed him wearily. Most Defenders he brought to Pearl's house to train them to control their craving for Watcher magic struggled, but few towered so far above him. Spells could render Rolf inert in a second, but still . . .

Rolf's reddened skin faded. He breathed easier. "Oh. It's . . . it's . . . passing."

Across the way, Pearl flipped another page. She patted her lips, legs propped up on a pillow, where she stretched across a hideous floral divan. She hummed under her breath. Every few pages, she'd slip back into the Watcher paths, stir the craving back up, then return to her book.

After an hour of practice, Rolf grasped it.

Pearl met Charlie's gaze. He nodded once. A distant expression overcame her as she slid back into the paths.

Rolf howled.

"Rolf, breathe."

More quickly this time, Rolf obeyed. His chest smoothed into an even rhythm. Time loosened the tension through his meaty body. Minutes later, Rolf nodded. Pearl slipped free of the magic, held a thumb up to Charlie, and returned to her tawdry romance novel.

Rolf's eyes opened. Elation brightened them.

"I did it."

Charlie beamed. "You did it!"

"I did it." Rolf swiped his sweating forehead with the back of his arm. "You said it gets easier?"

"Much easier. One more round at Pearl's and you'll be ready for headquarters. After that lesson, we'll transport you in. You'll never see where it is, and can only transport in and out, but it's sufficient. There will be more Watchers there, but they come and go. Eventually, you won't even notice them." He pressed a hand to his chest. "I don't."

Rolf nodded, his gigantic shoulders slumped forward.

"Good to hear."

Charlie clapped him on the shoulder. "Now, let's get you back home. I'll return tomorrow for your last lesson, then one of the others will clear you to help the Advocacy without endangering our support Watchers."

"They will trust me that soon?"

"I think so, but I'm only a volunteer here."

Rolf smiled shyly. "I'm . . . relieved. When Cecelia's cronies found me, they told me I had to help them and Defenders everywhere . . . it didn't feel right."

"It wasn't right."

He nodded emphatically. "Wasn't."

Pearl popped up from behind her book. "Great work, Rolf! See you tomorrow?"

With a smile, Rolf grabbed his hat and lumbered out the door. Charlie watched him go with a sense of relief. Once the door opened and Rolf disappeared, he turned to Pearl.

"Well, that was faster than I expected."

"He was nervous."

"Were you?"

She laughed, a giggly little thing. One foot bounced around. "Not at all. You'd never let him hurt me."

Charlie relaxed slightly. "Good."

"More Advocacy work today?"

"Always."

Pearl's gaze tapered in thought. A sly note entered her voice. "Max said the Advocate found out about another raid. He's planning a mission tonight."

"Good."

"Do you know anything about it?"

The transformation magic bled out of Charlie. He luxuriated in the lack of tugging energy for a moment before he shook his head.

"No."

Disappointment flashed through her features. "So, you still won't tell me who the Advocate is, either? Not after so many years?"

Charlie bit back a snort. How he loathed lying to Pearl! Yet, how necessary it remained. In five years of active Advocacy work, Max and Faye contained his secret.

"You think I have time to know those details? Work consumes my life. I can only contribute in small ways compared to those on the raids."

She opened her mouth to counter, then stopped. Truth lay in all parts of that. Just . . . not the *whole* truth.

"True." She sighed. "Very true. You are quite busy, and one of the most controlled Defenders I've met. Even if you don't do as much as Max or Lucey, I know it's appreciated. For myself, I'm inclined to think it's Lucey, but I can't prove it . . ."

A message appeared in front of him, thankfully drawing his attention. Max's handwriting. Another note from Faye, and a third from Council Member Stiles, shuffled behind the first. Always more messages.

He frowned, opened the two from Max and Faye with a spell, and skimmed through Max's first.

Reports of a third attack on the same night next week need to be verified. We have Dolly and Zander assigned to it, extracting a potential Watcher named Marvin from the Southern Covens. I suspect another attack, but on the opposite end of the Network.

· · ·

Easy enough to do.

Faye's letter unfolded next to the first.

We have two Watchers in Wildrose in separate basement rooms. They're both planning on leaving in the morning, just passed through because of rumors of a raid. They've taken the oath of silence and the forgetting potion to prevent them from remembering details about the basement.

Charlie shoved both into the fire and pushed Council Member Stiles note into his pocket. Pearl had already resumed reading as he grabbed his hat, mentally shifted back into the charade of Charles Dauphin, a barely competent Assistant to Council Member Stiles.

"Pearl, have a lovely day," he cried with jovial undertones.

Her hand snuck out, grabbed a sugar-coated sweet, and waved from behind her novel.

* * *

Council Member Stiles resembled a pine tree.

He had a narrow head, a bushy beard, and a blooming waistline, as if he'd pushed all the mass from his shoulders to his legs. He lumbered around with difficulty, snuffled when he thought, and had an obsession with drinking water that wreaked havoc on long meetings.

Charles adored him.

Charlie could barely stand him.

As the Council Member over the Western Covens, there wasn't a lot to do outside of currency hustling, tax audits, and meetings in the castle. The witches in the Western Covens were mostly self-sufficient and brought plenty of revenue to their little communities through ranching.

As the only true farmland in all the Central Network—thanks to expansive and sprawling growth from Letum Wood—Stiles was arguably the most important Council Member. Unfortunately, he cared too much about his reputation, and too little for his own flock.

When Stiles grunted and shoved out of his chair one bright afternoon in the middle of winter, Charlie perked up. He had pulled his red hair brushed out of his face and wore a tailored suit that felt as ridiculous as it looked. It almost perfectly matched Council Member Stiles in fashion, which delighted the middle-aged man.

Today, Charlie needed all the advantages he could find.

"Charles?"

"Yes, Council Member?"

"When does the meeting with Leo start?"

The sound of Leo's name sent a thrill through Charlie. *Leo Giuseppi*, he thought. *You have no idea what I'm planning for you.*

"Eleven o'clock, sir." Charlie fluttered over some paperwork, pretended confusion, spotted the calendar, and yanked it free from several others. "He'll be coming here, as requested, after your invitation."

Stiles huffed. "Amazing, isn't it?" Astonishment filled his voice. "That the Eastern Network Head of Guardians and I should both hold an equal pleasure in the same type of wine? I'm so glad you discovered the connection."

Charlie hid a smile. "Fate," he said with solemn gravity, "brings the best of men together in the strangest of ways. Sir, if I may extrapolate a few thoughts?"

Stiles waved.

Charlie stood, inched slightly closer, but not too much. Over the last nearly six years, he'd learned the gentle boundaries Stiles held for comfort. He didn't like too many witches near his body, but craved the attention all the same.

"I believe you hold a unique opportunity, sir, that no other Council Member has finagled. You are meeting with the Eastern Network Head of Guardians!" Awe thickened his voice. With delight, he continued. "I've never heard of such a thing. And in this political climate? A wonder."

"Yes, well . . . common ground."

"I imagine he has his own agenda," Charlie murmured, allowing the thought to fade.

Stiles frowned.

"Agenda?"

Charlie leaned closer. Stiles did the same. "Have you not heard of Watchers, sir?"

Stiles' expression clouded. "Watchers? Well . . . yes."

"Mr. Giuseppi has made no secret of his . . . distrust . . . of them. I believe that, should such a conversation arise, avoid it entirely."

Interest piqued in his beady eyes. "Avoid it? Why ever should I do that?"

Charlie nodded, pretended to sew his mouth shut and cut the thread. Deepening curiosity appeared in Stiles' gaze. Charlie spun around, hid a smile, and silently exulted when a knock came on the door.

Perfect timing.

An Advocate speciality.

"Oh!" he whispered to Stiles with unrepressed joy. "The witch in question has come!"

With a spare glance, Charlie confirmed that everything needed for lunch was in place on the table nearest the windows, overlooking a snowy, picturesque scene over Letum Wood. White filled the branches of the closest trees.

Stiles stood, straightened a strangling bowtie that looked too small for his wide neck. Charlie tripped his way to the door, mumbled apologies under his breath, and twisted the knob.

Leo Giuseppi stood outside, a pleasant-enough smile pasted across his face. Strands of white interspersed through his mustache, which had grown. Having stalked Leo for the good part of five years, Charlie had gotten used to his changing facial patterns.

Indeed, Leo morphed almost as much as he did.

What a thrill it would be to dupe him entirely. Leo sought the Advocate relentlessly these days. Inefficiently, as well. Today would give an unparalleled chance to study Leo face to face, without the Watcher-killer realizing to whom he spoke.

Delightful.

"Mr. Leo Giuseppi of the Eastern Network." Charlie bowed grandly at the waist. "It is a high honor to welcome you to the Central Network."

He stumbled to the side, caught himself by holding onto the doorknob, and swept out an arm. Leo stepped into the room. Two East Guards remained outside the door, one on either side, backs to the wall.

"Thank you," Leo said in the common language, rife with the roll of the Eastern Network. "I'm most pleased to be here."

Stiles hurried forward—as much as he could with his awkward walking pattern—an arm outstretched. Charlie pretended to fade into the background, puttering over the teapot, avoiding them entirely, while he canted a listening ear in.

"So glad to meet in person," Stiles said.

"I do love this wine."

"What part of the East are you from?"

The bland trivialities went from forced conversation to something far looser after the wine passed around twice. Charlie hovered at his desk, pretending fascination with his messages from the other side of the room. As planned, they forgot he existed.

Tidbits of mostly banal conversation flew around while sweat collected on the back of Charlie's neck. Hopefully, he had planted a firm enough nugget of curiosity for Stiles before Leo came.

Sitting in the same room as the man responsible for so many Watcher raids made Charlie's fingers itch. How easily he could break Leo. Drop him with a paralysis spell, then whisk him away.

The horrifying political ramifications held him in his chair. Eventually, they might trace everything back to him. By extension, the Advocacy, Wildrose, Max, and Faye. The remaining Eastern Defenders and the rest of Dante's forces would retaliate.

In the end, it would serve no one.

Leo worked a far greater machine. They had to fight the battle at the source, a problem Charlie hadn't yet figured out how to solve.

Whispers drew his attention back to their conversation. Muted tones that, with a quick spell, amplified easily enough.

"—Watchers."

The word, left as a whisper in the air, had come from Stiles. Leo straightened, brow high.

"Yes," Leo replied with some surprise. "We have a problem with Watchers. Fortunately, our leadership is quite proactive in their work to root them out and take care of them."

"A problem, are they?"

"An immense problem."

Leo's tone lengthened. He lifted a single brow, as if he couldn't communicate the depths of such treachery with words. Stiles' wide-eyed surprise was the only invitation Leo required. Charlie kept his head down, the quill moving in scribbled lines of nonsense.

"Watchers," Leo said, the word sliding out in a hiss, "are future-seers. They can affect the way the world operates. Can see what might happen and prevent it to whatever length they desire."

"That's . . . a lot of power."

Stiles sounded uneasy. He shifted in his chair, blotting his sweaty forehead with a handkerchief.

"Yes. In the East, we strive to control their ability to affect witches' daily lives. My Guardians and Cecelia Liam—do you know her?"

A shake of Stiles' head followed.

"A powerful witch in her own right. We have formed a sort of . . . system. She finds the Watchers, then the Guardians and I bring them to Carcere, where they can do no harm. It has rid the East of many potential issues."

Pride stuffed his haughty voice. Charlie swallowed back a swell of annoyance, nausea, and deepening hatred.

"I see," Stiles murmured.

A mournful note entered Leo's voice. "The problem? There are Watchers in the Central Network, and other Networks, that still work their mystical power."

"Well, yes. Of course we've *heard* of them."

"There are several we are tracking."

Leo cleared his throat. Charlie thought Leo cast a surreptitious glance his way. With his head bowed so low over the desk, it would appear as if he were sleeping. He gave a gentle snore.

Leo continued, more quietly than before. "I can't go into the particulars, but the Central Network has more Watchers than leadership may know. We've recently had a Council Member champion a law that requires all Watchers to register with the Network when their powers manifest."

"A plausible next step."

"Hmm, we hope so. If it proves to work for us, we would

be happy to share ideas and implementation strategies with you. Though we try to clean them out of the Eastern Network, they hide in other Networks. We seek witches that will . . . create alliances. Agreements, if you will, so that we might come into your Network and help you with your Watchers. We are highly trained, you see . . ."

"Of course."

"Do you think your High Priestess would be open to a discussion about this growing issue? Perhaps, if you sponsored it?"

Charlie repressed a smile.

Hook.

Line.

Sinker.

Sometimes, this was just too easy.

Stiles straightened in his chair, readjusting his jacket to better cover his girth. "I am close with the High Priestess. I believe I can make anything happen that you like."

Leo beamed, the teacup held in the air. "Then here is to us, Council Member! May we work together to rid the world of filth."

* * *

"Must you go, Charlie?"

Faye's quiet plea, whispered against his chest, broke his heart in half. He played with a curl of her hair, allowing it to wind his finger. The silky strands mesmerized him. Somehow, everything about Faye was soft.

Moonlight broke through the window, falling in ribbons and strands to the floor as it raced to the bed, lighting the dark room. The painted ceiling, obnoxiously elaborate, featured depictions of Letum Wood he could barely see through the shadows. The four-poster bed, with drapes pulled aside, occupied most of the space.

Wildrose.

Always so much bigger than it needed to be.

To his surprise, he missed the ancient manor with its creaky floors and constant protests. Living in Chatham Castle —an allowance because he served Council Member Stiles— kept him on the pulse of all things in Alkarra. He longed for home.

No, for Faye.

"I must go," he murmured against her hair. The tips of his finger trailed along her bare shoulder, skittered across her collarbone. "I have meetings in a few hours. Meetings where Stiles is going to ask Greta if they can work with the Eastern Network to plan raids on Watchers here."

She sucked in a sharp breath.

"But—"

"I know. It sounds dangerous, but it's exactly what I wanted. It gives us the insight we'll need to subvert them."

"Will Greta go for it?"

He shrugged. "It's impossible to tell. Her mood swings so wildly."

She snuggled in. The sweep of her bare skin against his sent a shudder through him. Faye lifted her head, propped her chin on his breastbone. The dig of pressure into the skin gave him a little thrill.

Her whisper affected him more deeply than he'd ever admit.

"I've missed you."

With dark eyes that matched the night, he felt lost in her. He reached up, trailed fingertips down the side of her face.

"I always miss you, Faye. When you're not with me, it feels as though a part of my heart walks around without me. I worry about you constantly."

"Mr. Advocate worries about little old me?" She gasped. Her eyes twinkled as she ran the tip of her finger over the bow of his lips. "I'm honored."

"You should be. You've always been my soulmate, Faye."

"Soulmate."

She stared into his eyes, ponderous. Then tilted her head to the side with a sigh. Her cheek pressed into his shoulder with the caress of her breath on his neck. He closed his eyes, breathed it in.

Drew her deeper to give him the strength to go on.

"Is this too much, Charlie? Are you taking on too much with your job, your . . . position as Charles . . . the Advocacy? It grows daily in some small way. New Defenders, new Watchers. The basement is never still, except at night."

"No. This is exactly what I wanted."

"Over time, though . . ."

"We'll be fine."

She sighed. "When will I see you again?"

He pressed a kiss to her forehead. "Next week, as we have the last five years."

Already, he felt Wildrose slipping away. Saw himself as Charles, the foppish Assistant that everyone liked, but not that well. The Assistant who tripped over every invisible hole in the ground and stammered his way into awkward situations with every opportunity.

A ruse.

A more exhausting, thrilling ruse he'd never imagined.

"Return to me?" she murmured, on the edge of sleep. He pressed a kiss to her hair.

"Forever, my soul."

Chapter Twenty-Three

MAXIMILLION

A buggy-eyed creature stared at Max with deep condemnation. He reached up, plucked it off his jacket, and squeezed.

The locust popped.

With his upper lip curled over his teeth, he stepped out of a teeming pile of the filthy bugs and onto emptier sand. Insect bodies crunched underneath his pristine shoes. Swarms billowed in the air, settling on trees, bushes, anything they could find. Frantic witches ran around, torches swinging, attempting to burn them away. More replaced those that shriveled in the flames.

At his side Dahlia muttered, "Disgusting."

Max peered to the West. The Western Covens of the Central Network skirted the river that created the border between them and the Western Network. The lush, rolling green hills of farm and ranch land butted against the borderlands in some places.

On the other side?

Desert.

Dirt.

Empty barrenness.

And more locusts.

"They're from Dostar," Max called over the buzzing sound of so many chewing monsters. "I can guarantee it."

"Clever, if that's true," Dahlia replied. She flicked a bug off her arm, then shuddered. "It's certainly one way to attack and weaken the Central Network."

"Perhaps in retaliation for the offense Greta gave at her last ball when she called him a boar's arse in front of the Southern Network delegation."

Dahlia's lips pressed.

Max drew in a deep breath and cast a spell. Two bubbles surrounded them, preventing the bugs from landing on their clothes. Other witches weren't so lucky, and the locusts teemed across any section of exposed skin.

Numberless.

"Well." Dahlia lifted both arms. "What do you want to do, future Ambassador?"

The yellowing pallor of her skin gave her away. Dahlia wouldn't work much longer. Her advancing sickness—which began several years ago with small lumps in her breasts, and held off only slightly by potions that made her violently vomit —meant she had little time.

She applied prodigious pressure on him to make the right decisions as an Ambassador. By a signed agreement, Max would take over as Ambassador when she retired. Which would be any day now, he imagined.

"We get rid of the problem before it becomes a bigger problem," he said. "It's still winter, so the impact is minimal."

"Unless you have cattle. The locusts are eating their stores of food, even the cows themselves. Entire orchards will decimate under such a force, and have in the past."

Max frowned.

"Do you address it to the West?" she pressed, almost cheerful now.

"Not yet," he growled.

"Why not?"

"I have no proof that it was Dostar's action. First, I'll apply to some local scientists on the reproductive cycles of this insect to see if this swarm may have been expected. I believe such creatures act cyclically. In the meantime, I'll send several samples to the Librarians at the Great Library of Burke in Letum Wood and ask them to help us identify any existing magic on the bugs. As it's winter, it seems unlikely that this is a normal course, but before I approach anyone in the West, I'll verify."

A pause. "Very good, Maximillion. I'll leave you to it."

She left.

He growled. Of course, he had this handled, though it wouldn't be easy. Fixing this problem would tire him significantly. Her not asking for the rest of his plan, proof of magic, meant that she trusted him to execute it without issue.

Chatham Chatterer journalists lingered in the background, dictating articles to enchanted quills while he attempted a few test spells, collected samples of the bugs, sent the messages to the librarians, scientists, and called for a witch. A young girl scrambled to his side.

"Sir?"

"How far do the bugs extend?"

She smacked a locust off her elbow as she motioned to the south. He extended the protection of his spell to her. She beamed, shoved a bug out.

"Thanks! All the way to the McPherson ranch, about a thirty-minute walk. They're chewing through the orchards there now."

"Fortunately, it's winter. There's no active fruit."

She shrugged. "We need the trees in the summer and they're chewing through the branches. They won't produce fruit if they're dead."

"Fair," he muttered.

A collection spell came to mind as he puzzled out what to do next. Normally, he used such a spell for dust, or to clean up shattered glass, or other undesirable messes. Today, he'd have to do it on a massive scale.

And then what?

He reached for his gloves.

"Any chance you have firewood?" he asked the girl, who occupied his thinking time by flicking the bugs off their protective veil.

"Sure."

"Can you have it brought right here?"

"All of it?"

He nodded once. "All of it. Tell your parents that if they want their barn to survive, we need an enormous bonfire and all the torches they have. These chewing locusts are going to burn."

Just another day in the life of a future Ambassador.

* * *

He returned to Dahlia's office two hours later with a buzz still in his ears. The power that such a large-scale collection spell required had utterly drained him. He needed something sugary, and a lot of water, immediately.

Three envelopes waited on the desk. A burning fire continued in the hearth, thankfully, steeping the space in warmth. Someone from the kitchens must have brought dinner, because a tray sat on a table off to the side, near the floor-to ceiling bookshelves. Historical books, notes from previous Ambassadors, references filled the spaces.

Though addressed to the Ambassador of the Central Network, he opened the first letter. A familiar-enough hand-writing filled the front. With a prickle of intuition, he studied it, flipped it over, and broke the wax seal.

To the Ambassador of the Central Network,

His Majesty, Dante Aldana, would be pleased to invite you to our Network for a discussion regarding the future of our relationships together, a problem of Watchers, and a sundry of other things.

The meeting is planned for three days from now as a dinner from 4:00 to midnight, with dancing and wine. You are welcome to stay overnight.

Yours,

Serafina Aldana
High Priestess of the Eastern Network

Max frowned.

"Well," he muttered, "I'll be damned."

He shoved the letter aside. Not his problem. Dahlia wouldn't be well enough to stay for the entirety, but she could do the negotiations. They'd accept, but he wouldn't attend.

No way.

In the nine years since he left the East, he hadn't once replied to her annual letters and he'd carefully avoided any meeting with Eastern Network leadership if it had any chance of Serafina attending.

The *Watchers* comment slipped through his mind again with greater intrigue, however.

Charlie's plan had worked.

He shouldn't have been surprised. Somehow, Charlie always read the situation just right. They would need to discuss it when they met together next to review Wildrose expenses, currency, and plans for the next Defender raid, which should be coming up soon.

The next message was a folded piece of paper. He flipped it open, distracted by thoughts of what sort of discussion they might have, and paused.

Dahlia's handwriting filled the note.

You're ready, Max. I've informed Greta. The title of Ambassador is officially yours. You are going to do it beautifully.

I never thought I'd bring a twenty-three year old into succession behind me, but I've never met a witch like you.

Make me proud.

The third wasn't a letter at all. It was a familiar parchment, signed by Greta and Dahlia and himself that swore him into position as Ambassador upon Dahlia's retirement.

Effective date?

Immediately.

* * *

Vague memories of Magnolia Castle filtered through Max's mind when he arrived with a crisp tuxedo in place, hair smoothed back, and a bumbling Charles not far away.

Council Member Stiles' beady gaze darted around as he mopped the moisture off his forehead and tugged at his jacket.

Max kept his distance.

Liveried footmen escorted them farther into the Eastern Network while Charles' exclamations rang through the air.

"A lovely bust! Tell me, is that the High Priestess, Vittoria? A brilliant flower in history, I tell you. Council Member, did you see that sword on the wall? Dashing, if you ask me. Might look nice at your side."

Stiles brightened, regarding the weapon with interest.

Max moved on.

He followed a determined butler whose stride didn't waver, grateful to put space between him and the others. Everything felt too close here. His necktie was too tight. The walls were too narrow.

Why did the air smell so brackish?

The butler paused in the doorway to a broad room. Soaring ceilings. Glittering windows. A ballroom with a wide, tiled floor that narrowed down to a single point—a giant banquet table, set for less than eight witches.

He paused at the cusp of the room, scanned. With little effort, he found her. Serafina stood near her husband. Her attention riveted on something at the table, oblivious to his arrival. He felt a swelling of gratitude for the moment to catch his own breath.

During the pause between seeing her and understanding, he had to remind himself that Mere was dead. Long dead. Lost to fists and misery and the anguish of a life she couldn't control.

Serafina looked just like the woman who haunted his dreams. His Mere, her younger sister.

On the other side of Dante stood Cecelia Liam. Elegant coifs of hair stacked on top of her head, billowing into an elaborate dress with layers in the skirts. Beadwork brightened the bodice, which tightened around an hourglass figure.

His favorite villain.

Dante smiled warmly at Cecelia. She blushed, glanced down, a rare smile on her features as she tipped him an openly adoring look. Serafina didn't seem to notice, and he couldn't help but wonder if she would care.

Dante and Cecelia were disgusting filth. He might harbor ill feelings toward Serafina for her abandonment, but loathed Dante all the more for his wandering lust.

Charles' prattling voice closed in from behind Max, announcing their presence. He didn't modulate—no, Charles never modulated for propriety's sake—as he approached. Stiles said nothing, content to let Charles have all the air.

Dante lifted his arms. "Central Network witches," he called with welcome. "Please, have a seat at our table."

Hatred curled Max's fingers into his palm. He tried to stuff it away, but couldn't hold it in place.

"Your Majesty," the butler intoned, "May I present to you Council Member Stiles, and his Assistant Charles. With them is Ambassador Sinclair, newly appointed to the Central Network."

Serafina's head snapped up.

Max met her gaze. The moment their eyes touched, he felt his entire body turn to stone. Only his heart beat a cold song. Shock widened her eyes. Wordlessly, her lips moved in the shape of his name. He transported a whisper next to her ear.

"Not a word in front of Dante."

A trembling hand rose to her lips.

From behind, a loud call broke Max's stone-like stance.

"Pleasure to meet you!" Charles cried. "Such a lovely home you have here. How many years has Magnolia Castle existed? You know, I've long known *Ilese* and adore the tones of it."

As Dante approached, Charles streamed into an eloquent rendition of the language. Startled, Dante replied. The distraction it provided allowed Serafina to compose herself. Her eyes followed him. He felt their weight. She'd want an explanation.

He didn't have one.

Not yet.

Chapter Twenty-Four

CHARLIE

Dante, High Priest of the Eastern Network, struck Charlie as something of a disparity.

Wealthy, powerful, with a beautiful wife and several small children. He lived in a sprawling castle, commanded armies, yet wore the perpetual appearance of bitterness. Proof that a witch could have everything, yet never enough.

Council Member Stiles released Dante's forearm from a friendly clasp. Dante's gaze darted over his shoulder, then back to Stiles with a wooden smile.

"The High Priestess has not come?"

Stiles pressed his lips, shook his head. "Ah, we're not sure, Your Majesty. She had verbalized—"

A shrill call near the doors interrupted his words. "Mr. Stiles! How dare you leave without me?"

Charlie pasted on a bright smile, eyebrows high. Greta's screeching voice had a way of carrying through the ears in a very unpleasant way. Despite the urge to scuttle out of her warpath, Charlie lifted an arm and pretended delight.

"High Priestess! Over here, your Highness. We're most pleased to have you."

Dante stiffened.

Stiles sighed.

Greta bustled closer, shoving past a butler. Her obnoxious dress, a mess of taffeta fabric, rustled as loud as a crashing tide. Peacock feathers bloomed out of the back of her head. Age lines wrinkled her face, drooping saggy skin around a wobbly chin. Her dress plunged down her chest as she bustled closer.

Thick brown hair, pulled out of her face in an ostentatious display, had clearly been bewitched. No gray lines lingered, though her eyebrows remained several shades lighter. Like a witch pasted together in the middle of a dark room.

She stopped a few paces from Dante, who wore an enigmatic smile.

"High Priestess."

She inclined her head in a brief nod, glanced behind him, then turned to Stiles. Her gaze flittered over to Max, then shrewdly to Cecelia.

"Well," she declared. "Shall we begin?"

* * *

Over a sparkling array of crystal and dinnerware, Max sent Charlie a warning glare.

Charlie ignored it.

Dante and Greta chattered with tight amiability across the table. Glimmering candles and goblets full of wine filled the tabletop. Tension rippled through the room with each passing moment. Greta spoke louder with each turn, which obligated Dante to match her volume. Her increasingly agitated responses would soon spell disaster.

Well, no one better than Max to fix it.

Cecelia, who sat to Dante's left, said little. The faint scent of plumeria wafted from her whenever she moved. He'd rather hoped Leo would appear, as Leo had coordinated this whole affair, but he did not.

Charles set down his napkin, leaned forward. Serafina, such a lovely witch, glanced up.

"Pray tell me," he murmured. "Where is the washroom?"

A smile followed, illuminating her graceful features and kind eyes. She pointed to the left. "Just down there, second door on the left."

"Thank you."

Max's gaze bore into his back, but Charlie ignored it as he first turned to the right, tottered, then finally to the left. His shuffling feet bore him out of the hallway with a little hum that he stopped as soon as he was out of earshot.

He passed the second door on the left.

Kept going.

A quick check revealed no familiar incantations active in this area. Which meant no hidden East Guards. Surprising, considering the importance of the guest list. Then again, they didn't have a Protector force like the Central Network.

One question lurked in his mind.

Where *was* Leo?

He cast an invisibility spell, then a transformative one. Time was of the essence. While his body slowly morphed into a small feline, he recalled the mental map he'd committed to memory before arriving. The Advocacy required animal transformation often enough that he didn't need adjustment time.

Paws hit the ground.

Slinking agilely, he followed the stairs up. There was a ballroom on the second story. Up he pranced past the third floor, ears cocked. The Head of Guardians office was on the fourth. The clink of Guardians' armor rang through his ears and a metallic scent followed. He ignored those and kept pace.

Less than a minute later, he jogged into the correct office.

Everything appeared unusually out of proportion when he

approached as a cat. Inspecting the underside of chairs instead of the top, for example. Such a perspective revealed interesting angles on everything, including hiding spots.

Leo's office remained as quiet as expected. No incantations to protect it, for why would they need it in the castle? Nor other spells present. Not even a curse to stop unsavory creatures like himself.

Charlie hurried around the desk, sniffing. Nothing alarming. Sand. Seaweed. Leo must have been on the beach, potentially Carcere.

Finally, he smelled it.

Plumeria, coming from the drawer on the . . . left. At the bottom. Under the desk, he removed the transformation spell.

Still invisible, he peered into the bottom drawer, riffled through the papers. Parchments that held little beyond Guardian formation trivialities and rotation schedules. Letters from Dante, with updates regarding recruits.

Nothing there.

The middle drawer was only the height of a thumb. Locked, too. Several attempts at spells yielded no result. Physically locked and protected with a spell that made it so magic couldn't undo it, he'd wager.

Easy enough.

He conjured a hairpin from Faye's collection at home, stuck it in a small hole along the side. The hidden lock only increased his curiosity. His teeth sank into his lip as he fiddled with it, held his breath, and *pop*, opened the drawer.

Scrolls lay inside. He closed his eyes, used a spell to increase the scent in the air, then confirmed.

Plumeria.

A noise in the hallway drew his attention. Hastily, he reached for the scrolls. The next thing he knew, he flew across the room, slammed into the far wall.

All went black.

* * *

A stinging sensation woke Charlie.

He groaned, pain reverberating from the crown of his head in long waves. Nausea welled up. He wanted to turn to the side and vomit, only that required too much concentration. His mind felt scattered, like feathers in the wind.

"Allo?"

His eyes flew open.

Leo Giuseppi peered at him, gaze tapered to suspicious slashes.

Leo?

What in . . .

Memory served. Charlie suppressed a bolt of panic. Like a fool, he'd reached for doubly protected scrolls without checking again for active incantations. The spell had tossed him away like a child.

The good gods.

Leo had found him.

"What are you doing?" Leo cried. "Why are you in my office?"

Charlie groaned again—more loudly this time. He had to think of something fast. An excuse plausible enough for . . .

Oh.

An idea sprouted in his mind. Wild. Precarious. There was little chance it would work, for it required exact positioning on society's belief that Charles was an utter fool.

"My head," Charlie moaned. "Oh, my head!"

"Thief! You are stealing my parchments!"

"Parchments?" Charlie cried. "Parchments! You have the nerve to accuse me of stealing your things when I have been brutally assaulted in your castle?"

Leo's rage cleared. He blinked several times.

"Assaulted?"

Charlie tried to open his eyes with exaggerated, long attempts. "Oh, the spinning room." He put an arm over his eyes. "An Apothecary, sir! Immediately, or this will be war. A lowly Assistant walks to the washroom only to be attacked! My High Priestess will *not* stand for it. You know Greta!"

Leo leaned back, stammering in *Ilese*. Half questions, uncertainties.

Charlie moaned.

With a bark, Leo shouted something. The sound of quickly retreating footsteps likely meant a nearby Guardian departed.

"Tell me everything that happened," Leo snapped.

"I shall!" Charlie cried, his voice pitched. He screwed his eyes shut. "When I can speak without this headache. Oh, why is everything so pungent in the East? Please, take away such fresh air! It insults my senses. I must sit in a chair, or will you expect me to recount the attack from the floor?"

Leo snapped orders to Guardians. Two arms came gently around his shoulders, lifted him into an awaiting chair. He slouched into it, a hand over his eyes. Narrowly, he cast a glance and spotted the scrolls.

Still in the drawer.

What a fool.

With careful manipulation and multiple spells, he could make them invisible, then transport them home. He'd have to do it under Leo's nose while maintaining this ridiculous ruse. The headache hadn't cleared, only throbbed when he complained.

"Now," Leo growled. "Tell me what happened."

Charlie angled his gaze toward the ceiling. "I stood up from the dinner," he began dramatically, "to use the washroom. Your wine here, sir, is quite potent, so I've had to drink a lot of water to dilute it. You wouldn't believe how weak the Central Network wine is in comparison."

"And then?"

"Oh, right. Yes, of c-course."

Another grimace, a sharp breath of pain. He issued the first spell, casting an invisibility incantation on the scrolls. At the end of his exhale, he spoke again.

"As I strode to the washroom, I thought I heard a noise. I spun around, but alas! No one stood there. Not a soul. I was barely out of sight of the dining hall."

"Ballroom."

"Right, that's what I said."

Leo gritted his teeth.

Charlie issued the second spell.

"Anyway," Charlie gave another agonizing groan, "when I turned back around and attempted to find the fourth door, for that's what Serafina said I should do, a witch appeared."

A light weight settled on his lap. Charlie's fingers itched to pluck at it, but he held off by sheer willpower.

All three?

He moved his left hand onto his lap, settled it on top.

One.

Two.

Three.

"And then?" Leo demanded. "What happened? What did the witch say, do? Did you see them clearly?"

"Oh, they appeared panicked. So . . . frightened. Oddly enough, they looked nothing like witches in the East. I thought nothing of it at the time. A hideous lad, if I must be honest. Garish eyes, sickly. Not at all a strong character."

Charlie lifted his head up, removed his hand from his eyes. A pretended squint gave him a full view of Leo, who was fairly salivating. His entire body thrummed with tension as he leaned forward.

"And then?"

Both hands lowered to his lap. The crux had come. He had

to send the scrolls back to the Advocacy without being found out, or the next mission would crumble. The Advocacy had weathered failures in the past, but not easily.

If Leo had any sense in his head, he'd have an East Guard in the hallway feeling for magic.

"Then." Charlie sighed, winced. One hand lifted back to his head, pressed into the skin. "Goodness, my memory does ache from such a blow. They said . . . something. I can hardly remember, what with the trauma of such an experience."

"What did they say?"

"The word . . . started with an A." He fluffed a hand in the air. "Can't remember. Said they worked for someone with an A and apologized. Told me *I need someone to blame my foolishness on* and promptly whacked me over the head. I almost fought them off, you know, but I sprained my wrist with a quill yesterday and—"

"Advocate?"

Charlie brightened. "That's it! That's the one." He grimaced, pressed a palm to his temple. "Oof, too much volume. Who is this witch, the Advocate? What an odd name. Mind if I ask? I took a blow to the head for him, which might qualify me for further insight into his character. Is he a good witch?"

Leo growled, body vibrating. His fists clenched at his side as he stared at the wall, fuming. "Of course!" he hissed. "Of course they come now, when they think I'm distracted. Those fools!"

Charlie sent the scrolls by another spell. They faded under his hand the moment it finished. He coughed, then groaned loudly and lay back down.

"Then I woke up here!" Charlie wailed. "In this room, with you yelling at me. I loathe being yelled at. It's not pleasant, and is bad for digestion, particularly after eating eels. Isn't it odd, though, that they should apologize before they hit me? Is the Advocate a gentle witch, do you think?"

Irate, Leo commanded another Guardian to enter. Several streamed into the room.

"Tell me!" Charlie cried. "Did they steal something and blame it on me? What scoundrels! I'll have you know I wouldn't touch the property of another witch if you paid me to."

Leo ignored him to bark orders. He issued a search of the castle grounds and securing the High Priest and High Priestess without interrupting the discussions. Breathless, Charlie went to work.

Final step.

He cast a deception spell, perfectly mimicking the three scrolls that had been there all along.

Two seconds later, Leo returned to the desk, glanced at the still-open drawer. Satisfied, he closed it, turned to Charlie. With a far more composed expression, he said, "The Eastern Network gives you our deepest regret, Assistant . . ."

"Charles. My name is Charles. I used to go by—"

"Assistant Charles. I will not rest until we find this scoundrel. An Apothecary will be here any minute to see your head. Will you stay to give us more details? I would most appreciate your help in this matter."

"Of course, good sir. Of course! I can see you're a man of judgment and respect. I will help however I can. Um, perhaps a bit more wine to aid with the headache?"

Leo's furious expression hardened.

"Of course. Thank you for your patience. The Apothecary will see you now, and I will ask my questions after."

Chapter Twenty-Five

MAXIMILLION

In contrast to the crowded floors, candlelight, torches, and loud discussions of the Eastern Network, the calm night at Wildrose soothed Max.

He stood at a window where husks of old roses clung to the trellises, their bodies gray. The souls removed, sucked out by winter's chill and a light coating of frost.

Flashes from the meeting filtered through his mind. Greta's escalation with Dante. Their arguments over allowing Eastern Network Defenders into the Central Network. Greta requested—fairly in Max's opinion—that the Eastern Network share with the Central Network the known Watchers and let them deal with the Watchers themselves.

Dante's expected disagreement followed. His insistence they do it *his* way and bring the Watchers back to Carcere didn't surprise Max. Eventually, it would surprise Charlie. When he could inform him, the absent miscreant.

Charlie had disappeared halfway through the dinner and hadn't returned for the fight that ensued between leadership parties. Irate mutters had given way to flushed faces and clenched fists. Max attempted to end the dispute by suggesting the Eastern Network leave the Watchers in the Central Network alone.

Dante didn't take that well.

Instead of peace, Max faced a contingent of East Guards promising to kill him should he speak another word.

All in all, the expected result for his first event as Ambassador.

During such a fracas, Serafina's hungry gaze devoured him. Studied him from across the table, though they never had a chance to speak properly. Dozens of questions filled every twitch of her lip.

He turned away from the nighttime grounds of Wildrose and lowered into a chair near the fire. Heat reached out in a soothing caress. Max leaned back, closed his eyes, and stepped into the paths.

An equally comforting darkness permeated the magic as well. After the debacle in the East, countless wisps populated. He ignored most, sought only those with Serafina, as he'd done several times in the past. She lingered in the possibilities more than ever.

Through his mind's eye, he wandered into the darkened shadows. Trails of light wound through it in lazy, jagged strands. The wisps populated here and there, illuminated. Charlie. Faye. Greta, unfortunately.

A little too often.

Finally, a witch.

The one he sought.

He'd found her again. In fact, he admitted to himself that she might have been what he sought. A sort of balm, a solace.

Tonight, she stood alone. Separated from the paths far enough she stuck out. She was bright-eyed, with a glint of curiosity that stoked his own. Blonde hair pulled back, revealing delicate features, but strong. In the gauzy representation, she appeared to glare right at him. Her nose wrinkled charmingly, though he'd never admit such a thing out loud. For what felt like eternities, he studied her.

No path ever lay at her feet, but she appeared all the same. He couldn't figure it out.

Realizing how long he'd been gone, how far he wandered, Max closed the magic.

Charlie awaited.

He sat in the chair to Max's left, deep in thought. Max stirred, blinking out of the stupor. A knowing smile filled Charlie's face.

"Anything?"

"Never," he muttered.

Three scrolls floated to Max. "Better send the Advocacy tonight if you want to save these Watchers. Leo will shortly realize the Advocate has duped him, if he hasn't already. Considering all the work I created for ol' Leo, he'll be occupied until the morning. It's a narrow window of time, but fairly concrete."

Max cast a look at a nearby clock. "That gives us six hours."

"Best get to work, my friend."

Charlie stood, strode toward the door. Max studied the three small scrolls, not all that surprised that Charlie had somehow turned the dinner into an Advocacy benefit.

Max hadn't been able to work out a deal that gave them the name of Watchers so they could protect them, but he'd known that had been a long shot. Dante knew about the Advocacy. He naturally feared the growth of the Advocacy's resources and power if he couldn't control the flow of information.

"Charlie?"

At the door, Charlie paused. He spun around, eyebrows high in silent question. Max set the three scrolls aside.

"How are you?" he asked, silently adding *my friend* to the

end. The words stalled on his tongue. They always had. He didn't need to say them. Charlie already knew how he felt about him.

But maybe he should.

Charlie paused, hand on the doorknob. "It's not too much, if that's what you're asking."

"I am."

"Then I'm fine. We'll continue. We'll get them, Max. Don't you worry. Somehow or another, we'll make Alkarra safe for Watchers."

CHARLIE

One year later

The sharp staccato of Greta's voice ripped through an Esbat meeting that Charlie would rather not attend.

"Council Member Stiles! Report your taxes."

Her reddened eyes, bleary gaze, testified to a long night. Several Council Members shared the same misery, having stayed up too late at the High Priestess' latest ball the prior evening. She had already canceled this Esbat five times. Greta, unwillingly, succumbed to pressure from her Accountants and attended.

All the worse for wear.

Council Member Stiles rose on shaky legs. He cleared his thick throat while his hands scrambled for the right parchment. Charlie surreptitiously slid it into his palm and Stiles straightened all the way.

"As requested, High Priestess."

The parchment soared across the room to the witch at her left. Stiles sweated, giant beads rolling down his jowls. He hadn't prepared sufficiently for this Esbat, though Charlie *had* tried.

Charlie pretended absorption with a fly on the paper. A half-smile lingered on his face, like an idiot. Meanwhile, his stomach simmered like a cauldron. He knew what the High Priestess would see when she received the report.

Just as he knew what the Accountant would say.

Spying within Chatham Castle had its own perks.

Most Council Members would assume that Greta's exhausted eyes revealed a hard night of too much ipsum and food. In fact, hours with a bevy of Accountants and a handful of other Council Members caused her fatigue. All part of her greater plan, which hinted to her diabolical interior.

A drastic showdown would take place today. It's why the room seemed to hold its breath. False reporting, amongst tax fraud, and other negligences.

Stiles' numbers didn't tally up, particularly against the last report, which had been two weeks late. Greta didn't care about mistakes.

Until they served her purpose.

The High Priest glared at Greta from where he stood against the far wall. He was an elderly witch with white hair slicked away from a tight face. His bristly mustache twitched. Greta noted his attention with irritated looks of deepest loathing.

An Accountant skimmed the report, as he had for each Coven present. Halfway down the page, he paused. His brow furrowed.

Stiles leaned his weight on one palm, gulped. Enough ipsum thickened his blood that he couldn't *quite* think through this situation. He seemed to know that something would happen, but couldn't puzzle it together yet. Far too many lies to track.

Max stood near the High Priest, his intense gaze fixed on

the Accountant, whom all in the room watched with bated breath. The Accountant leaned over to Greta, whispered something. The wretched planes of Greta's face smoothed out, then wrinkled again. She nodded once.

"Stiles," she called. "There are discrepancies."

"Oh?" Stiles gasped. "Oh. Oh, are there?"

"Several."

"I-I wouldn't know."

Another whisper from the Accountant. Greta listened, nodded. "Explain the sum of missing tax currency for the year, to the amount of 4,000 sacrans. Certainly enough of an amount for you to pay off that villa you purchased?"

Littered gasps punctuated the room. Stiles panted. Sweat saturated his collar as he sat back down, legs giving out beneath his bulk. Not even Charles would ignore the sober regard in the room. Charlie stared at the top of the table, solemn as the rest.

His stomach revolted.

If Greta challenged Council Member Stiles over blatant and sloppy forgery, Stiles could eventually lose his position and Charlie would lose his job. The flow of information to the Advocacy would have to come through Max, or direct spying. While Max remained capable of such a feat, it would force him to step back from management of the Advocacy, a position Charlie couldn't fill.

Not as the Advocate.

What would the Advocacy do then?

"You're forthwith dismissed from your position, Stiles." Greta set her hands on her hips with a frosty glare. "Leave the Esbat now."

Charlie's head snapped up.

Another Council Member gasped.

The High Priest glowered.

Just like that? No disciplinary council? No opportunity to

defend himself? Greta always thought herself above the law, but rarely to such intensity.

Stiles, breathing heavily, bobbed with open-mouthed surprise. Greta swung to the High Priest.

"Go with him, Albert. The gathered evidence puts you with the accused as well. I will answer questions in my office this evening. My team of Accountants will be ready with proof."

The word *proof* rang through his mind. Was it honest proof? Unlikely to be pure. While any fool could dig through the ledgers and find proof of Stiles' dishonesty, was the same true for Albert?

Albert had always challenged Greta. She might have manufactured a way to pull him out of the office in the midst of Stiles.

Charlie swallowed a rising knot. This ending for Stiles had been inevitable, yet it still invoked great stress. He hadn't expected Albert to be ripped from his position of power as well.

Two Guardians flanked a livid Albert as he shouted, fist in the air. Greta pinched the bridge of her nose with two fingers while they escorted him from the room. His dying shouts echoed down the corridor.

Stiles shoved to his feet. Weakly, Charlie followed. He didn't dare glance at Max. The absolute havoc this would wreak on—

"Stay, Charles."

Greta's voice halted him. He froze. Out of the corner of his eye, Max's gaze snapped to him. A prickling feeling raced through Charlie from head to toe.

When Stiles lumbered out of the room, Charlie faced the High Priestess. With terrible majesty—or perhaps hungover pain—she declared, "You are now the High Priest. Your empowerment ceremony will be tomorrow evening."

He gripped the table to stop himself from collapsing. The blood drained from his face. Collective gasps punctuated the silence. Wide-eyed, he could only stare at her.

"Y-your Highness?"

"Any Council Member that tries to play their position of power against me will receive the same fate!" she cried. "Albert and Stiles will be sent to the Northern Network instead of me having them fileted. The rest of you would do well to learn from their mistakes.

"In the meantime, we have bigger issues at our Western Border to deal with. We will shunt the recovered taxes from the Western Covens to provide more Guardians along the river. If Dostar thinks he can take all the water he wants and bleed our crops dry, we'll prove him wrong."

Her furious glare reached every corner of the room. No voice of opposition rose, not even Max, who constantly rebuffed her in a variety of ways.

"You're dismissed."

* * *

Four more Covens had yet to account for their own taxes, yet no one voiced dissent as the room rose, shuffled toward the door. Greta disappeared out the door first, her frantic Assistant scrambling after her.

Charlie didn't move.

What had once been fear now solidified into absolute terror. Of all the results he had imagined . . . what witch in their right mind would appoint *Charles* as a High Priest? A Council Member Assistant, not quite twenty-five-years old?

A witch that wanted no interference and unparalleled power.

Charles Dauphin, the dimwitted gardener who loved to be around witches but loathed responsibility, would now be the second most powerful witch in the Central Network. Equal parts terror and elation coursed through him. Weakened by the onslaught, he could only breathe.

The room emptied, leaving Max, two Guards, and a couple of shocked Assistants. One of them eyed Charlie, shook his head in disgust, and strode toward the door. Max stopped at the doorway, spun around. In an even tone, he said, "Congratulations, High Priest."

"Th-thank you, Ambassador," Charlie whispered.

Max left. Charlie sank into the chair and stared at the wall, lost in an eddy of thoughts.

* * *

Despite his love for buildings and structure, Letum Wood often felt like the only safe place in the world. Ready to destroy, even as it healed. Shock bolstered Charlie in these terrible moments after Greta's announcement, when disbelief permeated like a fog.

She couldn't . . .

Surely, she . . .

But, no.

High Priest? Would he go down in history as the youngest?

He hoped not.

And yet . . .

Thoughts of how the Advocacy might benefit followed close at the heels of those ideas. Unparalleled and easy information. Greater power in social circles across all Networks. The good he might do outside of the Advocacy.

Couldn't he?

The character of Charles was ironclad. Could he compromise Charles' cover by being productive?

Perhaps.

Did he want to? Greta certainly wouldn't desire it.

These questions circled his mind as he waited for Max to find him. They'd stew it out together. At some point, he'd have to tell Faye. Soon, too. The *Chatterer* newsscroll already updated articles.

His gut clenched thinking about it. High Priest meant he'd see less of her, certainly. Greater social responsibilities existed as High Priest, and the exhaustion of living a lie would take its toll faster.

Charlie leaned against a tree when the snap of a twig came from behind. He waited. Max would intentionally make noise to alert him. His heart banged in his ears when he spun around, words on the tip of his tongue.

Faye stood back there, bleary-eyed. Her normally healthy hair hung in ragged locks on her shoulders. Wrinkles below her eyes testified to long nights. She blinked several times.

"Max is on the way," she said. "It's . . . just me."

"Never just you, my love." Charlie held out his arms. "Faye, I'm so glad to see you. His message said he'd bring you with him to discuss . . ."

She didn't budge.

Faye lingered just out of touch, fingers squeezed so tight they blanched. Like a specter from his dreams, the ones he'd always thought haunted Letum Wood. His arms trembled when she didn't close the distance. A dark feeling crept up his back.

Why didn't she rush to him immediately?

"Faye?"

The tenuous pleas spread like a ripple.

"Is it true?" she whispered.

"What have you heard?"

"That Greta made Charles the High Priest. She doesn't care that Council Members are protesting her display of power. The *Chatterer* says there's proof of tax fraud from Stiles and Albert, but the High Priest claims it's false."

Ah.

The fight over the High Priest title had begun. With such a dramatic dismissal of two high-ranking witches, Greta all but guaranteed more drama.

Charlie nodded. "Yes, it's true. It just happened. I haven't even spoken to Max about it yet."

She swallowed. Tears filled her eyes.

"I have."

The quiet admission, riddled with knowing, arrested him. An icy feeling shivered through his arms, down his fingers, to his toes. His entire body clamped. Such a loaded statement could only mean one thing: Max had looked into the paths.

His voice was hoarse when he asked, "And?"

"She wins. You remain High Priest. He said it's overwhelmingly obvious. There are no paths that reveal otherwise in what he sees. He says he can feel it."

The relief that followed revealed more to him than he expected. He should have met with terror or madness.

Yet opportunity struck.

The entire Network thought Charles Dauphin an idiot. No one held a modicum of respect for him, except maybe Max, but only in private. Faye never interacted with Charles. In several ways, Charles misrepresented everything that Wildrose stood for. Outwardly, at least.

The Advocacy would thrive because of this.

Faye's expression sank, as if she could read his thoughts. The trouble that brewed in her eyes faded to disbelief.

"You're happy about it, aren't you?"

"Yes, Faye. I am. In some regards. Overwhelmed by others. It's access and hope the Advocacy and Watchers haven't had before. If I focus on that, the rest doesn't feel so overpowering."

"At what cost?" she cried. Branches cracked under her feet as she stepped closer. "Where is the end, Charlie? Where does the Advocacy pick up and you end?"

"That's not fair."

"You're right, it's not fair! It's never been fair. I work myself to the bone to care for Wildrose, for Watchers and Defenders and witches I will never meet. And I do it because I know that, at some point, I might see you."

The vague euphoria of this chance shrank away, crinkling as it withdrew. His heart beat faster.

Faye wiped a tear off her cheek. "And now I'll never see you. You'll have even less time as High Priest and . . ."

The word *Advocate* died before it appeared. Faye ran a hand over her eyes, shoved locks of hair out of her face. Charlie scrambled to find reassurance. Promises that life apart would be better. Different this time. The words wouldn't rise.

He had no promises to give.

"Don't you have something to say?" she demanded. "Anything?"

He held out empty hands.

"Faye, what *can* I say? You're correct. This will be harder before it gets better, and I need you."

"What if I need you?"

"You always have me."

"You are many things to many witches, Charlie, but a liar isn't one of them. Don't start now."

Silence fell.

In fact, she understood it more clearly than he wanted to. His vague promises, agreement to make things happen, hadn't manifested as much as they should have.

Faye closed her eyes. Her thick lashes fanned her cheeks as she pulled in a breath. When they opened again, they latched right on him. Deep exasperation, coated with something like misery, crossed them. She existed far away, disconnected from the present moment.

"I love you, Charlie. I have always loved you, and I always will. But I'm tired. I can't do this anymore. The back-and-forth. Missed messages. Days that stretch into weeks, which might evolve into months, without seeing you. This hidden half-life? I never asked for it and I don't want it. I will never be the most important thing to you, the way you are to me, and that's not something I can live with."

A lump rose in his throat, intensifying the erratic staccato of his heart. "Faye," he murmured, "Please—"

She held up a hand. "I've held on through everything you asked of me. Everything you have required, I have done. Whatever I had to give, I offered. There is nothing left for you to take."

Terror struck him. A life without Faye was no life at all. Yet the hold of the Advocacy, the requirement to save other witches . . .

He summoned the only words he could find. "What . . . what does that mean? You're leaving?"

She softened. "Not yet. I promised to help the Advocacy with a few more things on their next mission, and Max with Wildrose."

"Then what?"

Her chin notched a little higher.

"I'll stay at Wildrose for two more weeks. When the missions have finished and the Watchers are safe, I want to go home to the West. I know I promised you I'd take you with me," she quickly added when he opened his mouth to protest, "but you've had years, Charlie. I want to find myself again. To take care of myself. Think of myself. I don't want to wait, I just want to *do*."

Tears streamed down her cheeks. Her lips twisted in an almost-sob, like a half-wrought scream on the edge of release.

"Charlie, my love. You are chasing a conclusion that you can never attain. Until you let go of your need to keep *everyone* safe, you will never be mine. And all the waiting, hoping, and supporting in the world will never change that."

Her name stuck on his tongue. It filled his throat, his head, and swelled through the empty recesses.

Not now, he wanted to plead. *Please, Faye. I cannot hold myself up without you. There is too much on me, too much complication. How will I ever unthread this tapestry?*

He couldn't.

He had no more power to beg her, rebuke her, than to stop the wheel of madness he'd pulled himself into.

"You deserved better," he whispered.

The image of her blurred. The space between her eyebrows knitted together. With a sob, she disappeared.

A moment before he dropped to the ground, a firm hand clamped on his shoulder. Max spoke. His heavy tone broke the tunnel-like trance.

"Let her go. It's the only prayer you have of ever getting her back."

"Max, I—"

"I know."

The words fell apart in the quiet air. He could go into the paths, rewind it all. With enough searching, he could find the paths where he *didn't* do all this Advocacy work. Where he and Faye lived in Wildrose. They might chase scampering children while Pearl and Max visit on the holidays. Cozy winters with falling snow, lean years because his work wouldn't be so encompassing.

A dream, all of it.

He'd tortured himself in the paths before. Glimpsed times when he might have helped Papa heal. When the Apothecary had made a different decision and Papa survived longer. Or he'd chosen differently and not lost an Advocacy member to a

Defender raid. The pain of what *could* have been was its own exquisite torture.

Oh, how he loathed the paths.

"Come, Charlie. We have business to attend to. Our wicked High Priestess has exercised control she shouldn't have, and you have an empowerment ceremony to attend tomorrow. Give Faye time. That's all she needs."

Chapter Twenty-Seven

MAXIMILLION

One Year Later

Max jerked awake.

His shirt clung to his chest as he shoved out of the tangled blankets, panting. A cool floor against the pads of his feet escorted him out of strange dreams. By instinct, he settled onto a chair and slipped into the paths.

Light, darkness. The clash of the two soothed the prickling that lingered like a malady. Flashes of a memory from when Pere used to hit him over fifteen years ago still haunted him.

He's gone, he told himself. *You're twenty-five years old. Pere is gone. You're an adult and far more capable than him.*

Logic offered no solace.

With a blink, he regarded the paths. They held comfort only by familiarity. And, perhaps, something else. A quiet effect of the magic, maybe. Soothing steadiness, though the paths always changed and the wisps dissolved and no certainty lived here.

Max lingered, cooling his whirling mind by the disconnection from his body. He began to leave, but stopped. There, in front of him, stood the girl.

He hadn't seen her in almost a year now. As usual, she'd advanced in age. Blonde hair. Green eyes. Freckles so light they hid themselves. Something in her presence *felt* different this time. Inevitability, maybe.

That made no sense either.

No paths linked her to him concretely. She seemed to live in the forest, as greenery almost always swamped the background. A forester for the Advocacy, perhaps? Then why was there no path?

Seeing her eased the rest of his harried stress.

"Who," he murmured, "are you?"

As always, the paths gave no response. Rippling changes moved through the wisps, altering the landscape.

The girl—no, young woman—disappeared.

* * *

Lucey bustled around a middle-aged Watcher, lying on a table in the middle of headquarters, with practiced and certain hands. She probed around a bruise on his head near the right temple.

Her lips tugged into a frown.

Max stood nearby, chest heaving. Chasing Defenders had nearly torn his shirt off his shoulders when they ripped it down the front. Blood smeared his right jaw, though it didn't hurt much. Two women flanked him on either side, wringing their hands.

"Will he make it?" one woman asked through a breathy gasp. A cap covered part of her head, hanging over one ear.

"I believe so," Lucey murmured. "His breathing is regular, his heart strong. We have potions that will wake him up."

Max appreciated her quiet confidence all the more because

he remembered how frightened she'd been when she first arrived. She had appeared only a few years ago, half-dead and quiet as a mouse. This alternate version of her, with a calm confidence of where she stood in the world and what she could do, gave him a silent thrill.

The Advocacy needed all the help they could find.

Despite attending the raid, Charlie hid in the far corner behind an invisibility spell. Max could feel his magic, which meant he must want to speak with him. Charlie so rarely observed the Advocacy members at their jobs. A year as the High Priest, and he still ran the Advocacy from the very top. Only their frequent interactions at work, and secret messaging on the side, kept the Advocacy from crumbling to dust. He saw Charles constantly, but not Charlie. Only once had Charlie returned to Wildrose in all that time.

No, Charlie hid.

For Charlie without Faye was no Charlie at all.

Torches and floating candles on plates cast shadows into the corners of the room. A lamp illuminated a small table filled with parchments. On top of it sat a discarded meal, left in haste hours ago.

The headquarters had more than found its full use over the last several years. Divans, tables, and full shelves packed the once-empty space. He could hardly recall it when he first stumbled on it as a boy. A mere cellar that smelled of dirt and mold, with muddy walls and leaky doors.

Charlie had transformed it into a place of healing, refuge. Here, in the headquarters of Wildrose and the Advocacy, both of them found purpose in the chaos.

Calm, too, despite near-constant upheaval.

Lucey spun, skirts swirling. Behind the exam table waited shelves packed with tiny bottles that ranged from bulbous, thick, petite, and thin. The shelf below housed drawers where cotton, droppers, and disintegrating herbs awaited. All of it was created or donated by Advocacy volunteers.

Sixty-something witches supported the Advocacy in various capacities. Rumor-gathering. Spying in the Eastern Network, the Central Network, now the Western Network. Many hosted Watchers in danger, particularly foresters. So willing to open their home. Witches in the East feared Letum Wood and avoided it at all costs, Big Leo included.

Which made things all too simple for the Advocacy.

Max conjured drinks of water on the table for the two ladies, another for Lucey, and the gentleman. Last, for himself.

Lucey wafted a thin, oblong potion bottle under the injured Watcher's nose. Three thready breaths later, he sputtered awake with a cry. The two women at his side released sobs. Their cries gently descended into snuffles and exclamations of gratitude after Lucey promised to give them a room to stay in for the night.

Powerful magic that Faye cast before she disappeared to the West prevented witches from transporting into the rooms after they left. Advocacy members alone could transport in if they gave blood to the recognition spell.

Max exited through the door, hidden behind a bookcase and back into Wildrose. Silently, he continued down the hall and up a wide staircase padded with thick carpet. At the top of the staircase, a wall. Certain no one but Charlie followed, he cast a silent spell, walked through the wall. As the quiet of Wildrose greeted him, Max caught the trailing thread he'd been silently chasing all evening.

Safe.

That's what he felt here.

In the study, he allowed Charlie to enter behind him, then closed the door. Once a sealing incantation prevented listening ears, Charlie appeared.

Max stood at the fire.

"Well," he drawled. "We're up to fifteen total Watchers saved from direct raids on the Eastern Network since the Advocacy began. Many more raids were thwarted, and we've yet to lose an Advocacy member this year, the good gods willing. Somehow, despite being High Priest, you've kept up."

"You're a champion at this, Max."

Max sent him a wry, sidelong glance.

Charlie looked worse for wear, with jagged lines down his face. He must transform daily into the healthy skin and appearance that the Network knew as empty-headed Charles Dauphin.

"Dunford was supposed to go tonight, but we couldn't find him." Max's nose wrinkled with poorly suppressed concern as he faced the fire. "His wife said they pulled him into the Guardians to fight at the Western Network border."

Dunford was a quiet fellow that often helped extract Watchers out of hard situations. Max's second favorite witch, outside himself, when he must go.

"Not surprising," Charlie murmured. "There are so many witches pulled into the war with the West right now. Greta is . . . a tiresome woman."

An edge entered his voice.

"And more battles on the way," Max muttered darkly.

For several minutes, not a word was spoken between them. He waited, feeling the silence out. Stinging flagellations lingered on his tongue. *By the good gods, Faye's been gone for a year,* he wanted to say. *Your life continues with more havoc than before. Move on, already!*

He bit his tongue.

Unable to bear it any longer, he whirled on his friend. "Well?" he demanded.

Charlie's brow lifted in genuine surprise.

"Well, what?"

"How are you?"

"Fine. You?"

"Don't pander. How are you really?"

Charlie's expression darkened. He cast a quick glance around the room, then back to Max.

"I hate being back here, if that's what you're asking."

Perhaps it would be heartless to ask, but Max couldn't hold back the burning question.

"Because of Faye?"

Charlie flinched. He held his hands behind his back, shoulders pulled tight.

"Yes."

His lack of extrapolation told the full story.

"It's been a year, Charlie."

"So it has."

"You must be over it."

"Never," he whispered. "You never finish mourning a soulmate, Max."

"She didn't die."

"She did to me."

Charlie's gaunt expression sent a knife through him. The good gods, but he hated seeing Charlie in pain.

Max shook his head and reached for the end of his sleeves, which he rolled to his elbow. "Since you haven't spoken to me as Charlie in half a year, the question bears asking again: how are you, really? Is the weight of the Advocacy and the High Priest's mantle too much yet?"

"No."

"Would you tell me if it was?"

Charlie laughed dryly. "No."

"Then I can't trust you."

"That's something only you can decide. I can't tell you what to do, Max."

Max whirled on him. "This is insanity. You must stop. Stop being the Advocate, stop telling yourself you're fine. Stop

. . . something! You never come home anymore. You go on too many raids, you work too hard. This must cease for the good of the Advocacy."

A stricken expression crossed Charlie's face. He drew in a breath, swallowed.

"I cannot, Max."

"You'll work yourself into the ground. Ranulf wanted better for you."

"Then Papa can come back and tell me that himself," he said blankly.

Irritation spread through Max. He fought off a growl.

"This is it? You plan to destroy yourself, and for what? To pine for a woman who possessed enough courage and independence to give herself what you could not give her? Or is that what's eating at you? Instead of fighting for her, chasing after her, you remained here to lick your wounds and sulk?"

Pain broke through his jaw like the slam of a shooting star. He caught himself from falling by staggering back. A disorienting whirl tilted him sideways. Momentarily blind and dizzy, he groped for a chair.

Charlie shook out a fist. "Demmet, Max, but you've a jaw like iron."

Max pressed a hand to the pulsing bone. The initial shock wore off slowly. By the good gods, but Charlie had punched him.

"Perhaps I deserved that," he muttered and fought back a grimace.

"You did," Charlie said firmly, wincing. "You absolutely deserved it, but so did I. You're right, Max. I failed her. And every day that I don't find her, I fail myself. I fail her. But I can't let go of this charade, not with other lives on the line. So I live with that agony, and it is my punishment."

"You're a toad."

Charlie laughed brightly. "Best friends with one, too, I'd wager."

The ratcheting tension calmed in Max's chest. With a sharp intake of breath, he worked his jaw. It would sting like the fires of Halla for a few days, but no teeth were loose. Max glowered at him.

"I say this from a place of caring. A place of . . ." *Brotherhood* lingered on his tongue, but he shoved it back. "Of friendship. Can you, Charlie? Square with me. You owe me that much for running the Advocacy, the manor, while you attempt to save the world with some unrequited need to prove yourself."

Charlie sobered.

"Even if I felt I couldn't keep this up, I must."

"*Can you*?" Max barked. "We're about to get involved in a war with the Southern Network while the West continues to advance in ever more creative ways. Everything is going to be more difficult, Charlie. Everything. Beyond what you've ever had to do before."

"I must," he said again, this time more firmly.

Not convincingly at all, but enough.

Max paused, took Charlie's measure. Seeing no wavering, he let out a long breath, rubbed a hand over his weary face.

"The good gods help me for saying it, but I agree with what Faye said before she left. You ask too much of yourself. You can't save everyone. Maybe it's time you stop trying."

"You first," Charlie muttered.

With a scowl, Max opened his mouth to reply, then snapped it shut. Charlie waited, smiling.

"Well?" he drawled.

"It's different!"

"How so?"

"I'm an Ambassador. It's normal for me to go to the

Eastern Network, to the Western Network. To disappear without having to account in the same way as a High Priest."

"Max," Charlie said sharply. "Keep this line of questioning up and you will seriously insult me. I will punch you again. In the nose this time and mar that handsome profile, if I must."

Max pressed his lips together, and sighed through his nose. "Fine."

"You've always trusted me before. What's changed now?"

Max glared harder than ever, vexed that Charlie should reduce this to the barest bones.

To the emotions of it all.

"We are all each other has left. The weight of this has worn on you. I can see it and I'm . . . concerned."

"About?"

"You're going to make me say it?" Max growled.

"Yes!" Charlie chuckled. "You won't disintegrate, Max. Words can't eat you, though you certainly look as if you believe they might. My goodness, it might do you a world of good to use them."

"Fine! I'm afraid for *you*, Charlie. You're my best friend, my family. I don't want you to get in over your head once issues with the South escalate."

Charlie crossed the space, tossed his arms around Max. Max stiffened as Charlie slapped him on the back with several thuds. A smile wreathed his face when Charlie shuffled away.

"See? You survived."

"You almost didn't," Max muttered. "Embrace me again and you'll have your own sore jaw."

Charlie sobered. "Thank you, Max. You must see, as I do, that we all have a role to play. Charles is mine. You understand?"

Reluctantly, he nodded.

The requirements of generations of Dauphins had always been a heavy burden on Charlie's shoulders. Ranulf expected

Charlie to carry on the family legacy of picking up the broken bodies and mending shattered hearts.

Though he said little of them, Max could tell that ghosts pressed on Charlie to continue. The trail had been drawn, fate decided. He couldn't go back now. In this, Wildrose fulfilled its potential. In this, Charlie fulfilled his own.

Charlie no longer fled from the ghosts.

He carried them.

The sound of approaching feet came from behind the door.

"Lucey," Max said. "Reporting, no doubt."

Charlie saluted.

"Until next time, my friend."

* * *

Irritation washed through Max when he realized, yet again, he had returned to the Eastern Network.

And Serafina.

This time, she'd cleverly finagled the two of them alone in the same library thanks to an insistent butler. Books ringed every available space in the two-story room. Most of them were taller than tomes in the Central Network, because witches preferred large-text books in the East.

Serafina held three titles that made absolutely no sense for her to read.

Walking at Night Along the Beach and Other Horror Stories.

Dephila Gonzalez.

Remember What You Forgot After Your Hex and Other Memory Tricks.

A curious part of him wanted to peruse the shelves. Before diplomacy and the Advocacy sucked up his life force, he had enjoyed reading. Or perhaps he loved that witches tended to leave him alone when he held a book.

The sounds of quiet revelry and gaiety issued from the ballroom down the hall. Dante, in an ever-increasing desperation to create peace, had amassed all Networks together for a delegation to stop the wars.

Dostar and Greta participated in a silent challenge and glared holes into each other from across the room. Mikhail, from the Southern Network, spoke too loudly about everything—particularly his plans to construct a wall that spanned the northern border of his Network—which irritated those around him.

Greta, of course, annoyed all of Alkarra with her penchant to ignore diplomacy and say exactly what she thought.

Which was, consequently, wrong most of the time.

Max should thank Serafina for the momentary reprieve, but couldn't bring himself to say a word.

Somehow, he'd always known this confrontation would come. Had always known there would be a time when he couldn't avoid her. Wasn't that family, though? Always catching him by surprise. Would Mere have had the same features at her age? Unlikely. She had lived a hard life. Time wore differently on the desperate.

"Serafina."

Her neck tightened as she pulled in a breath. He'd startled her. Didn't she expect him to speak? Considering how much he'd dodged her in the past, probably not.

"How are you?" she asked.

"Tired."

"Things are not good in the Central Network, I hear."

"Are they anywhere?"

She said nothing. Guards might lurk, unseen. Defenders, for all he knew. He kept a tight lock on his magic, which he'd satisfied before he came. It purred quietly inside him, content. If he didn't use it, they wouldn't sense it.

"Thank you for speaking with me."

He chuckled darkly. "I hardly think I could have avoided it. You coaxed me in here with a butler."

Amusement lightened her tone. "Would you have come if I hadn't?"

"No."

"So I was wise. Please," she said quickly as he turned to leave. "Allow me to apologize. Max, I have spent the last twenty years atoning for the message I sent during my sister's funeral. I wanted to come. I begged Dante. He locked me in my room. He wouldn't—"

She broke off, unable to speak.

"You could have sent for me. Could have taken me out of the hellhole that Antonio . . ."

He stopped. The anguish in her watery eyes halted him entirely. He fought not to care. To put her in the same box as he did every other witch. The one that didn't matter. Business only.

He couldn't.

Deep in her gaze, he saw it. The inklings of love he'd craved for so long. In the depths of the darkest nights, surrounded by nothing but space and fear and the feeling that everything would fall on his young chest and crush him, all he'd wanted was an anchor. A stable-something to tether him.

Serafina held it in spades. He felt her affection in the way she looked at him, half a sob stuck in her throat. A tear cascaded down her cheek, chipping away at his resolve. He swiveled away from her.

"I . . ."

"I tried, Max! You were gone when I sent Guardians after you. I snuck you baskets of food and medicine."

His head jerked up. "What?"

"Did you not receive them?"

"No."

"Then your pere must have hidden them, hoarded them. I don't know what he would have done with them, but I sent them every month. Toys. Clothes. Messages. Anything I could think of."

The question he'd always wanted to ask occluded his throat. Sat there like an elephant in the way. He could hardly breathe until it rolled out of him in a raspy rush.

"Why?"

Serafina closed her eyes. When they opened, tears glittered. "Dante demanded my utmost capitulation to life as High Priestess. An erasure of who I had been before this. I couldn't go back on my word, on my marriage vow. I had to obey. Witches snuck the baskets to you. East Guards who gave me loyalty because I knew them once in the streets. That's all I could do for you, Max. The letters, the worrying."

She pressed her fist to her lips to stop a sob. His pere, Antonio, had even deprived Max of Serafina's love. The simple acts from Serafina that would have bolstered and reassured him when he felt like a boy falling through a never-ending giant hole.

He gave an irritated breath.

"Does Dante know who I am?"

"Yes. He knew I had a nephew named Maximillion that I wanted to search for. Maria gave you our surname, not Antonio's. Maximillion Sinclair. Twenty-one-years-old when he strolled into the Eastern Network as an Assistant to the Ambassador, was unabashedly one of my family members. You look like your grandpere, Mansfeld. A man whom I loved very much."

Before Max could respond to her or the welling it created deep in his chest, a familiar screech, then a smashing of glass, sounded from the other room. All sounds ceased. Serafina startled.

"Forgive me, Serafina. I believe my High Priestess is about to dissolve all my hard work. Allow me to deal with her."

With a blank nod, she gave him permission. He turned to go, stopped. When he glanced back, she hadn't moved.

"All is forgiven," he whispered. "I know all about your family, your children. Perhaps, one day, you can introduce them to me."

Hope brightened her voice, made it wobbly.

"Thank you, Max. Thank you."

The sound of smashing plates, a massive *bang* as if a table had been flipped over, and cries of shock followed.

Charles' high-pitched voice, loud with fear, called out, "Oh dear! Do avoid the glass, please! Well, look at that. A perfectly ruined tablecloth. And all that crystal!"

Max steeled himself for the worst.

Chapter Twenty-Eight

CHARLIE

Charlie stood in front of a basil plant at his office window. Flickering torches illuminated Chatham City and winked in the distance. The chaos of another failed delegation behind him two days ago, he released a long breath.

Max's words, cutting as they had been, followed him. *Instead of fighting for her, chasing after her, you remained here to lick your wounds and sulk?*

Charlie sighed.

If possible, he'd never return to Wildrose and all the rampant expectations there. The incumbency. The pressure of family members staring down at him from perpetuity, demanding he make something of himself to continue their legacy and their name. A legacy he cared less and less about every year.

Without Faye, what did it matter?

Perhaps he'd abandoned Wildrose for too long, leaving it to Max's overly capable and adoring hands. He should appear there more.

Should.

Wouldn't.

Despite attempts, he couldn't tear his thoughts away from Max, Wildrose, and Faye. He swallowed rising nausea at the thought of her. A year. A year of his life without seeing her face, feeling her touch. Twelve months without softness or the steady connection that her laugh provided.

The good gods.

He *should* let her go.

Release her from his mind and heart. As if that was so easy, or an opportunity that he controlled. Blessed be, but he'd tried. She had effectively tacked herself into the planes of his soul. He couldn't rip her away. She'd integrated too far.

Charlie reached for his cloak. He'd go spy on Carcere, or Magnolia, or Big Leo's personal townhouse in Necce. He couldn't think when the world had no noise. The sight of a silhouette near the fire stopped him. He whirled, crouched, summoning a dagger with a thought.

Astonishment stopped him.

Faye stood near the fire, silhouetted against the flames. Her hair haloed behind her head, braided at the top, spiraling in the back. A small silver circlet sat in her right nostril that hadn't been there before. The angles of her face were more smooth, defined. Her eyes, dark as midnight, appeared strained.

"Faye?"

He dropped his arm to his side. Had he summoned her ghost? Did he hallucinate? Had his longing gained such power that it brought her?

"Charlie."

Her whisper sent a shock through him.

"You're real?"

A twitch of her lips replied. "I'm real. I wouldn't be a proud member of the Advocacy if I didn't know how to find my way around an old, drafty castle." She eyed the far wall, where a lesser-known hidden passage lurked behind a pair of drapes. "Helps that Max mentioned an alternate entrance to your office."

Words failed him. He could only stare. How many nights had he dreamed of this? Had his tugging heart hoped for her to return?

"You spoke with Max?" was all he could manage.

She sobered. "No. He told me about it before I left last year. Said . . . he hoped it would come in handy for me one day."

A slight pulse of regret for slamming his fist into Max's jaw slipped through him. Not *that* much regret, though. Despite good intentions, Max had deserved it.

"Oh."

She'd lost some of the roundness he loved about her. The full cheeks, gentle shoulders. Life in the tribes had hardened her physically, at least a little. She would never lack the buzz of life in her smile, however. The amusement at life, even at its worst.

Faye drew in a deep breath, shoulders expanding.

"I came because . . . well . . . a lot of reasons." Her gaze dropped momentarily. She ran her bottom lip through her teeth. "Mostly? To apologize. I've hardly been able to live with myself the last year. Abandoning you when you needed me most. I . . . it was wrong. I'm sorry."

"Faye—"

She held up a hand. "No, allow me to speak. Please. Charlie, I should have told you sooner that I struggled. I should have given you an opportunity to fix it before I just left. But . . . I think I needed this time to find myself, my family, in the West."

His breath hitched. "Did you? Did you find them?"

A full smile followed. "Yes. It took me longer than I wanted, but yes. I found them. My parents are both dead, as I suspected, but I have an uncle that's alive. Several cousins, whom I love now. They accepted me back with open arms."

Relief flooded him. He released his first genuine smile. "Faye, I'm so happy to hear that. I had hoped . . ."

Tears glittered in her eyes.

"I know you did, Charlie. That's what destroyed me the most. I knew you'd be happy for me, hoping for me. You have a good heart under all that hero's obligation you hoard. The best heart I've ever known. Without you, I haven't been myself. I thought I'd find myself in my tribe, but I only found pieces. Missing pieces, of course. Important ones that I will always cherish. But I realized that, if I wanted to be my full self, I needed you at my side."

He hesitated, ready to throw himself across the room, gather her in his arms, and dissolve there until night turned to day. All his restraint held him back. His hands trembled.

"What does it mean?" he asked, desperate now. "What does it mean, Faye?"

She held out two hands.

"Will you have me, Charlie? Can you forgive me? Is this a gap we can bridge, or have you already moved on?"

With a cry, they collided.

He clasped her to him, clawing her closer. Her arms wrapped around his chest with a sob. The press of her face into his neck sent a jolt of disbelief all the way through him. He weakened, nearly fell.

"I'm sorry, Faye," he whispered. Tears spilled onto his cheeks. Her fingers found his hair, his lips, his cheek. "The good gods, I messed up. You deserve better than me. Better than I've given, and I've promised myself every day that if you came back, I'd be the man you deserve."

Faye pulled back, pressed a hand to his cheek. The gentle chastisement, layered beneath amusement, had returned to her gaze.

"Charlie, you already *are* the man I deserve. Here, in your arms, I've finally come home. I want to go back to Wildrose, the Advocacy. The goddess of desert help us," she muttered dryly. "I've even missed Max."

He laughed; he couldn't help it.

"Don't tell him that."

She sobered. "Do you think he'll take me back? Will he forgive my departure?"

"He'll take you back, but he won't forgive you."

She laughed this time. He joined her, buoyed by disbelief. With Faye in his arms again, light zipped through him like electricity. It hummed along his nerves, danced down his spine. He felt alive, free. Able to take on the world with no questions or doubts.

"Faye?"

Her hands framed his face.

"I'm here to stay, Charlie," she whispered. Their foreheads pressed together. "If you'll have me, I am yours forever. No matter what the Network, the Advocacy, Wildrose asks of you. I am ever at your side, my love. My soulmate."

Chapter Twenty-Nine

MAXIMILLION

Four years later

Max's jaw tightened as he stared at the same page, read the same paragraph, for the tenth time. A tickling sensation lurked in his mind, like a tug. A tap on the shoulder from the magic.

With a growl, he gave in.

He opened the paths. The darkness sank like the rapid close of night. The relentless sensation ebbed as soon as he entered the magic. Never had the magic *insisted* on anything. Not like this.

Instead of dozens of paths at his feet, only one awaited. Since the magic began with him, there had *always* been multiple paths. Too many to make sense of.

At the end of the singular trail, a familiar blonde witch grimaced, a hand to her forehead. She leaned against a tree. Pain, he recognized right away. The depths of Letum Wood, if the low light, mossy trunks, meant anything. His heart sped up with a gallop. Over the years, he'd grown fond of her, though he had no idea who she might be. To see her in pain created dissonance in his chest.

How could he fix it?

At his feet, a single point of light brightened. It inched toward the girl, illuminating a bright line from his toes to hers.

She'd never had a path before.

"What?" he called. "You want me to find her?"

No answer, though the communication was clear enough.

"Fine," he growled. "This one time. Then I have another war to prevent, thank you *very* much."

* * *

After transporting eleven times, Max had no luck.

With a growl, he returned to the paths, saw the same image. Irritated, he closed the magic.

"This is my last attempt," he hissed. "You want this to happen, you make it happen!"

As he issued the magic, a pull accompanied him. The pressure and discomfort of transporting followed, but with an additional nudge. Oddly, just like the night he left the East, when Charlie found him.

He landed with a grunt.

Verdant forest surrounded him. Thick trees, heavy with green drapes. Sultry air. He paused, breath held, when the crack of a branch sounded nearby. The witch in question approached him on a thin track.

After years of seeing her in the paths, to find her in real life arrested him entirely.

The good gods.

She was exquisite.

A young woman, of course. She had been for several years, but seeing her brought it home in a new way. His heart missed a beat. He swallowed back a rush of panic.

No.

No, he couldn't feel this way. He didn't know her; had

never planned to know her. Never had he, never would he. Care, compassion, affection. Those emotions belonged to men like Charlie.

He had business to conduct.

Tucking aside the nervous thrill that consumed him, he straightened his shoulders back. The moment had come. The magic wanted them together, for some reason. He'd make it happen, then leave her alone for good.

A perpetual wince filled her features as she navigated down the thin path. A low bun pulled her blonde hair away from her face. She stopped and studied several purple bottles in her hand.

A simple dress, clearly homemade, covered a thin waist, lithe arms. Mud coated the bottom of the skirt, but she demurely pulled it a little higher anyway, revealing sturdy boots beneath.

Definitely the same witch.

"Finally," he muttered.

She gasped and dropped the bottles in her hand. They shattered against a rock. Fright crossed her pretty features. A hand lifted between them, as if that would stop anything.

"Who are you?" she cried. "What are you doing here?"

Her voice had a firm, but lyrical, melody. Better to get this over with. He had things to do, and something about her peculiar gaze made him uneasy. Max cast a spell to repair the bottles.

"I'm not here to eat you. You dropped those."

Her eyes widened with shock, then delight. "Egads. That must have been a complicated spell!"

Egads?

The good gods, but the magic had sent him a forester. A Watcher, perhaps? Why would the magic be invested in this witch? Better yet, why should *he* be invested? The young woman snatched the dangling bottles and shoved them into her pockets. One fell out through a hole in the bottom to shatter again.

He rolled his eyes. "Your eyes are two different colors. That's very odd."

Disdain crossed her bold features.

"So are yours."

He ignored the inherent defensiveness. If a forester, she wouldn't likely know what her two differently colored eyes meant.

Watcher, then.

"Odd, but defining. How interesting."

She crouched, fumbling in the grass until her hand found a branch. She tried to lift it with a grunt, but vines anchored it to the ground. With a guttural cry, she wrenched it free and waved it in front of her.

"Go away."

"Or what?"

"I'll call down a lion."

"Sure you will."

"I will!"

He yawned. "Go on, then. I'd love to see it."

"Who are you?"

"Maximillion. Not Max. Not Max*well*. Maximillion. It's important you get that right."

She rolled her eyes, branch still held aloft.

"Why?"

"Because it's rude otherwise."

Clearly, the magic brought him here for something. Even more clearly, she'd been in the forest, probably playing all by herself, for far too long.

"What are you doing here?" she insisted, drawing him back to the moment. She'd braced her legs, crouching slightly.

He lifted an eyebrow. "Do you own this forest?"

"No."

"Then why does it matter?"

"You shouldn't be *in* here."

When she motioned behind him, he noticed a sort of wall. Built of . . . piled stuff. Greenery. Logs. Moss. Rocks. Some of it blackened, charred by dragon fire, perhaps. Double interesting.

He held up his hands as if to say, *Then why am I here?*

She leaned on a tree and grabbed her head, eyes clenched shut. "Please leave."

Ah, another good sign.

A *transitioning* Watcher.

No wonder the magic brought him. It must protect its own, though it had never done it like this before. He shook his head.

"Not yet."

She growled, teeth slightly bared. By stomping one foot, she attempted a brave show. "G-go a—"

He'd had quite enough. Max stepped closer. Her screwed-shut eyes flew open. She took a step back, but a tree prevented her from leaving. This close, she smelled like a bundle of herbs. Pleasant, but subdued. Unlike the witch herself, apparently.

"You're in pain," he said.

She snarled, but it held little energy. "Get away from me."

He deflected a weak attempt to shove him with a hand. Annoying that his glare didn't faze her. Other witches succumbed to his demands far more quickly. Of course, the magic would choose an irritating witch for him to help.

"Calm down," he snapped. "I'm going to press my fingers to your head. Don't try to bite me, or I'll remove all the hair from your head with a spell."

The tips of two fingers pressed into her temple while he murmured an incantation. Heat collected under his fingertips, pulling the pain free. An ancient spell, hardly used anymore, that over time had proven useful against the transitioning headaches that Watchers often complained about in headquarters, or places like the BLAUS.

Her tense neck eased, and mouth dropped open. Some of the cloudiness had left her gaze.

"What did you do?"

"Magic. Please tell me you've heard of it."

"Of course I've *heard* of it. But we aren't allowed—yes. I've heard of it."

Not allowed to do magic? The good gods, this grew worse with every passing second in her presence, for more reason than one.

"Mildly reassuring," he drawled. "You'll have a hard time of it later, should things move that direction with us."

"How did you know what to do? Can I do it? I-I know a little magic. Simple spells. But still . . . "

"Don't ask stupid questions."

"No question is stupid!"

"I assure you, there are stupid questions."

She scowled and stepped back. "Why did you help me?"

A fair question, one he had yet to answer himself. Obviously, a transitioning Watcher. Perhaps a powerful one, if the magic brought him to her. He'd been seeing her for years, which likely meant something.

Hopefully not a sign of things to come, at any rate.

"Because you're of more use to me when—and if—you're competent. Now, I've answered your question; you will answer mine."

Instead, she pointed to his wrist.

"What is that?"

"You are clearly a creature of advanced intelligence. It's a cufflink. Not steep fashion by any means, I assure you. Although, considering the state of your dress—"

She folded her arms over her piddly fabric. "My dress is perfectly functional."

A wry glance at her broken potion bottle brought a rise of heat to her cheeks.

"Clearly."

"You must leave. Now."

"I must not."

"Then why are you here?"

"To get you out of my head."

"What?"

"This meeting has been inevitable for a while now. I'm glad to be rid of it. Answer my question, and I'll leave."

"What are you talking about?"

Frustration nearly overcame him. He slipped back into the paths. There had only been one trail for him earlier—a clear insistence that he do nothing *but* this. Now, others proliferated.

Indeed, so many others.

All of them with her.

He closed out of the magic, too overwhelmed to comprehend it right then. Seeing her back in Letum Wood, staring at him as if he had two heads, only made it worse.

"Cursed witch. Just my luck. You're on *more* paths now than ever."

She shuffled back, hands held up.

"You're insane, aren't you? You're a wanderer who's lost his mind and isn't fit for society."

"The good gods, you're dramatic. I control society, for that matter, and am more *fit* for it than half the witches in the Network. Yourself included. Who or what I am is not as important as who you are. What is your name?"

A defiant glint entered her eyes. "I don't have one."

"I'm not surprised."

"What's that supposed to mean?"

"You're a confirmed heathen."

"Heathen?" she sputtered. "By Drago, you—"

"There's no possible way you could misconstrue what I just said," he snapped, at his wit's end now. "You probably share rooms with a sibling, too, don't you? I had hopes for someone of greater intelligence. Can't imagine why this had to happen."

"What are you *talking* about?"

"Tell me about yourself."

"Absolutely not."

"You're eleven?"

"Fifteen!"

"Your older brother is named Alfred, correct?"

"What? I don't have a brother."

"Your sister was Alice?"

"No!"

"Ah, a sister it is."

A squeak popped out of her with livid steam. She folded her arms across her chest. "You're not going to get any more information out of me with your sneaky game."

"Damn," he drawled. "You caught me. How often do you have headaches? How advanced are they? Do you see a gray cloud yet?"

Terror filled her gaze now.

"If you aren't gone in two minutes, you'll never leave alive. I may not be able to call lions, but there are worse creatures to fight in Letum Wood that—"

He scoffed, rolling his eyes. "Call your dragons. I can't imagine they care much for a witch like you."

The girl stumbled over a tree root in her haste to get away, but didn't make it far. "What are you? A poacher?"

"Do you really think I'd admit it if I was?"

"Ah. . ."

"Do I look like the kind of witch who cares a whit about

animals or blood?" he snapped. "You couldn't get me near a giant lizard if you paid me. The dragons won't come here for you. Not today, anyway."

"How could you possibly know?"

Another return to the paths confirmed it. No immediate dragons which, he could hardly admit, gave him relief. Other things showed, however. Things he didn't like. The two of them discussing parchments—the Ronan Scrolls, he believed—in a school setting. Wide-eyed shock on her face with an ocean backdrop.

Too much.

He left the paths behind, humming with annoyance now.

"That is something for us to discuss later," he said sharply. "I've done my duty today by simply meeting you. The paths will dictate the rest. Perhaps you'll never see me again."

"Sounds lovely."

"I agree. What's your name?"

"I'm not telling."

"Grogda it is."

She recoiled, nose wrinkled. "Grogda?"

He lifted his brow in silent question.

She paused for a long time, then finally asked, "Where are *you* from?"

"The outside."

"Can you teach me more magic?"

"Someone must."

She leaned closer, hungry hope in her bright-eyed gaze. "Get rid of my headaches?"

"Inevitably."

"Today?"

With a roll of his eyes he said, "No, not today, you impetuous thing. It's not time."

Determination filled her voice when she said, "Isadora. My name is Isadora."

"I prefer Grogda."

Max left as she issued an irate huff.

Good riddance, he thought, and returned to work, if only to hide from the inevitable lurking in the shadows of the future. As he turned his mind from her, his heart raced like a wild thing.

Chapter Thirty

CHARLIE

Max stood at the head of the table in headquarters, a plethora of papers around him. He'd transformed himself into his usual Advocacy caricature—a young, cheeky boy, not much older than twelve. Whether or not it bothered Advocacy members to discuss their missions with a pipsqueak of a kid, Charlie could never tell. The child was certainly nothing like Max's true self.

Which only made it more amusing to Charlie. A twelve-year-old barking commands, so serious about life.

Hilarious.

"The Defenders stopped the raid at the end," a woman named Naomi said, her voice wobbly. "We escaped with the Watcher, but . . . just barely. It's almost like . . . like they wanted us caught."

Max's quill paused when he glanced at Naomi. Though the effect wasn't obvious, he softened his features.

"Are you well?" he asked.

Naomi, a stalwart woman with control that most witches never achieved, nodded. The muscles in her neck remained taut. Something wasn't right, and Max seemed to sense it.

Charlie, transformed into an uneducated female from Chatham City that most knew as Tabitha, watched from Max's side. Naomi's gaze roved over Charlie entirely—most Advocacy members ignored Tabitha.

Naomi reached into a pocket of the trousers she wore, pulled out a small, rolled parchment.

"One Guardian grabbed me. He held my arm, said I was to bring this message back to the Advocate. Then he let me go. After that, all the East Guards disappeared."

A thrill ran through Charlie.

Ah.

How interesting.

"A setup?" Max murmured, taking the scroll from her hands. Naomi shrugged.

"Must have been."

Advocacy members gratefully accepted the foremost rule that they should never appear as themselves. Only in rare cases were actual identities known. Faye, of course, knew the major volunteers by name, real and fake, in order to contact the appropriate witch if needed. Not even Max had kept track at that level of detail.

Max hesitated, then tucked the letter into his pocket. "Thank you. I will pass it along to them when we meet tonight. As always, you performed admirably, Naomi. We appreciate your efforts and hard work."

A hint of disappointment flashed through her eyes just before she smiled. "Thank you. Everyone thinks it's you, you know."

Max's adult disdain carried through the young lad's voice when he scoffed. "Fat chance I'd want the weight of this organization on my shoulders. I'll pass on the accolades, thank you, Naomi."

She nodded, then turned to leave. Halfway out the door and into the basement hall, she glanced back.

"The raids have lessened a little, haven't they?"

Max had already turned his attention back to the paperwork in front of him. Details for future raids. Assignments. Mission flow charts. Other witches patched these together, sent them to Max for approval. Before the final plan, Charlie reviewed all of them.

For now, Charlie pretended a cursory interest, reminding himself that he was neither Charlie nor Charles in this moment. It had become a tangled web he could hardly keep track of anymore.

Max, still focused on the paperwork, called out, "A little."

"Will they continue to lessen?"

"I should hope so," he said crisply. "Most witches have turned their attention to surviving all the wars that our High Priestess has antagonized into being with her fair wit."

His cutting sarcasm deepened the grooves on her forehead. Max didn't glance up, so missed the telltale sign of concern.

In a lithe feminine voice, Charlie said, "The Advocate told me they hope attacks should slow, Naomi, and they will keep us informed."

A lessening of the tension in her shoulders followed. The door wheezed shut behind her, latching firmly. Only a witch with the right incantation could enter from Wildrose.

Max flickered a wry glance Charlie's way. "I didn't reassure her enough?" he inquired coldly.

"The day you reassure anyone is a day that shall go down in history books, my friend."

Max leaned back.

"The current plans for potential raids are fine with me." He shoved the parchments farther away, met Charlie's feminine gaze as he lifted the small scroll. "Shall we see what old Leo has to say now?"

"I'm quite certain the Advocate is dying to hear his thoughts."

Max snorted, opened it.

Blocky handwriting filled the interior.

To the Advocate.

This business of raiding and attacking back and forth grows tiring. I believe we might be better off to meet in person and work this out one-on-one.

If you agree, please visit Carcere, top of the building, in two days' time.

Formally,
  Leo Giuseppi

Charlie hooted.

Max rolled his eyes.

"Can you imagine writing such a letter?" Charlie cried, laughing. "Faye will have a laugh at this one. I can't imagine a man sitting down to think this sort of thing would work."

Max tilted an eyebrow. "You're not going to go?"

"Of course I'm going to go."

"Naturally," he muttered.

"But I won't go when he *asks*. I'll be there to observe, perhaps . . . test a few things . . ."

Ideas flooded Charlie's mind. Ways to trick Leo, have fun with such an invitation. Undoubtedly, ulterior motives lurked behind it. They wanted to plan a farce of a meeting, then follow him home as he transported, perhaps. Or ambush him, but that seemed far too simple for Leo's taste.

"I think you're a fool to go."

"And pass up this opportunity?" Charlie slapped a knee. "Leo knows the Advocate well enough by now. I'd never pass up an exciting challenge like this. You know they're lessening attacks to help us feel safe. Probably while they try to figure out *who* the Advocate is."

"Don't be a fool."

"I've always been a fool," he said lightly, in the droll tone of Charles. Max sent him a withering glare. Charlie nudged him with an elbow.

"Lighten up, Max. Leo has something up his sleeve, and so do I. I'll take Advocacy members with me, if you don't mind, and we'll have a bit of fun. Some of them could use some sport, you know. They're getting bored, they say."

To that, Max had no reply.

Charlie heard his condemning judgment all the same.

* * *

"Charlie?"

The quiet voice appealed to him from the other side of the room. Charlie startled, half awake, and pushed up.

Faye's silhouette stood near the door to his bedroom at Chatham Castle. Seeing her here always caused a flutter of concern in his belly. He didn't like the mixing of the two worlds.

Too much risk.

"Faye?"

She bustled over, moving silently as a cat. After years of treading the halls at Wildrose, she had quietness down to an art. He lifted the covers, and she slid in between. She reached out, shivering against his side.

241

"Are you cold?"

"A little."

He wrapped her in his arms, warm from the heavy coverlet. She sighed against his shoulder. He breathed deeply of her hair. She smelled like dust and Wildrose and sharp apothecary potions. The scents swirled around inside him like all the lost pieces he kept trying to pull together. They fell back out as quickly as he found them.

He wasn't sure which pieces belonged to him, Charles, Wildrose, or the Advocacy anymore.

Once the little trembles subsided, he tucked a stray wire of hair out of her face and peered at her through the moonlit room.

"My love?"

Ridges cut across her brow, testimonies to concern.

"Charlie, I don't want you to go to the Eastern Network tomorrow. Not even with the Advocacy members. It must be a trap. Leo might suspect that you'll show up early or try to be there."

He scooted away to better see her.

"Why?"

"I'm worried for you."

"We have made promises, my love," he whispered. "Promises to witches who cannot protect themselves."

"At the expense of your life?"

Troubled, he pulled her closer. "No, of course not. That's why we're taking precautions."

"And if this is a wiser trap than you think? What if he doesn't want to trap you there, but at Wildrose?"

Charlie frowned. "What do you mean?"

"You're always subverting him, Charlie. You anticipate what he'll do, get information before he gives it. Every now and then, they're able to trick us, but rarely. What if this is a retaliatory prank? Maybe he won't try to capture you—because he's never been able to—but to get information?"

"I can't say it's not possible."

"Then how will you keep us and yourself safe?"

"I have a careful plan, Faye. The Advocacy will be with me —I won't be alone. We'll be careful and abandon the moment I suspect a single problem. Why are you worrying about this raid over all others?"

She swallowed, shaking her head. A hand lifted to her face, pushed tendrils of hair out of her eyes.

"I don't know."

She pressed her hand to his chest. Her fingers toyed with the edge of his open shirt as she molded back into him with a sigh. The flutter of her eyelashes closing followed.

"Leo addressed that message to me, Faye," he whispered. "The responsibility is mine."

"I know."

"I would never do anything to separate us again."

Faye pushed away. Her dark eyes, the same as midnight, studied him. Unshed tears glimmered there.

"I know, my love," she whispered. "Sometimes, I'm afraid for you. That's all. This one feels different."

He wanted to run his finger along the curve of her nose, the hollow of her cheek. To memorize her with touch until he could recreate her in the back of his mind forever.

The last four years since her return had passed in her face alone. He tried not to see the stress lines and crow's feet. The frown marks. Her cheeks were too thin, her shoulders tiny inside her dress. Greta's escalating wars had been difficult for the Advocacy, but Faye had always given more than her fair share now that they opened Wildrose to the increasingly needy souls that found it.

He wanted to soothe this away, but knew he could not. Perhaps that's what hurt most of all.

"I love you, Faye."

"I love you, Charlie."

He pressed a kiss to her forehead, her nose, her cheek. She melted, softening like butter in his arms until he rolled her onto her back, pressed his body against hers, and carried her away with a love that bubbled from the depths of his own terrified heart.

* * *

The smell of sand and surf and sea filled the air.

Charlie tilted his head back, sniffed. Usually, he observed Carcere from the air as an *aquila* bird. Over the years, the *aquila* bird had become his favorite disguise. Such intelligent creatures. Some days, the temptation to remain an *aquila* and fly away nearly overwhelmed him.

Faye would follow.

Today, he stood on top of Carcere as an East Guard. A cool breeze rustled along the back of his neck, ushering his thoughts to the present moment. The top of Carcere was a most boring structure. Not as dull as sitting in the High Priest's office, though.

A deception spell slept in his chair back at Chatham Castle, transformed into a sleeping Charlie. His Assistant had strict orders to direct any surprise appointments away for the next two hours. If she peeked inside, she'd see the false spell.

He hoped that would be enough.

For now.

Two days had passed since Leo's letter arrived to the Advocacy. Charlie had issued no response. Leo would, at this point, merely hope that the Advocate received the challenge.

They had stationed three Advocacy members at the top of Carcere since Naomi handed the note over. The three of them alternated between different animals with transformative magic, observing, passing messages: *aquilas*, mice, and cats. One attempted to observe boat movements and Guardians as a dolphin.

So far, nothing to report.

Unfortunately, several East Guards had fallen ill—thanks to a bottle of fresh ipsum passed around that night. The Guardian in charge of Carcere transported a message back to Magnolia Castle, requesting more Guardians.

A loyal Magnolia Castle worker, grandmere to a Watcher the Advocacy had saved last year, intercepted said message before Leo received it. Which meant that Charlie and Tomi, a woman in her early twenties with a deep love of terrifying challenges, appeared as East Guards instead.

Almost too easy.

Which had Charlie on edge.

Faye's warning and concern from last night kept him more alert than usual.

A scuffle of movement on the other side of the tower drew his gaze. An *aquila* soared past the turret. It was Rhiannon, another Advocacy member, if the black and brown feathers meant anything.

Charlie the East Guard kept his position near the northern edge of the turret, surveying the north side of La Torra island. With a clearing of his throat, he signaled for each Guardian to move.

As one, all four Guards present on top of the tower walked in a counter-clockwise circle. A quarter of the way around, they stopped.

Surveyed.

As the dozens of times before, nothing to see.

The routine dulled his brain. It would have been maddening if he didn't have so much attention to give to his surroundings. No familiar magical signatures around him. No sign of Leo.

Nothing.

Nothing at all.

A prickle along the back of his neck bothered him. Intuition? Fear? Had Faye's concerns rooted in his mind and now sabotaged the success of the mission? Never had he let fear get the best of him. Today, he couldn't help but agree.

Something wasn't right.

A voice called from down below. "Oi! News from the mainland."

He peered down the stone exterior. A thickset gentleman waved both arms. Charlie didn't know him by name, but had seen his brawny form before. A chef? No, that made no sense.

"What of it?" Charlie called in *Ilese*.

"The High Priestess of the Central Network! She died!"

Charlie's stomach clenched. Nausea welled up. Sticky, nearly overpowering. For a breath, he couldn't contain his thoughts. They scattered everywhere, all at once, like an explosion.

"What?"

"News just came from Magnolia Castle. They said to be on alert, in case it's a trick from the Advocacy. We're to lock down, send the two of you back to Magnolia Castle to double up security on the High Priest."

Charlie's brain lifted his arm in acknowledgement. Across the way, Tomi, her male disguise firmly in place, stared at him in muted shock.

"We must return to Magnolia," Charlie called. "News from the mainland. Our new assignment is there. See you at the castle."

She grunted, shrugged. She would have heard the news report—she had uncanny hearing—but did an impressive job hiding it.

The other two Guardians stared out at the water, clearly bored.

Charlie clenched his sword, issued a transportation spell. Habit took him first to the Western Covens, then to the northern fringes of Letum Wood. He stood there a moment, listened. No one followed. Tomi would take a different route, because no Advocacy members traveled together if they could avoid it.

He paused, took a moment to catch his breath. Greta, dead? No, it couldn't be. Nor could the timing be accidental. Faye's worries rippled through his mind as a reminder.

But how?

What could Leo possibly learn from this?

He removed the transformative magic, stepped away. A trick. This had to be a trick. He'd return to his office before anyone discovered his deception spell and all would be well.

He couldn't be the Highest Witch.

Not at twenty-nine.

No . . .

Yet something heavy in his gut countered his denial.

Chapter Thirty-One

MAXIMILLION

The dining hall couldn't have been any stuffier than it felt at this moment.

Max longed to undo his necktie and pitch it into the fire. At the top of the long-running table, Greta presided like a coy queen of cats. Council Members listened, some of them enraptured, while she extrapolated on her foolish plans to manage Dostar in the West. Others napped, snoring gently while Greta enjoyed the sound of her own voice.

Imbeciles, all of them.

His thoughts strayed to Charlie, potentially in a trap with Leo, at this very moment. He drummed his fingers on his thigh, trying to force aside thoughts of Isadora. Only a few days passed since their last teaching session as she learned to use her powers, during which she'd taken him by utter surprise.

Her voice, curious though demanding, filled his head now. *Tell me one thing about yourself that I don't already know.*

The request filled him with righteous indignation then and now. He'd almost transported away on the spot and left her to her magic. What right did she have to *demand* anything? In the end, the same inexplicable draw kept him rooted to the forest at her side. Almost like he *wanted* her to ask.

Why do you care? he'd snapped.

I don't know.

I don't like to be touched.

I already knew that.

Witches annoy me.

I also knew that.

That's all there is.

You're lying.

Then what don't you know?

Why are you helping me?

Several moments had passed before he could answer that question. Finally, he said, *Because it's the right thing to do.*

Infuriating woman.

She could never know how much more compelled him.

He firmly escorted himself back to the present moment. Recollections such as these wouldn't help anything. He needed to center himself.

Here.

In the Central Network.

He had business to conduct, and then he'd find Charlie. Once Greta stopped speaking long enough for him to nudge in a suggestion, he'd leave.

Servers passed out the third course. The clank of china added a quiet symphony against Greta's horrendous voice. Creamy soup with flecks of potatoes and clams. The smell made his ravenous stomach water. If he wasn't so demmed hot, he might—

A choking sound drew his attention.

Greta, spoon in one hand, bloomed a bright red from the bottom of her neck through her cheeks. She dropped the silver spoon, which clattered back to the bowl. A gagging sound followed. Drool appeared at the corner of her lips.

"High Priestess?" inquired a timid woman at her elbow. "Are you quite all right?"

A grunt.

Flailing hand.

Max shot to his feet, nearly shoving his chair into a server. "Call the Apothecary!" he snapped.

In four strides, he stood at Greta's side. Cries of shock rippled through the room, compounded by a general paralysis. Her thick, choking sounds punctuated the unexpected quiet. The frothing at her lips intensified, tinged pink. Wild eyes glared at him, bulged out. She grabbed his lapel.

Her eyes rolled back in her head.

"The High Priestess has been poisoned," he cried. "Call an Apothecary this instant!"

Max reached for a glass of water, tipped the High Priestess's head back on his arm, and attempted to trickle the water into her mouth. She lay inert against his bent elbow, becoming more slack with each passing moment. The water cleared the foam, but nothing more.

Cursing, he reached for a napkin.

Panicked voices escalated through the room. He swore under his breath, attempting to lay her down. Her heart still beat, but slowed. The choking sounds had ebbed because she didn't breathe.

"Greta," he growled. "If you die on us now . . ."

An Apothecary appeared at Max's elbow. He stepped back, recounted the events as best he could remember them. A second came, then a third. Before too long had passed, a crowd of Apothecaries transported Greta somewhere less public, floating potion bottles following in their wake.

A half-silent room remained behind.

Council Members flanked the table, amassing in morbid

fascination. Helene cried. Johnson snored away. The rest rustled back, horror in their eyes. High-pitched cries, gasps, running bodies hurried from the room as servers and Assistants panicked. Max drew in a deep breath, a horrid weight sinking through his gut.

The good gods, but what just happened?

"Where is the High Priest?" a shrill voice shouted. "Where is Charles?"

"Don't bring that idiot in," another snapped. "That's all we need is the dimwit knowing he's about to be in charge of our Network. And at such a delicate time."

Max's cheek twitched. Two *Chatham Chatterer* journalists stood in the doorway.

"Attack from the Western Network!" one of them called, waving an arm. The spreading pandemonium cooled as Council Members whirled around to face them, mouths open. "The Western Network is attacking all over the Central Network. Rumors say that Dostar is beginning his assault in Berry and working his way down."

The room stalled.

Unwittingly, each pair of eyes turned to look right at Max. Whether he stood in the correct spot, he'd taken action when no one else had, or they were simply that idiotic, remained unclear. Obviously, they sought his leadership.

Well, at least they weren't totally lost causes. He had a Network to defend, a High Priest to find, and an Advocacy to keep hidden.

"I'll find the High Priest and tell him." Max straightened, searched for his Assistant against the mess of frightened faces. "Wally, find the Head of Guardians and send him directly to the High Priest's office. Tell him to mount a defense where attacks are occurring and come prepared with a plan. Each Council Member will secure their coven. Have your High Witches report whether they are safe or under attack. We need a broad picture of what's happening. And, in the name of the good gods, if anyone finds Dostar, let me know immediately. *I will deal with him.*"

* * *

Charlie opened the office door just as Max reached for the door handle.

Seeing his best friend hale and alive, relief flooded Max. Charlie breathed, for one. Here, for another. Maintaining cover for the Advocacy would be far easier if Max didn't have to interrupt a mission and hold the Central Network leadership at bay.

Charlie's disheveled hair, bright eyes, and slight aura of terror told Max all he needed to know.

Charlie already knew.

The ugly truth brewed a hideous potion. Somehow, this entire debacle must have been a setup. Dante and Dostar might have worked together to pull the Advocate to the East at the same time that someone poisoned Greta's soup. To what end? Max's brain moved too quickly to focus on that now.

Stop Dostar's advance first. Political machinations, later.

Seeing Max, Charlie's tense shoulders unwound. He stepped aside, the brightness of the Charles character subsiding.

"Come in, Max. We have things to discuss. Please—"

"Your Highness, all Council Members are currently securing their coven. The Head of Guardians is on the way. We're tracking down Dostar as we speak. If I might suggest that we send several Protectors to key cities?"

Charlie recoiled.

"Dostar?"

Max blinked, tilted his head.

"The West is attacking, Your Highness. You didn't know?

Leadership is assembling now. They're coming here to speak with you. Greta has also died."

"The rumor is true?"

"Yes, Your Highness."

A bloodless expression followed. After a beat, Charlie nodded once.

"Very well. Let's talk. Sadie," he called to his Assistant, wide eyed at a desk just outside. "Please send the Head of Guardians and Head of Protectors in as soon as they arrive. It appears we have a confirmed war on our hands."

Chapter Thirty-Two

CHARLIE

Berry lay in burned piles.

In the smoldering ashes of the city, Charlie thought he smelled tar. Pitch. Inflamed hay with rancid smoke billowing out. The charred scent of living things, destroyed. Hands folded behind his back, he strolled through the empty square.

Once so happy.

Now gone.

Charlie swallowed as he roved over the last of the burning cinders. Would Berry reclaim itself? He hoped so. The legendary orchards would grow, perhaps stronger than ever for the nutrients the char and ash would provide.

He couldn't bring himself to leave. Something in the smoke, in the depths, felt all-too-familiar. The unexpected appearance of a message floated in front of him. He blinked, recognized Faye's handwriting, and accepted it.

I'm worried about you. Please come home.

Charlie crumpled the paper, pitched it to the coals. The parchment caught to flame, consumed in moments, and tumbled away in a restless trail of wind. Steps came up from behind him. He didn't turn around.

He knew that tread.

"We appeased Dostar for now," Max said, his voice hoarse. "You managed yourself with impressive authority, Your Highness. Considering."

Charlie's nose twitched. His upper lip curled in disdain. Max's generous compliment cut deep. Charles had done nothing to advance diplomacy tonight, not really.

"How I loathe Charles."

"He's a necessary means to an end," Max said, overturning a burning coal with his toe. It smoked, illuminated, faded out.

To what *end?* Charlie thought.

"Thank you, Max, for saving the girls' school and Berry. You stopped Dostar at the beginning of his path and handled his negotiations with the finesse of someone that knew exactly what he wanted, and how to get it. You saved many lives tonight."

Max snorted. "You don't give yourself enough credit. Even as the fool, Charles, you created a deal, negotiated favorable terms, and convinced him to leave without further damage. How you maintain such a character and produce results, I'll never know."

A gracious response.

One he potentially didn't deserve.

"I believe Leo is behind this," Charlie said.

Max frowned. "Leo? But why?"

"I don't know," Charlie murmured, gaze tapered. A swirl of embers blazed from the ground. He welcomed the heat and discomfort. Something in it pushed him to think harder.

"It seems convenient that the two events should happen on the same night," Max said.

"I've been torturing myself in the paths, trying to see what would have happened if I hadn't left Carcere to come here right away."

"Anything?"

He shrugged. "Of course, potentials exist. Strange, most of them. Anything from a tropical storm whipping out of nowhere to Leo and I fighting on top of Carcere to what appears to be a quiet night. Nothing that convinces me that Leo showed up, and no Advocate appeared, anyway."

"Leo may have called it off, considering the information."

"Perhaps."

Max turned to him, arms folded across his chest. "How would Leo have known to coordinate this day?"

"Dante would have been involved."

"Dostar and Dante are not friends."

"They don't have to be. Common enemies, and all. Somehow, it would seem that one of them would have revealed their plan. I very much doubt Dostar is keen on revealing anything to the East."

"Or Leo stumbled into the information, took advantage of it. Why, though?" Max warmed to the discussion now. "How does Leo gain an advantage by being involved in this?"

Charlie's jaw tightened. Exactly the question he couldn't answer.

"I don't know, Max. It's how I feel. I sense in my bones that something moves that we can't see. I don't like it."

"You just became the Highest Witch of the Central Network. That has to be uncomfortable enough. Perhaps you're projecting your fear. You've done it in the past."

Brutal, but honest.

As Highest Witch, rumor had it the Esmelda Scrolls were supposed to appear to him at some point. The bracelet that stated SAC ERO DOS SUM MUS had already attached itself to his wrist, sometime in the chaos.

Everything blurred together.

Perhaps that's why he hadn't returned to Chatham Castle yet. He didn't ask for the responsibility that waited. His negotiation with Dostar seemed lifetimes away, almost as far as standing on top of Carcere and waiting for something to happen.

"It is uncomfortable, but it's reality. There's a sense of relief, to be honest."

"Greta is gone." Max exhaled. "There is that."

"Earlier, you reluctantly mentioned that you dealt with Isadora tonight, around the time you saw Dostar. What happened?"

Max's taut expression turned deadly. "Nothing I desire to relive. That wretched woman is going to get herself killed."

Charlie suppressed a smile. With an even voice, he said, "Oh?"

"Impudent, never listens. Thinks she knows *everything* there is, and so much more than me. Mark my words, Charlie. If I didn't suspect that woman had more power than any Watcher I've ever met—perhaps all of us combined—I'd take her back to Letum Wood and gladly give her to a troll."

"Would you now?"

Something in his inquiring tone drew Max's attention. He glanced up, soured, and turned his back.

"I have things to do, Your Highness," he said coldly. "Please, grant me an audience before lunch and we'll discuss more then. Wouldn't be a bit surprised if Dante tried to spin a yarn about meeting together for peace talks after this."

After Max left, Charlie felt part of the tension that held him upright dwindle. Like shock swept his legs out from under him. He wanted to sink into the ash and mud and soot and disappear. Let someone else be the Highest Witch.

Papa's memory forbade it.

The weight of Wildrose, the Advocacy, kept him standing. The momentum carried him back to Chatham Castle, back to Charles' apartment, and into the life he loathed more than anything. Once there, a wild idea struck. With it, a rush of zest and rebounding verve that might serve him better than the loathing.

Could he?

But what if . . .

No.

He shouldn't.

A thrill buoyed him. He *would*.

He sent a message to Faye with a prayer on his lips.

Look for me at lunch. I will come to you.

Voices called through the door. Fists pounded on the wood. Charlie straightened his skewed vest, pasted on the empty smile that used to thoroughly amuse him, and forced himself to steer toward the waiting hoards.

Lunch, he told himself. *I have only to survive until then.*

* * *

Hours later, Charlie hustled invisibly through Wildrose, silently chanting Faye's name.

Not in the room of curiosities. Not near the gargoyle grandfather clock, nor the room of scrolls.

Not in the greenhouse, either.

Healing Guardians with varying capacity lurked in their individual rooms. Some of them sat upright, others lay down, stared at the ceiling. The representation of Greta's legacy, laid bare through the injuries of these witches, filled him with smoke and fire.

All the more reason to be a better leader.

When no sign of Faye appeared in headquarters or in the kitchens, he hurried outside. Instead of transporting, he jogged down the driveway, hooked a sharp right, and rushed down the lane.

Halfway to Pershington, he skidded to a stop.

Faye hurried along the road, a basket draped on her right arm. A long piece of grass twirled in her left hand. She hummed, he could hear the ditty from here. A song she'd brought from her tribe in the West.

He slipped into his usual transformation disguise, removing the invisibility spell. Faye startled when a body appeared, then stopped. Relief flooded her expression when she noticed him. A smile wreathed her features.

"Merry meet," she called, holding the basket with both hands now. Adoration infused her face, a giddiness he only saw in his presence. It wrenched his heart. She still didn't see him enough.

"It's been awhile since you've come here, stranger," she sang, in that lilting way that no one else ever had.

Charlie rushed to her, crushed her to him. He swung her around, scattering the contents of the basket. She issued a cry, then a shocked laugh. Her arms came around his shoulders.

"What are you doing?"

"Holding you," he said fiercely.

With regret, he set her down. Lowering her put space between them, and he lamented they couldn't merge bodies, be one forever. Her twinkling eyes stared at him with trapped laughter, a breathlessness in her voice.

"What's wrong? Besides the obvious, of course. Dostar and Greta and . . ."

She reached up, pressed her fingertips to his cheeks. Soberness stole over her, banishing the levity he craved. He leaned into her palm, closed his eyes. Her healing touch opened all the wounds. Everything barreled past him now. The Network. The Advocacy.

His own ideas and plans for his life, none of it truly belonged to him anymore.

His eyes flew open.

"Handfast me, Faye."

She stilled.

Astonishment glued her to him. Her lips parted, but no sound came out. Finally, a whisper.

"Charlie?"

"Handfast me, my love." He ran his finger through her kinky hair, transfixed by its texture. "Let's be one. One heart, one mind. Inseparable, except for . . ."

Life, he silently thought.

Understanding flooded her features. She exhaled, a long breath that never seemed to end.

"Handfast you?"

"Now. Right now. We'll take the night, be together without stopping. Before the floods, before the chaos really descends. There's nothing I want more in this moment, right now, than you."

Her long, thick lashes blinked several times. She closed them, pressed her forehead to his. He cupped her face in his palm, cradled her close with his other arm. Her heart thumped against his, a sweet and steady anchor.

"Faye, be mine? The only thing that truly is? I cannot do this without you, my love. The weight. I . . . I cannot."

"But the High Priest—"

"Not allowing the High Priest to handfast is a tradition, not a rule. Besides, we won't tell anyone. It'll be our secret. No one has to know."

Another interminable pause. He couldn't guess at her thoughts—didn't believe he'd want to. He risked everything in asking.

"Yes, Charlie. Of course."

Blood flushed in warm currents through his body. He gently grabbed her shoulders, pulled her back.

"Faye?"

Tears sparkled in her eyes. A languid smile followed.

"Charlie, yes. You . . . yes. You have me, Charlie. Always. We'll do this together, my love."

They sealed the promise with a searching kiss. What courage he sought, she gave. The power he required, she imparted. Faye folded into him like a collapsing sand castle. He didn't know where he ended and she began.

When he pulled away, she laughed. A breathless, wild thing that made his heart flutter.

"Faye?"

"Right now." She tipped her head back, still giggling. "Let's do it right now."

"You know what I'm asking?"

"Yes."

"No one will ever know. Max, only. Just us. Maybe Pearl."

"I understand."

"One day, I'll give you everything you dream. Greta is gone. Now I can actually make good things happen for the Network. Do you see the dream, the possibilities?"

"Yes. Yes, I see it, Charlie. I see you in it. I see Wildrose and us and forever."

He twirled her around. The frantic terror of the night subsided in Faye. In the feeling of her in his arms.

Castles, manors, political upheaval. None of it mattered. Only Faye. And home.

Faye was home.

* * *

Charlie trailed the tip of his finger along Faye's shoulder later that night. A sheet covered her bare back. Hair spilled across his pillow in loose locks.

"My wife," he murmured.

She snuggled closer.

A plate of raisins, thick crackers with seeds, and crumbled chunks of yellow cheese lay on a nearby table. The thick bread Faye recreated from her roaming tribe left crumbs behind. Cups of sweating cold water sat next to it.

The excitement of finding a High Witch in a far-away forest town to handfast them hadn't wavered. Faye didn't even care that he handfasted her while transformed to someone else. Charlie breathed deep the scent of wild roses that tangled in her hair. For the first time in his life, he never wanted to leave Wildrose.

"We're sleeping in Ranulf's room." She giggled. "I never thought of what our handfasting might mean . . ."

Charlie cast his gaze around the ancient room. A giant, four-poster bed that nearly swallowed the two of them housed a creaky mattress. Maids kept the cobwebs and dust at bay, but only barely. Age lingered in the walls, as if time had a scent.

The room occupied the entire uppermost floor, which sat on top of the manor, only a quarter-size to the rest.

"You'll stay here now, Faye."

Faye propped herself up on a bent elbow, stared at him. He met her inquiring gaze with a smile that she mirrored.

"Husband. You're giving me your father's room? What if witches ask?"

"Then they ask. Tell them you're making space for more Guardians."

"No one really thinks of you and Wildrose anymore." Reasoning layered her voice. "That is . . . Well . . . "

"And I'm not giving you Papa's room." With a growl, he rolled her onto her back. She laughed, accepted his weight.

The tangled blankets locked around his knees as he stared down at her.

Faye. She had always been a part of him. Always his.

"I'm giving you Wildrose, Faye."

"I didn't ask for Wildrose." Her nose wrinkled. "I love this manor, you know that, but I don't want it."

"I know," he whispered. "Ties."

Reluctantly, she nodded. "You are the only tie I want, Charlie."

He smiled to clear her concerns. She tweaked an eyebrow, so he grabbed the back of her neck, pressed a kiss to her lips.

"Soulmate."

Faye giggled as he sank back into the pillow. The tips of her fingers explored his nose, his cheeks, the contours of his face. He closed his eyes, reveled in the warmth.

The night inched away, past midnight now. The few hours they had left lay before them like scattered petals blowing in the wind. At five o'clock, he'd return to the castle to meet Max and his Assistants and prepare for the day. The Network would officially be his responsibility. He'd have to search for a High Priestess, deal with riots, and allow the Network to mourn a leader whom no one had liked.

He reined those thoughts back in, locked his gaze on her.

"I'm sorry, Faye."

Understanding warmed her expression. One side of her lips lifted in a half smile. "I know."

"I wish it were different."

She pressed her palm to his cheek, swamping it with her hand. The tips of her fingers rubbed his hairline with a comforting pressure. "It's not, and we're doing the best we can. No one can ask for more than that."

"Tell me what you want to do."

"What do you mean?"

"What do you want to do together? We might need to

keep our love a secret until I can wrestle out of this position, but that doesn't mean we can't experience our life. Tell me, Faye, whatever you want."

Interest piqued in her expression. She blinked several times before saying, "I want to jump off a waterfall with you."

He laughed. "Really?"

Her white-toothed smile widened. "Yes, really."

"Then we shall." A quill and piece of old parchment bounced to life from the far side of his room, where their clothes lay cast off on the floor, draped across the back of a chair. "What else?"

She eyed the scratching quill with some amusement.

"Hmm . . . well, I would also like to return to my tribe." Her expression softened. "I want you to meet my family."

"Consider it done."

Faye chuckled as the scratch of the quill on parchment continued in the background. "You and that pale skin and red hair in the Western Network sun? Can you imagine?"

He chuckled, ran a hand through his hair. "It will be a disaster, but you are worth all of it."

Faye pressed a hungry kiss to his lips. Just as he sank into it, eager for more, she pulled away. The gentle brush of her lips whispered against his as she said, "I want babies, Charlie. Lots of babies. I want a big house where the forest meets the desert. We can live by a river or stream to access water. My soul longs for the dryness, the barren landscape. I want goats and chickens and to not see another soul for days."

The edges of her dream ripped through him.

"Me too, Faye."

She curled her arms around his neck, pulled herself into him. He lay on his back, brought her with him. He rubbed her shoulders, tucked the blanket under her, and used a spell to send another log onto the crackling fire.

"Charlie?"

"Hmmm?"

"I love you."

He pressed a kiss to her hair. "I have always loved you, Faye. I didn't think it was possible to feel this depth of emotion. Your list, we'll do it together. I vow it. This will not be the rest of our life. I won't let it."

She settled in with a little sigh.

"I trust you."

Chapter Thirty-Three

MAXIMILLION

Six months later

Isadora looked like a bedraggled mess, and she smelled like one, too. The woman must have rolled in a bog.

Literally.

Her drawn eyes testified to her exhaustion.

While Akesha, a member of the Advocacy, disappeared into the forest with the young Watcher Alessio, Max regarded Isadora through the blue eyes of his typical child disguise. His hair lay tangled in blonde strands around thin shoulders.

Isadora had brought Alessio through the attack, at least. As her first true move with the Advocacy, she did well enough.

Better than that, but such admittance wasn't strictly necessary.

Except for one question: where was Lucey?

Isadora turned to walk into the forest. He trailed behind her quiet shuffle as his transformative magic slid free. She ignored him, though took care to move quietly and gaze around often. Did she do that naturally after living in Letum

Wood and around dragons her whole life, or was it based on Advocacy training?

Did she always hitch her breath when tired?

No end to his questions existed regarding Isadora, a fact he'd rather not admit. Attempts to dismiss the questions only led to greater frustration, so he let them stew and simmer until they finally came back on track.

Irritated with himself, he snapped, "And where in the name of the good gods is Lucey?"

Isadora's shoulders tensed, then slowly eased. He caught up, striding at her side. Several moments passed after she regarded him with a sidelong glance before she replied.

"I haven't seen Lucey since the ambush."

"Something went wrong."

"Nothing outside our plans."

"Tell me everything."

With surprising detail, Isadora obeyed. It wasn't often she listened to his commands without some witty attempt to best him. A testament to her exhaustion, no doubt.

". . . then we made it to the forest. Thank Drago—I mean the good gods—that those vines helped. The forest itself gave us aid, unless a witch commanded those vines. Somehow, I doubt it. It was strange."

"Impossible," he countered. They stopped walking. Max forced himself to face her. She met his sharp gaze without fear.

Then rolled her eyes.

"Obviously *not* impossible, considering this is a magical forest, but that's beside the point. Once I smacked the fairy house and made Alessio and myself invisible, the fairies drove that Defender, and hopefully the others, out. An hour later, and here we are. I haven't seen or heard from Lucey."

She spread her muck-strewn arms.

A shot of concern for Isadora's health came out of nowhere. What sort of illness might she acquire with such goop smeared on her skin? He suppressed the thought as quickly as it came.

"Interesting. Well, no doubt Lucey will be fine. It was a . . . decent first run, despite a plethora of mistakes."

"Don't choke over the compliment," she muttered.

"Regardless of your many failings, you still managed to save Alessio's life. That's something, at least."

"I'm glad of that."

Nonplussed by what he said, she sighed. Concern for Lucey distracted him away from Isadora for the moment. A blessed reprieve when he normally couldn't stop himself from noticing her.

Irritating witch.

"Go home," he said. "Take a bath. Get some rest. I won't expect your full report until tomorrow morning. Lucey will have contacted me by then."

He left, or else he might never go. When he returned to Wildrose, the boggy scent of whatever she rolled in continued to fill his head. The office lay quiet. Winter signatures frosted the window panes as he strolled by, sending firewood onto a banked fire. He locked the door with a spell, sat on a chair near the hearth, and rested his head in his hands.

The paths lay in their usual scattered disarray. Unfortunately, he couldn't see for *other* witches, but he could find likelihoods of Lucey in his paths.

Or not.

Assumptions always came from looking into future events. All of them were, indeed, assumptions. Fate and time appeared to rest on the power of agency. Witches decided the future by their actions, intrepid or stupid, like it or not.

"Lucey," he murmured.

Speaking gave no variation, no change. He didn't command this magic, he simply stood as a bystander. Lack of Lucey in anything immediate lent greater concern.

He returned to the office to find a letter from Charlie waiting. Max summoned more appropriate clothes from his room—these breeches and white shirt would shock anyone used to the Ambassador side of him—and commanded the letter to open.

Soiree tomorrow evening.

I will confirm swirling rumors about Vasily's plans to erect that ridiculous wall across the Southern Network boundary. The Council desires a discussion around escalating tensions with Dante, as well.

Big Leo has been unusually quiet. I'd love to attribute the lacking Watcher attacks to the business of war, but it seems too simple.

More later.

Max cursed under his breath. By the gods, he'd almost forgotten another social engagement because of Advocacy business.

Any more of this, and they'd be found out.

Muttering a curse under his breath, he tossed his shirt off and reached for the clean one. He shoved Isadora into the furthest regions of his mind, with her spunky eyes, lack of fear, and dubious expressions. Instead, he allowed Lucey to simmer at the front.

As always, Isadora refused to go far.

"Max?"

The crisp voice, so fluidly stated, startled him.

Max straightened, peered back over his shoulder. Faye waited near the door, arms hanging at her side. She appeared no less gaunt than anyone else. Continual rotations of Guardians through Wildrose had settled. Steady Apothecaries, volunteer villagers from the outlying towns, came in more regularly.

Whether the presence of more witches helped Faye, he couldn't be sure. Didn't have the time to figure it out, if he were honest.

"Yes, Faye?"

"I have some concerns I'd like to share." Her hands folded in front of her. "I think there are witches outside of Wildrose."

"There are always witches outside of Wildrose."

Her brow scrunched. "Yes, but this seems different. These witches only appear at certain times. I thought I detected a magical impression somewhere near the old cellar door last night."

Suspicion drew an icy finger up his spine. He shivered.

"You saw nothing?"

"No."

"What magic did you detect?"

"I'm . . . not sure. I've only just started detecting magic. There are intricacies to it I hadn't expected, but once you learn how, it's difficult to ignore."

He paused, feeling this situation out. For Faye to speak to him at all was a bloody miracle. They'd spent too long assuming the other one was competition for Charlie, though neither had implicitly stated as much. He was inclined to believe her. Faye gave him no reason not to.

Except for her novice magical abilities.

"Is there a magical system you might suspect, even if you can't confirm?"

"Invisibility, because I saw nothing. A detection incantation?"

"That makes less sense," he said carefully. "A detection spell would be autonomous, without a witch present, and harder to identify in open air like that. Do you use detection magic often?"

"Hardly ever. Only for Advocacy work."

The spell she spoke of was inadequate in most cases, and hard to recognize over great distances.

"Where were you?"

"My room."

"The opposite side of Wildrose from headquarters?"

She nodded.

"I'm inclined to think it a mistake." He turned his back. "I'll have a few Advocacy members stay in Letum Wood over the weekend, see what they might observe."

"It only comes erratically. So far, it's been unpredictable."

"When?"

"I don't know."

His voice sharpened. "Then what would you have me do other than posting sentries, Faye? I have incantations on Wildrose that prevent fire, outside attack of certain dark magicks, and transportation within the basement. Some witches with a specific mark that we give them, or after a certain potion, would see only trees. We have Advocacy members taking every precaution, and the protective screen of Guardians constantly coming in and out."

Her jaw tightened, but he sensed her capitulation. Could almost taste her fear. His nostrils flared as he pulled in a deep breath, forcing himself to patience.

"Is this due to a lack of security?" he asked.

"No. I can sense witches out there, Maximillion."

"Again, I'll post sentries—"

"For how long?"

"A few days? That's all we can ask. Witches are desperate to protect themselves, their families. There's no time to ask more."

"It won't be enough."

"Then you may do it yourself," he stated with more venom than intended. "This is all I have to give, Faye. Lucey is missing, Isadora thankfully returned Alessio on her own, and I am attempting to keep the Eastern Network from declaring open war on us."

All emotion left Faye's face. She nodded once, expression like glass.

"Best of luck to you, Ambassador."

Faye departed. Max stared at her back, growled, and returned to his fire with an uneasy feeling. He'd do anything to protect Wildrose. Anything.

So why did he feel as if he wasn't protecting anything at all?

Chapter Thirty-Four

CHARLIE

Charlie lifted a goblet with a delighted laugh.

"Yes, yes! Thank you, thank you."

The Council Member to whom he raised a toast bowed, then faded away. Max stepped forward, out of the shadows. Charlie pretended to be startled, then lurched closer to Max, as if drunk.

"Ambassador," he said crisply, lifting his glass. "To you."

Max ignored him.

A barren soiree milled in the hall. Cheery music played, but the notes rang false, too brilliant in overtures and melody. Each musician carried a heavy drudgery in their composition, as if they, too, felt the weight of fabricated gaiety.

Wars threatened on each side of the Central Network, yet Charles threw another party. A lacking one, at that. Not much food, but lots of illumination and stiff smiles to go around. *Going through the motions*, as it were.

Though the Network ran more smoothly and efficiently than before Greta took charge, they still hated him.

Dostar continued to surge from the West. Dante pressured them to support his anti-Watcher cause in blatant rejection of the edict Greta had passed. Meanwhile, Vasily hogged resources along the Southern Network wall he began in a poor attempt to keep witches out.

Pressure, pressure, all around.

Not even a soiree with weak appetizers, a lackluster showing, and limp music could stop those details.

"Merry meet," Charlie drawled with a twinkling smile to a woman across the room. His gaze roved on, belying the dead, hollow pit inside. He missed Faye. Longed to have her on his arm at these events. Could imagine her gleeful laugh, whispered jokes.

"Your Highness," Max murmured. "I come with difficult news."

An austere gaze amplified his hard expression, more solemn than usual. A knowing chill darted up Charlie's spine.

"Bad news with our friend?" Charlie asked around a fake sip of wine. Such a dire expression must concern Lucey and the latest Advocacy raid. Nothing else would plague Max with the same lines in between his brow.

"Yes."

"Do tell."

A couple shifted by, called several greetings, then veered away from Max's unforgiving glower. Most witches gave them a wide berth. Far enough they could speak quietly. Charlie would have laughed if the tension hadn't tripled in the last twenty seconds.

"Confirmed capture. At the place you so love to transform, taken by the ringleader, but not yours. Mine."

Charlie translated the cryptic phrases immediately. *The place you love to transform* was La Torra island. Carcere, to be exact. Missions at Carcere tended to be more successful, simply because so many Watchers ended up there. Defenders had very little space to hide them.

Taken by the ringleader, but not yours. Mine. Cecelia was a ringleader, but so was Leo. *Mine* meant Cecelia had Lucey, not Leo.

Cecelia had long been Max's challenge.

Leo belonged to Charlie.

"I see," Charlie said, then waved exuberantly across the room. His smile was too wide, too fixed, but no one noticed. They didn't look close enough. After all these years, he'd developed a numbing effect to being Charles. No one ever wanted to look deeper, so they didn't. Such distance allowed him to put the show on with greater force.

He pretended to have another gulp of wine, but transported it to a bush in the far gardens instead. By degrees, his cup emptied. Yet another grand scheme to have witches believe what they wanted.

"So," Charlie drawled, "tell me the plan to retrieve her. Do you need me to make myself available?"

"Not yet. I have a plan that involves Marguerite. The ringleader gave me three months before she kills the captured. Dante plans to speak with her himself."

Charlie's grip on his wine glass tightened.

"Torture?"

Max's voice sharpened with bitter regret. "Of course. She wouldn't be the ringleader without her lacking a moral compass."

"Naturally."

"Marguerite will replace a *lavanda* maid who will soon become ill."

"How tragic."

"She'll report back. I'll attempt to infiltrate as much as possible."

"Don't go alone."

"I'll call on you if needed, Your Highness."

Charlie cast him a sidelong glance, his first sober expression of the evening. His thoughts continued to iron out, revealing more and more.

"I know you think this is about Cecelia," he whispered, knowing Max would hate that he used her name, "but I don't think it is. Leo is involved in this. I believe *he* told Cecelia that the Advocate is Lucey."

Max frowned. "It's possible."

"It means he's getting closer."

"Perhaps. Allow me to find Lucey first, then take whatever action you want. Not before. We can't risk it."

With a sigh, Charlie relented.

"Let me know if I can help."

Max eyed him askance. "You're wavering."

"I'm not."

"You look exhausted."

He said nothing, because he wouldn't lie to his best friend.

"Let Leo go, Charlie. I'll deal with him and Cecelia."

Charlie scoffed, momentarily losing the brightness of features that Charles required. "As if you're any less busy?" he hissed quietly. "You now have a protégé that you're training, on top of Ambassadorship, and working with a flop of a High Priest. I didn't even include all your other duties."

When a witch glanced his way, Charlie affected as empty a smile as possible. It felt too easy, sliding into the idiocy of the High Priest.

"Leo will dissolve when she is overthrown," Max muttered with a warning glare. This conversation should be reserved for later.

Yet, there never *was* a later.

"Impetuous hope has never been a forte of yours, my friend. Now is not the best time to try it."

To that, Max had nothing to say.

Charlie cleared his throat. "I hear there are witches in the forest outside of the manor at night."

"So I've heard. We've set patrols, but can't see or find anything."

"I'll watch."

"No need. If they see something, it might be worth investigating, just in case. If they don't . . ."

Charlie loosened his necktie with a grimace. "I'll take care of it."

A warning drawl overtook Max's voice. "Char—"

"Don't bother," he said brightly. "I've got this handled, if nothing else. You take care of your problem, do what you must. I'm always available to help. In the meantime, I'll monitor issues in the West. Rising Defenders, and all that."

"Wise."

"Talk soon."

With a nod, Max faded away.

Charlie slid into Charles with some relief. There was a sense of escape in becoming the High Priest. Letting go in order to hide. Even if the room felt too stuffy, his cravat too tight, the stretch of his hideous shirt across his chest as thick as a vise.

The band of his life, tightening, tightening.

* * *

The wind stirred against Charlie's wings.

He closed his eyes, soared into a cloud. The damp moisture collected on the feathers and slicked back. *Aquila* birds could change size and form as much as they wished. He preferred a larger wingspan on calm nights, though it made it easier to track him in the air.

Fortunately, the Eastern Network had a bad habit of never looking up.

La Torra lay in quiet repose. Several magical auras lingered on top. Basic security spells. He'd been soaring overhead, diving for fish, long enough to know that Cecelia resided within.

By some twist of fate, Isadora as well.

Cheeky witch.

He rather liked her.

He cut into a transportation spell as an *aquila*. Minutes later, he soared above Magnolia Castle. Transporting while in a transformed state was the height of idiocy. Crossing the magicks, not maintaining the spells, could cause an untold number of effects. The thrill of a risk reminded him he was alive.

It helped.

Charlie pivoted around the elegant white structure. *Aquilas* weren't common this far north, but not so rare as to draw suspicion. A few wary looks, pointing from Guardians, tracked him at first. He continued to wind in and out of the foggy beach, taking a tally of patrols. One of them laughed when he issued a high-pitched scream.

When the fog rolled just right, obscuring the beach from the castle, he dove.

Seconds later, he alighted just below a window. His *aquila* form shrank. He maintained his mental faculties as different wings and razor-sharp talons emerged. He transformed into an alternate bird of prey.

The eagle.

Giant legs, an elegant white head. The space to think was restricted, but he didn't need complicated thought work to finish his task. Leo required a reminder.

A test.

Voices came from a window that he fluttered below.

Leo and a Captain that Charlie recognized, but didn't know by name. Within moments, Leo dismissed the Captain and sat at his desk, alone.

Charlie rose to the window ledge on sprawled wings. With

his beak, he pounded on it. The glass fractured in a spiderweb, drawing the old man's gaze. A spell brought an already-prepared parchment to Charlie's foot, tied with a ribbon.

The Advocate had never issued a letter, or a response to any letter, before. Surely, if Leo caught on in time, he'd never expect the Advocate to deliver the letter himself.

Leo scowled as he comprehended the bird of prey, but stood. Curiosity glittered in his dark gaze. He pulled a knife from his belt, then used the tip of it to flip the lock on the window. The delicate metal arm swooped back, slipped round, and released the glass. The window canted open.

Charlie screamed.

The screech sent Leo stumbling back.

Charlie could so easily rake his talons down Leo's face. Could transform to a witch and dispatch him without a word of explanation. Leo was the fool that had opened himself to such a straightforward attack, simply because of a rare and beautiful bird. Witches were so easy to distract.

But he didn't.

Because the real issues would continue. He could only destroy Leo—and his power in the East—after Cecelia was defeated. Dante had to lose the love of his life, to feel no ability to continue, before he would negotiate for peace with Watchers included.

Dominoes.

Yet, Leo needed to know that the Advocacy didn't cease, and would never bow to his whims. They might hold Lucey, but Leo would understand that they didn't break. That pressure and pain and torture wouldn't stop them.

Nothing.

Nothing would stop them.

Which explained the desperation of this circumstance. The sheer audacity in going through such a simple plan to make a perhaps unnecessary point.

Was this a game?

Or was this real?

The lines blurred. When Leo advanced with greater hesitation, eyes on the dangling scroll, Charlie forced his annoyance and hesitation to cool. The complicated emotions were too much for the bird. He couldn't maintain it for long.

Charlie flicked the thoughts aside, strengthened the transformation spell. The old man plucked the dangling string that unwound the knot and the letter fell in his hand. Charlie fluttered out of reach. Leo kept a wary gaze on him as he unrolled the parchment, which stated,

Wrong witch.

The move is now mine.

Leo's face morphed from astonishment to fear, then a glittering challenge. When his gaze lifted, Charlie met it.

An understanding passed between them. Maybe Leo knew more than Charlie expected. He might understand that the Advocate issued the declaration. Or maybe he tasted Charlie's desperation.

Leo snarled and advanced. His meaty hand reached out. In a thought, Charlie transported away. He relocated into the ocean first, then more quickly to the forest. Letum Wood enveloped him in darkness as he leaned back against a tree. Water streamed down his face, his shoulders.

A tug of magic flowed around him.

Someone followed.

Charlie transported to the frigid bowls of the Southern Network.

The Western Network.

He transported more times than it should be possible for

Leo to follow. Sand thickened his hair. Seaweed wrapped his ankle. He moved like a hot coal bouncing from place to place. Pursuit would be impossible.

Exhausted, he waited on a tree branch in Letum Wood for thirty minutes.

Sixty.

No stir of magic.

No cracking tree branches.

Confident he'd lost Leo, Charlie now strode invisibly across the grounds of Wildrose to avoid more powerful magic, easier to track. He attempted to draw peace from the old manor, but thought only of Papa. Of headquarters. He'd created a force he couldn't even acknowledge or own. They didn't know him, yet couldn't successfully function without him or the guidance and information he provided.

The Advocacy wasn't really his.

Yet, he had to sacrifice all to protect it.

Charlie sat on the stairs, deep in thought, until the sun hinted at the horizon. Before the manor stirred, he returned to Chatham Castle. His butler greeted him at the door in surprise, but Charlie breezed past with a laugh, acting half-drunk, and collapsed into bed.

Sleep took him away.

Chapter Thirty-Five

MAXIMILLION

A bundle of envelopes trembled in his pocket.

Isadora appeared no worse for wear, despite living as a secret spy in Carcere for months, being tied to a seven-pointed star that Cecelia would have used to torch her to death, fighting Cecelia head-to-head with her Watcher magic, and coming out the victor.

Despite himself, he had to give Isadora respect.

Silently, of course.

She might detect what else lay behind his show of approval, and he couldn't afford distractions. By the good gods, though, she was the most difficult witch he'd ever encountered. A bundle of trouble. The truest test of his reserves he'd ever met.

He grabbed the envelopes, thrust them at her.

"Here."

Isadora blinked, regarded them, and accepted. "Thank you."

He hesitated. "They're from your family. I . . . this is the safest time to give them to you."

His stomach clenched in pain. She accepted them with a

radiant smile, despite all her fatigue. How she could experience all that terror and still smile stymied him. Why she smiled at *all* was something he'd never figure out.

"Thank you, Max."

He bit back the urge to correct her. Like Charlie, it did no good. She'd never call him Maximillion, except for when he exasperated her, which happened often enough.

"I must return," he said stiffly, uncertain what to do now. The moment of affectionate weakness while Isadora had been in the depths of unsafety on La Torra plagued him. Why had he kissed her? Felt the warmth of her mouth on his? The depths of her heat, her touch? Like water in a desert.

He craved more.

Could hardly imagine it never coming again. But it must not. She was an Advocacy member, practically a servant to his cause. He couldn't—no.

Couldn't go there.

Isadora had the gall to appear slightly amused. "Of course you must leave," she said dryly. "You love escaping awkward situations, am I right, Max?"

"I've no idea what you're talking about. Nothing about this is awkward. Stop wasting my time."

She indicated around them with a wave and a poorly hidden smile. "No one is stopping you from transporting away."

Though he had more to say—scads of it. Enough to fill eons of time—he did just that. Left before he could speak another word. He'd only betray himself, and he had enough on his plate as it was.

Besides, she'd open those letters soon.

Then she'd thoroughly hate him.

Instead of going back to Wildrose, he appeared at Pearl's. Leaves scattered her front porch as he rapped on the door, not entirely certain why he'd come. His thoughts lay heavy with

Isadora, Cecelia, the weight of death and all that lay ahead of them. Cecelia had taken her own life, which significantly improved prospects for Watchers.

Only Leo remained.

He'd proven to be a patient, wily old man so far. Without Cecelia, would that change? At most, they must have taken the wind out of his sails. Certainly not the boat from the ocean. Leo would still fight, but with less recruitment now.

As hoped, this would gut Dante. Challenge his ability and will to press on with the same degree of hatred. Dante's adoration for his mistress had only been part of the reason they pressed so hard against Watchers.

The Advocacy had to give this transition time.

Space.

During which Isadora would grow to hate him, Leo would amass his next massive trick, and Max could do nothing about it.

The door blew open, revealing a red-cheeked Pearl with a hat on top of her head. Her plump cheeks had long-since faded to thin bones, but she carried joy with her, regardless.

"Well! Merry meet, Maximillion! Come in, come in."

She bustled out of his way and waved him closer. He stepped inside, greatcoat billowing around him as he entered. Romance novels littered the table, the chairs. She kept a different book for each sitting spot. A teapot whistled from the fire.

"I . . . came to check on you."

Pearl beamed. "How lovely! I'm fine, fine. The Advocacy keeps me apprised of any dangers, and I haven't heard of any in little old Berry recently. After Dostar burned it down, witches have been ignoring Watchers entirely."

She brought a chair over with a spell. He ignored it. Now was not the time to sit down. He had business to conduct. Issues to straighten that would wreak havoc with his status as

Ambassador. Currently, Charlie would be directing Advocacy members to new jobs through messages.

With cleanup from Carcere taken care of, he could breathe. Work through the morass of emotions about Isadora. Himself.

Just one moment to reconsider his place in the world . . .

"I've . . . done something I'm not proud of, Pearl."

The words issued out of him before he knew they were there. Pearl attempted to hide her astonishment as she lowered the tea kettle. Steamy water slowed to a trickle, then individual drops. She spelled a cup to his side, followed by a sachet of tea. The smell of bergamot followed. Despite himself, it soothed.

"What happened?" she asked.

Her lack of searching made it easier to speak. He couldn't have stopped the admittance should he have wanted to. It barreled out on its own force.

"I've hurt Isadora."

"Isa? What are you talking about?"

"Her father died weeks ago." He cleared his throat. "I kept the news from her."

Pearl's tea cup plummeted to the ground. He caught it with a spell a second before it would have shattered. She blinked, hand halfway poised to her mouth still. Her ashen face matched her breathy voice.

"What?"

Max stood, batting the floating tea cup aside. Pearl's tiny house allowed him three steps to pace before he had to turn back around.

"He died. A dragon fight or something. I read the letters from her sister because I didn't want them to distract Isadora while she was on a mission. If they had been normal letters, I would have sent them on."

Pearl lowered to a chair. "Lucey. Isadora was at La Torra, trying to save Lucey."

He nodded, hands on his hips. "If I told Isadora any sooner than now, she might have gotten herself killed. If she left Carcere unexpectedly, we would have compromised our ability to save Lucey. He died. There wasn't a thing she could have done to stop it."

"Her family would want her, Max!"

"I know."

Her mouth bobbed open, then closed. She sighed, shaking her head. Several long moments passed before she broke the quiet. "You did what you had to do. You were in a hard position."

"She'll never forgive me."

Giving voice to the terrible notion turned his heart to a swamp. He didn't want this to be real. Didn't want to care for her the way he did. Ranulf, Pearl, and Charlie aside, he'd never worried about the opinion that another witch carried for him.

Why now?

Because Isadora mattered, as little as he wanted it to be true.

Pearl set her hands in her lap, a troubled expression on her face. Her lack of immediate, soothing, reassurances spoke worlds to his instinct. Indeed, Isadora would hold a grudge.

He hated himself for it. For what she went through. Tried to tell himself that death was a natural part of life, and she'd better get used to it, but it didn't help. Memories of Mere, Pere, even Ranulf, flittered through his mind.

No. One never *got used to it*.

"I feel regret it had to happen that way," he continued, "but I did what I must in order to protect her."

His walls returned with sturdy strength around his heart. He let them grow, deepen. Pearl watched with a troubled brow, as if she saw what was happening and felt regret for it, too.

"Eventually," Pearl said, "she will understand."

Max tightened his jaw, took that in with a nod, and said, "Thank you, Pearl. I'm glad you're well. You know where to find me if you need anything. Now, I have a mess to clean up. The Advocate believes we've bought ourselves a little time before Leo strikes again, but he will strike. The fate of Alkarra rests on a couple of hot headed Highest Witches and an idiot."

Pearl smiled, eyes sparkling.

"Sounds like a fun challenge for you to fix, my boy."

With a scowl, Max transported away. Indeed, *he* wouldn't fix it. Charlie would, but Max would get the credit.

Oh, how he tired of this game.

Chapter Thirty-Six

CHARLIE

6 months later

The High Witch of Ashleigh Covens peered at Max and Isadora's retreating forms as they stepped out of Charlie's office, a bemused expression on his face.

Lucey and Charlie stood on either side of the High Witch. A feeling of uncertainty—one could almost call it amusement—clouded the air.

"Well," the High Witch murmured. "I don't think I've ever handfasted a couple that seemed so reluctant. She wasn't a real happy bride, was she?"

The question remained unanswered. Charlie couldn't help a twitch of his lips. The very *idea* of Max being handfasted almost made him laugh. As both Isadora and Max took a great deal of responsibility in hand by volunteering to go to the Southern Network and represent the Central Network, however, the idea required far more solemnity than he wanted to give.

"I think," Lucey said slowly, hands folded in front of her,

"that Isadora might be the only witch who could do this with him."

Charlie canted an eyebrow with a beaming smile worthy of Charles himself. "You think so?"

"Hmmm."

She nodded, deep in thought.

Charlie folded his hands behind his back as the High Witch made a few apologies for having to leave and bustled toward the door. Charlie walked him out with his usual prattle, but felt the depths of the screen that such conviviality truly was. The High Witch left, a relieved appearance on his face as soon as he made it to the hall.

Witches couldn't wait to get away from a High Priest who loved to chat. Never failed.

Once the door closed, Lucey spoke again. "Do you think they'll be able to do it, High Priest?"

"No one's better than Max! Isadora's such a lovely witch. She doesn't take his guff, either. You know her better than me. What's your assessment?"

Lucey pressed her lips together for a moment, then nodded. "Isadora comes from a good family, with high morals. She's willing to voice her opinion, even though that wasn't a tenant of her childhood. She does seem to irritate him, though," she added with a dry smile.

Charlie laughed, thoroughly amused.

"I think they'll be fine," she concluded. "It will be interesting, however. I never thought a woman could unseat Max, but I believe we've found the one that could."

"A wonder she is, too."

Lucey straightened, releasing a sharp breath.

"Please, High Priest, do let me know if I can be of assistance. Maximillion told me that you're privy to the Advocacy and all its . . . work. If anything comes up while Maximillion is gone, I've agreed to run most of the behind-the-scenes work while he's in the Southern Network."

"Most kind of you!" he cried, then motioned toward an array of plants that lined the window. They looked meager in the low winter light. "I have a few meetings, and will be busy here with my garden, but yes. I'll keep you informed should anything appear."

A hint of annoyance—perhaps even a question—filtered through her unfettered gaze.

"Thank you, High Priest. I would appreciate the help. Maximillion has taught you how we send messages?"

He almost laughed again. The criteria for sending messages had been his own. Instead, he responded with due gravity.

"Yes, of course." He patted his vest pockets. "I have the instructions written somewhere."

Her gaze flared with shock, but he held up a placating hand.

"No, no. Not here. At my apartment, where no one could access it. I'd never write those things down here for others to find. Max forbade it."

Relief filtered back through. She nodded, only slightly mollified. Her discomfort lay palpable in the air, but he pretended not to notice.

"Well, thank you, High Priest. I better be going. Witches to check on, and all that."

He smiled. "Very good. Thank you! We'll see if Isadora gives Max the run of his life, eh?"

A half-hearted smile appeared as she edged toward the door, gave a wave, and stepped outside. The silence rebounded in her absence. He closed his eyes, breathed deep, grateful that confrontation was over with.

Like Max, Lucey had developed a straightforward way of interacting with witches in all the years that had passed since she stumbled into the Advocacy. Indeed, she'd been the turning point.

Without Lucey and her willingness to heal witches, step up to stop all the injustices, the Advocacy may have never taken off. He owed her prodigiously for realizing his dream.

She might never know it.

The temptation to shuck aside the mask, tell Lucey everything, and thus gain her genuine respect, nearly overcame him. It wasn't often that he felt the need for approval. The Advocacy required him to sacrifice a certain level of his pride in order to run it. He'd long ago accepted that.

Sometimes, though, he wanted to be seen.

Craved it.

Without Faye, all of this would have been utterly unbearable.

His mind moved on to Max and Isadora in the Southern Network. To a certain Head of Guardians in the Eastern Network that had been lying low for too many months. Cecelia died half a year ago. In that time, the Eastern Network had stopped all Defender attacks on Watchers.

The lull of safety had been welcome.

Now?

It felt downright suspicious.

Charlie cleared his throat, checked his calendar. With Max gone, he'd have to pretend his way through meetings, then help actual results realize for the Network without being tied back to him. A good deal of Max's messages from Council Members would route to him through a spell. They'd never know they spoke with him, not the Ambassador.

For now?

As it should be.

His next meeting started in two hours, which gave him just enough time to do a little exploring.

* * *

Charlie sat on the edge of a roof, legs dangling.

He hid under an invisibility spell, though the bright sunlight would make it almost impossible to spot him, with the way it shone off the white stucco. A cool breeze drifted off the ocean, twining his way. He closed his eyes, breathed deeply.

Lovely.

Ahead of him lay a sprawling mansion. Two stories, with a turret-like front that boasted several spires and a man with a constantly roaming gaze. Not an active Guardian, as not even Leo could post Guardians at his private residence. Charlie wagered this witch had retired from the Guardian force, then switched to work privately for Leo.

Which begged the question: what did Leo have to fear?

Or *whom*?

Behind the Guardian waited a quiet house with closed windows and a tomb-like interior. Not a hint of movement within. A maid left out the back door and disappeared half an hour ago. Leo wasn't at his office, and La Torra had been all but deserted, save for two Guardians watching the prisoners in the depths of the top floor.

Where are you, Leo? Charlie thought.

Gulls cawed, pecking at discarded food not far away. In the distance, to the south, lay Magnolia castle, resplendent against the giant sky and constant waves. The crash of the surf reminded him of Faye.

Did her home in the Western Network stretch along the sea?

Did she miss it?

His thoughts meandered there only a moment before he turned back to the house. Still no movement.

Well, time to confirm.

With a spell, he transported into the house, landing invisibly and silently. A cursory glance clarified Leo ran a tight ship. No pleasantries cluttered the walls or empty shelves. A table, two chairs occupied the floor space near the kitchen, with only a white tablecloth to provide a splash of color against the hardwood floor. Near the hearth lay a stack of firewood.

Charlie used a hovering spell to avoid creaking boards and moved to the other side of the room. If the Guard upstairs had any worth, he'd detect Charlie's magic soon. With such a barren space, it wouldn't take him long to encompass whatever hid here.

Nothing downstairs.

No stirring from the roof.

Charlie hovered up the stairs to find mostly-empty rooms. Several swords hung on a wall near a cracked shield protected by a glass case. He hurried past. Those wouldn't be all that important. Upstairs, he discovered a similar state of lacking life.

A faint stirring in the air meant a door, or a window had opened elsewhere. The stairs above him groaned so faintly he almost didn't notice. Charlie froze, turned an ear toward the sound. The Guard had noticed him, then.

He didn't use another spell to avoid layering the magic. Instead, he rushed to the final room.

Charlie swept his way into Leo's personal quarters on the same spell. The sound of a groaning stair, quickly silenced by a spell, followed.

No rumpled bed.

No scattered clothes.

Not a hint of shaving soap or fresh razors or even a chamberpot abandoned. No life, whatsoever.

Leo wasn't here.

So where was he?

Charlie transported out as the scuff of a foot came near the landing. For good measure, he transported several times, splashing into water, the heart of sand dunes, and eventually back to Letum Wood.

He shook the sand free, rubbing it from his strands of hair, and waited. The forest soothed him as he fell into concerned thought.

Where *was* Leo?

He returned to the castle, unrolled a hidden map. Candlelight bounced to life around him, casting shadows. He bent over his desk, peered at Alkarra. For years, he'd been tracking Leo's movements. Noted each spot he found him, and for how long. La Torra, Magnolia, home. Those had been his three principal places to sleep, though he traveled the Network. Particularly the borders, where Guardians amassed.

Charlie trailed his finger around the triangular markers. He'd go to each and check, of course. The Advocate was always thorough.

He had a feeling he wouldn't find Leo that way.

Where had he gone, and why?

A letter popped into view. Folded a specific way, with a slight tear near the bottom left. A message from the Advocacy to the Advocate. Lucey's handwriting. With a spell to close all the drapes in the room, seal the door, he sank into a chair.

His heart fluttered.

Found Defenders in the clans of the Southern Network. Not yet turned against Watchers. Sending two of our Defenders to them now to see if we can prevent them from falling to the East.

No signature, as always.

He scrawled his reply along the bottom before sending the message back to Lucey.

Very good.

Charlie leaned back, stared at the fire, and fell into deep thought. Where was Leo?

And why was he hiding?

Chapter Thirty-Seven

MAXIMILLION

"Tell me, Max. How is married life?"

Max glared.

Charlie laughed.

The robust sound further soured Max's mood. A thousand other questions about Network affairs and Advocacy meetings and other issues cluttered his mind. He wanted to ask them all, remove the weight off his chest, but there were too many. With the pressure of Southern Network negotiations and Advocacy concerns, too much ground to cover existed.

Yet Charlie asked about married life?

As if Charlie read his mind, he blew a raspberry. "All business is taken care of, Max. I've been attending to all the Network correspondence in your name, as well as the Advocacy. Lucey is far more on top of Advocacy business than *you* are. Given the opportunity, I might put her in charge instead of you next time."

"Please, feel free."

Charlie continued as if he hadn't spoken. "Lucey keeps me

apprised of a few things, even as she loathes me . . . well, she loathes Charles. She's very careful to message the Advocate in thorough detail. All that is to say . . . I can't find Leo. Though I only have an hour to look per day. The Network continues on, and all is well."

Max snorted. "Lucey doesn't loathe Charles. She just doesn't respect him."

"Same thing, if you ask me. Regardless, focus on what you're doing in the South. Let me know if you have questions. I sent you some ideas about diplomatic suggestions. Did you receive them?"

"Yes. They were good."

"I know." Charlie grinned. "I'll keep searching for Leo. The minute I find him, we'll capture him, stop this foolish Watcher-chasing business, and question him. Though we should consider that he might be out of our hair now, Max. For all I know, he's dead."

"Don't hold your breath. Another Head of Guardians hasn't been appointed."

Charlie frowned. "Which is what is so perplexing. How can a Head of Guardians disappear?"

"I haven't any idea. It's plausible that he knows he's our next target. Having removed Cecelia, he's wise to fear for his life."

Charlie waved it off. "I'll find it out . . . somehow."

"And Wildrose?"

He couldn't keep the quiet fear from his voice. Charlie chuckled at his concern, as he knew he would.

"Fine."

"Nothing amiss?"

"No," he said, laughing. "You'd think me incapable of running my own ancestral home, the way you say it, Max. Goodness."

"And you?"

"Fine, Max! Go. Go back to your lovely wife and pretend to have a real life. The type that most witches crave. You never know. Isadora could be the one."

Another scathing glare did nothing to stem Charlie's amusement, a fact Max highly rejected. No, Isadora would never want him. He'd thoroughly stopped that from ever happening.

"Next week, Your Highness, you are invited to a ball and dinner."

"I have it on the calendar."

"You'll make it?"

"I shall."

"Be careful. Watch out for Pearl?"

"Always."

* * *

"Is something on your mind?" Isadora asked, hands held to the warm flames. The turret at Zamok Castle held the two of them in a tight grasp. He hated the circular walls, the heights, the darkness.

He loathed the Southern Network.

Energy coursed through his body, borne out of sheer nerves. Observations, thoughts, concerns cluttered his mind. The last week had moved like a weird dream. In front of the delegation, he established tenants of his plan for the Central Network, one concept at a time.

Vasily spoke up often enough during the multi-Network discussions. He appeared to have genuine interest. Dante contributed too much for Max's taste, but it wasn't his responsibility to tell the High Priest to close his mouth.

Dostar said almost nothing, unless forced, and Max couldn't decide *which* was more irritating.

Almost as grating as his own concepts proven moot by

Dostar today. The Central Network needed Charlie here to represent them. He had a brilliant mind for strategy and dealing with difficult personalities. Though Max agreed they must uphold the integrity of the Advocacy, it didn't change him not wanting to be here.

He stood, legs jittery.

"Dostar made an excellent point today. My plan to deal with the black-market witches will never work. I hate it when he does that."

Isadora chuckled quietly. "Glad you've realized it. Now what?"

"Sending witches to the dungeons if they've crossed the border will only burden us. We can't have borders so strict that prisoners can't return. That would leave us to feed or kill whatever witches are desperate enough to cross. We have to send them back. But there are too many holes in that. I have to figure out an alternative."

Pacing didn't help. He wanted to loosen his cravat, but had more social affairs to deal with today.

Drat responsibility.

"Would you like some special help?" she asked.

He scowled. The word *special* meant his aunt Serafina. If he said yes, Isadora would quietly let Serafina know he required an audience with her. No, he didn't need Serafina to give him any ideas.

That time might come soon enough.

"Not yet," he growled. "We can puzzle this out easily enough."

A tap sounded. Isadora turned around and called, "Come in!" A tray entered the room with a spell. Max turned away, lost in the tenants he'd present tomorrow, while Isadora lifted the platter lid.

"A little food may help you feel better. Come. Eat. The brown bread is crusty and delicious with soup, no doubt."

"No."

He stiffened when she put her hands on his shoulders and forced him to the closest chair. Her touch created a whirl storm of exquisite agony.

"You're unbearable when you're hungry and stumped. Then we can talk this out together."

Questions built behind her inquisitive eyes. Before the conversation gained any speed, a knock interrupted it.

"Who is it?" he called.

"Visitor for you, sir," said a maid. Max motioned Isadora to stay. As he rose back to his feet, he reached into his jacket. The end of a knife waited at the tip of his fingers as he closed the space between him and the door.

"Coming."

Once there, he glanced back in silent question. Perplexed, but calm, Isadora nodded. By some miracle, she'd listened and hadn't followed. He reached for the doorknob, pulled it open. A smallish maid with light hair and invisible brows stood there.

Lucey stood behind her.

A storm appeared to have ravaged his friend. Her face was pale. With each inhale, she winced. Her eyes barely met him before gazing away. Fear and panic washed through him.

"Thank you," he said to the maid. "She's welcome."

Lucey stepped inside, greeted Isadora, then scuttled back. Max surveyed her over Isadora's calls of concern.

Something was wrong.

Dread settled into his gut when Lucey finally turned her full attention to him. "I'm sorry for this."

"Not at all. What happened?"

"I-I came as soon as I could."

Isadora fetched a chair with a gentle command for Lucey to sit. Lucey complied, lost in thought for several moments. Her pale face trembled slightly, hands loose.

"It's the Advocacy," she finally said, through half a gasp. "I-I just came from the rendezvous point."

Max crouched next to Lucey, a gentle hand on her arm.

"What happened?"

"Around the time you left, rumors of a resurgent group of roaming Defenders circulated. I sent out a notice to all Advocacy members, but nothing happened, so I didn't tell you. All the reports came back fine. Everything has been . . . so quiet since La Torra. A note came from one of our Advocacy members in Berry just an hour ago."

"Sophie?"

Lucey nodded.

"*Sophie*?" Isadora cried, pale. "As in Miss Sophia's School for Girls?"

"Yes," Max muttered in vexation. "What did she say?"

"I don't know!" Lucey said. "You know Sophie. It was something vague and cryptic about *birds* and *flowerpots* or something inane like that. I went to check it out, and she . . . she was . . . she was already gone."

His eyes widened.

Lucey nodded in affirmation. "Dead. Someone destroyed everything. Not a board of the old school remains. Not even that horrible shack she lived in. Nothing."

* * *

The old school lay in a charred pile of ruins.

Max surveyed the former Miss Sophia's School for Girls with a pit in his stomach. Advocacy members had already come by and removed Sophie's body. The devastation appeared complete.

Utterly destroyed.

He ruminated on the attack, his thoughts tugged back to the Southern Network.

Why would Defenders surge now?

An itch took him back to Chatham Castle, just outside the High Priest's office. All lay deceptively quiet here, despite what chaos must wage within the Advocacy now. He tapped with his knuckles.

"High Priest?"

A shuffle. Charlie's steps moved closer to the door, then paused. It opened an inch a moment later. Surprise, but not that much of it, filled his gaze. He pulled the door open and quietly said, "Come in, Max."

He already knew.

Charlie shut the door behind them, sealed it with a spell while Max charged into the room. For a full minute, Max paced with all the grace of a bull. Lampshades clattered. Quills trembled. He didn't care. He strode past the desk a twelfth time and let his thoughts run out.

He had no love for Sophie, but felt regret that they should slaughter her in such a way. The misery in Charlie's gaze showed a similar sentiment.

"Yes," Charlie said a bit needlessly, "I am aware of what's happened. I was only just informed. Several messages from Advocacy members. It's not just Sophie. Raids are popping up here and there. Brutal ones."

As he spoke, more messages arrived.

"You think it's Leo," Max said.

"Who else?"

"Rogue Defenders, Lucey said."

Charlie shrugged. "Perhaps."

"They're easily enough subdued, Charlie. Not indicative of anything with Leo."

"They murdered Sophie. There was no capture. Sophie was a warning, and I expect more to come."

The thought sent a shiver of darkness down his spine.

"I see."

Charlie sat on the edge of a chair, elbows propped on his knees, hands clasped at his lips. Max continued pacing, too full of thoughts to iron them out.

"I'll deal with this, Max," Charlie said, straightening. "This is my fight, not yours. Return to the Southern Network, but first give me a quick update. Anything I should know about?"

"It's been two weeks of negotiations," Max said, peeved. "We've hardly made any headway. Dante occupied far too much time presenting his inane plan. Now Dostar is attempting a different one, and it's all the disaster I expected."

"But is there hope?"

"Minimal."

"Then we continue."

He bent Charlie a long-suffering glare that he hoped would quell the relentless optimism. Charlie met it without apology or change of expression.

Blast Charlie's ability to ignore his wrath.

"Max, we have to press toward hope. I know you don't like it, and they're difficult personalities to negotiate with, but any chance of peace we will foster. Not just for the Network, but for the Advocacy. In peace talks, we can advocate for Watchers differently."

Duly reminded, Max mentally backed down. He didn't like it, but he had no counterpoint to give. There had been no reason nor time to prepare one. Charlie stood, clapped Max on the shoulder.

"Keep at it. It'll shake out. While you distract them, I'll take care of Leo."

Max frowned. "Where do you think he is?"

"Not sure, but I have ideas."

"Has something else happened?"

Charlie's hesitation meant that yes, something *had* happened, but not enough to burden Max with the details.

"Go back to the South, Max. Isadora will be worried. Tell her the Advocate is personally looking into it."

CHARLIE

Charlie stopped first at Wildrose.

Slate gray snow clouds, thick as ice cream, hung overhead in tempestuous promise. An icy wind drove through his thick wool coat. He'd transformed to his usual Advocacy disguise.

No one spoke to him as he strode down the basement hall, headed toward the bookshelf at the end that hid headquarters. Tonight, it lay open, bridging the worlds. Rarely did Faye allow such a thing to happen, but Charlie recognized everyone here. They were all trusted, sworn members.

Watchers cluttered the room. Open doors revealed some of them grouped together, talking in low tones. One woman cried softly, handkerchief to her cheek, while a young man soothed her with murmurs. Charlie caught the words *Sophie* and *not safe* before he sped by.

Bodies packed headquarters with Lucey amid them. She stood on the largest table, speaking over outcries. She had transformed herself into a woman that, frankly, looked only slightly different from her true form. Darker hair, fuller cheeks, and a taller body, but little else altered.

Not enough energy, perhaps? Her gray pallor, saggy eyes, testified to a harder night than he expected.

Why did she appear so ragged?

"Please," she called. "Our headquarters manager, Faith, will give out room assignments. Be patient as the Advocate and I work through this."

A transformed Faye stepped up next to her. With a bark, she commanded silence. Lucey's gaze caught his as he approached, but soon dropped it. No, she'd assume he was just another Watcher.

Lucey left.

"We have room assignments for the evening, and food on the way. Water is in the second door, on the right. Please, use the same cup."

Faye briefly looked his way. A moment of relief appeared in her expression before she continued on, in an altered tone, as if nothing was out of the ordinary.

Minutes later, the uneasy crowd dispersed. Well-known Advocacy members, hidden in their transformative disguises, helped calm hysterical Watchers as they passed into the basement of Wildrose. Charlie waited until Faye approached. Only a few witches milled around by the time she waded her way through.

"Do you have a moment?" she asked. Her lips pressed into a thin line. She carried a handful of opened scrolls, behind which she hid a hand.

The hand trembled.

He nodded.

She beckoned with a wave of her fingers, and he followed her into the hall.

* * *

Faye's shoes clacked a crisp staccato on the stairs as they climbed to the master bedroom on the top floor.

Charlie couldn't help but think of Papa as they passed through the wooden double doors and into the master suite. Normally, he only came to these rooms in Wildrose to see Faye and meet with Max. Occasionally, he'd transform and slip into headquarters to listen. Mostly, he avoided all Advocacy members, and focused on Faye.

Darkness coated the room. Only a filmy, muted light came from outside the windows, filtering through sheer drapes. Frost etched a twirling design along the edge of the shivery panes.

Charlie removed the transformative magic while Faye waved a hand toward the hearth. Fire sprang to life on a waiting stack of dry firewood. The tang of smoke and sap filled the room seconds later. In the middle of the floor, she spun around.

An envelope sat in her shaking hand.

"This arrived."

Charlie reached for it, filled with dread. "A note?"

She nodded once.

"Why do you appear so frightened by it?"

"I think I know who it's from. Tonight, I felt them. The magical signatures that I've detected outside Wildrose? They were here again. Outside the manor. This envelope was on the top step just . . . waiting."

Charlie tore through Big Leo's wax seal and flipped the envelope open.

Dear Advocate,

. . .

I feel it is necessary to bring a cessation to our war. I believe we all grow battle-weary. Your Watcher friend, Sophie, is the first of many who shall die over the next ten days.

We know all your Watchers. We know where they live. Where their children live. Most importantly, we know where you live.

Wildrose will not be a safe place for them if you don't surrender yourself. The murders will stop when we have you.

Sincerely,
  Leo Giuseppi

Charlie resisted the urge to crumble the note in his palm.

Lovely.

His mind raced with questions, ideas as he passed the note to Faye. She read it, trouble brewing in her expression, until she handed it back.

"Charlie," she drawled.

The terror in her voice drew him out of his thoughts.

"I have no intention of surrendering myself yet, Faye. We can . . . strategize our way out of this, while still preserving life for everyone involved. Give me a second to think, then we can discuss my plan."

Faye didn't move. She stared, wide-eyed, as he shuffled closer to the hearth. Charlie stood at the crackling fire, one hand on the ledge. The heat rolled over him in a languid, calming way that allowed his thoughts more freedom.

Max.

He *needed* Max.

No, this couldn't leak out to anyone. Only he and Faye could know about this contact from Leo, lest panic break out. More lay at stake than just the Advocacy. With inter-Network negotiations ongoing, the fate of the entire Central Network lurked in the fringes.

Undoubtedly, Leo planned to out the Advocate while the peace negotiations continued in the Southern Network. Likely to discredit Max's assertions, potentially remove the Central Network from the voting, and allow Dante greater control over outcomes.

One question flared brighter than the rest: did Leo know the Advocate's identity?

Or did he have a strong suspicion?

Leaving a message at Wildrose didn't mean he knew about Charlie, or even headquarters. It might have been a wild guess. If Charlie didn't act carefully, he would play into Leo's hands.

For weeks, Charlie had unsuccessfully attempted to find Leo, but to no avail. Wily old witch hid himself just in time. Not only could they have come after him after breaking Cecelia, but at any moment after. Leo was the last pillar in their Watcher defensive tactics.

Dante knew this.

Just as both Leo and Dante must know that the only way to break the Advocacy was to find and break the Advocate. They might have trails that led them to Wildrose, but barring a traitor, they'd have only supposition.

Certainly, they didn't know *him*.

He had to stall. Buy the Central Network time to work out the peace agreements and also stop Watchers from losing their lives. The Advocacy had to be faster, and more clever, than Leo and his Defenders.

"Of all the times," he muttered, shaking his head. Of course. Of *course*, Leo pushed to make a move now. The Central Network unwittingly leaned on Charles, the Advocacy on Charlie, and no one even knew it. Two behemoth stones pressed on him from either side, and he trembled from the weight.

Charlie turned. Faye hadn't moved. Her soulful, frightened gaze remained riveted on him. Beneath the teeming fear, he caught a hint of her resilience. Her stubborn endurance against difficulties.

"We tell no one about this letter, we gather the Advocacy, and we find Leo," Charlie whispered. "That's what we're going to do. It's time for the Advocacy to rise as one in our own power to make this happen."

The troubled expression didn't fade.

Faye clenched her hands in fists, closed her eyes, and pulled in a breath. Several seconds paused in which she stood like a statue before her eyes fluttered back open. Resolve filled her again.

"What can I do?"

Charlie forced a calm smile. "I'm going to give you a list of Advocacy members that I want to help me search for Leo. If possible, we can force a confrontation with him on *our* terms. Then, I want you to choose six Watchers that you trust and have them spread the word. We want every Watcher to come to Wildrose. Every single one. Not just the basement, but all of it. We're going to have to fill it up in order to keep everyone safe."

"But . . . what will that do?"

"We'll have a whole manor of Watchers, Faye! As one, we direct each other and use all their abilities to our advantage. We can do this by anticipating what could happen. Combined, we can keep others safe, watch ahead. Together. *This* is what I made the Advocacy for."

"But then they'll know about Wildrose and headquarters and—"

He held up the envelope.

"Leo already does."

Energy infused Charlie again. He leaned into the ideas populating through his mind like wisps of the past. If he had more time, he'd search to see if the potential for something like this had ever happened before.

Besides, if all Watchers congregated here, it would force Leo to do something desperate. Using the paths, they could predict what he'd do. The Advocacy simply had to pull together, make Leo truly irate, and buy Max time to negotiate in the Southern Network.

Faye sighed.

"Very well. I'll get to work."

Charlie grinned.

"If Big Leo is going to pick a fight, tell the Advocacy that we are going to be ready. The Advocate has spoken. I will be amongst them."

* * *

The door to Charlie's Chatham Castle office opened with a creak. He cast a spell to hide the Advocacy letter he wrote, reached for a magnifying glass with his right hand, and lifted it up with his head as he peered up.

His Assistant, a girl named Cherry, stood in the doorway with a *Chatham Chatterer* scroll in hand. She startled, no doubt shocked by the size of his eye, and held out the scroll.

"Your updates for the day, Your Highness."

Charlie turned back to his desk. Plants lay on top, scattered leaves of different varieties, accompanied by blank paper and a pot of sticky glue near his left hand. He pretended fascination with a rare leaf out of the Southern Covens.

"Thank you, Chalaine."

"Cherry, sir."

"Right, so sorry. Once I finish this identification, I will be ready for our next meeting. You can leave the scroll there, please."

"Your next meeting is not until four o'clock, Your Highness."

"Yes, yes. Very good."

Cherry closed the door behind her. Once she left, he sealed it with an incantation and summoned the still-floating scroll to his hand. The top headline caught his attention.

FIRE OUTBREAK IN WESTERN COVENS

A suspected arsonist set fire to several homes in the Western Covens yesterday evening. They immediately quelled the conflagrations thanks to buckets of water waiting in the backyard that were ready, "just in case," according to a local witch.

With repairs to the roofs, no lasting harm was done. The houses were empty.

Ah, of course.

Another successful thwarting of Defender attempts. Charlie grabbed a knife, dragged it down the side of the article to cut it out. Doing so ruined the scroll—which is why he ordered a new one every day. Cherry's exasperated face whenever he asked for another *Chatterer* scroll showed her annoyance. She assumed he lost them each time.

Once the article cut free, he pulled the others out of his drawer and set it with those he'd collected over the last five days.

ATTEMPTED ABDUCTION

Attempted abductors of a fourteen-year-old boy were caught while trying to drag him away from his home. Two witches wrestled them to the ground before they disappeared into a spell.

Renditions drawn below.

They appear to be of Eastern Network origin. Ilese was spoken amongst them.

HOME ATTACKED BY ROGUE CRIMINAL

Malcolm, father of five, states that two men attempted to break into his home. "They spoke with Eastern Network accents, had their swords drawn, and used magic to break my doorknob."

Malcolm fought them off with a burning torch and a "hunch that they'd try to head to the stairs first."

Three other waiting armed household members cut them off, forcing the criminals to flee.

If you have more information, please visit your local High Witch.

MISSING WITCH

Cordelia James of the Northern Covens would like to put out an alert on her friend, Alice, who went missing four days ago.

"Just up and left! Not a sign of her. She always had the most accurate weather reports, and we'd like to know where she went."

According to Miss James, Alice has, "Light blond hair the color of straw, an eye that's pale blue, and one that's darker blue and also green."

Contact your local High Witch for any information.

. . .

Eight successfully thwarted Defender attacks lay at their back. One per day, at first, but increasing desperation seemed to lead Leo to act more quickly. All Watchers, working with non-Watcher Advocacy volunteers, quelled the violence. Max gave no sign that he knew of the underlying machinations.

So far, so good.

But nothing lasted forever.

Leo had to be fuming, and Faye's management of so many witches hung by a precarious thread. Watchers packed Wildrose Manor. Every day, one or two more arrived, though they'd long since reached the capacity of known Watchers. Watchers from the West, the South, even one in the North, found Wildrose. One could barely think with all the noise and bodies.

Charlie flipped the article over, scrawled a note across the back, and sent it to Faye.

Keep an eye out. Send updates my way. No news from Max, but I won't pressure him. Dante is no doubt attempting his own path to getting power. We have to balance this from both sides.

Five days down.

Who knew how many more to go?

Chapter Thirty-Nine

MAXIMILLION

Frost coated the veranda of Zamok Castle. The glittery layer glimmered in tones of brightest white, almost blue, and enveloped every available space. Beyond the veranda lay the tundras of the Southern Network. Vast, barren swaths of land he'd rather not spend time looking at.

Snow twirled onto his shoulders, his hair. The bitter cold of days before had faded, leaving a subtle warmth behind. Still, not *warm*. Not like summers in the East, when the air thickened to the point of hot, painful gasps.

Max held onto a banister, felt the cold stone bite against his palms. It grounded him apart from the whirling dances inside. The shuffling feet, murmured voices, fake laughter. Even the stuffy candlelight felt overwhelming and dense.

Here, he breathed more deeply.

Freely.

Isadora stood at his side in a contemplative quiet. For having just inspired his deepest jealousy while dancing with Charlie—of all witches—she seemed nonplussed. Perhaps she frequently, and intentionally, inspired such baser reactions in other male witches.

The thought made his jaw tense.

"Can I ask you a question?"

Her query, so boldly stated, was more a demand than anything else. No, he didn't want to answer questions. Yet, he couldn't bring himself to refuse her. Max lifted a hand as a signal to continue.

Meanwhile, he tried to draw some courage.

"That night on Carcere . . . were you afraid of me?"

His stomach twisted. The good gods, *that* was her question? She wanted to discuss the evening when Defenders strapped both of them to seven-pointed stars and soaked the wood in flammable liquid?

Consequently, the day Isadora seemed to truly grasp her power. Max, as well. He felt the magic in her. Deep, eternal pools of it. Enough to frighten anyone, Isadora included.

Of course, he'd been terrified.

Of *losing* her.

"Yes, but not for the reason you're thinking."

Isadora fell silent.

Without question, he owed her more than he'd given. Both of them had been forced into a situation that neither asked for, but that didn't mean he had to be a cad. Isadora had been gracious during his foul tempers.

And perhaps a small corner of him wanted to give her more.

"Serafina is my aunt. My mother was her younger sister. The two of them were close at one point. Reputedly, anyway. My mother died when I was young, so I rely solely on the recollections of other people."

Isadora stiffened, but didn't breathe a word.

"My mother's name was Maria. She lived in the slums, working as a flower girl—even lower in status than a *lavanda* maid. She would find flowers in the fields, then try to sell them. A difficult enough job in the summer, it left her starving in the winter. When the call issued from Magnolia Castle that the High Priest was searching for his son's future wife under the Law of Vittoria, my mother and Serafina both tried to get his attention. Serafina, with an interest in politics and an extensive education pushed by her father, Mansfeld, despite their poverty, succeeded. My mother had never held on to a thought for more than a few seconds. Flighty, they called her, but passionate."

Max drew in a breath through his nose, tipped his head back to the night sky. The good gods, but he'd never spoken this out loud.

Not even to Charlie.

When he looked at Isadora, he saw the young girl that haunted his future paths for so many years, and he wondered if there wasn't a deeper reason for it. If her appearance in his life, for so long, wasn't a weird twitch of the magic but a statement.

Tonight, garbed in such a dazzling array, with her exquisite features wholly focused on him, he couldn't help but wonder if *he* would ever be enough.

"Desperate with jealousy," he continued, "my mother married a hotheaded man named Antonio. She became pregnant with me and missed the Network-wide handfasting of Serafina and Dante. The two sisters rarely spoke afterward. My mother died not long after my seventh birthday. After her death, Antonio, already a difficult, belligerent, *angry* witch, became nearly unmanageable. I attended Mere's funeral, prepared to ask Serafina to save my life by taking me away. She never came."

He heard the ghost in his own whisper and felt the shocking reality yet again. The gaping hole that existed in his chest afterward, as he stared into the endless chasm that housed his mere, nearly overwhelmed him again. Black earth swallowed her up, and the world moved on.

Max ran his bottom lip through his teeth, shook away the memory.

"She sent a letter saying that Dante wouldn't allow it and that she was sorry. I lived with Antonio until my twelfth birthday, when I finally hit him back. The blow broke his nose, shoved the bone into his brain, and killed him. After that, I ran away."

"And eventually found Pearl in Berry," she whispered.

Max nodded.

A pregnant pause followed. Relieved for a break, he sank into it, though he didn't have the courage to see her face. Would his past matter? Would she find parts of him loathsome? Antonio ran through his blood, he could never change that.

Which meant he could never trust himself wholly, either. Monsters lurked unseen everywhere.

"Emilia is your cousin, then," Isadora said.

The banal, safe topic brought a rush of relief.

"Yes."

"It makes sense now, seeing you. Seeing them. But I never would have guessed it otherwise. Do you miss your parents?"

Max snorted. "I only wish I'd killed my father sooner. To my memory, my mother was a jealous woman who wanted more than life had given her. Antonio had a knack for beating me when he was angry at her, so she distanced herself from me. But . . . she did care for me."

"Thank you for telling me."

He forced himself to meet her gaze. The strength it required almost cracked him in half. What if he saw disgust? Horror? Instead, he comprehended compassion. Perhaps a touch of respect. Surprise. Or maybe he just hoped to see such emotions.

She shuffled closer, placed a hand on his chest, near his beating heart. He didn't move, didn't breathe. Her warmth bled through his clothes, searing the skin beneath it. Tingles swept him from heart center to toes.

The good gods.

She'd never know the effect she held over him. He'd give anything to her.

"When I first started to learn the magic, it showed me something about you. I can ask to see a witch, and they appear before me. The magic then gives them a word. My sister, for example. Her word is *courageous.* Hardly surprising. Pearl's? *Goodness.* You were the first witch I saw. I'm not sure why it was you. It showed you as a broken, beaten little boy, then a furious teenager, then now. As a man."

"And?"

"Merciful."

The word nearly broke him.

Taciturn, focused, determined. Any of those he might have expected. He'd been called far worse and didn't care.

Merciful?

The truth touched him, even as it horrified him. How clearly did she see him? What depths existed to her access to the magic? If she truly had such visibility to witches and their core being, did she see the darkness of Antonio swirling in him?

Max wanted to turn away but Isadora cuddled into his chest, wrapped her arms around him. The caress of her breath against his neck as she spoke sent electricity firing all the way down his skin.

No one had ever held him before.

"You're not your father, or your mother. And, for what it's worth, the magic hasn't been wrong yet. I, for one, find you infuriating, impossible, and the most lovable man I've ever met. I don't know how you accomplished it, but you've done the impossible and risen above the ashes of your past. I think you're wonderful, Max, and I'm honored to be here with you."

The most lovable man I've ever met.

I think you're wonderful.

I'm honored to be here with you.

A joke, certainly. She couldn't be serious and actually mean something so . . . heartfelt.

About him.

For too long, Max debated over whether or not she could be sincere. He sensed no disingenuous emotion in her. No, Isadora wasn't that witch. She didn't have that ability.

Unable to help himself, Max placed his arm around her shoulder, pulling her closer. His eyes closed. He pulled in a breath, drank in her heady scent. Something subtle, but bold. Isadora responded in kind.

He clung to her.

Equal shots of misery and love coursed through him. He loved Isadora. He'd loved her the moment he discovered her in the forest, with those ridiculous purple bottles in her holey dress. All those years of seeing her in the magic, then in person.

Their training sessions.

Her sassy retorts.

The good gods, but he'd never loved anything more than her, and wasn't that the worst of it?

Love led witches to terrible decisions. Horrifying places. It wrenched away control, understanding, and security. Love is the reason that witches like his mother convinced themselves to be with men like Antonio.

Thoughts of his pere zapped him from the life-giving haze of Isadora. The crash of the door opening, and a trilling laugh, jolted Max. He stepped away, stunned.

What had she done to him?

Isadora peered at him, questions in her eyes.

No, she deserved better. A man that could tell her the same things back. That knew how to form love, to live in it. Max understood strategy and obligation and performance, and none of that had any place with love.

He had to make this easier for her.

"Your loyalty to your Network is appreciated, but you should know I'm not interested in love or happy endings."

Her lips parted.

He continued before he lost all ability to speak. The words choked out, barely viable from the depths of their frost.

"When this is over, we'll return to our lives as acquaintances. Our professional relationship can go back to the way it was, and you will be free to find a man who truly deserves you."

Rage filled her besotted gaze.

"If you think we can go back to what we were before, you're a bigger fool than I thought."

No, Max thought as he turned to go. *This will end entirely, and that is what's best for you.*

Chapter Forty

CHARLIE

Ice shivered down the length of Charlie's spine.

He trembled in his fur-lined coat and did a poor job of hiding it. Three witches stood in front of him, regarding him through thin eyes. One of them couldn't stop looking at Charlie's hair. The other hadn't blinked once, not even in this piercing chill.

Did *all* witches in the Southern Network have such famed tolerance to winter?

His teeth ached when he opened his lips to smile. None of them smiled back, and too late he remembered it as a sign of weakness. Charlie sucked in a sharp breath. Here, he didn't bother to transform much. His hair color, freckles, remained the same. He wore the traditional clothes of the Southern Network, but altered his facial structure.

"You are protecting Watchers?" he asked in *Yazika.*

The eldest, indicated by the plentiful wrinkles around a wind-worn face, nodded once.

"Why?"

None of them spoke. He waited, feeling it out for length. How long *could* they go without explaining anything?

Southern Network Advocacy members—all three of them —had been transporting to these Defenders to speak with them about Watchers, their powers, and the lies from the East. Once Leo re-entered the picture with his attacks, the Advocacy members lost contact with these men.

Charlie sought them out today to find out if they needed help, or if the seven Watchers they had been protecting had survived. Having thwarted most of Leo's attacks by pulling Watchers to Wildrose, some Advocacy members had wandered home, updated neighbors, and answered questions. Like Pearl, who kept zipping home to grab another romance novel or twelve.

The more fluid nature made Charlie nervous, but ten days had passed. He could hardly force them to stay at Wildrose, not with an unknown deadline looming in the future.

"We don't like the Eastern Network," one of them finally said. "The East doesn't like Watchers."

"They stole our friend," said the middle.

An icy fist of dread formed in Charlie's gut. "I'm sorry?"

"Yesterday."

Charlie swallowed a rise of panic. "Have you any idea where they went?"

The three shook their heads as one.

"No. The rest are safe."

"You're sure?"

Another mutual nod.

"Who was it?"

"Ch'pak."

Ch'pak. Charlie had met her only once, but Faye had regular correspondence with her. She'd been wary and uncomfortable in headquarters. With these vast, open tundras for a dwelling, who could blame her? Though headquarters had a high ceiling and a lot of light, it was an underground box.

"You fight?" the one on the right asked.

"Yes."

"We fight, too."

"Enemy of my enemy," Charlie murmured.

They didn't ask what that meant.

"Thank you for protecting the other six. Will you send me a message if you hear from Ch'pak? It's of utmost importance that we find her."

More nods.

Charlie tapped the side of his head. "You see the past?"

The one in the middle that still hadn't blinked nodded once. "We will protect the Watchers."

The other two said nothing.

Clearly, they weren't related. Their difference in their height, ranging from very short to taller than Charlie, was nearly comical. Varying face shapes, but similar black hair, gave each witch away as from the clans.

"Why do you protect them?" Charlie asked. "If you don't mind me asking. I want to make sure the Watchers are safe for more reasons than you hating the Eastern Network."

His translation was appropriately done, but perhaps not as well executed. Twice, he repeated himself before feeling satisfied that they understood what he meant.

Finally, one of them shrugged.

"It's enough."

Charlie, unsatisfied, but willing to accept whatever help they'd give, nodded once. "Thank you."

One of them lifted a thin eyebrow, rising against a wide forehead. "You are a past-seer."

"Yes."

"Powerful?"

"No."

The man narrowed his gaze, as if he didn't believe him, but said nothing else. Charlie took it for a good sign and shuffled back. The tallest one seemed to relax as he put space between them.

"If you need anything, please contact Cho. He will help you."

Another nonresponse. A letter popped up in front of Charlie, then another. He grabbed them both, then a third and fourth, recognizing Advocacy handwriting on all of them, with a lurch in his stomach.

Oh, no.

Correspondences sent that quickly, from more than one Advocacy member, could only spell out disaster. He collected all of them, stuffed them in his pockets, while the Southern Network witches regarded him with growing curiosity. He chuckled awkwardly as another appeared, and their annoyance deepened.

Pearl.

Not folded, no envelope. He couldn't help but see the single word when he snatched it out of the air.

Attack.

"Pleasure," he cried, then transported away.

Fear propelled the spell faster than usual, increasing the pressure. Leaving the Southern Network for the Central Network was no easy feat. The discomfort, breathlessness, heady sense of ripping apart time, made him stumble when he landed at Pearl's house.

All lay quiet within.

Heart slamming, he rushed to the back door. Through window panes, he caught sight of Pearl bustling around, rushing back and forth. She shoved food into a bag, followed by more clothes.

With a frown, he rapped on her back door. No need to transform. She knew Charlie helped with the Advocacy, just not to what extent. Hesitantly, she cracked the door open.

Seeing him, she pulled it the rest of the way, jerked him inside, and slammed it shut.

"What's happening?"

"Attacks," she cried, hustling as fast as her squat body would allow her. "There are Defenders infiltrating all over the Central Network. They're setting homes on fire, all of them. They're pulling witches out, too, but mostly destroying everything."

A stab of fear shot through his stomach.

"Go to headquarters, Pearl," he murmured with a hand on her shoulder. "The Advocate will take care of this."

With a distracted nod, she heaved the food onto her shoulder and disappeared. Several romance novels went with her, tossed in amongst the meager pile of bread and old tins of sardines. So little food circulated anymore. It was no wonder she came back.

Quickly, he dove into the other messages. Similar panicked words had come. The last one caught his eye. From Lucey

Advocacy infiltrated after a Watcher was tortured and gave some names. Defenders attacking in all Networks. It happened quickly. We're trying to locate and warn our members, as well as Watchers. Both are targeted. Will update you soon.

Heat, maybe fear, rose in Charlie's throat.

But how was it possible?

Ch'pak, perhaps?

Advocacy members weren't supposed to give their real names or faces. Then again, they might. He didn't deal with them every day. Hardly ever, truly. That rule might have been lazily applied outside of Wildrose, which led to circumstances like this.

Quickly, he ravaged Pearl's house. Knocked belongings over, scattered clothes, overturned mugs, plates. Any attacking Defender would pass by, assuming she was gone. Broken glass, torn sheets, scrawled scrolls. It was all he could do. Pearl would be safe at headquarters again.

For now, he had to give orders to Lucey and the others, secure whoever the Defenders tortured, and let Max know. This was no random attack or burst of hostility. Leo's final push had begun. However Charlie could manage it, the Advocate would confront Leo and stop this war once and for all.

Charlie left, Chatham Castle bound.

* * *

Messages bombarded Charlie.

With them, a death count.

Five.

Eight.

Sixteen.

Heart in his throat, he calculated twenty deaths so far. Attacks strung all over Alkarra, from the Central Network to the Western, executed all at once instead of stealthily. Wildrose overflowed again with Advocacy members and their families.

Faye, Lucey, they could manage it.

Carefully, he kept control over the flow of his responses. Sent orders to Lucey, commanded quills to write a general message to all Advocacy members. A warning, a command to gather at headquarters if they hadn't already.

His fingers itched to notify Max, but he stopped himself. Max had enough on his mind tonight with the first vote over plans to move forward with a peace treaty. The most important night of all the negotiations had finally arrived.

Escalating tensions around Dante and . . .

Later.

Once this resolved, he would update Max.

As he sent off the last response, prepared to transport away, and check on some lesser-known Watchers in the northern East, a knock came on his office door. Aiden, a Guardian he rather liked, stepped through. His heavy brows, nearly converging in the middle, knitted together.

"High Priest?"

"Ah . . . yes?"

"There's a woman here to see you."

"Woman?"

"Isadora, I believe?"

Shocked, Charlie strode across the room, opened the door. Isadora stood outside, eyes wide with fright, face pale but determined.

"By the good gods," he cried, "what are you doing here?"

"Your Highness, I apologize for the unexpected visit. If I may speak with you alone?"

Charlie nodded and stepped back to allow Aiden to return to the corridor. Isadora stepped demurely inside, chin high. He closed the door behind them, motioned her into the chair across from his desk.

"What can I do for you? Is Maximillion all right?"

"Fine. I came on . . . well, Advocacy business."

His initial surge of shock had since faded. If something were wrong with Max, she wouldn't have been so calm. The two might be in denial about their feelings for each other, but they'd never fooled him.

With a gentle smile, he said, "I assumed so."

"Why is that?"

"What can be done? Twenty deaths reported already."

She paled, eyes closed. When they opened again, she looked even more frightened. "I received the news. My contact said Defenders were on the rampage, killing Watchers. So I went to check on Pearl and . . . found her house ransacked."

A moment before it might have been too late, he reminded himself that Isadora didn't know. He was Charles, the High Priest.

Shock coated his reply as he jerked his shoulders back, eyes wide. Somehow, he sounded sincerely surprised.

"She's practically Max's mother!"

"Yes. There was no sign of her. I-I can't be sure whether she's been taken or—"

"Frightening. And you came here after?"

"Yes. I . . . I don't want to tell Max until we know more. I fear Dante has done this to distract him from his work there. The first vote was just cast, and Max's plan is up against Dante's. It makes sense that he'd be more desperate."

Relief that he and Isadora should see this the same way weakened him.

"Agreed," he murmured. "Max cares deeply for her. He would be distracted, at best. More likely livid. He's a man of impressive control until he's sufficiently goaded, and then he isn't."

Isadora wrung her hands as she said, "I would search for Pearl myself, but I can't, and I don't dare bother L—my contact, who has enough on her plate now. I thought since you are the High Priest . . ."

Lucey, he thought.

Oh, the intricacies of this web. Isadora did a fair job of maintaining secrecy, the way the Advocacy taught all members. Yet, she didn't know that there was nothing she could hide from him. That he, the idiot High Priest, remained the lynchpin behind all these careful machinations.

Her words rang through his mind. *I would search for Pearl myself.* Her genuine concern struck him.

How *much* he liked Isadora!

If only, in different circumstances, she could have known it all . . . they might have been friends. Max and Isadora, living with Faye and Charlie at Wildrose. With a shake of his head, he set aside those thoughts.

"I can take care of that," he said firmly. Isadora deserved some peace, else she wouldn't be able to support and help Max. Maintaining his position as Charles remained as instinctual as ever.

"Really?" she cried, her voice uplifting in shock.

He gave a wry smile that he couldn't help. "I may not be as efficient and useful as Max at these kinds of things, but I am kept apprised of the things happening in my Network. I shall seek out the Advocate and let them know."

Isadora's eyes widened. "What?"

Startled, he stared back at her. "Max hasn't told you who the Advocate is?"

"No."

He couldn't help his amusement. Of course Max hadn't. He'd known this, but enjoyed throwing Isadora even further off the track.

"It's hardly my place to tell you, as I'm only a small cog in the vast Advocacy machine. I'm sure Max will betray them. One day."

She nodded, albeit reluctantly. "Then will you let me know what the Advocate finds out about Pearl as soon as you can? In the meantime, I'll try to keep Maximillion focused. He doesn't know about any of this. I . . . I hate lying to him."

"Immediately. As soon as I receive word myself. In the meantime, I'll see that someone goes to her house and watches for further movement. You've done the right thing, Isadora, allowing Max to concentrate."

"Thank you, Your Highness. I can't tell you what it means."

Isadora swayed away with a steady clip until she reached the door, then stopped. She glanced back. He stood there, hands in his pockets, until she gave him a small smile.

Without another word, she slipped into the hallway. The moment the door closed, he flipped the lock, used a spell to draw all the drapes closed, and prepared to transport away. Just before he left, a message appeared. The familiar handwriting on the front sent a chill down his spine.

Leo.

He snatched it out of the air, slid the folded message open. All the blood in his body turned to slush.

We have your wife.

Chapter Forty-One

MAXIMILLION

Dante, that insufferable witch, preened like a rooster. Had the man any feathers, they'd bloat out in a wild array.

The altogether too-smug expression on his face made Max want to slap it off of him. He kept his fingers curled into his palm, trying not to worry about how unwell Isadora looked when he left the turret. To consider the cool detachment of her face when she asked not to come to the dinner. Feigned a headache.

Indeed, she didn't look well.

Then again, she hated him. Not that he could blame her all that much. His cold handling of her open heart the other night hadn't been fair. She genuinely attempted to be kind to him. Tell him how she felt honestly. She shared feelings he wanted to acknowledge, to experience, to feel himself.

Belonging.

Warmth.

A place to fall at the end of the day. Surety.

Also desperation. The lost sensation of abandonment. When emotions and stability and certainty came into play, disaster always followed. He couldn't go through that again.

Wouldn't.

Though Isadora tempted him more than any other witch in his lifetime.

With a frustrated growl under his breath, he turned his attention back to the insufferable dinner. Serafina watched him closely from the other side of the room. Like always, he avoided eye contact with her. Working with Serafina had been . . . revealing. Nice, to an extent. If he had contact with any blood relative, she wasn't the worst, despite his former beliefs about her. He had a particular fondness for her children, whom he saw now and then.

Emilia, especially.

The Southern Network High Priest, Vasily, sat at the head of the table to Max's left, looking for all the world like a squat, lordly High Priest set against a backdrop of tension. Diamonds glittered in a nauseating display of wealth and power along the tables. His wife, Arayana, appeared pale, as if worried about something.

All leaders of the Networks, aside from Dostar, who remained in the capital city, Custos, to deal with issues in the West, clustered around a circular table that brought them closer than usual. A boon, for it made tracking the tension in Dante's gaze simple.

This last-minute dinner was a farce. A chance for Dante to hear himself speak again, something the man should have had enough of thirty years ago. Dante pushed to his feet, wine glass held high.

"Might I say, High Priest, that this is a lovely night for us to come together? Thank you for hosting such phenomenal peace talks within your castle. Because of your gracious hospitality, we can pull together and unite Alkarra in a new way."

Max toyed with the stem of his wine glass, nauseated at the sound of Dante's voice. His hair stood up on edge, but he didn't know why. What *didn't* he see? When his instincts sat up, he usually listened.

"If you don't mind, Your Highness," Dante said. "I would like to tell all of you a story. One that you might not believe."

Serafina caught Max's gaze.

A note of panic underlined her pinched expression, which hit him with heavy force. Her eyes widened, head tilted slightly toward Dante. Max tapered his gaze in silent question. A clatter from behind drew his attention. All eyes in the room snapped to the double doors that led inside.

Isadora stood there, panting. Her shoulders heaved up and down. A high flush filled her face as she stared at him, then the rest in the room. Slowly, Max stood. All signs of a headache had left his wife.

Suspicion flared freshly.

Isadora's brow wrinkled in confusion. Her lips formed a question, though she said nothing. Unable to help himself, Max reached for her with a hand. He wanted her *out* of here. She needed to flee this strained room and the danger that lurked with such proximity to Dante . . .

Dante spoke before he could.

"Just as expected! Please, Mrs. Sinclair. Sit down and join us. I was regaling the company with a story you may enjoy. You look like you need to recover your . . . power."

Isadora froze.

A near-invisible movement almost drew Max's gaze to the right, away from Dante and the table. A magical, ethereal bird landed on his shoulder. The kind that Lucey always sent. He listened, heart seizing.

Advocacy infiltrated, Lucey's voice whispered. *Watchers dying everywhere. Get Isadora out of there. Dante isn't her match. I am.*

Shock rippled through him.

Dante isn't her match.

I am.

Impossible.

"The story," Dante continued without tearing his gaze from Isadora, "is about a witch named Cecelia. I believe you knew her. Of course you did, for it was *you* who murdered her. Carcere. La Torra. And a Central Network mission that not only infiltrated my prison and freed almost forty guilty heathens, but resulted in the murder of my Ambassador."

Max spun to face Dante, edging closer to Isadora with each breath. Not close enough. Isadora was too far away, and the edge of mania in Dante's eyes didn't reassure him for an easy way out. Somehow, he had to tell Isadora about Lucey without revealing anything to the rest of them.

A spell?

Transported whisper?

Did he dare?

Guardians moved into place along the fringes of the room.

So, this is how it would happen.

A two-fold attack.

"Your Ambassador killed herself," Max snapped. He shifted closer to Isadora but was still half a room away. Shadows moved along the edges. East Guards, likely.

Dante's face hardened into bitter lines. "Cecelia was confronted by a Watcher far more powerful than she and pulled into the magic. Something that no one knew to be possible. Shouldn't be possible. Whatever the Watcher did to her there pushed her to take her own life. I have that on good authority."

Isadora called from behind Max. "Not on the authority of the Watcher in question. The only other witch who would know what actually happened."

A wretched, triumphant smile crossed Dante's face.

"Not until now," he murmured. He swung toward Vasily. "Your Greatness, as promised, I brought the little usurper here. I present to you Isadora Spence, handfasted wife of Maximillion Sinclair, and the most powerful Watcher in Alkarra."

Max closed the distance between him and Isadora. He pushed her behind his back, relieved for the minute chance to touch her. The reassurance, though small, gave him courage. Vasily studied her with narrowed eyes.

They'd be lucky to make it out of this alive.

Isadora stepped out from behind him and called, "He speaks the truth, Your Greatness. I am a Watcher, and the most powerful in Alkarra now."

Max suppressed the urge to growl at her to be quiet. Dante spoke first.

"As a Watcher, she can see the future. And as a Watcher of her demonstrated power, who knows the end of her sight? Is that why you handfasted Maximillion right before you came here?"

"My being a Watcher has nothing to do with my presence here. I . . . care deeply for Maximillion. I love him."

The firmly stated words gave him a moment of shock.

I love him.

No varying. No question.

His breath caught.

Dante chuckled. "An insult, if you expect us to believe that you came to the most important meeting in modern history without the intent to manipulate the negotiations. A quick handfasting to Maximillion ensured her a place here. She walked amongst us and interacted with our wives. No doubt her husband told her of our discussions, allowing her to see the future and pivot everything to the benefit of the Central Network."

He waved a dismissive hand toward her.

Isadora ignored him, spoke to Vasily. "I don't see the future, Your Greatness. I see possibilities for the future, and I don't need to be present to do it. I could have done such a thing in the Central Network. It's a moot point. Besides, the magic isn't certain. Most possibilities I see never come about."

Max shifted closer, calculating. Their best escape would be to transport. Dante and his cronies would follow, without question. The usual avoidance tactics might work, but Dante salivated over this opportunity, which would lead him to greater magical power.

No, he had to think of something else. The fate of the Central Network also weighed in the balance, and he couldn't let go of that for the tunnel vision of love.

Another strike against the worthless emotion.

Isadora didn't make it easier, not while she bantered back and forth with Dante and Vasily. She couldn't *talk* her way out of this one. No matter what they did, the accusation had been set.

Not even an Ambassador had that power.

Dante turned to Vasily, eyes glittering with dark promise. "Your Greatness, I believe we have all been played by the Central Network. This violates the terms of the summit and immediately disqualifies them from any say in the future of Alkarra."

Max snarled.

Vasily hesitated.

"Your Greatness," Dante called, spinning to face Arayana, who sat wide-eyed next to Vasily. "Did Mrs. Sinclair declare herself a Watcher to you?"

After a long hesitation, she murmured, "No."

"Is it not true that, by law in the Southern Network, a Watcher must declare themselves in advance of a political meeting?"

"Yes."

Dante grinned, hands spread. "I think it's very clear we have a spy in our midst, Your Greatness. Any plan she has been a part of cannot be considered fair. Our wives, I believe, have suffered the most. To protect them and our children, we must ask the Central Network to leave this summit."

Ah, the plan unfolded.

Attack Watchers while he kept the leadership busy. Double whammy. Get rid of those he hated the most, obtain all the power Alkarra had to give.

Wily bugger.

"An act of war," Max snapped. Condemnation filled his voice. "And *fascinating* timing. With Dostar in the West and the Central Network so conveniently removed, you have an open opportunity to enact your one-ruler plan without opposition."

"By majority vote," Dante said coldly. "Even if Dostar were here."

Vasily and Dante constituted a majority as long as they removed the Central Network. How Dostar voted didn't matter, so long as Dante could get rid of him.

"I ask a personal favor of you now, Your Greatness," Dante called. "Mrs. Sinclair murdered my Ambassador, Cecelia Liam. It's only right that she meets justice in the Eastern Network, where she committed her heinous crime."

Serafina leaped to her feet. "Your Greatness, may I—"

"Silence," Dante snapped.

Serafina's mouth bobbed open and closed without a sound. A surge of rage rushed through Max.

Isadora pushed forward. "Cecelia killed herself! She threw herself off the top of the castle in despair, not because I harmed her in the magic."

"Silence! She would have never removed herself from this life or from m—" Shaking, Dante turned to Vasily with a gaze full of meaning. "A personal favor, Your Greatness."

Vasily fell silent.

Max's thoughts sprinted through options while Dante

extrapolated another issue with Isadora. Vasily debated. Max could grab her, take them out of there. Play the odds. But where would they go? The urge to look in the paths almost overwhelmed him, but that would make everything worse.

Panic spurred him on. He couldn't let harm fall to Isadora. They couldn't have her. Dante had taken Serafina from him as a boy. By extension, his Mere. Many of the lonely horrors of his childhood he could trace back to Dante.

He wouldn't have Isadora, too. Not her. Of all of them, she mattered most. Which meant there was nothing for it. His attention snapped back when Vasily muttered, "Take her."

Max sucked in a breath.

Isadora pressed a hand to her chest.

"Mrs. Sinclair," Vasily called, "you will go to the Cage while Dante arranges transport back to the East for your trial. You may do as you wish with her."

An approaching South Guard stepped forward. Max pulled her near, his back to her chest, and growled. The gleam of a knife, and his low promise, paused the South Guards steps.

"You will kill me first."

East Guards marched into the room with Vasily's permission. Defenders, expressions rabid. A deep hunger seemed to compel them closer, closer. They almost salivated over Isadora.

He increased his hold. "Been busy in the paths?" he muttered. To Dante, he called, "Over my dead body, Dante."

Dante shrugged. "Your decision, Maximillion."

East Guards circled them with a bevy of short swords. His odds weren't great. He thought of Charlie—he had deft skill with small weapons—but he would be focused on the Advocacy attacks Lucey mentioned right now.

Isadora's murmur haunted him.

"Max, let him take me. They can't hurt me."

"They can. They will. He'll keep you locked up like a plaything, forcing you to tell him what you see or endure torture you can't imagine. Physical pain. Rape. You name it. There will be no breaking you out this time."

"But it will buy you time to negotiate something for the Network. This is spiraling into a disaster. You may have a hope of saving all of Alkarra if I'm not here. I trust you to break me free. Even if it's eventually."

Max swallowed past the rising lump in his throat. "He cannot have you, too."

"Max, I've seen this in the paths. This *must* happen."

"You're lying."

Her voice was soft when she asked, "Will you take that risk?"

Dante shouted impatiently, "Let us have her and I will agree to discuss keeping the Central Network in the summit."

She ignored Dante, speaking only to Max. Her warmth permeated his back. A tantalizing reminder.

"If you don't, the world will fall. My life isn't worth it."

It's worth everything I have to give, he thought.

East Guards closed in.

He snarled, knife at the ready.

"If you want my wife, you'll have to take her from my cold, dead hands."

Dante sighed. "Very well."

Isadora let out a cry. A firm shove came onto his back. Splitting pain in his head, and a second-long realization that they couldn't possibly survive.

The world went dark.

Chapter Forty-Two

CHARLIE

Wildrose lay in utter stillness.

Charlie tore through the front doors, raced into the foyer. No candles, no torches. A bruised layer of shadow filled everything. All the Advocacy bustling should be in the basement and headquarters, but for several days Watchers had infiltrated up here. Incantations kept the noise from shuffling higher.

He hoped.

His throat ached with the desire to shout Faye's name. Not knowing if Leo was in Wildrose or not, however, he held back. He sprinted up the stairs, taking them two at a time, as soundlessly as possible.

Leo must have used a spell to send the letter to the Advocate. Or did he have Faye send it? How did he know Faye was his wife?

Did Leo know that Charles was the Advocate?

The questions clogged his thoughts as he searched. Where were they? Stillness echoed down the corridors, reverberating off empty walls. His ancestral home carried a nefarious feeling, as if it conspired against him. Charlie raced faster, heart slamming as he searched.

The note could have been false. A test. An ambush. They might use this to out him, but the panic in his gut said otherwise. The sinking of his stomach, the backdrop of attacks, the months and months of quiet before all this buildup, created a darker context.

He thundered down another set of stairs after clearing the upper floor. A hint of light down the corridor drew him closer.

Enraged, he slinked along, feet quiet on the long carpet running the length of the hall. Down the stairs, on the first floor, was the kitchen. A sound came from near there. He paused, listening.

A whistle.

Ice crawled through his body as he transported to the next floor down. Candlelight and torches flooded the kitchen as he stepped into a room full of East Guards.

Weapons lifted. Swords. Shields. Spears. They pointed right at his trembling heart. Twelve visible, at least. He sensed magic all over this room. It vibrated with power, too many incantations to be certain of which he should detect first.

In the midst of them, Faye.

A cloth bound her mouth. Blood stained the edge. Her unbound hair hung ragged around her face. Swelling closed her left eye, and blood trickled down a split lip. They tied her hands behind her back, and Leo held onto her. Fear widened her eyes.

Charlie's rage swelled. He held himself back with the silent promise to avenge every hurt. Leo peered at him with undisguised annoyance.

"So," Leo drawled. "You came. We had a feeling that the High Priest worked with the Advocate after all. I haven't forgotten the incident in my office, nor the thwarted raid that came after. Those scrolls in the drawer were deception spells all along."

Faye cried out something indistinguishable and lunged forward. Leo's grip released ever-so-slightly. With her momentum, Charlie summoned Faye in the breath of a chance he had. The spell jerked her out of Leo's slackened hold.

Faye hurtled across the room.

The stunned Guardians could only stare as Charlie caught her. She slammed into his chest with another cry. A foot braced back prevented them from falling.

The heavy weight of her in his arms, alive, breathing, gave him a moment of relief. Beneath it bubbled righteous wrath borne of love. Each mark and bruise on her lovely body would require a price.

Paid by Leo.

Without taking his eyes off the Head of Guardians, Charlie ripped the rope from her wrists. She wrenched the gag free. He nudged her behind him and edged to the side, where he filled the doorway with his body.

"Go."

Faye hesitated. With a flick of Leo's head, two tentative East Guards advanced. Charlie tossed a forceful spell that sent them slamming into the wall. Wood cracked. Hanging pots fell on top of their heads and both lolled in unconsciousness. Faye sprinted away, her footfalls ebbing thuds against the quiet night.

Leo raised a hand to stop the two other Guardians. "Wait," he called.

Uncertainty threaded his voice. He stared at Charlie with studious intent, head canted to the side. The Charles that Leo knew as the Highest Witch had no physical capability at all. Stammering and fear, with a touch of diplomacy and flair.

Now, Leo met Charlie.

Charlie smiled. "You wanted the Advocate? Here I am. This is between me and you, Leo."

Leo drew in a deep breath, eyes wide. "It can't be."

Charlie gave a little bow.

Leo blinked.

His gaze slipped to the stunned East Guard closest to him, then back.

"Not . . . *you.*"

Leo's disdain made Charlie laugh. "I tell you," he cried, "all these years may have been worth it for just that. Your shock and surprise makes it all the more fun for me, I promise."

Leo scoffed, his bluster poorly presented. "You? The pathetic High Priest? How much damage could you do?"

"For being the Head of Guardians, you're not all that bright." Charlie tsked. "I am the Advocate, Leo. I am the witch you've been hunting, fighting, seeking for years. My evasions have been epic. My powers, relentless. My thirst to have revenge on you knows no depths, and it comes to a pinnacle tonight. Fight me if you dare. I've prepared for this night my entire life. I will not disappoint myself, my soulmate, or my family."

A flicker of uncertainty slipped through Leo. He may not have wavered had Charlie not dealt such an unbelievable blow.

"I didn't . . ."

"No one did. That was the point the entire time. Do you remember the meeting with Council Member Stiles? I engineered it. The night at your office? I found those scrolls, and you fell for the foolish Charles disguise like everyone else. The eagle at the window? The *aquila* bird flying overhead at Carcere? Me. All of it."

Poorly suppressed panic swept Leo's face.

"I will let the whole Network know!" he cried.

"Please, try."

"You . . . this . . . it changes nothing! Removing the Advocacy will be even more rewarding if the idiot High Priest goes down with it."

"Yes, yes," Charlie drawled, "you've convinced me you're a great and powerful witch and Dante will be so proud and likely give you a lot of currency. If we can skip all the boring parts, please? I'd like to resolve this once and for all."

"You are not controlling this conversation. *I* decide what we discuss. The Advocacy is here," Leo said with a renewed and bolstered confidence. "We are certain that Wildrose Manor harbors these magical demons and we will burn it down."

Charlie spread his arms. "Then I invite you to search. You'll find nothing, I assure you."

No one moved.

"If you're here to kill more Watchers, you've come to the wrong place. Leo, you will not make it out of here alive." Charlie's expression hardened. "But I will give you one chance to save your Guardians."

Magic shifted behind Charlie. He sensed it briefly. Faye's voice whispered at his back.

"It's me."

"Guardians!" Leo called. "Destroy the Advocate, then burn this place to the ground."

Leo barked several commands in *Ilese* as six Guardians disappeared, leaving four visible. One of the two that had fallen groaned. The other didn't stir. Rags trailed out of bottles of ipsum, painted in *Ilesan* words, revealed their other plans. They were going to light the rags and set this place on fire.

Such a brutal show of force wouldn't be enough to stop the Advocacy, but to break its spine. To kill the Advocate, burn the headquarters, wouldn't remove the witches from the Advocacy.

Nor their willingness to fight the evil in the world.

Charlie never loved Wildrose the same way as Max, but he wouldn't allow Leo, of all witches, to incinerate his legacy.

Four witches sprang into view behind him. Shouts, calls, terrific noises followed. The shifting magic in the room revealed three other Advocacy members who had been hidden all this time.

The Guardians hesitated.

Charlie crouched, lifted a hand, and beckoned Leo with a curl of his fingers. "Come on then," he called. "Let's get this over with. Send your Guardian dogs, if you must. The Advocacy will take them out one by one. Wildrose is the last place you'll ever see in this life."

With a nod from Leo, the Guardians advanced.

Chapter Forty-Three

MAXIMILLION

Max returned to consciousness in fits and bursts.

Waves of pain and shadows undulated above him as he sifted through each waking step. Head-splitting agony. Concern, but he couldn't remember why. His wrists and head pulsed with pain.

Memory returned like a slap.

Isadora!

His eyes flew open. He gasped. A low chuckle filled the space in front of him as he struggled to right his vision.

Dante.

"Ah, our hero awakens."

Two East Guards stood just behind Max. He lay on the ground, hands bound behind him. Attempts to shove to his knees resulted in more waves of agony through his head. A sticky liquid poured down the back of his neck, dripping to the floor. The metallic scent of blood filled his mouth like old cotton.

"Your wife has been taken care of, Maximillion. We have politics to discuss."

Max blinked, clearing the blurry image. Arayana and Serafina huddled close on the other side of the table. Vasily glowered at Dante, cast reluctant stares at Max. Uneasiness filled Vasily's thick features.

Fear for Isadora spurred Max to greater pain tolerance. Serafina winced as he struggled upright. A wave of nausea ripped through his stomach. Time to do the impossible.

He had to resolve this whirling feeling, talk Dante off a power-hungry ledge, and find Isadora. Charlie could clean up the political mess later. He was the only one with diplomatic ideas and . . .

Max's scattered thoughts trailed away, too confused to come back together with sufficient intelligence.

"Call this madness off, Dante," he barked.

"Gag him."

With a jerk of his hand, a South Guard complied. A filthy rag filled his mouth. He grunted against the searing pain it sent through his skull. The throb faded into a faint pulse. Enough to think through them, at least.

How long had he been out?

Long enough that Arayana trembled on the floor, propped against Serafina. A hint of bruising showed on Arayana's swollen cheek. No servants lingered. The presence of so many South Guards meant he might have been out longer than he expected.

Not good.

He set aside fears for Isadora, otherwise concern for her safety would overwhelm. A spell removed the gag.

"Dante, we need to talk. This is madness."

The South Guard stepped forward, replacing the gag with a growl. A fist to the cheek from another Guard sent Max flying backward. His teeth clattered.

Renewed pain through his mind put him into a deeper stupor. For minutes, he struggled to regain full consciousness.

The ripples of swelling agony escorted him in and out a numbing darkness.

Eternities later, he grappled his way back to his knees. Each move cost him energy. He almost stepped into the paths, but couldn't focus long enough.

Would the magic restore him?

Drain him?

Dante prattled on, speaking incessantly to no one. Vasily's discomfort grew with each passing moment. Madness lingered in Dante's voice. Grandiose ideas. Serafina paled, staring hard at Max. If nothing else, he had to notify Lucey. Tell her to come, find Isadora. Do . . . whatever powerful matches did.

What were the ends of this magic?

What did all of it mean?

For the second time that night, the crack of slamming doors interrupted Dante. His head jerked up with a glower as a pair of familiar, quick steps entered the room.

"Dante!" Isadora cried.

The following quiet rippled like a gentle touch of water.

Relief and terror tripled through Max. He wanted to shout at her, but the gag, now reinforced with magic, didn't budge. Isadora advanced, eyes flashing. The doors thudded to a close behind her again. Ice and wind and scoured cheeks stirred her up, giving her a ragged, but bold, appearance.

"This is between you and me, Dante. Let them go."

Dante scoffed, livid now.

"No."

"I won't let you steer the Networks onto a disastrous path. A one-ruler solution populates millions of possibilities, none of them good. The evidence is overwhelmingly against it."

"So you *did* come to influence the outcome."

"I came to support my husband, and I bring you the truth now. I don't believe in trying to predict the future based on possibilities, but there are trends that can be useful."

"And you expect me to believe you when you say that isolationism fares so much better?"

Quietly, she said, "No. I don't expect you to believe that."

"Until you can prove it to me, we are at an impasse."

A dark feeling welled up within Max. The glint of interest in her eyes, a sign that she had a new idea, followed. She thought Dante was her match. She'd want to test it. Overwhelm him, throw him off. Weaken him in this last moment . . .

Resolution settled over her visage. She pulled her shoulders back, drew in a deep breath.

Oh, no.

She could only have one idea with that expression on her face. He tried to explain, but the cottony fluff of the gag nearly made him vomit. When he shook his head, his brain sloshed around.

No! He wanted to shout. *No, it's not him! Don't take him in the paths like you did with Cecelia!*

Isadora held out an arm. Max screamed, shook his head, endured the nauseating sensation of his brain about to burst from pain, to no avail. Isadora's offer to Dante exploded through the room.

"Let me show you what I see."

Chapter Forty-Four

CHARLIE

Chaos followed.

East Guards surged forward at the same time. A formation they'd clearly practiced before, if their synchronized steps meant anything. Distant expressions lurked on several Watcher faces in the room.

They were in the paths.

A second before the East Guards fell on them, the Watchers snapped out of it. Two in the middle disappeared. One dropped to his knees. Another leaped into the air.

The chaotic movements startled the East Guards, who slid to a stop. Attacks on the Guardians came from all sides. Invisible witches appeared. The witch on her knees slammed a previously hidden knife into the calf of the nearest East Guard. He screamed, toppled.

Charlie summoned the fire poker, and cast an immobility spell. Two Guardians froze. With the five seconds of purchased time—they'd overwhelm it with their own spells quickly—he slammed the poker into the knee of the closest Guardian.

It cracked.

He toppled with a shout.

The other two roared back to life and ran at him together. He ducked, dodging the first. With a shove of his legs, he flung the leader into the hearth, where a spell issued a bright flare of fire. Flames consumed him.

While Charlie grappled with the third Guardian, Watchers swarmed the others who rushed into their space.

Charlie kept the kitchen wall at his back as he slunk toward Leo. The Guardians formed a wall around their leader. A slight sheen likely meant a spell to prevent transportation lingered between the backs of the Guards and Leo.

Clever coward.

Charlie threw up a defensive wall that a Guard knocked into and wheeled back. A waiting Watcher, ready with a sword, sliced into the tendons at the back of his legs. The Guard screamed, collapsed.

A behemoth of a Guardian transported into view. Meaty shoulders. Growly face. A thick beard slipped all the way down his neck, nearly connecting with an equally hairy chest.

The Guardian locked on Faye.

Charlie transported behind him, landing on his back. He slithered an arm around his neck and pulled. A kick to the elbow sent a knife flying out of his grip and safely away from Faye's back.

The East Guard whirled around, grabbed Charlie's arm, and hauled him off. The tabletop slammed into Charlie's back, robbing his lungs of air. He skidded over the top and dropped to the side. The bench collapsed beneath him in splinters that sent pain spiraling through his ribs.

He couldn't breathe.

The Guard chuckled as he strolled over. Each footfall crashed like boulders. The floor trembled.

"Hiding, are you?" the East Guard growled.

Charlie rolled off the bench and closer to the wall. The

Guard leaped next to him and slammed a foot onto the floor by Charlie's face. Black dots crowded his vision from the edges. If his lungs didn't work soon . . .

Air rushed in.

Gasping, Charlie dodged a spear end by tumbling shoulder-over-shoulder away. He moved under the table, out the other side. The East Guard planted a foot on Charlie's ribs. Bones began to strain. Charlie grunted as the East Guard reached down and almost jerked his arm out of socket. Charlie kicked out, attempting to slam into the knee, to no avail.

Chuckling, the gigantic man grabbed Charlie by the throat, lifted him in the air. His legs dangled paces from the floor.

"Not so brave now, Advocate."

Charlie conjured a burning shard of wood from the fireplace, shoved it in his right eye. A popping sound, followed by a squelch, followed. The Guard shrieked, hand scrabbling over his eye. Charlie dropped as the flailing Guardian screamed again. Blood dribbled down his face as he crashed into the dangling frying pans overhead. The half-blind giant ran into the wall, then fell. The kitchen shook from the force.

Charlie whipped around.

Where was Leo?

Frantic searching led to no sign of the weakling Head of Guardians. An Advocacy member screamed, hair on fire.

Charlie sent a spell to douse the flames, leaped to his feet, and jumped onto an approaching Guardian, taking them both to the ground. Leo appeared amidst the chaos while Charlie grappled with the Guardian on the floor. As soon as he saw him, Leo disappeared.

Charlie bit the finger of a Guardian attempting to asphyxiate him. Another Advocacy member came from behind, stabbed the Guard in the neck, then gave Charlie a hand. He pulled Charlie to his feet.

"Thank you."

"High Priest," he said, a twinkle in his eye.

Charlie grinned.

Guardian bodies cluttered the floor. Advocacy members cleared their fallen friends, which left more room for the bodies of their enemies. Either more manifested themselves, or Leo called for reserves.

At least twelve lay on the ground. Seven fresh Guardians formed a half circle around the Advocacy members present, all of them snarling with curled upper lips and gleaming swords. Leo stood behind, a gloating smile on his face.

Candles had tipped over in the fracas, spilling wax over the tabletops. Fire licked along the edge of a chair, and spilled ipsum chugged free in the corner. Someone had uncorked a barrel of vinegar, and it flowed.

Behind Charlie, only four Advocacy members remained. He recognized none of them—they didn't transform to their usual hidden appearances. Like him, they revealed themselves in full forms.

Pride filled his chest.

He'd fight alongside this tattered army any day. He couldn't extrapolate odds. Too much magic filled this room to tell which belonged to Leo and his Guardians, and which to the Advocacy. Hidden witches lurked.

Leo advanced. His low, humorless chuckle moved ahead of him.

"You and your pathetic little force can transport away, Advocate, yet you do not."

Leo nudged in between two of the Guardians, who let him pass. Charlie watched warily. Only five paces to Charlie's left lay the abandoned fire poker. Just behind it, propped against the hearth, was a metal shovel. Charlie eased his weight that way, but didn't move.

"Well," Charlie drawled, "I wouldn't want you to get bored now, would I?"

Leo laughed.

"Sure, sure. That is what you're staying for. You are the Advocate, are you not? These witches are your followers?"

Sensing a trap, Charlie inclined his head once. Leo ambled forward, careful not to move too close.

"The Advocate protects all Watchers, does he not?"

"And Defenders."

Leo shrugged. "As you say. So if you could leave an overwhelming fight, and you do not, what logical conclusion might I draw?"

The dangling truth that hung silently between them dawned on Charlie then. Leo still hadn't confirmed that Wildrose was the headquarters. Undoubtedly, while they grappled here, he'd sent runners through the manor.

"Your Guardians are such poor researchers, are they? You don't trust them when they say that the Watchers aren't here?"

Leo returned the smile. An arch, spiked, horrendous thing that sent a shudder down Charlie's neck.

"You mistake me," Leo murmured. "I'm not looking for individual Watchers, or even the Advocate. I'm looking for the *Advocacy*. It's not enough to have you, though you are a greater prize than I expected." Leo leaned forward. "I want *all* of you."

Charlie paused, waiting for something to fall.

Then he smiled.

"Leo, you pathetic butterfly. You cannot kill the Advocacy. It is not a thing, it is not a place. It's an idea. A movement."

Leo recoiled.

Charlie continued, warming to the idea. "I am the Advocate for now, but there will be others after me. Murder me, if you like. Another will follow. We have some of the most brilliant, justice-oriented minds amongst our ranks. Perhaps they will do a better job than me. Because, if there's anything I can promise you, it's that the Advocacy is not mine. The idea may have started with me years ago, but it has grown beyond me."

A dawning came, and Charlie laughed. Isn't *this* what Papa wanted Charlie to understand about Wildrose, and their familial obligation, and the power they held all along?

When he died, the Advocacy would continue on.

Like Wildrose.

The manor was the symbol of his family, but his family never truly left. They would always be a part of him and Alkarra. Dust and bones and spirit and breath and that's all Papa ever wanted him to know.

You create opportunity and place goodness, then let goodness run wild, Ranulf once said. *That is the legacy of Wildrose.*

A sound from the hallway caught his ear. Instinct compelled him to pause, to wait. Faint whispers followed the light scuff of a foot.

Charlie tilted his head back, giddy as the revelation continued to unroll.

"Kill me, Leo! Out me to the Network. Tell everyone the truth, if you must. You can review all of our missions, all the idiotic stints you tried, the idiotic ones we tried. Reveal it all. Because no matter how hard you try to kill the Advocacy, or even me, it won't die."

The skin above Leo's nose wrinkled like a fat raisin. He glanced out of the corner of his eyes to the Guards, who hesitated.

Charlie held up both arms.

"You can try to find Watchers and Defenders for the rest of your life, but you know the futility of that mission as well as I. The magic continues regardless of whether you kill the Watchers or not. Why? Because it's *bigger than you.*"

Charlie ran a hand through his hair. The Guards lifted their weapons a little higher, their wary gazes tracking his every movement. He laughed harder. They thought him mad. Totally unhinged.

When, in fact, he'd never seen the world more clearly.

Leo opened his mouth, closed it again. In fury, he shouted. "Then you will die! And we will extinguish all of those that hold the idea with them until the Advocacy dies!"

A firm voice came from the doorway.

"You'll have to kill *all* of us."

Leo whirled to the side.

Faye stood in the doorway, torch in hand, a wrathful expression on her face. She wore the red war paint from her tribe in the West. Black charcoal lined her eyes, darkening them until they blended with her brown skin. Circles of red swelled out from it. *Blessings from my ancestors,* she once explained. *We wear them with us in all our fights.*

His breath caught. Faces, bodies, eyes filled the hallway. Witches crowded the door, attempting to spill inside. Five. Ten. Twenty.

The Advocacy.

Without the magic hiding them.

Shouts arose from the hallway, populating back. Faye held up her torch—a sharp spear at the other end, and shouted.

She rushed into the room.

Advocacy members scurried behind her, moving fast. Guards attempted to swell against them, but there wasn't space.

One Advocacy witch climbed on the table, grabbed a copper-bottomed pot, and swung. She hit a Guardian in the back of the head. He toppled, crashing into a second as he lifted his sword against a young Watcher recently rescued. The Watcher twirled out of the way, grabbed a rolling pin from hooks on the wall, and smashed it into his nose.

He howled.

Clamor arose. Faye wielded her spear against a Guardian

who attempted to jump out the window. Another Advocacy member conjured fire with a spell, then blew it onto the beard of an East Guard.

Leo backed away, eyes wide.

Charlie transported until he stood in front of Leo, smiling down at the little old man. The cowering Head of Guardians was a dream he never dared to dream.

"Welcome to Wildrose, Leo. I'd like you to meet the Advocacy. We've spent a long time waiting for this moment, and we appreciate you bringing it to us."

Leo shrank, lips blubbering. A Guardian attempted to defend him, but another Advocacy member conjured ropes at his feet. The ropes snaked around his ankles, tied themselves, and tightened. The Guard crashed and slid across the floor.

Leo snarled. "You'll never get away with this."

Charlie laughed, grabbed Leo by the shoulder, and yanked him away from the wall. A paralyzing incantation sent him to the ground in a puddle of vinegar. Charlie conjured two pairs of manacles, tightened them from wrist to ankle on each side, and left him on the floor.

When he straightened, Advocacy members filled the room in a heady crush. The Guardians, some of them wrangled out in the hall, others bound against the fireplace, appeared in varying stages of disarray. Swollen eyes, scowling features. Three of them hadn't yet regained consciousness.

"And that," he cried, arm lifted, "is what happens when you mess with the Advocacy."

A shout rippled through the room. Several screamed with near-hysterical relief. Others struggled to meet his gaze. Some stared, mouths slack. A woman named Kate gaped. Her lips formed the words, "Is this real?"

Pride surged through him. *The* Advocacy. Not *his* Advocacy, because it had grown far beyond that now.

The Advocacy belonged to all of them.

Once they tied the last Guardian, Charlie nodded to the lot of them. "To the prison, in Chatham, if you please."

A former Central Guard stepped forward. His gaze lingered on Charlie with an uncertain, but hopeful, appraisal.

"Your Highness?"

"Separate cells, if you don't mind. I think level four, cells ten through twenty-one should do it. James, Ahab, Georgette, can you help? Please, I must go to check on Max. Has anyone seen Lucey?"

"*She* is checking on Max!" called a voice from the back.

A rush of worry overcame him. He didn't know what, but he knew it wasn't good. Amongst the crowd, he searched for Faye. Not seeing her there, and feeling the press of urgency yet again, he transported away.

MAXIMILLION

Isadora lay on the floor, limp.

Max scrambled closer to her, shouting through his gag. Dante slumped over the table, staring at the wall. Serafina rose on shaky legs. When Dante made no correction, no bark, she rushed to Max's side.

The gag faded.

"The ropes," he gasped.

She obeyed, using a spell to yank the ones around his legs free. They budged, resistant, until Max conjured a knife, slipped it through them, and shoved them off. Isadora didn't respond to his touch when he lifted her off the ground and carried her to a divan.

The South Guards didn't move.

Once he set her safely aside, Max whirled around.

"You have a choice now, Vasily! What will it be? There's no chance Dante can survive against Isadora. Her power is truly unparalleled. She has a match, and that match will join her. I don't know what that means, but I know it's the end of Dante. Somehow."

Vasily scowled, mustache bristling.

"It is too late!" Vasily cried. "I made the decision already, Maximillion. You cannot stop it now. Dante will survive."

Max snarled. "Wrong decision."

"Get him!" Vasily screeched.

South Guards surged forward. Max crouched in front of Isadora, summoning his favorite knife. Ranulf's knife. It sat in a display case for too long, waiting for purpose. He hoped that something of his adopted father's tenacity lingered in it. Max's fear for Isadora, for the Network, was a vibrant heat in his chest.

South Guards advanced more cautiously this time, forming a circle around him. He gritted his teeth. This was it. The final stand. Somewhere else, Charlie must be taking his as well. The thought gave him a moment of courage.

He might stand by himself, but he didn't fight alone.

A shimmer of movement manifested out of the corner of his eye a second before a familiar head of hair appeared. Charlie stood at Max's side, a similar knife in his own hand. His disheveled red hair, torn shirt, smears of blood, and uneasy grimace testified to his own problems.

Charlie took the scene in with his usual alacrity, then cast a wry, sidelong glance at Max.

"I've seen something like this before," he said brightly. "In the Eastern Network. You're always negotiating your way into problems, aren't you, Max?"

A dark smile crossed Max's face.

"It would appear so, Your Highness."

Seeing the High Priest, the South Guards paused. One glanced at Vasily in silent question.

"Your Highness!" Vasily cried. "What are you doing here?"

"From the look of things, Maximillion has made a point that you don't support, I would assume," Charlie called.

"The Central Network will not survive this outrage! Dante will come off conqueror!"

Serafina appeared at Max's other side, a petite knife, almost like a letter opener, in hand. He opened his mouth to command her to leave at once, but she stared him down.

"I didn't listen to my protective instincts twenty years ago," she whispered, tears in her eyes. "I will never do that again. Max, I stand with you."

Something welled up inside him.

Gratitude. Love. Relief. A healing balm that he'd craved his whole life. He didn't have the time—nor the desire—to figure out emotions. South Guards advanced with another command from Vasily.

"Thank you, Serafina. You are of no use to the Eastern Network if you're dead. Dante won't survive. Go to Arayana, keep her and yourself safe. You have made your position clear. I . . . appreciate you."

With great hesitation, she obeyed.

Behind the Guardians, Arayana clung to Serafina's shoulders with a light sob. Vasily's red face, splotchy with purplish veins, brightened from the other side of the room. He held a sword in hand, two beefy South Guards at his side.

"Well," Charlie sang, "nothing like a sword fight to finish things off. You know, I've seen a few brilliant things done with cast-iron? I might rethink my weapons cache later this month."

The South Guards came in swinging.

"If," Max muttered, "we live that long."

Charlie laughed.

Despite half a dozen South Guards attacking, the two made an admirable duo. The wintry nights practicing in the basement of Wildrose, before headquarters became what it was now, must have paid off. Charlie moved at Max's side like a song. Each tracked the other one, moved with finesse. Staved off South Guards, and took light blows instead of deadly ones.

All this time, a building presence filled the room.

Light.

Darkness.

More light.

The brilliance grew, throwing vague shadows and shapes on the ground. Fallen South Guards littered the floor as Max winced, ducked another swing from a desperate Guardian.

Isadora disappeared from the divan. Max whirled.

"Isa?"

Neither he nor Charlie strayed from where she once lay, protected within their reach.

Dante also left.

"Where is she?" Charlie cried, ducking under a swinging cudgel. The overeager South Guard grunted as the momentum of his swing carried the weapon into his own back. He screamed. Charlie kicked him in the groin, shoved him over.

"I don't know!" Max cried.

Light exploded.

The physical force tossed all of them against the wall. The replenishing South Guards slammed into marble busts, chairs, and the wall. Paintings toppled. Max groaned, head pulsing yet again. Charlie moaned next to him, pushed to sitting.

Max stopped, breath caught.

Light extended from the middle of the room, falling through a foggy, open space. A path snaked before him. Not of light, as in the paths, but something firmer. The faintest hint of a green backdrop—a forest—lingered in the back-ground. He thought he saw the outline of branches. Bushes.

In the line, wisps.

Himself. Charlie. Isadora, her strange sister. A dragon? No, that couldn't be right. Nothing about these wisps felt fragile or uncertain. Only firm. Capable. He pushed himself higher to see better. The light spread out, almost like a fog, obscuring his vision for anything else. Charlie had disappeared. So had the entire room.

The magic enveloped him.

The wisps faded, removing those he loved. They reappeared in a mass meeting in the Central Network. All the delegation leaders except Dante. Serafina stood in his place. Maps sprawled on the table to show Network boundaries. Closed borders. A wall along the Southern Network from east to western edge.

Peace, for now.

A map of Alkarra zoomed out, showing boundaries, lines, and shaded colors.

As if . . .

Isolation.

Max drew in a sharp breath. The light collected into itself, pulling together from the inside. It collected into a circle, collapsing like a dying star, until it disappeared with a silent zip.

Shadow returned.

Presence.

He saw the room again. Charlie crouched on one knee with a knife at his side. He lowered his arm to find Isadora standing next to Lucey. Dante lay at their feet. Lucey trembled. The pale haggardness had left her face. She stood resplendent, normal. Like the Lucey he had known for years.

Max shoved to his feet.

"Isa," he murmured.

The magic closed.

Dante jerked, as if waking up. He leaped off the floor, eyes wild. His hair mussed on end. His upper lip curled as he locked his gaze on Isadora. Max rushed toward her, heart in his throat.

No.

She didn't make it through whatever happened just to lose

her now. Fear propelled him to cross the room at a sprint. Dante, focused solely on Isadora, didn't see him coming.

"I have seen it all!" Dante cried. "It is mine to know and to conquer!"

Dante lunged.

Max arrived first.

Hand on Dante's throat, he shoved him to the ground. Dante slammed onto his back with a resounding *thud*. Max released him, shoved his foot to his neck, and snarled back.

"Touch my wife and you die."

A spell knocked Dante unconscious, though the pale planes of his face, his bloodshot eyes, the jitter of his teeth, likely meant he wouldn't have been long in consciousness, anyway.

Charlie grabbed Max's arm, tugged him away from Dante. A rope coiled in his hands. "Let me bind him."

Max whirled, reaching Isadora just as she fell. He gathered her in his arms. For the first time that night, his soul released all the tension in a sigh.

Magic swirled away from the room as Isadora pressed her forehead to his chest. Hints of the forest vanished. A looming branch became a chandelier again. Leaves morphed into rubies, emeralds. All the world became a quiet sigh, leaving horrified witches in its wake. Max saw a path. His path.

Did the others see the same?

Isadora released a shaky breath. Had she meant to speak? Her hands rested near his heart, gathered close, as if she wanted to tuck herself inside him.

"The good gods, Isa. I thought . . ."

He couldn't even speak the terrible words in his throat. The dreadful truth that he'd almost lost her, and the more shocking truth that he realized in the folds of terror.

He loved her.

As she loved him.

He couldn't decide which frightened him more.

Isadora attempted to speak, but no words came out. She leaned into him more heavily, her fingers slack. The more weight she gave him, the more fright rose within. He pressed his cheek to hers, whispering against her temple.

"Hang in there."

The others stirred back to life, but he didn't see them. Didn't care what the noises meant. He understood only when Isadora whispered something about her sister, then passed out. Max pulled her into his arms. Charlie appeared, grim-faced.

"Take her, Max. I'll get the details from Serafina. We'll discuss all of this later. Let me manage from here." An exhausted smile followed. "Rumor has it I am the High Priest, you know."

CHARLIE

Charlie didn't bother being quiet when he returned to Wildrose.

Sunrise hinted at the horizon, edging the sky in blue. Soon, it would wash with pink, like a painting left to its own devices. For now, it settled into the place where day was neither morning nor night.

Charlie hurried through the achingly quiet manor.

"Faye?" he shouted. "Faye?"

He jogged past doors, up the stairs. Didn't matter who slept over or whether they'd be angry or what they had to say. His heart led him.

He had to see her.

"Faye?"

The door to the master bedroom opened up at the top of the stairs.

"Faye? Faye!"

He ran faster, desperate now. The night pressed him toward her. Leo and Guardians and his revelations about the Advocacy shed away behind him. How smug and arrogant he'd been to assume he was the most important part of this entire organization. To shoulder the burden in his mind in such a way. He longed to tell her how wrong he'd been.

A door at the end of the hall opened and a familiar form slipped free. Shadows moved, then stopped.

"Charlie?"

Relief slowed his steps. "Faye!"

He skidded to a stop, opened his arms, and Faye collided into him with a sob.

She had messily wiped the charcoal and war paint from her face. Remnants dotted the shell of her ear, her cheek. Her hair hung around her shoulders, limp from the fight. She clung to him, banishing space.

A sob wrenched out of her. "Charlie," she whispered. "Charlie, I was so—"

"I know." He tightened his grip. "I know. Me too."

He picked her up, sprang up the stairs to the master suite, and shoved through the double doors. They slammed behind them. Their lips locked in a heated kiss as he lowered to a chair close to the fire.

She pulled away, pressed her forehead to his. Her dark lashes closed against her skin. Tears slipped out from underneath. He curled her into his chest, whispering things he didn't even know, until the panic dissolved. Faye framed his face in her hands.

"They know," she whispered. "Your secret is out. All the Advocacy knows and is talking about it."

"I know. The Central Guards should be giving the East Guards potions in the dungeons. They won't remember Wildrose, just the fight. Or details of it, anyway."

"Leo?"

He laughed darkly, threading a piece of her hair through his finger as he tucked it behind her ear. "He won't even remember his name, I hope. For now, he's going to rot in our prison until I negotiate a deal with Serafina. Regarding some *very* interesting facts that I just learned about their daughter, Emilia, I think Leo might end up a forgotten old man in the dungeons until time takes him."

"But—"

"Dante will never know," he whispered, smiling. "I have so much to update you on, my love. So much to tell you. All of it can wait. Right now? I just want you."

She hooked her legs around him, pulled them close. "Tonight," she murmured, "Can we be Charlie and Faye again?"

He pressed a kiss to her forehead.

"Forever, my soul. Forever."

* * *

The potted plants had, by many miracles, survived.

Charlie surveyed them with a tilted head. Starts, most of them. With the right spells, temperatures, and care, they would eventually grow to impressive tomato plants. Magic could keep a start alive through the winter and into the spring, when the sun did all her own magic, but it required more energy than he desired to give.

Instead, Charlie spelled the plants to Pearl. She'd be happy to take care of them. The High Priest had better things on his mind.

A knock on his office door drew him around. He called out, but Max had already entered. Max crossed the room, hair slicked back, suit coat perfectly pressed, as usual. Some of the stressed gauntness had exited his face in the last week since the closing of hostilities in the South.

Charlie frowned. There couldn't be much to say. He'd just left the final delegation meeting himself.

"Well?" he asked.

"Nothing new," Max said with a huff. "As you know. The

conclusion of the Mansfeld Pact, where the Network leaders unite to integrate and implement the isolationist agreement, will be a week or so from now. Assuming the best."

"I'll be there whenever it occurs."

Relief showed in Max's expression as he nodded. "Thank you, Your Highness."

Charlie shot him a dirty look. Max returned the vexation. He'd been vastly more ornery lately than expected, for having defeated their foes and set the Network and Watchers on a safer path.

Charlie hadn't been able to peg the reason down until just this morning, when he heard Isadora had been staying with Pearl since the debacle in the South, attempting to restore Pearl's house. Advocacy members spoke of sightings while she volunteered at refugee camps, too. Her current status as Max's wife had *everyone* talking.

A few gossip columns in the *Chatterer* attempted to speculate, but Max shut them down immediately.

In all that, Isadora hadn't spoken to Max at all. The fear in his best friend's eyes, his loyal protection of Isadora during those harrowing last minutes, replayed fresh through Charlie's mind.

Ah, but miracles never ceased.

"So," Charlie drawled. "How are you?"

"Fine."

"Really, Max."

He lifted an irritated eyebrow. "I'm fine."

"Good. Because I thought I'd let you know that I'm going to die."

Max blinked. Stared.

"I'm sorry?"

Charlie suppressed a laugh. Thanks to years of experience, he didn't crack a smile as he reaffirmed his original statement. "Charles is going to die, Max."

Max opened his mouth, closed it again.

"Eventually," Charlie tacked on with a drawl. "Once the Network has stabilized, the Mansfeld Pact firmed up, and we have a solid High Priestess in place. Several candidates come to mind. I'm not in a hurry, mind you. But I figure that, in a year or two or four, Charles is going to die."

Understanding flooded Max's expression. With a droll voice, he asked, "And when you die, will your ghost and Faye's be seen roaming the Western Network?"

"Most likely."

"And will the Network know to mourn you?"

"Charles will be dead, dead."

"I see."

"You, however, may visit your old friend Charlie whenever you like."

"You'll be in the Western Network?"

Charlie smiled. "Perhaps. Perhaps not. Faye has an extensive list of places to travel, and I have promised her the full run of it. Who knows where we will go?"

"You do realize you are the Highest Witch putting into place an isolationist pact the likes of which Alkarra has never seen? The requirements against border crossings are as strict as they get, short of death."

"I am."

"You feel no remorse of conscience that you'll break said pact?"

"None whatsoever. I feel I've earned a vacation."

Max didn't argue.

Charlie grinned, allowing full rein of his emotions. "I'll tell you when, Max. As I said, a stable Network first, then Charles will die. I think something dramatic and à propos. Walk off a cliff. Hit too hard in the head by a library book. Something of that nature. I'll require your help."

"Naturally."

"I'm quite looking forward to it. It's the ultimate prank, you see. Faking one's own death and getting away with it? Particularly as High Priest."

Charlie reached down to his desk, where paperwork littered the top. He reached for a scroll, handed it to Max.

"For this reason, I officially bequeath you this. You can protest all you like, but Harry has already made it official. Might be his dying act," he added in a mutter. "The man has survived all manner of difficulties thus far."

Max's face turned to stone as he read the scroll. He lifted his gaze.

"I cannot."

Charlie laughed. "Don't be an idiot, Max. Wildrose has always been yours. That is simply the deed that turns it over to you in name. Now, before you try to tell me that Papa wanted me to keep it in the family, you can stuff that idea. You are as much a son to him as me. Max, you love that manor. I've never felt half of what you do for it, and if you have it, my ancestors will be glad. Charles would probably light the demmed thing on fire."

Max's hands shook slightly as he regarded the paper. His lips parted, then pressed several times. Finally, he lowered his hand. Several searching moments later, he nodded once.

"Thank you, Charlie. I accept with gratitude."

"A relief. I was prepared to fight to the death again, and win, and I'd have regret for killing you too early, you know."

"I'd win," Max muttered.

Charlie laughed. "Well, let's face it, old boy. You, more than me, are in a better place to care for it. Isadora will love Wildrose once you introduce it. And might want to have the vinegar scrubbed out of the floorboards in the kitchen. Powerful stuff."

Max shot him the dirtiest glare he'd ever seen, which only brought more laughter. Charlie couldn't help it.

"Oh, come, Max! Don't tell me you aren't fighting for her?"

"She hasn't spoken with me."

"Petulance is not a good look on you."

"I'm not petulant."

"Then you're pouting."

"I am not. I'm . . . giving her space."

Charlie rolled his eyes. "Ever think that she might not want space? Did you ask her whether she wanted it?"

Max frowned. "It was implied."

"The good gods save you, Max. You're the biggest idiot I've ever met. Brilliant, but an idiot. Are you going to fight for her or not?"

"I'm . . . I'm not sure."

"Are you going to tell her you love her?"

Max squirmed under his suit coat. Charlie nearly exulted. When was the last time Max showed the human trait of discomfort?

What a delightful situation.

"I haven't. I'm . . . on my way to Letum Wood to discuss our future now. Thank you very much."

Charlie clapped him on the shoulder. "Very good, as I wanted to head that way as well. The Advocacy members that helped us fight Leo have all taken a blood oath to keep my secret, you know? Faye administered them myself. I'm passing the responsibility of Advocate to Lucey. Think she'll take it?"

Max nodded once.

"Good." Charlie let his hand drop to his side. "She'll be better at it than me. The Mansfeld Pact, and the laws to protect Watchers that are embedded within it, will make the Central Network a far safer place for them."

Charlie fell deeper into thought. "I found a grimoire that will allow us to combine magic, stabilize it for an unknown amount of time. A powerful thing from the library of Burke.

The South has requested steep consequences for breaking it. Widespread loss of magic. It'll be an exhausting weekend, requiring much work from me. All worth it."

"Hmm," Max said, and Charlie thought he heard relief. As long as Max didn't have to go, he'd be pleased.

"The East will be safer for Watchers now, too, though that stigma might exist for a while," Charlie continued, deepening in thought. "Lucey as the Advocate will allow me to stabilize the Network, woo my soulmate properly, and figure out how to live one life again. Can't remember how, to be honest."

"You should come with me," Max said. "Reveal yourself to Isadora. She'll need to be brought into our trust if . . . well, let's just say that she's earned it. With her powers, anyway, she might know."

Charlie brightened. "Not a bad idea. I'll do that. Are you on your way now?"

"Yes."

"Give me a moment. I'll be there. Oh, Max?"

Max stopped, halfway turned to the door.

"Yes?"

"When you approach Isadora, try not to be your usual cranky self? It's not very inspiring, even for a woman who clearly loves you."

* * *

Though Max expected him in Letum Wood soon, Charlie lingered at Wildrose.

Duties at the castle called. Several Council Members wanted to speak with him about Mansfeld Pact negotiations and Harry held pending signatures for signing the deed over to Max.

Before he left Wildrose, Charlie paused.

Papa's old room lay in quiet repose. All of Faye's belongings had left. The stalwart possessions remained. The glass lamp. Bookshelves full of dusty old tomes that no one read any more. Shades, blankets, pillows.

So much, yet nothing really.

Faye would move into a secluded house on the outskirts of Chatham City, with guaranteed privacy. Charlie would transport home to her every day until the time to transition to a new Highest Witch arrived. He didn't know when that would be, but the moment would strike when it was ready.

Then?

They'd find the world.

"Papa, I hope you're proud."

A settling occurred as the weight of generations blew away. The pressure of the Dauphin name went with it. Wildrose lay in the hands of those who would love it most. Max, who had always been the witch for this home.

"The Advocacy has fulfilled the mission I set for it, and my underground headquarters met its destiny."

A note of amusement lingered in his voice. Charlie shuffled a foot, gaze cast down. Past the watercolor scene that Mama painted before she died. Papa had stared at it endlessly while alive.

"I'm going to do what I can for the Network, make you proud, and then I'll leave and live a happy life with Faye. Of all that I have accomplished, I feel that is what you would be most proud of."

A feeling, not unlike a warm embrace, flooded him. He swallowed past the gathering knot in his throat.

"I love you, Papa, and I love Wildrose. Maximillion will continue its reputation as you always desired. Now, perhaps, I can truly let you rest in peace."

Not a sound followed. Only the gentle creak of the house. The groan of it settling—constantly settling. Charlie lost himself in the silence, the drifting dust motes in the air, until a gentle *tap tap tap* came from the door.

He lifted his head.

Faye stood outside with a half smile. Relief flooded him as he opened his arms in wordless invitation. With her bright grin, she stepped into his embrace and wrapped her arms around him. He held her so tight it might have hurt, yet he couldn't bring himself to pull away.

"Manors and reputations and inheritances and the dead don't matter as much as my soulmate, the woman I have always loved. Faye, you are the most important thing to me. I can't wait until I can choose you first, always."

Her arms tightened.

"I will always be yours, Charlie," she murmured against his chest. "We'll get through all of this together."

She tilted her head back. He pressed a kiss to her lips, brushed a lock of hair out of her eyes.

"Are you ready for the next phase of your life? For something different, new, and exciting?"

A full smile split her lips.

"Only with you at my side."

Chapter Forty-Seven

MAXIMILLION

Never in his life had Max felt such terror as he did at this moment.

It gripped him around the chest, tightening like a snake. He attempted to breathe around it, but barely wheezed air in or out. Charlie's carroty hair wandered into the greenery of Letum Wood, his parting words fading in the air.

Almost forgot. The obliteration of your handfasting. I'll put that through tonight. Should be final within a week.

Obliteration.

Isadora had taken the reception of Charlie as the Advocate surprisingly well. With amazement and shock, as expected. She appeared equally stunned. To his consternation, he couldn't tell whether the look on her face was relief or . . . something else entirely.

A dozen things he could say now ran through his mind, then back out. Charlie's advice not to be his usual self only made it more impossible. He'd never been one for caring words.

Or words at all, for that matter.

Isadora was an independent witch that knew her own

mind. She wasn't afraid of him or life on her own or anything, really.

Drat her.

While Max stewed in the silence, she cleared her throat. Her gaze caught up with him, reservations thick. She smoothed a hand down her skirt.

"Well, I suppose there's a few things we need to discuss."

Relieved to have the burden of starting the discussion off, he nodded once. "Indeed."

She shuffled around to face him, the folds of her dress swaying. She held her hands in front of her, fingers clasped tight, the tips of them blanched.

"Ah, I meant to thank you."

"For?"

"You were a perfect gentleman. You kept me safe and were . . . my friend. I needed that. I-I needed someone on my side after—"

My father died, he finished in his head. That sick feeling arose again, but he batted it away. Time to cut this agony off. Max drew in a shoulder-expanding breath and forced himself to say the words.

"What do you want, then?"

Her brow lifted in surprise. "What do I want?"

"What will you do now? What is next for Isadora Sin —Spence?"

Isadora deflated slightly. "The Head of Education reached out to me. They're thinking that a Watcher who can see personality traits in witches would be a good qualifier for admission. Identify quality students they can start preparing to serve in the Network, instead of the ramshackle way they find Council Members now. Charles wisely wants to start from the ground up in rebuilding the Network, emphasizing competent Council Members."

"Sounds perfectly boring."

"I know. Isn't it wonderful?"

Her beaming smile cut all the way inside him. He hesitated, brow furrowed. "After all this war? Yes, it is."

She sighed, crossed her arms across her chest, and peered into the forest, as if she could look into the future that way as well.

"But that's not what you really asked me. You asked me what I wanted. I want a cottage in Letum Wood. Close to Sanna and Mam. I want a job that makes a difference for the Network, and I want a house full of the teacups that Mam and I paint together. Then, maybe, it will feel like our lives haven't totally ended. As if . . . Daid could still be with us. What about you? What does the great Ambassador Maximillion Sinclair desire?"

His throat gummed up.

You, he thought. *I want all of you. Everything you have to give. I want to wake up to you every morning and see you in the evening. I want you to come to Wildrose and love it as I do.*

He paused, finally managed to say, "Peace."

Idiot, he told himself.

Isadora nodded, as if such a response made sense. It didn't. There were a thousand other things more important than *that,* but for the life of him, he couldn't get past this ugly dread in his throat. The fear that choked his heart.

"You have that now," she intoned. "The new plan is—"

He couldn't stand it.

"Are you going to leave?"

Startled, she reared back. Her eyebrows rose.

"Leave?"

"Are you . . . do you want something else?"

"What do you—"

"The good gods, Isadora!" he cried. "You *know* what I mean. Do you want to remain handfasted or not? Because if you want to go, I won't stop Charles from granting the obliteration. But if . . ."

"But if?" she whispered.

Max reached for her arm, unable to hold back now. All the longing for connection to her, the hope for more, poured out of him. The distance closed between them until he could almost feel her heart against his. The thready *thud*, the racing anticipation.

By the good gods, he wanted to kiss her.

He wanted nothing more.

"But if you didn't want to go," he whispered. "If you wanted to stay. With me. Then . . . I believe we could build something together. Something . . . peaceful and real and . . . not empty and cold."

Questions filled her bright eyes, and a dozen other things he couldn't hope to understand.

"In the South," she said slowly, "when I asked you whether you were afraid of me after Carcere, you said yes, but not for the reason I thought. What was it, then?"

Carcere.

The mere memory of that place brought up emotions he'd rather not deal with. His reply came out a hoarse whisper.

"I thought I had lost you. That I couldn't protect you, and it almost destroyed me. It was then that I realized the depth of my feelings, and that frightened me."

"Do you really want more, Max? Can you handle me being near you every moment?"

"I crave it, Isadora." He gripped her more tightly. She fell under his touch, her hands on his chest. "Like a dying man. I . . . I don't want you to go. Will you stay? Will you endure a man as insufferable, arrogant, and terrified as I am?"

His heart leaped into his throat.

The agony of the following moments ripped him to shreds until her expression softened. A half smile appeared on her lips. She reached up, touched his face with the tips of her fingers.

"Yes. I want you, Max. I believe I've loved you since we first met."

His heart collapsed.

She drew closer as he kissed her, giving vent to the steam of desire that had built for ages. It's all he'd wanted to do while in the South, since Dante's attack, and through every moment until this one. With Isadora in his arms, he could do anything.

After a blissful eternity, he pulled away.

Her kiss-teased lips parted as she stared at him, dazed and blinking. A laugh nearly rolled out of him.

"Come with me," he whispered, tucking a piece of hair aside. "Come with me to Wildrose, Isadora?"

Confusion clouded her features for a moment.

"Wildrose?"

"My home. My . . . sanctuary. It's a part of me that few have ever seen, nor truly understood, what it means. It's what I have to give to you. I won't . . . I won't always be able to give myself."

The words trailed away.

"Take me, Max. Take me to Wildrose."

Also by Katie Cross

All books are available in ebook, paperback, and audiobook at www. katiecrossbooks.com and on all online ebook, audiobook, and paperback retailers.

The Dragonmaster Trilogy

FLAME

Chronicles of the Dragonmasters (short story collection)

FLIGHT

The Ronan Scrolls (novella)

FREEDOM

The Dragonmaster Trilogy Collection

The Sisterwitches Series

The Sisterwitches Book 1

The Sisterwitches Book 2

The Network Series

Mildred's Resistance (prequel)

Miss Mabel's School for Girls

Alkarra Awakening

The High Priest's Daughter

War of the Networks

The Network Series Complete Collection

The Isadora Interviews (novella)

Short Stories from Miss Mabel's

Short Stories from the Network Series

Hazel (short story)

Alkarra (short story collection)

The Network Saga Suggested Reading Order

1. The Parting (novella #1)

2. The Lost Magic (full-length novel)

3. The Lamplighter's Daughter (novella #2)

4. Merrick (novella #3)

5. The Rise of the Demigods (full-length novel)

6. Priscilla (novella #4)

7. Viveet (novella #5)

8. Prana (novella #6)

9. Derek (novella #7)

10. The Forgotten Gods (full-length novel)

11. The Returning (novella #8)

12. Regina (novella #9)

13. Leda (novella #10)

14. The Sister (prequel to WOTG #1)

15. The School (prequel to WOTG #2)

16. The Council (prequel to WOTG #3)

17. The Goddess (prequel to WOTG #4)

18. War of the Gods (full-length novel)

19. The Finales (a collection of novellas)

20. Marten (novella #11)

The Historical Collection

The High Priestess

The Swordmaker

The Advocate

The Reader Request Series

The Gods

The Plummet

The North

The Wander

The Return

Viveet Forged

About the Author

Katie Cross is ALL ABOUT writing epic magic and wild places. Creating new fantasy worlds is her jam.

When she's not hiking or chasing her two littles through the Montana mountains, you can find her curled up reading a book or arguing with her husband over the best kind of sushi.

Visit her at www.katiecrossbooks.com for free short stories, extra savings on all her books (and some you can't buy on the retailers), and so much more.